THE MARK OF AMULII

PATH OF SEGOLIA

Aeron Dusk

Publisher's Note: This is a work of fiction. Names, characters, places, and incidents are a product of the author's imagination. Locales and public names are sometimes used for atmospheric purposes. Any resemblance to actual people, living or dead, or to businesses, companies, events, institutions, or locales is completely coincidental.

Ordering Information:
Quantity sales. Special discounts are available on quantity purchases by corporations, associations, and others. For details, contact the "Special Sales Department" at the web address above.

Cover Design: Alexandre Rito
www.designbookcover.pt

Developmental Editor: Gary Smailes
www.bubblecow.com

Copy Editor: Jean McConnell
www.thewordforager.com

The Mark of Amulii/ Aeron Dusk. -- 1st ed.
ISBN (Paperback) 978-1-7378433-0-6

*To all those that encouraged me through the years,
this is dedicated you.*

When I wrote this story over a decade ago, I was at my lowest point, and it was my way of escaping an existence I hated. I rewrote it last year, and the story now contains fragments of myself throughout a time of growth and tragedy. It's a still frame of people I've loved and lost as well as the people who have scarred me.

For good or bad, the experiences shaped the person I am today.

I warn you, this is not a conventional romance, and I have never been a conventional person. The Mark of Amulii is a story written for people like me. Those that have experienced years of loneliness and loss, hoping to find meaning in the meaningless, love in the loveless, and magic in the mundane. Those that shy away from the norm and long to be something else, something better, far beyond this reality.

Mom

Though you're gone now, you were always in my corner. I miss your smile and the way you made everything special. I told you one day I'd write a book; just wish you were still here to read it.

Seth

You were a fan from the first draft many years ago when I had no idea what I was doing. You've been a source of inspiration and comfort throughout the years and a true friend.

My Followers, Betas and Critique Partners

Many of you were very passionate about this story, volunteering your time to sometimes read through multiple drafts. You all helped shape this story into what it is today.

*The greatness of humanity is not in being human,
but in being humane.*

– MAHATMA GANDHI

A LIFE UPENDED

There's a special kind of anxiety that accompanies a call or text after midnight, a sense of cold dread that makes your palms sweat and chest tighten. That's what happened to me when *We're leaving Calgary* popped up on my home screen with no further explanation.

I kept rereading the message, each time thinking I'd misread something. This was so sudden; what the hell happened? When some of the shock subsided, I began mashing out a series of panicked responses that got angrier the longer they sat unread.

"What's wrong?" The tip of a finger poked at my upper arm, but I swatted it away.

"Hold on a minute," I said, chewing on a fingernail while staring at the phone screen, which had dimmed to conserve what little battery life remained.

After another minute of nothing, I dropped the phone into my lap and leaned back against the bed. The water-stained ceiling of my best friend's room rolled into view, and I rubbed my forehead before glancing at Mike who was sitting cross-legged on the floor next to me.

"I don't know what's going on with my parents."

"Breathe, man. You always make things worse when you get like this." Mike settled his hand onto the base of my neck, moving his thumb over a tense muscle in a firm circular motion. Every inch of my body buzzed and heated at his touch, most notably my face, but I forced that feeling back into exile, like I always did. We'd been close friends for years, but once puberty hit, everything got weird.

All the girls went crazy for Mike and all the guys wanted to be him. He was six feet of toned muscle, hardened by three years of football and off-season sports. His skin was olive-toned with a small patch of brown from a birthmark on his left cheek, and his eyes were deep caramel, though they always seemed a little brighter when we were together. It was hard to believe that the once lanky, awkward middle school LARPer who played Magic the Gathering would end up an Adonis his senior year.

Though he'd left me far behind physically, we never stopped being close. There were times I wanted to blurt out what I really felt about him, but I didn't want things to get awkward between us—well, more awkward, anyway. Sports and clubs had taken most of his free time, and I dual-enrolled in college courses. Whenever we did have time to hang out together at school, I was always the background noise while everyone else took his attention. No, I'd carry this to my grave.

"Are they talkin' about divorce again?" Mike removed his hand from my shoulder and raised an eyebrow, his fingers now fidgeting with the remote control. It was hard for him to understand what my family life was like, considering how happy his home was.

"Nah, it's not that, I don't think," I responded, my tone wistful. I jumped when the phone vibrated in my lap before holding it up so I could see the response I'd been dreading.

Jasper.

"Shit," I said through clenched teeth before tossing the phone in a fit of anger. It bounced off the wall and fell to the cream-colored carpet, the rubber case hopefully protecting it from my temper.

"They're at it again." My eyes watered as I looked up at Mike. "I guess things are bad enough that we're moving."

"What? Where?"

"Jasper."

The room got uncomfortably quiet again, save for the gentle hum of a humidifier in the corner.

Mike finally opened his mouth to speak. "What the hell's in Jasper?"

"I don't know. She's being vague, which means they're probably fighting right now."

"It's your senior year." I felt his muscles tense as he leaned against me. "You know my folks'll take you in, right? You wouldn't have to leave everyone, and I don't care if you share my room."

Heat flushed my face again, spreading from my forehead to the base of my jaw as I thought about sharing this small bedroom with him on a more permanent basis.

"Hello? Have you met my mom?"

We both let out loud sighs.

"Damn it," Mike muttered as the television screen went black. "Damn it," he repeated through his teeth a little louder. The evening had started out light-hearted, with us watching another hilariously awful horror film. It took one text to send my social life crashing to the ground in flames. "I don't even know what to say about this."

"After everything they've done, this bullshit sits in the top tier." I raised my knees and folded my arms over them. "You're so lucky."

"At least you guys got money."

"Money doesn't make things any less shitty, Mike."

He draped a sinewy arm over my shoulders, and I couldn't help but smile.

"Hey," he said, giving me a slight shake. "Promise me you'll keep in touch, and I don't mean every once in a while."

I wiped my eyes with the sleeve of my shirt. "Of course, I will."

CHAPTER ONE

CLOSE ENCOUNTERS

Calgary never tried to kill me, but I couldn't say the same for Jasper. A dank, ferrous odor wafted past my nose in pulses as I froze on the bottom porch step of our 'new' cabin home. Yellow eyes locked with mine, and I couldn't help but find the situation morbidly hilarious.

It was pointless to call for help. My parents were screaming at each other, and there weren't any neighbors for kilometers this far outside of town. It was just me and the biggest freak of a wolf I'd ever seen.

A wet nose touched my cheek, cold as the rough frost melting on the wooden railing under my hand. Despite its monstrous size, the animal was beautiful. Its fur was tar black, yet had an oily shimmer where dappled sunlight touched it. Thankfully, it showed no signs of aggression, its gaze full of intrigue as it waited for my next move.

After swallowing what little moisture I had left in my mouth, I balanced a trembling foot on the edge of the step, holding my breath as I climbed, never turning my back to the giant predator panting in front of me.

All it took was one careless move and the wolf's curiosity could turn into a prey drive. It was strange to be in a situation like this so close to the house. Wolves around here were timid and rarely seen, but this one was far from typical.

The curious animal stalked closer, hollow snorts of air roaring through its nostrils, and I struggled to climb fast enough to widen the space between us.

"Whoa," I shouted, my heel slipping against the icy edge of the top step, which caused me to trip backward. I caught myself before falling. The creature didn't stray or panic at the sudden movement, and the ridges of its smooth, black lips angled into what I could have sworn was a smile. One massive paw after the other bowed the wooden planks, and as the beast inched forward, I could see it was male.

"You're a big boy, aren't ya?" He cocked his head to the side like a confused pet while I continued the painfully slow trek toward the front door. "C'mon, stay back." The panic in my voice grew as the air in my lungs vanished. A silent gasp filled them again when my back grazed the gray, wooden door. The wolf's thick tail pounded the rails, but his glaring, pointed expression worried me.

He wasn't afraid of humans. Why would he be? His paws dwarfed my feet, and he could have carried two of me on his broad, muscled back.

The puzzling behavior continued as he advanced, eyes now closed and snout flaring as if he were savoring something delicious. There was an awareness on his face that freaked me out. I'd never seen such human-like facial expressions on an animal.

The doorknob clicked under my hand, and he charged before going airborne. A high-pitched shriek broke the momentary silence as I shielded my face.

I expected knife-like teeth to tear into my neck; instead, skittering claws tapped a playful rhythm in the opposite direction accompanied by the pounding of heavy paws. A slice of blurry scenery flashed through my fingers in time to see a black tail vanish over the railing.

I released a long, drawn-out breath through my pursed lips. Every muscle that held me upright turned to noodles, and I slid against the front door to the splintery deck below.

Dad and I had experienced close calls with bears over the years when we hiked the trails near Banff, but we were always prepared. This wolf came out of nowhere, and its size and boldness almost made me reconsider my trip to the lake.

Thunderclaps on the other side of the door rattled the windows as my mother swore at my father. The shattering of glass that punctuated his bellowed response put to rest any hesitation I had. I welcomed a chance encounter with a man-eating wolf if it meant being away from here.

With all the grace of a newborn colt, I rose to my feet on wobbly legs and tripped down the front steps, getting a mouthful of dirt before standing again. I dusted myself off and hurried across the lawn to the rickety shed in the distance. Glossy red paint peeked through holes in an old tarp. As much of an asshole as Dad was, he felt terrible about pulling me out of school my senior year. This was the first apology gift I'd ever received.

I loved my mother, but the only consolations she gave were unwanted criticisms and lectures. It made sense that a former trauma surgeon would be neurotic when it came to her child, but it was worse now that she was homeschooling me. If it weren't for the wilderness, there'd be no escape from this new hell my parents had dragged me into.

With a cautious stride, I glanced around the corner of the shed to make sure there were no more rogue wolves. The blue plastic tarp crackled as I pulled it away, revealing a cherry red ATV with black trim and a mesh-style cargo rack at its rear. It was big enough to carry two people and could be hard to control, but it was a blast to drive.

As I hopped onto the seat and tapped the ignition switch, the engine sputtered to life. The four-wheeler lurched when I knocked it into gear, tearing through the yard while kicking up grass and dirt behind me.

Lodgepole pines and bright yellow aspens whipped by in a blur as I sped over well-trodden trails of fallen leaves and needles. The terrain was hilly here, but the forest obstructed most of the mountain view. When I ascended into a clearing, the vast sparkling waters of the park's most famous lake slipped into view.

Maligne was long and narrow, surrounded by some of the most picturesque mountains in the park. Some had gentle slopes leading to snow-covered, broad peaks, while others were sheer, glacier-worn steps.

My vehicle dipped and shuddered along the jagged banks, and I glimpsed Spirit Island less than a kilometer in the distance. It was an island in name only, little more than a crumb of land that protruded into the lake, attached to the mainland by a narrow strip of soggy grass and sand. Tall, skinny lodgepoles jutted unnaturally from the center, like an unfinished latch hook rug. Spirit Island had such a mystical appearance, it may as well have been ripped straight from a fantasy movie.

It was my favorite place to get a panoramic view of the mountains. Since it was off-peak season for tourism, there weren't many man-made noises, aside from the occasional boat tour.

I cut the engine and admired the portrait of perfection that surrounded the valley. The tranquility of the forest had a calming effect, melting away the stress from earlier. No matter how many times I visited the lake, the rush of serotonin was always the same. It was my addiction.

I stood and took in a deep breath of crisp mountain air before kneeling to pick up a smooth stone from the sand. With a sideways toss, I skipped it across the water, disturbing the glassy blue surface. Circles rippled outward from each impact, distorting the almost mirror-like reflections of mountains and trees.

The fall breeze nipped at my skin as it carried a familiar scent of the holidays: pine mixed with a kiss of smoke from cabin chimneys in the distance. Sun-soaked evergreens along the slopes swayed in golden waves as stronger high-altitude gusts whipped through them.

The soles of my shoes scuffed along the stones as I approached a strange boulder decorating the shoreline. It always seemed out of place, like it had been purposely put there. With the aid of a small crevice that fit my smaller feet, I climbed to the top before reaching into my wilderness bag. I grabbed a handful of trail mix and funneled it into my mouth while listening to the creaking and whistling of the trees overhead.

Moments later, the sun touched the horizon, and the snow caps around the valley ignited as though they'd been resting all day in a forge. The trees below the timberline went from gold to black as the line of twilight from the western mountains extinguished them.

A sudden, uneasy feeling raced through me. I wasn't alone. Bushes rustling along the shore caught my attention, but I saw nothing.

After my encounter earlier today, I didn't want to leave my fate to chance. I jumped off the boulder and dashed toward the ATV but stopped when a man in baggy clothing appeared from behind the trees.

"Hey," he shouted, bounding toward me. I walked a few steps closer to meet him as he approached the shore. He was several inches taller than me, with golden brown hair clipped into a short crew cut. His face was slightly sunburned; it was easy to get those at higher altitudes. Camouflage cargo pants and a thick army-green jacket gave his lean frame a bulked-up appearance. His facial hair was neatly trimmed into a short beard.

"Hey," I replied, feeling a bit relieved as I walked closer to him. He was younger than many of the people I'd seen around this part of Jasper, perhaps in his early twenties. My smile faded as I caught sight of the rifle strapped to his shoulder. "Uh, can I help you?"

"Nah," he said, holding out his hand, his piercing green eyes locking with mine. "I saw ya up here and wanted to say hi." He spoke in a thick accent typical of the American South, but it had a twinge of the city in it as well.

"Oh." I reached out to return the welcoming gesture, eyeing the weapon again. "You know firearms are illegal in the park, right? My dad's a ranger."

"We're out keepin' these parts safe." He shrugged off my concern with a slight laugh. "We've got permission."

"We?" I asked, scanning the area. "There are more of you?"

"Oh yeah, we're camped out all over these parts." He narrowed his eyes. "It's pretty out here, ain't it?"

"Uh, yeah." This was why I didn't enjoy meeting new people; the awkward small talk always made me reel inside. "That's why I come out here."

"This place . . ." The man paused and looked toward the island. "Brings back memories. My older brother used to take me hiking around the lake whenever we'd come to visit. Dad's business is oil, so Alberta's kinda a second home in a way." There was a touch of melancholy in his voice, and his eyes seemed to wander beyond the lake to the mountains.

"Why are all of you here? People don't like hiking where they might accidentally get shot."

"We're all trained." A blast of icy wind raced over the lake, and he shivered, raising the hood of his jacket. "Question. You ain't seen anything unusual out here, have you?"

"Aside from people with guns? No."

He pursed his lips in annoyance and nodded. "Alright, the gun bothers you, I get it," he muttered. "What's your name?"

"Alex, yours?"

"Liam," he said, shuffling under the light hiking pack he wore. He reached into his pocket and pulled out a wrinkled card, handing it to me. "Here. This is my cell. Call me if you see anything out of the ordinary. It can be tracks, scat, animals—anything."

A chill went down my spine as I remembered the giant black wolf from earlier. Was that what he was hunting? I hated trophy hunters, especially those that killed wolves. They were hard enough to find in the wild as it was. I grabbed the card and tried to force a smile. "Sure."

"You still pissed off about the gun?" He crossed his arms and rolled his eyes. "You wouldn't last a day in East Texas."

"Well that's fine, considering absolutely no desire to go there," I replied, leaning against the seat of my four-wheeler.

He clenched his jaw and looked across the lake again. "There might come a time when you see something dangerous that you can't explain, and you'll wish you had something to protect yourself with. Especially out here."

Perhaps it wasn't wise to piss off a man holding a deadly weapon with no witnesses around.

"Alright," I said, my tone softer. "I'll let you know if I see anything." I held the card up and put it in my pants pocket.

His eyes brightened. "We ain't the enemy here. We just wanna get what we're lookin' for and leave. You're welcome to join us one day and see what we're all about if you want."

"I'll think about it," I said, hopping onto the four-wheeler. "You don't believe in Bigfoot and stuff, do you? Is that what this is all about?"

Liam grabbed my shoulder. "This ain't some bullshit hunt for the paranormal. If you'd seen what I have," he said, choking on his words, "you wouldn't be out here ridin' around." He let go of my shoulder and gave it a light pat before turning toward the trees, raising his hand to wave without looking back. "Good night, Alex. Be safe."

"I always am," I said dismissively, watching the thick brush of the forest swallow him as I started the ATV. What the hell was that? He seemed friendly, but there was something off. His parting words and unhinged expression had me even more on edge.

///

"I'm heading out," I said, grabbing my bag before tiptoeing over creaky floorboards. The cabin was smaller than our house in Calgary, but big for what it was. Contemporary living room furniture may have worked in the upscale suburbs, but here, it clashed with the cabin's wooden interior in a boxy gray and black mess. The colorful abstract paintings and minimalist decor seemed out of place with the scarred pine and cedar. This ordinarily would have driven Mom crazy, but I could tell she knew this wasn't permanent, despite her pretending the move was in our best interest.

This place got smaller every day with no one to talk to but arguing parents. I'd been escaping to the lake often since the wolf encounter, hoping to catch another glimpse of the rare animal before the hunters got him.

These days I was better prepared, keeping my bear spray close in case I had to use it. Occasionally, I'd see the odd rifle-wielding hunter or two around the lake, but they kept to themselves. I never did see Liam again.

When I passed the couch where Dad was sitting, Mom stepped in front of me.

"I'm leaving for the conference today, remember? Plus, we had this discussion yesterday. You're not going out there by yourself anymore."

Mom, as small as she was, commanded respect from anyone that crossed her, excluding my dad of course. She was petite and stylish; her brunette pixie cut perfect for someone twenty years younger.

It wasn't as though she looked old. On the contrary, at forty-four, she could have easily passed for someone in their early thirties. My friends used to embarrass me by making gross comments whenever Mom came to school. She'd wear low-cut, tight-fitting jeans and sweaters or blouses that showed off a little more than I was ever comfortable with my friends seeing. Since she was going to a medical conference, she was dressed more conservatively today, though not by much, opting for a low-cut plum blouse and a pants suit.

She eyed Dad before tossing a full suitcase onto the sofa cushion next to him, pulling his attention from the hockey game.

"Damn it Sally, let the boy go," he said, leaning forward to mute the game. It was easy to see why he and Mom looked like the perfect couple from the outside. Dad was a pretty good-looking guy, heavily muscled and tan with a scruffy beard and a bit of gray in his short black hair. Why didn't I get those physical traits? "Hiking out in the woods toughens him up." He glanced at me and scoffed, an air of disappointment in his eyes. I'd grown accustomed to that look over the years.

"I'm not having this argument with you," she replied, lightly biting her upper lip as she often did during their arguments. "It's common sense. You're a park ranger and you warn tourists about this all the time. Plus, all those guns out there. You know how dangerous it is right now. Go with him."

"I don't have time. I'm on fire watch for a few days, and I need to be at the tower by one. He's got his four-wheeler and his bag. He'll be fine."

"Why are you telling me this now?" Mom huffed and shook her head. "Damn it. We were supposed to get jobs with better hours. You're home less now than when you were on the force."

"The marriage counselor suggested we get less stressful jobs, and the less I hear of your shrill, harpy screams, the less stressed I am," Dad said with a slight chuckle before cranking up the television volume.

Mom snatched the remote from his hand, throwing it against the wall. "I'm sick of your shit, Robert. We both agreed to move out here because we *don't* want to get a divorce, remember? If you're not going to bother trying, let's just get it over with."

"There you go, breakin' shit like usual. I swear, towel-heads in Iraq were easier to deal with than you."

I crept closer toward the door, unnoticed, but glanced back to see Mom's face redden as she clamped her fists.

Dad's racism made the family look bad when my friends were around. No one ever felt welcome in our home, even me. The irony was, he was half Spokane.

"When did you get so hateful?" Mom slipped from anger to disappointment as she sighed. "I don't want Alex here all by himself."

"The boy's gonna be eighteen in five months. How long are you gonna keep your tits in his mouth?"

The rage returned as Mom's face got redder.

I slipped out the front door, letting it come to a silent rest against the frame before carefully releasing the knob. The moment the door clicked behind me, round two started.

Today, I changed things up and hiked along the ridges of Maligne canyon before making my usual trip. Excursions through nature were therapeutic, and no matter where I went, I'd always end up back at the island by sunset. It was hard to explain, but the place had an unusual magnetism.

There weren't any hunters around to avoid, but I wanted to circle the woods close to the lake to make sure. Evergreens and aspens whipped by in brilliant greens and yellows as I rode down the hillside toward the rocky lake shore. The sun was already setting, so I cut the engine before making a mad dash toward my usual spot. I locked up just before stepping onto the land bridge when I heard a rustling come from the dense trees ahead.

"Hello?"

The knot swelling in my throat made it hard to swallow as I pulled out a can of bear spray. Dad had taught me a lot about survival and safety when hiking through the park, but now that I faced possible danger, my stubborn legs wouldn't move.

"Liam?"

A few twigs snapped before steady human footsteps crunched toward me. Fear seeped from my nostrils in a loud exhale, and I tossed the can into my backpack as a different man emerged from the bushes. He was much taller and built like a bear, with short, messy black hair and a light dusting of stubble along his dirty, chiseled face. His ears were unusually pointed which made him look kind of wild.

He wore mismatched clothing, baggy cargo pants, and an uncomfortably tight, dingy white T-shirt. It was as though he'd grabbed them from a lost and found bin twenty years ago while blindfolded.

Dirt and rust-colored finger smudges covered the stranger's outfit, particularly along the sides of his pants. He looked like he'd been hiking for days, but he was barefoot.

A broad maroon crystal dangled from the leather strap necklace he wore. Aside from the dirt and the clothes, he wasn't a bad-looking guy. In fact, with his muscular, rugged appearance and tanned complexion, I found him pretty hot.

I expected him to return my greeting, but he just stood there examining me. His eyes were colors I'd never seen on another human being: honey amber that faded to gold near the pupil. They appeared both beautiful and unruly. He reached toward me with his grime-covered hand, wanting to shake mine.

His strange body odor and lack of proper hygiene made me hesitate, but I didn't want to seem rude either. Ignoring my discomfort, I grabbed his hand and shook twice, cringing before letting him go.

There was a stickiness that clung to my skin, and I wanted to shove my hand into the lake.

"I see you often," he said in a calm, deep voice, his eyes never leaving mine. "You come here, stay long."

"Uh . . . yeah." He'd been watching me? He didn't have a gun and was barely dressed, so he couldn't belong to that group of hunters. In the few moments I stood there studying him, I couldn't get a proper read on this guy.

He motioned me to follow as he walked back toward the island. I'd need to find somewhere else to go if I wanted to be alone. I wasn't the type of person who enjoyed small talk with unfamiliar people, especially people that creeped me out like this guy did.

As I turned to leave, a sturdy hand gripped my arm.

"Stay." His voice seemed to drip with impatience. He towered over me, and judging by the vice-like hold he had on my arm, he was insanely strong. I wasn't able to pull away.

"Come, sit with me. I . . . not talk to people here unless they . . . interesting."

"C-can you let me go, please?" Any calm that remained soon evaporated, my trembling body and squeaky voice giving me away. He looked at me as though he'd never seen another person before.

"I sorry," the stranger said as he let go, arms rigid at his sides like he was trying to control himself. His hand left behind a stain on my tan sweater similar to whatever was all over his clothing. First, I thought it was clay, but upon closer examination—was that dried blood?

He turned away, footfalls silent as he stepped toward the island with me following from a distance. Clearing my throat, I tried to think of questions to ask.

"Do you live around here?"

"Yes, close," he grunted. Wolf howls I once looked forward to, now added to the spine-chilling ambiance, causing me to jump. The man glanced back and smiled as I pressed a palm against my fluttering heartbeat. After some chuffed laughter, he focused on an area near the lake before jumping on top of the boulder like it was nothing before sitting. "You sit here as sun sets. You like sunset too?"

"I don't mean to be rude, but you're kinda creepy."

"Ah, fear smell. I do not mean scaring you." The man's slow, broken English added more mystery, but his softer expression quieted the voice in my head screaming at me to run. "Sit with me. Wolves sing for us. We share this spot."

The howls were louder than before as they echoed long and mournful throughout the valley. When I peered back up at the stranger, he was distant, seemingly lost in his thoughts.

As I tried to ascend the boulder, my shoe lost traction, and I slid. The man snatched my arm faster than I could fall and lifted me as though I weighed less than a doll.

After shuffling around on the rock, our shoulders touched. That questionable scent from earlier wafted from him and got stronger as time passed. I couldn't tell whether I found it pleasant or nauseating.

It was hard to enjoy the sounds, smells, and sights of nature with him next to me. The woods all mixed with his intense musky scent, making it hard for me to focus on anything but him. I continued to watch the man through my peripheral vision, in case he did something unexpected.

"You said you lived around here." I turned toward him, but that didn't tear his attention away from whatever he saw in the distance. "Where exactly?"

"There." He pointed to a random area near the lake.

His cryptic, non-answer irritated me. If he didn't want to have a conversation, why ask me to stay?

"What's your name?"

The silence was dreadful. If I didn't keep talking, the tension between us would smother me like a wet quilt. The stranger wore a slight grin, but the intensity of his stare stirred more anxiety. He had a gorgeous smile, though. There was an uncanniness about it I hadn't noticed until then. His canines were longer than average, which I wouldn't have thought unusual if it weren't for his eyes and ears. Why did I get this sudden sense of déjà vu?

"Amulii."

"That's kind of odd. Is that a nickname?" I looked down at my lap, catching myself. "Sorry, I didn't mean that to sound as rude as it did."

There was another lengthy pause. "You not rude," he said, shaking his head. He placed his right hand on his chest before turning to me with a grin. "Not nickname, Alex. This name given to me when born."

The significance of what he said took a few moments for my brain to process, but when it did, the internal screaming started again. This guy, who I'd never spoken a word to, somehow knew my name. It was the last of a series of warnings that I should have heeded earlier. I jumped from the boulder and hit the ground, bolting toward the shore.

When a thud, followed by rapid footsteps grew louder, I sped up. It didn't matter. He easily outran me. There was no choice but to turn around and confront the man.

"Leave me the hell alone," I yelled, reaching for the bear spray in my bag before aiming it at his face. I was so petrified that I forgot to remove the pin from the trigger.

He stopped and put his hands in the air.

"I not . . . understand why you scared. I sorry. Will not chase anymore."

He slumped forward and walked back to the island. The stranger's disappointed expression and somber body language made me wonder if I had misunderstood his intentions, but all I cared about was getting away from him. Shaky and out of breath, I climbed onto the seat of my ATV and sped back home.

///

A yellow sticky note clung to the front door with the words *CALL ME* scribbled on it. Sighing, I crumpled it before stumbling across the threshold into the living room. My heavy backpack slipped from my shoulders onto the floor, and I walked toward the kitchen. There was no cell signal, so I had to use the cordless phone instead.

After tapping Mom's number on the speed dial, I knew I was in deep shit when the speaker clicked before I heard a ring.

"I was about to drive back home." The shrillness of her tone made me move the receiver a few inches from my ear. "I told you not to go out in those woods, but you did it anyway. Your father doesn't listen to a damn word I say, and you're just like him."

That hurt.

"I'm fine, Mom," I said, trying to hold back an argument I wasn't prepared to have. "I had my emergency kit with me." I paused, gritting my teeth. "Plus, I'd rather take my chances in the woods than listen to you two bitch at each other all day long."

"Watch your language," she shouted, releasing a heavy breath before clicking her tongue. "Promise me you won't go back out there until your father or I get home. Please."

"Don't worry, I think I'm done going out there." The strange man's face flashed into my head, causing me to shudder.

Her voice lowered. "Did something happen? Are you okay?"

"Nothing happened, just weird people out there." I scrambled to the front door and locked it, peeking through the window in case he'd followed me home.

"That's another reason why I don't want you out there. Those people are nuts. Your father's been fighting with city hall to get them out of the park, but no one seems to care."

After a scan of the yard, I closed the curtains and walked back to the kitchen. I was alone in a cabin in the woods. How many slasher movies started out this way?

"Are you listening to me?" Mom asked, pulling my wandering attention back to the conversation.

"Yeah, sorry."

"There's a lasagna in the freezer, and some lunch meat. There's cash on the counter in case you need to run to the store. You'll have to make do until I go grocery shopping, okay, sweetheart?"

"Yeah, okay."

"Hey," she said as I pulled the phone from my ear. "I love you."

"Uh, love you too," I mumbled before hanging up. As embarrassing as it was being treated like a child, she was the only one who said those words. After setting the phone on the cradle, I dragged myself upstairs.

I walked into the room, grabbed the television remote from the nightstand, and hit the power button. It was already tuned to the local news, and Liam's face appeared on the screen. I turned up the volume.

"People are nervous," the reporter said, holding the microphone between her and Liam, who wore his camouflage outfit. His greasy, unwashed hair reflected the film crew's lighting and his unkempt beard and dirty face meant he likely hadn't bathed since our last encounter. "Everyone's started calling you 'the myth-hunters.'"

"This ain't a myth," Liam said casually. "There's a monster near that lake. Half man, half wolf, and he's lookin—"

The TV went black as I cut the power. It was the first time I had ever felt embarrassed for someone else. I already suspected the man wasn't all there, but that confirmed all I needed to know. Perhaps it was better if I didn't run into him again.

I stepped into the bathroom and undressed, exhausted. Another of mom's angry sticky notes clung to the mirror: *CLEAN TOILET.* There was a bit of a pee smell. It wasn't like I couldn't aim, I just hated turning on the light when I needed to get up in the middle of the night.

I leaned toward the mirror and examined a pimple forming on my chin. My acne hadn't flared up since my early teens, but with all the stress lately, it was inevitable.

Small patches of peach fuzz sprouted from my baby face. "Forever a twink, aren't you," I muttered to myself. Mom often reassured me that I was a late bloomer, but that never made me feel any better. My father's imposing, masculine voice was the dominant one in my head for years. No matter what I did, I was a disappointment in every way to him.

A few months ago, I had the dumbest idea to go from dark brown to platinum blonde, a decision I regretted after everyone teased that I looked like a male version of Ellen DeGeneres. Thankfully, my natural hair color had grown back out and most of the blonde had been cut away.

Spotty brass knobs squealed as I turned them, and hot water poured from the showerhead. I stepped in and ran a soapy washcloth over my skin before looking down. Dad was tall and tan and easily put on muscle, but Mom's thin, pasty-white genes were annoyingly dominant in me.

After showering, I dressed and grabbed a blanket before walking downstairs to the larger living room television. I wanted to watch a thriller before going to sleep, but my encounter earlier made me opt for a classic Disney movie instead.

///

The sound of banging threw me from the couch, startled and disoriented. I glanced at my watch, which read half-past six. The neighbors were far away and mostly kept to themselves.

"Who the hell?" I whispered to myself, standing on my toes next to the front door before peeking through the hole.

All the blood drained from my face when I saw those wild amber eyes.

CHAPTER TWO

BEAUTIFUL STRANGER

The assault on the front door continued as I pulled the curtains aside. After tapping on the window, the man snapped his head toward me. He flashed a toothy smile and pounded faster, happily staring me down while he did it.

He wore different clothing today, and it was a drastic improvement from the fashion crime scene yesterday. A faded blue T-shirt clung tight to his sinewy upper body while well-worn cargo pants with a hole in the right knee covered the rest of him. He was much cleaner now, and most of the grime that repelled me yesterday was gone. It looked like he'd hand-swept his greasy black hair into a much neater style. His feet were still bare, which baffled me because the ground around here was rough, not to mention freezing.

There were visible dents where his fists made contact, and I knew I needed to stop him before he broke down my door with his freakish strength. I threw open the window, and he rushed over, his face nearly touching the screen.

"What the hell are you doing here?" My voice cracked and pitched upward, like it always did when I was trying to act tough.

He flashed another grin, probably holding back laughter after I squeaked at him. It was a shame the guy was such a creep because damn he cleaned up nicely. He puffed out his chest and held a hefty blood-soaked hare to the window by its feet. Something was off about the wound on its neck, like he'd stabbed it several times with an ice pick.

"I sat on rock and thought a lot. I was sad because . . . wanted more talking, more knowing you, but you ran. Then I knew what I missing." His smile and eyes got wider as he gave the dead animal a light shake, thick blood roping against the log siding of the house. "Food. Everyone love good meal." There was a child-like inflection in his voice, in hilarious contrast to how deep it was.

"Uh . . ." He offered a dead, bloody animal as casually as a neighbor would a casserole. This was over-the-top redneck, even for rural Alberta. "You chased me yesterday, and now you're at my house, which means you've been following me. Give me one reason I shouldn't call the cops."

He tossed the carcass on the porch table outside, splattering blood everywhere. The mesh screen wasn't enough to block some of it from spritzing me in the face. The warm, wet feeling and iron smell alone made me gag as he held up his dripping red hands.

"I not harm you. Look. I look like you, yes? Human, both of us."

I couldn't help but squint at him after that. It was hard to equate "harmless" to the gore being displayed through my window. And what was up with that human spiel? The voice of reason in my head repeated not to let him in as I wiped the remaining blood from my face with the collar of my shirt. I sure as hell wasn't about to ignore it.

"Get out of here," I shouted, slamming the window shut and locking it before fastening the chain bolt on the door.

When I heard the pounding again, it became all too apparent that he wasn't going to listen. Clutching the phone tight with my left hand, I unfastened the deadbolt, keeping the chain in place. Nine-one-one was on the digital display, but I hesitated to send the call. I tried to remember the man's odd name to give him one more warning, but it slipped my mind.

I cracked the door open, but it swung all the way in with a snapping sound, barely missing my face. The sudden motion made me trip backward over my feet, and before I knew what was happening, my ass hit the hardwood floor with a thud. The receiver flew from my hand and slid far under the couch, almost out of reach.

I lay there, bewildered, staring at the red cedar ceiling with some of the air knocked out of me. When I looked toward the splintered section where the lock used to be, I knew I was in trouble.

"Oh," the intruder said, poking his head through the opening. "Alex okay? Sometimes it hard to hold back."

"What the fuck is wrong with you?" I shouted while furiously feeling around under the couch for the only lifeline I had. His huge, dirty feet were already next to my face by the time I got a firm grip on the phone.

"You opened, and I thought knocking change your mind," he said, reaching out his crimson-stained hand to help me off the floor. "Knocking what you do when . . . want to get in, right?"

The sweet iron odor turned my stomach. I held down vomit as I knocked his hand away, using the couch as leverage to stand. The way he behaved made me wonder if he had a mental disability. If that were the case, I felt bad for yelling at him, but this was scary.

"No, when I said you need to leave, that meant leave." I tried to appear more furious than terrified, but that shifted to confusion when his eyes glazed over. "You know you did something wrong, right?"

The stranger paused a moment before remorse overwrote the confident grin he wore. "I . . . sorry," he said, breaking eye contact with me.

My demeanor softened as I walked backward toward the kitchen counter, setting the phone in its cradle. Despite what he did, he was sweet in the way he apologized. If he had any intentions of hurting me, he could have done it by now, and given our size difference, fighting him off would have been impossible.

His body odor and the scent of rabbit's blood wafted back into my nostrils as I walked by him through the living room. Perhaps the man had suffered brain damage at some point. He seemed desperate for a friend, and I could have used some actual conversation that didn't devolve into an argument.

"Alright, you can stay, but don't touch anything." I pointed to the kitchen. "Go wash your hands."

The front door groaned as I pushed it shut with my shoulder. The forced entry loosened the hinges, tearing some of the screws from the wood. Dad was going to bitch about having to fix it when he got home. I turned back to see the man still standing in the middle of the living room, watching me.

"Hello? Dude, wash your hands. They're gross."

He gave me a sideways glance before rubbing the blood onto his shirt. I wanted to stop him, but his spaciness made me wonder if he understood anything I was saying.

"Damn," I groaned, grabbing his arm while pulling him toward the sink. "Come here, uh . . . what was your name again?"

"Amulii," he said with another soft smile as he followed.

He was solid, and his heft took me by surprise as I led him through the room. He must have been at least six-foot-eight considering my head only came up to the middle of his chest.

"Oh." Amulii's expression brightened as a rush of water poured from the faucet. He placed his hands under the stream, rubbing them together until the puddle in the sink turned vermilion. "My . . . understanding of your language is . . . simple. I fast learner though, learning much every day."

"Where are you from?"

"There." He pointed out the kitchen window over the sink toward the woods. It was the same vague answer he gave me yesterday.

"No, what country? And what language do you speak?"

"Country? Language?" He paused for a moment, his eyes shifting to the side. "I . . . from here. Speak English."

His snarky half-grin hit a nerve. Amulii wasn't the innocent "special" person I thought he was. He was being secretive, and I could see right through it.

"How did you find my house? How did you know my name?" I fired off one question after the other, faster than he could understand them. I paused for a moment as I thought of the last thing I wanted to ask. "Why are you stalking me?"

"Hmm . . ." He hesitated again, thoughts slowly turning to words as the cogs began spinning. "Hunting days ago, maybe. I still hungry, out for food and heard shouting, took me from my track. I saw you and someone inside shout 'Alex', and I remember. You very upset that day." He held his hand to my chest, and my face burned. "Sad, I could feel. You need friend, yes?" He removed his hand and stared expectantly.

The story seemed plausible; except I'd never seen him walk by my house. Was he hidden in the trees? He also said he was "out for food," and my mind raced back to the dead hare on my front porch.

His ingenuous way of stringing simple words together made him charming. A familiar feeling washed over me, just like the other night at the island. How could someone scare the hell out of me and calm me down at the same time?

"I lost prey, but I instead follow you."

And with that sentence and creepy grin, any calm I had morphed into chills.

"I come back to say a greeting, but something noisy carry you." He made an engine noise with his lips while making wild gestures. "Fast into the trees. I follow from far because I not know what to say."

"You followed me while I was going seventy kilometers per hour?"

His expression turned spacey. "I not know meaning of that, but I follow easy. I fast. When I saw you sit on rock . . . in our spot, I very happy. You like special spot too."

"Dude . . ." My tone grew serious. "You just admitted to stalking me."

He stood silent for an uncomfortably long time, looking so deep into my eyes he could have fallen in. For a moment, an absurd thought crossed my mind as we stared at one another, which I shrugged off as nonsense. Why would I make *that* connection?

"I . . . not have friends, and I looking for someone being friends with often and be very close. Sorry I scare you. I follow to see who you were. I not always trusting of others." After another lengthy pause, his stare went from intense to something I couldn't grasp. He stepped uncomfortably close. "I have . . . strong desire to know short-tempered Alex. Knowing more about you."

The breathiness of Amulii's voice caught me off guard. It could have been a bit of wishful thinking, but I got this *more-than-friends* vibe from him. Whenever I took a step back, he would shorten the distance between us again, sniffing the air. I didn't know whether to be creeped out or turned on. What was this?

"Yeah, we uh . . . we could get to know each other better," I said, examining his face as I spoke. "I just moved here myself, so I don't have any friends either." I trailed off while watching Amulii casually inch even closer. I took another step back and off to the side. "I'm also homeschooled." When he shuffled toward me again, I had to say something. "I don't mean to be rude, but—personal space."

"I sorry," he said as he looked to the ground with that same sad expression he wore earlier. "I not smell you from too far away. Too many smells in this place."

His words made me shudder, and I raised an eyebrow before shoving him away from me.

"Are you seriously sniffing me?" I shot him disgusted glare. "Why the hell are you so damn creepy?"

He looked back up at me, perplexed.

"I not understand. This how my people are when smelling someone nice. Today you not smell as good. Smell strong and harsh, all mixed up. It confuses. Not natural."

He seemed to get more alien by the moment, and when I heard the animal growl in his stomach, it was the perfect diversion from the current discussion. Thank God.

I cleared my throat. "Are you hungry?"

His face lit up as he shifted his attention toward the front door, like he had remembered something important.

"I *am* hungry, and I brought meal for us. I wait so we it eat together."

"Hold on—you were gonna eat that?"

He nodded in excitement. "We both will. They so delicious, but so hard to catch." I followed close to Amulii as he raced across the room with a slight skip to his gait. "It a little old, but it good." He pulled open the warped front door with such gusto I thought he'd fly away, but his mood shifted when he glanced at the empty patio table. His shoulders slumped forward as he sulked. "Hmm . . . forgot father's rule. Never leave meal unguarded."

"Oh, yeah, we get wild animals all the time. I mean, I saw a wolf a while ago, so he might have gotten it." I gave him a slight pat on the back. "It's okay. I've got lasagna if you want some. I wasn't gonna eat that, anyway."

I wondered how long he'd spent hunting that poor animal, and what he'd hunted it with, considering he had no weapon on him. How had he planned to skin and butcher it with no tools?

I grabbed the frozen dinner from the freezer and sat it on the counter. "It's a little early for this, but whatever."

He strolled up behind me, his body lightly brushing against mine as he reached for the box. The knot in my stomach returned now that he was closer.

He lifted the cold packaging to his nose and gave it a curious sniff, as if he'd seen nothing like it.

"I not sure of this. Smells funny, but . . . trust you." He was uneasy at first, and I didn't understand what he was about to do until he tore into the cardboard with his teeth.

"Stop playing around."

I snatched the box away and opened it. The clueless act was cute at first, but it was grating on my last nerve. After making a few slits in the plastic with a steak knife, I popped the lasagna into the microwave.

"Last night, I nervous but wanted asking you to dinner. But you left fast, and you upset, so I . . . not think it right time to ask."

"You scared the shit out of me," I said, tossing him another wary glance. "And you still do."

"No," he said, his voice pitching upward to sound more friendly. "To scare you is never what I want, only knowing you better." Every part of me shrank as he took up more of the room. My face burned, and I had to look away and change the subject again.

"Are you messing with me right now?" I asked, pushing an uncomfortably close Amulii away again.

He went blank.

"Hmm . . ." he muttered, watching the food spin around in the microwave. After smacking his lips, he shifted over to the sink. Remembering what he had done earlier, he lifted the faucet, but this time he stuck his head underneath.

"You're definitely fucking with me," I muttered, grabbing a plastic cup from the cabinet. Water poured from his face as he leaned back, dripping down his chest and onto the floor. I looked at the puddle and groaned before droplets hit my face as he shook his head dry like a dog.

"Damn it, Amulii. Stop," I shouted, tearing off a few paper towels to dry myself. "Use the cup." I held the cup under the tap. "Don't they have these where you're from?"

"I sorry. You always angry at me."

I paused for a moment and thought about what he said. It wasn't the first time someone said that to me; I'd even heard it from Mike. It was something my therapist always tried to get me to work on.

"Are you being real with me right now?" I asked, scrutinizing his face for any signs of bullshittery but was surprised to see only more confusion. "You don't understand any of this, do you?"

Amulii shook his head and grabbed the cup. "No, but I learn. I promise."

He guzzled down the drink and filled the cup several more times before leaning back and belching. With his light blue shirt soaked, I could see the outline of muscle all along his midsection. The fever returned as I handed him a wad of paper towels.

"You must have been pretty thirsty," I said, averting my gaze so he wouldn't notice me ogling him.

"I so excited coming here. I forget stopping by lake to drink first."

Despite the weirdness, he seemed to have a charming personality, and there must have been something about me he liked. Gay guys usually had a tell I picked up on, but I couldn't get a read on this one. If there was attraction, I wasn't sure how I felt about it. All of this was fresh territory and not exactly something I could explore while living in a house with my dad.

Amulii may have been attractive, but his hygiene and serial killer vibe left much to be desired. Still, I wanted to pry a bit and see if he was single. What could it hurt?

"So . . ." I said, patting out a nervous rhythm on my hips. "Do you live alone, or do you have someone?"

There was that irritating blank stare again.

"Someone?"

"You know, a partner? Lover?" My voice got a bit softer as I examined his reaction from the corner of my eye. "Girl . . . friend?"

His eyes widened. "Oh," he said, shaking his head. "No mate yet. But soon, I know it."

"What about family?"

He leaned against the countertop, looking thoughtful.

"I alone for now, no family. But during long night, I go home to visit."

"Long night?"

"I . . . hmm," he said, rubbing his chin. "Solstice?"

"Ah, Christmas. You only visit for a week or so?"

Amulii frowned, and his eyes shimmered as though he might actually cry. He reached for the red crystal that hung around his neck, clutching it in his palm.

"Only a day. It is only time when I see them. Cannot go back until I have what I need."

"What are you looking for out here? There's literally nothing."

Amulii reached into his pocket with his free hand as if to grab something, but instead, he let it fall empty to his side. He didn't look away as he continued rubbing the crystal he held with his thumb.

I cleared my throat, pretending to look at something else through the kitchen window. The awkward silence had returned.

"What I needing is here. I hope finding it soon because I do want to go back home one day."

"What are you looking for?" My voice lowered as I awaited his response.

"That is—" the teary-eyed expression he wore turned to a teasing grin, "—secret for now. Agree to know me better and I tell you."

I slammed my hand on the counter.

"I'm trying to get to know you better, dumbass. How the hell do I do that when you're so goddamn cryptic." I picked up the plastic cup and dropped it into the sink and took a few steps back, crossing my arms. "If you're gonna keep messing with me, then go away."

He grimaced as we stood in silence again. The microwave beeped, and Amulii jumped at the noise, which broke a bit of the tension. I opened the door and grabbed the cooler corners of the container before pulling it from the microwave.

"You have much anger." Amulii crept up from behind and squeezed my shoulder. I wasn't expecting him to rub the base of my neck with his other thumb, and I tingled all over as he worked his hands lower. "Anger dangerous for us. I like you, Alex. I make you smile, okay? I know how, if you let me."

"Oh, you do?" A slight moan escaped my mouth as I tried to remain stoic, but I was melting with every stroke. Why couldn't I stop this? He spun me around, his body now up against mine. All I could do was breathe him in as he placed his hand under my chin and leaned down.

"I do," he whispered. "I learn this from father as pu—child when I sad or angry. Look at face and no blinking."

We stood face-to-face for about twenty seconds and I thought my heart would explode as I waited for whatever flirty move he'd make.

"What is this? What are we doing?" I asked, not breaking my gaze.

"Shh." He leaned closer to me, and since I was already against the refrigerator, I couldn't back further away. He parted his mouth, and my eyes widened. A slight smile crept across his lips, before his cheeks puffed out, and he crossed his eyes. It was the dumbest face I'd ever seen anyone make. I let out nervous laughter, all while wondering what the hell had just happened to the mood.

His suggestive attitude shifted as he moved away and gave me a friendly pat on the back. That was insane. Thank God I hadn't acted on my thoughts and kissed him because I don't think I could have survived the humiliation.

"Much better with laughing and beautiful smile." He turned and walked toward the table.

My hand shook as I sliced into the layers of pasta and meat sauce with a metal spatula I pulled from the drawer. My every nerve was shot, but Amulii seemed pleased with himself. Why wouldn't he be? He'd succeeded in turning me into a confused pile of goo. Deep down, I knew what he was doing; I just didn't know how many signs I'd need to be completely sure.

After shoving a fork into the meal, I brought it over to my eager guest. Amulii pulled the utensil out and held it close to his face.

"I need to get changed. You eat, I'll be back down," I choked out.

He sniffed the plate and looked up at me. "Alex not eating?"

I shook my head. "I'm not hungry." There was a slight quivering in my voice as I turned toward the stairs. He grabbed my arm, gently pulling me toward him.

"Come with me. I not only come for eating with you. Want to show you my home. You ask, but never like answer I give, so I show you." His mood shifted to something more serious. "I not show many, only those I trust."

Something changed; there was no more naivety on his face. Amulii was testing the waters to see how I would react, but I kept as calm as I could. He wanted to bring me to his house, alone, with no witnesses. There was no way I'd be stupid enough to agree.

"Uh, sure." It was an automatic response as I stumbled upstairs like I'd been drinking. What the fuck did I just do?

There were the voices in my head again, screaming out warnings, and I knew this was incredibly stupid, but it became all too apparent I wasn't thinking with my brain. Years of being a thirsty, closeted teenager had finally caught up with me.

An imaginary debate continued to rage inside as I got dressed. I repressed it, convincing myself that if he wanted to do something terrible to me, he'd have already done it. After taking a calming breath, I grabbed my wilderness bag before casually strutting down the stairs.

"Just so you know, if you kill me, there's enough evidence here for—" I groaned and dropped my bag. "Really?"

Sauce not only covered his hands and face, but part of the table in red fingerprints. The food was gone, but the fork, of course, sat unused at the side of his plate. "Food good, but hot. I burn mouth." His reddened palms faced me. "And hands."

"Christ," I muttered, grabbing the plate off of the table. "You're supposed to use the—forget it. I'm sure you remember the routine. Don't wipe it all on your shirt this time."

He stood and gave me an apologetic glance before trudging toward the kitchen sink. I turned to grab my bag again and heard water pour onto the floor. His head was back under the faucet.

The hike to the forest started well enough; it was when Amulii decided on a *shortcut*, that things went downhill—or more accurately, uphill. I was not out of shape by any means but power walking up steep grades with no visible path was not something I was used to. The terrain didn't affect him at all as he sprinted along, still barefoot. I gasped for air like the fattest guy at the gym and had to stop, leaning forward while holding my stomach. Amulii was so far ahead of me, I didn't bother calling out for him.

I stumbled onto a rocky outcrop and sat. It was embarrassing to admit, but there was no way I could keep pace with Amulii, who had an entirely different degree of athletic prowess.

I turned to see Amulii bounding toward me, sliding and jumping from rock to rock before skidding to a stop half a meter away from where I sat. My mouth fell open as I wondered how the hell he moved like that. He appeared to overexert himself but wasn't the least bit winded.

"I sorry," he said, extending his right arm. "I not notice you fall behind. I go slow."

"Thank you."

I grabbed his calloused hand, and he pulled me from the rocks. As Amulii lifted me with ease, I was reminded of yesterday when we were at the lake. Though I was already standing, Amulii gave another tug, and I fell into him, my face brushing against his chest. I flushed before pulling away. Did he do that on purpose?

"Make sure only stepping where I do. Ground loose up here."

"Okay."

He placed his foot on a small rock and looked back to see if I was paying attention. I did the same, following each step he took. The slower speed was exactly what I needed, but my legs were still weak.

I fell into a rhythm as we climbed, and my mind wandered. When I slipped a little on scree, I should have stopped, but my focus was on Amulii.

As my full weight bore down on what I believed was sturdier ground, the rock underneath gave way. There was an audible snap as my right ankle took the brunt of the fall. I remember the pain shooting up my leg, but everything after that seemed to slow to a stop.

A Crimson Friendship

Seething pain tore from my lower leg as I fell. There was nothing I could do but brace for the inevitable tumble down the steepest part of the small mountain. In all the panic, I hadn't noticed a pair of bulky forearms wrap tight around me.

I stopped screaming when I slammed against Amulii's solid chest, my body stiff as I dug my fingers into his arm. He must have been five or more meters ahead before I fell. How did he get behind me so fast?

The shock of near-death wore off the longer I leaned against him, and I tried to remember what happened.

"Alex hurt?" Amulii asked, loosening his hold.

As I bore weight on my right ankle, it bowed slightly and electricity arced through it. I cried out, and Amulii caught me again, supporting my weight with his.

"I think it's broken." I clenched my jaw, forcing out hisses of air while my knuckles whitened from gripping him harder. "Why did we go this way?" I loosened my grasp, trying to balance on one leg, which was nearly impossible at such a steep angle. "You knew I was having trouble, and it's not like we saved time."

"But—there are people on usual path. I not go near them. It seems I make many mistakes. I forget you lack abilities I have." His slightly insulting apology married with the realization of my hopeless predicament fired off every livid neuron in my brain.

"Thanks a lot," I muttered, falling against the side of the steep hill while trying keep myself from sliding in the scree. "There's a reason why no one goes up this way." My watery eyes squeezed shut as I rocked from side to side. "You're an idiot. There's no way down now."

"I carry you. It easy to do."

Even I could appreciate the vote of confidence he gave himself, but I wasn't about to literally put my life in his hands.

"Again, you're an idiot," I muttered, using his body as leverage to stand on one leg. "Look at how steep this is. It was hard enough to walk up this thing on two good legs. We need to take this slow." I grabbed my backpack and handed it to him. "I need to wrap my ankle when we get down. Can you hold this?"

"You so stubborn." That was the first time I'd heard him raise his voice. He snatched the bag from me and put an arm through the strap, swinging it over his shoulder. "I strong. You will see." He scooped me up, and before I could react, I fell back against him.

My muscles tensed as I looked down behind us, my ankle screaming as I jerked it in surprise. "We're gonna fall."

"Trust," he shouted. The gruff tone of his voice grew more irritated as he ran. "I never let you fall."

Everything got scarier as I realized we weren't even going back down. The larger, unsteady rocks under his feet broke off and rolled toward the valley, but he remained as calm as ever, kicking against the gravel as he bounded effortlessly up the slope.

He wasn't taking me back home; instead, he was still determined to take me where he wanted to go. Maybe he thought it was safer to ascend with me in his arms.

The longer he climbed, the more I got used to the sensation of being carried. Amulii sprinted faster than when his arms were empty. He was a horse of a man, his massive muscles flexing with every leap and dash. All of this went well beyond being physically fit. There was nothing normal about his strength and speed.

"How are you doing this?"

Anger toward him dissolved into disbelief as he jumped to another outcrop while I clung to the back of his neck like a frightened baby koala. His intense focus never shifted.

"I sense where ground solid and not slip." He misunderstood the meaning of my question. "This nice to carry you." A wolf-like grin widened his mouth, his larger canines peeking from under his lips. The enamored expression didn't disappear as he looked forward again, inhaling deeply through his nose.

My skin flushed hot against his, and my guts had that familiar knot from earlier. There were only so many hints Amulii could drop, and this one was the cartoon anvil that landed on my head. Did I give off an unconscious signal? Maybe there was something in my voice or actions that gave me away, but whatever it was, he knew.

As the land flattened near the small peak, I began feeling comfortable in that position. I lay my head against his sweat-stained T-shirt, the scent of musk and perspiration making a heady combination. Was it gross to be so attracted to that smell?

Amulii slowed when we reached the summit before lowering me against the trunk of a thick pine. He sat close enough that our shoulders touched. Maybe he thought I'd be more receptive since I'd spent the last several minutes clinging to him.

My injury put me in a vulnerable position. I didn't know this man and had to trust him to get me back home safely after carrying me a kilometer or so in the wrong direction. The situation got scarier when he said nothing for a minute, instead giving me a wild, hungry stare.

"I liked your scent."

My eyes shifted, but I didn't turn toward him. The growly timbre of his tone caused my heart to race.

"Th—thanks?" I didn't know how else to respond to that. The longer we sat in silence, the more oppressive the vibes he gave off. It made me want to shrink away until I was invisible. "Uh, my ankle really hurts. We should probably head back so I can put some ice on it."

"Wanted you in my den. We talk and eat and I tell you secret, but since you injured and not run away, now good time to tell."

I swallowed the dryness that lumped in my throat as he continued.

"That day our faces met, I very . . . curious. I track your scent to island. Such pleasing smell you give and interesting feelings." The innocent, benign cluelessness at the house earlier seemed to mutate out of control into a pulsating mass of disturbing.

"Please stop." Everything about his personality shifted in another direction the more he spoke. "I wanna go home."

"Calm yourself," he said, reaching into his pocket like he did earlier. "Cannot explain in good words. Fear, I smell. I very bad with talk."

Normalcy returned to his voice, putting me somewhat at ease.

"Stuff you say really freaks me out."

Amulii stared blankly. "I not understand."

"That whole smelling me thing needs to stop. That shit's weird and makes me want to get the hell away from you."

He paused for a moment, a predatory smile inching up his face.

"Even if you run, I catch you. You not good at running."

"That right there," I shouted, pointing at him. "Stop saying creepy shit like that."

"Frustrating." He slumped forward, staring at whatever he was clinging to. "This language hard. Making you afraid . . . not what I wanted."

He grabbed my hand and dropped a leather-strapped gemstone into my palm. It looked a lot like the necklace he was wearing.

"What is this?" I inspected the blood-colored crystal, noting how unusually warm it was before meeting his gaze again.

There was a second or so of hesitation, but a half-smile replaced the wary expression.

"It is . . . chélanc," he said, clearing his throat. "A, uh, symbol of friendship in my land. You desire friendship, yes?"

So that was his intention all along. Still, he was being intentionally careful with his words for some reason. He used a different inflection this time, unlike before, when he was merely fumbling through the language.

The crystal was beautiful. Smooth, bulbous beveled edges that lifted toward the center gave the gem a slight hand-cut appearance which contrasted with the natural cracks in a few places along the surface. There were beaded red droplets suspended within that appeared to glow, even in the shade.

"Wow, thank you. What is it again?"

Amulii slid the necklace out of my hands, pausing once more before draping it around my neck. The heavy jewel fell to my chest, and an odd warmth flashed across my skin.

"Chélanc." He took my hand in his, and I noticed a slight tremble. "Ché'cané alta ko'ho," he whispered, squeezing before letting go. I couldn't place the language he was speaking. It had a bit of Germanic throatiness but flowed from his tongue like a Romance language. "A mark of friends it is, if easier to understand."

I nodded, wincing as I moved my leg. If I remained still, the ache was little more than a light throb. My shoe was tight, and I knew it would be difficult to remove from my swollen foot. The slightest movement knocked the air out of me.

"I so careless. Idiot, as you said." He rolled my pant leg to get a better look. My ankle was almost purple. "I fix this." He pulled an amber-colored crystal from the leg pocket of his cargo pants.

Being the son of a doctor, I rolled my eyes, but he was only trying to help in his own ridiculous way. I didn't want to sour the moment by being a dick about it.

He laid the flat end of the chunky mineral against my ankle before wrapping it in twine.

"Your eyes very loud," he muttered, casting a squinty glance at my face before tightening the knot to keep his crystal secure. "You not believe me."

"No, I don't. What the hell is this thing supposed to do?"

"You see soon." Amulii leaned against the pine, crossing his stretched-out legs. He closed his eyes and cracked a half smile, folding both hands over his stomach with annoying confidence.

It was peaceful on that mountain, and I leaned back to close my eyes as well. The natural spice of autumn peppered my nose as gentle breezes pricked at my face. Despite the cold, it was my favorite time of the year.

Amulii shuffled next to me. "You saw me outside your house, but not same me as I am now." My eyes snapped open and shifted toward him. Amulii's expression was much more sincere this time.

"No, I would have remembered seeing you."

"There was fear smell, so I ran. But we met." He grinned. "I remember good. Was hunting and heard angry shouts. You ran out, catch me by surprise. At first, I not know what to do, so I stay still. You afraid, but you not scream or try to run like many humans. Your smell was good, and I not meet many humans so friendly, even if you afraid."

The conversation with Liam that night echoed a warning.

"Holy shit," I whispered as earlier suspicions I once thought of as absurd returned. No one saw the brief interaction I had with that giant black wolf, but he described every detail as if he experienced it from the animal.

Amulii's odd behavior, the dead hare, how he looked like he'd never seen the inside of a house; there were so many things about him I subconsciously picked up on, but who in their right mind would have ever put that together? I wasn't crazy; his eyes *were* familiar.

My chest tightened, and I flinched when he grabbed my hand. "You understand. I know it. I ran after when I gave up on prey. That thing you rode was fast and loud, like the things on the lake. I not smell you because of it."

Amulii stroked my hand as he told his story, trying to calm me. When I tried to pull away, he pressed my palm harder into the grass.

"You stopped, and stink cleared. The wind blew. You all I smell then. It not confusing. Real, sweaty, natural. After that, I follow you for days, waiting near human den in mornings, hiding. I wanted to meet but I nervous."

"This is crazy," I cried out, trying to lift myself from the ground, but he grabbed my arm, pulling me back in place.

"No," he said sternly. "You in pain. Stay."

Every awful scenario involving werewolves raced through my head as I locked eyes with him. Did I smell delicious? Was that why he followed me? Tears trickled down my cheeks as I thought about how he'd kill me. Was I going to end up like that carcass he held up earlier?

"Please, no crying." He pulled me close, not so much talking as growling. "I . . . feel like I hunt you. You prey to me. You have been, but not for eating. Does that make sense?" he whispered, leaning in closer. "You know I . . . not good at your words."

It wasn't my finest moment as I cried more, trying to hide my face from him.

"Please don't hurt me. Just let me go."

I could feel Amulii's breath hot against my neck as his rough hand grazed my chin. The gentleness of his touch did little to allay my fear as he turned my head to face him, his once amber eyes glowing yellow.

"No fear, Alex. Never want hurting you." He placed one hand over my broken ankle and leaned in, tilting his head. There was no mistaking what he wanted now. "I make you feel good. No pain. You will see."

There was a slight tingle as his lips brushed against mine. A jolt of electricity stole my breath, stopping my heart for a moment. I squeezed my eyelids shut and wanted to pull away, but my body wouldn't cooperate as unique sensations hummed through every nerve. My ankle warmed under his hand, and my lips burned against his. As if by instinct, I opened my mouth. Time slowed and the sounds of nature faded when his tongue gained entrance, slipping against mine. Our mouths seemed to dance to an untamed rhythm. He moved faster than my mind could keep up, and as scared as I was, I couldn't stop this. The way he kissed was savage, and it awakened the volcano in me that I'd kept dormant for years. As his fingers trailed up my leg, I wondered what he would do next. Before my mind could wander to much darker places, our mouths separated.

I wiped my lips with trembling fingers, my fear turning to shock at what just happened. That was the first time I'd ever kissed a man.

"Feel better, yes?" he asked, his eyes still glowing. There was a breathlessness to his voice, like he had run a marathon.

"What . . . just happened?"

There was no more pain in my ankle, and I reached forward to grab it. Amulii grinned as he removed the crystal.

"You healed."

The moment whipped by without allowing me time to take it in. "Let me get this straight, you're a wolf that turns human and kisses people to heal them?"

"No, crystal healed. Kiss, you wanted."

"What? No, I didn't want it. You did something freaky to my head, didn't you?"

Grunted laughter shook his stomach. "All you. Very good kissing you do, and I smell things you not good at hiding." He pointed to his nose. "I said I like your scent. Scent different feelings you give off. If you fear, I smell." He took two quick sniffs through his nose. "Happy or sad, I smell. This is not first time smelling scent like this." He turned away, his tongue wetting the lips that moments ago locked with mine. "When I close to you, arousal strong."

He violated my mind. The playing field wasn't even at all. He knew the entire time, and he toyed with me. We'd only known each other a few hours, and he was already certain I wanted to have sex with him.

"Let's get one thing straight: I am not, in any way, aroused by you."

Amulii sat quietly, his eyes travelling downward for a second before narrowing on my face. Why did I bother telling that lie if he already knew?

"Hmm . . . nose never lies. Nose smells what bodies want."

"Stop saying that you know what my body wants!"

"Okay," he said dismissively.

"No, none of this is okay."

"I sorry. I—" He groaned while crossing his arms against his stomach. Black hair sprouted from them in thin strands at first before exploding outward in an onyx wave of fur, growing longer and denser as it crept up his arms to the top of his head. Amulii panted, and his wide eyes glowed brighter yellow than before. His human hair thickened into an unruly mane on his head, spreading to his neck. "I . . . too hungry."

He scrambled to his feet and arched his back, appearing to be in either pain or ecstasy. A painful snarl racked Amulii's expression as bones shifted and popped in and out of place. Swelling muscles stretched the tight blue shirt he wore, splitting it along his chest. The groans and crunching noises coming from him made me cringe, but morbid fascination rendered me unable to look away. All of this should have been impossible, but as the transformation continued, my reality crumbled further.

Amulii's face distended into a snout, and trickles of blood launched from his blackening lips as human teeth quadrupled in size. Sharpened canines jutted from his bloody gums, growing longer than when I first saw him. Pulsating muscles expanded and his height increased; the shirt he wore fell to the ground in tatters, and the button on his ragged pants flew off with a muffled pop. I understood then that he wasn't turning into the wolf I saw the other day. This was way different.

His giant hands turned rough, now covered in the same pitch-colored fur as fingernails snapped and lifted from their beds, sharp claws replacing them. Amulii's heels pulled upward as his feet elongated, becoming a part of the leg. His feet turned to massive paws that sank into the ground under his new heft, and his big toe shrank, pulling up into a dewclaw as other sharper claws grew from the other toes.

The change took less than ten seconds from start to finish, and the creature before me defied anything I'd ever known about biology. Amulii loomed overhead, his eyes the same as when he was human, but his gaze untamed.

He kneeled next to me and sucked in a deeper rush of air through his huge, dog-like nose.

"You very scared, I understand." Amulii's voice was deeper and guttural, sounding nothing like it did when he was a man. He pointed to his snout and stood back up. "Smell such big fear. You not have to stay with me, but I no different now. Still feel same way."

My mouth hung open as I stood stunned. What the hell was happening?

"This is . . . a lot to take in," I choked out, my vision clearing as I rose from the ground. He was a real werewolf, and none of this was a dream. "So, you're still in there—the same person? No man-eating bloodlust?"

He tilted his head as an ear flicked away a fly that had landed on it.

"Hungry. Holding human form uses much. If you want to follow to my den, it make me happy. Have dried meat. Still be friends, yes?"

Amulii smiled at me through two rows of deadly teeth. He looked like a monster on the outside, but there wasn't much beast in him, and he was as calm and friendly as before.

I couldn't help myself as my fingers carefully traced along his broad arms before running through the silky, thicker mane of fur on his chest. Werewolves were real, and this one wanted to be my friend.

A shudder rocked me as I remembered the kiss from earlier. This creature wanted much more than friendship, and as I took in more of his monstrous form, I wondered how that would even happen. It was par for the course with my shitty luck: the first man that found me attractive turned out to be a mythical beast. What were the odds?

"Yeah, we can be friends," I said, letting out bouts of nervous laughter. I wasn't sure if this was wise, but there was no stopping my curiosity now. I had to know more about him.

CHAPTER FOUR

SWEET MEATS

Amulii stalked over the dead leaves blanketing the forest floor on two padded paw-like feet. Despite his enormous size, the ground may as well have been cotton. The only sound on that mountain came from my clumsy footsteps as I tried not to fall too far behind.

I couldn't stop staring at his tail, which he threaded through a torn hole in his pants. It swayed as he walked, whisking along the backs of his legs. Whenever he'd looked back at me to slow his pace, it would wag.

"I thought werewolves only changed with the full moon?"

I jogged to keep up with his longer strides until I was beside him. For every step he took, I needed three. Amulii peeked at me, his ears folding to the sides of his head.

"What is werewolf?"

That was a strange question coming from him, but I wasn't surprised.

"Well, it's what you are. A human that turns into a half-man, half-wolf," I said, tearing my eyes away to get a sense of where I was. This side of the mountain was less steep as we continued our descent. "They're just stories, though. Well, I thought they were."

He threw back his head and half-howled a laugh. There were muscles in his face that the average canine didn't have, giving his expressions uncanny human characteristics. "Not human and not wolf; maw'cha. This what I am. Can take human, wolf form, but not what I am." He gave me the toothiest grin I'd ever seen. "I make sense? I not know how to explain."

"You haven't made sense from day one," I said with a laugh. The werewolves I'd seen depicted in movies were nothing like Amulii. His explanation did, however, help me put another piece of the puzzle in place. "Well, at least now I know why you didn't know what a damn fork was."

Amulii slapped my back, nearly knocking me to the ground.

"This make me most happy." The giddiness in his tone was the opposite of what anyone would expect from what was essentially a monster. "You not run and are by my side. Humans say they friends but run when seeing real me."

There wasn't a soul around happier than this werewolf, which made me wonder how many humans he'd actually gotten to know. He wasn't threatening, and I'd always loved wolves. In fact, I found his wolf-like features adorable, especially his ears and tail.

"Well, you're kinda cool-looking," I responded, poking at him again to make sure for the umpteenth time he was actually real.

The white peaks of the Queen Elizabeth Ranges to the west dominated the distance as we descended into a clearing. Sunlight glimmered from the azure, wind-disturbed waters of Maligne nestled in the valley below. The lake was like a long crevasse filled with sapphires, dancing and sparkling as a tour pontoon floated by Spirit Island.

"Fur keeps me warm. You are cool-looking. If you cold, I keep you warm."

As unfamiliar as I was with werewolf facial expressions, the one he gave needed no explanation. It was unsettling being hit on by an eight or nine-foot-tall wolf man.

"Uh, thanks. I'm already warm though."

"Only in case," he said, his ears dropping to the sides of his head again.

Near the bottom of the slope, there was an unexpected bulge along our path, and the grass disappeared as we stepped over smooth sandstone. After rounding the craggy formation, an entrance to a shallow cave seemed to pop up out of nowhere. It was within thirty or so meters of Spirit Island. Why had I never noticed?

An unusual warmth hit me as we entered, and yellow-orange light emanated from what appeared to be fist-shaped cracks in the sandstone. They each had sizable irregular-shaped crystals shoved into them; some were jagged and oblong while others were smoother and fatter.

Much of Amulii's life lay sprawled along the floor with ratty, torn clothing strewn about in messy piles mixed with the occasional dried animal hide. The hide was probably used to make the simple leather sacks that lined the back wall of his cozy den.

Two leather-bound tomes stacked on top of each other adorned a makeshift wooden stool in the middle of the room. To the right of that lay a fur-covered pallet on the floor, plush with aspen leaves and pine needles that poked from the sides. Amulii's thick, earthy odor clung to everything, mixing rather pleasantly with the leather and pine from the bed.

"This home for now," he said, a twinge of melancholy in his voice. "You welcome anytime. I not get *wanted* visitors." Amulii's tail fanned the dust that had collected on some of his belongings.

"Those people that you were trying to avoid by walking up the mountain . . ." I watched his ears press back against his head aggressively. "Have you run into them while you were like this?"

"Once," he snarled. "Always humans with their little noses and noisy weapons near my den." His ears pointed up again as he grinned. "You good human though. No one sees now but you."

How did he hide such a prominent structure? When I first asked Amulii where he lived, he must have pointed to this place, but I couldn't see it.

He yawned, plopping on his bedding while loose fur and dust swirled and shimmered in the rays of morning sunlight pouring in from the cave's entrance. He leaned back and grabbed one of the sealed leather satchels along the wall before sitting up and patting an empty place beside him.

"Sit, please. You cold. My fur keep you warm."

My face flushed and I nodded before sitting on the scratchy bed, trying to keep a sliver of space between us. This wouldn't have felt so weird had he not kissed me just twenty minutes ago. He grabbed a handful of what appeared to be jerky from the bag and held it in front of my face. "You not eat earlier—have some. I hunted it five days ago, but it keep long."

Movies often depicted werewolves as violent, disfigured, sometimes hunchbacked creatures. Amulii was gentle and had a majestic quality about him as he sat straight and proud, but that made sense considering he wasn't really a werewolf as we knew them. He called himself a *maw'cha* earlier, and I wondered how long his kind had been around people. Perhaps I'd ask when we could understand each other better.

The rest of his coat was coarse, but the thicker fur on his head, neck and chest, trailing past his abdomen was silky soft. It had a natural shine, and I'd have thought he'd just bathed if not for his pungent smell.

I looked at the offering he placed in front of me. It was hard to refuse such a friendly gesture; I was his guest after all. The meat resembled beef jerky, but it was covered in something fuzzy and green that almost resembled mold. The thought of putting it in my mouth made me squeamish.

"I'll, uh . . . have one. You need it more than I do," I said, peeling away a tiny sliver of the questionable meat. A snort followed by wet smacking echoed through the cavern. Amulii stuffed an entire handful into his mouth, gnawing while stringy saliva dribbled onto his lap.

That was gorgeous. It certainly didn't help with my nausea.

It felt wrong to watch, but I couldn't tear away. He gave an expectant glance while nudging me with his elbow. Both the dank smell of the cave, and the copious amounts of drool made everything so much worse. After swallowing the sour taste that traveled up my throat, I gave it a sniff, expecting the worst. Surprisingly, it had no scent.

I took a few deep breaths to steel myself before the fuzzy meat landed on my tongue. At first, it was peppery, but then a flavor I wasn't expecting intensified with each chew. It was savory and spiced with something unfamiliar but delicious.

"Whoa." Whatever zesty seasoning he used made every salivary gland open at the same time. Slobber trickled down my chin as I gnawed the tough jerky into tender mush. "You made this?"

He nodded, devouring more from the pouch before handing it to me. "Take."

"I can't take your food from you. I've got plenty at home." Earlier, there was a listlessness to his gait as we got closer to the cave, but I'd be lying if I said I didn't want to stuff my head into that bag.

"Amulii, how long do you stay human?" I sat the pouch in his lap.

"I . . . not often take that form. It uses much energy and is weakest. Not good for hunting," he said. "Please take more." He gestured to the pouch. "I have much."

When he insisted again, I couldn't help myself. I grabbed as much as I could, cramming two pieces into my mouth, moaning as the flavor exploded. He patted me on the back as I continued to stuff my face. Before I could swallow, I'd shove more in.

"This is amazing," I sputtered while drooling everywhere. My eating was just as sloppy as his, but I didn't feel embarrassed about it around Amulii. In fact, sitting there with him was rather pleasant.

"You have maw'cha appetite." He grinned; bits of meat stuck in his teeth.

As I ate more, a strange heaviness hit me out of nowhere. My head spun, and I couldn't lift my arms. I stared widely at Amulii as my mind raced to the worst possible places.

"W-what's in these?" I asked, letting what was in my mouth fall to my lap. Amulii floated further away as the cave got smaller.

"Alex?" His speech sounded slow and slurred as his face faded into clouds of ash. There were weights on my eyelids, and it was a struggle to stay conscious.

"You . . . know what you . . . did." Everything sank as the back of my head slammed against his bedding.

///

I peeled open my eyes and blinked them into focus. I tried to move, but my legs and arms were tied to the ground by something. An icy draft lapped at every nook of my naked body.

"Finally. I was waiting for you to wake up." Amulii's growl was seductive, coming from a corner of the cave I couldn't see. His clawed feet raked across the stony floor, inching closer to my head as he stood over me and grinned before kneeling next to my face.

"Where are my clothes?" My voice was raspy as I struggled to free myself. "What's happening?"

"You're not gonna need clothes anymore. You're mine now, human. You'll be like me soon. But first, I want to have some fun with that little body of yours."

He spoke perfect English. Was he pretending the whole time? No. . . this couldn't be right.

"Please," I begged, turning away as his long, canine tongue trailed from neck to cheek, licking away my tears.

"This is what your body wants. I can smell it." His rough hand traveled the length of my chest. "You'll love it, and you're never gonna leave," he continued as sharp claws grazed my abdomen, traveling lower. . . .

My eyes shot open and every ragged breath I took shook me as I examined my surroundings. Amulii wasn't there. Recalling my vision, I inspected myself to see if he had done anything. Sweat-soaked clothes clung to my skin under my jacket, and there were no bite marks, though I noticed an uncomfortable situation happening below the waist.

Why in the world did something so fucked up turn me on?

The cave was toasty and well-lit, but beyond its mouth was a starless void that would swallow me if I left. There was no way of knowing the time, or how long I'd been unconscious. Had it been hours or days? I couldn't safely navigate the forest by myself with no flashlight.

Where was Amulii?

My stomach gurgled, and my mouth was sandpaper. I crawled to my feet, feeling my way through freezing, pitch-black darkness as I left the safe glow of the cave. My vision adjusted as I trudged along the sandy path toward the shore, a rippling reflection of a dull half-moon getting brighter the closer I got. The lake was always clear, but I didn't know if the water was okay to drink, though that didn't matter at the moment. I felt like I'd been spinning in a drier set to high.

Thousands of icy needles pricked my fevered skin as I dunked my face into the water. I slurped up mouthfuls that occasionally trickled the wrong way down my throat. The cold-water shock made it hard to catch a full breath to cough.

I choked the lake down until I thought I would explode. My thirst may have been quenched, but liquid hell churned in my stomach. Hearing light footsteps, I turned to see a monstrous silhouette and a pair of glowing yellow eyes.

"You awake."

"What did you give me? Did you do this on purpose?"

"I not know what happened. When you not wake, I worry."

"Amulii y—" A trickle of vomit cut short my words before I let loose an acrid, caramel-colored fountain, just missing his feet as he jumped out of the way. Everything I'd eaten earlier lay on the ground in a sour, meaty puddle.

"I not understand your sickness. Meat was good. It not make me sick."

He had a point. If he drugged the meat, why wasn't he on the ground with me?

After what felt like an eternity of retching, I spat trickles of mucus, gagging once more before the agony ceased. I dipped my hand into the lake and washed my face. Sweet water poured over my tongue, and I swished it around, spitting out the taste of stomach acid and jerky.

Amulii extended a hand to help me off the ground, and I wobbled to my feet, following him back to his den.

"What did you season that meat with? I think I may have had a bad reaction to whatever that was."

"Pun'chei, from my land. Delicious to maw'cha. Full of nutrients." His tail hung between his legs and he stared at the ground. "I not do right things, it seems. Mess up much, not knowing humans like I should." He let out a short, high-pitched dog whine which melted my heart. "I sorry, many times."

I'd have hugged him to make him feel better if I wasn't so sure he'd get the wrong idea. We sat next to each other on a boulder near the cave entrance, basking in the glow of the warm crystals.

"You didn't know," I said, scratching between his shoulder blades. His ears perked up as he turned to look at me. "It's okay, I'm not mad. I'm just a little scared, and I don't know you that well. Sorry I jumped to conclusions there."

"I stay close long, keeping you warm in my fur, but was still hungry, so had to hunt. I had thoughts to carry you to your home, but I did not want others seeing me in the day. I not leave without knowing you okay."

What was that malevolent creature I conjured into existence in my dream earlier? There wasn't a mean bone in Amulii's body as far as I knew. The way he cared about me was endearing.

"Oh, fuck it," I muttered, standing in front of him before wrapping my arms around his neck. I didn't care that he looked like this, or that he wanted more than friendship. For the moment, he was the only true friend I had in Jasper. "You're a good guy, Amulii." I pulled away before rubbing his head. There was that grin again as his tail went crazy.

"I hate parting, but very late, unless you wish staying the night with me," he said.

His tone wasn't suggestive, and I was so exhausted that I wanted to take him up on that offer. We hadn't had a chance to talk much before I passed out, but it was late.

Way too late.

My chest grew heavy as I remembered something important.

"I am so fucked right now."

"I not understand this word, fucked," Amulii said. Though it was kind of funny hearing him say it, I wasn't in the mood to laugh.

"We may as well enjoy this walk together because I won't be leaving the house for a while." Sighing, I followed Amulii as we trekked closer to the trees near the shore. I noticed something odd. As we got further away from the cave, the crystal light no longer illuminated anything. I could see the glow from the entrance when I looked back, but the light didn't travel and there were no shadows. "My mom is going to kill me."

Amulii grabbed my hand while dragging me back toward the cave. "Human mothers kill offspring?" he shouted, genuinely horrified. "My mother never ever kill me." We were almost going at a sprint. "You living with me now."

This time I laughed at his misunderstanding, tugging his shaky arm back toward the path home.

"Why laughter? You not scared? How I not know such horrible thing humans do?" He was adorable, his eyes wide with concern as one ear fell to the side of his head.

"It's just a saying," I said, having trouble catching my breath. "She's not actually going to kill me, dude. I'm just in a lot of trouble because she's probably worried."

With his head tilted and bushy brows furrowed, his eyes locked with mine for a moment. I flashed him another reassuring smile before his features lightened.

"I need getting better at your language," he said, relief in his tone as he let go of my hand.

///

We neared the forest clearing, and the seriousness of the situation strobed blue and red through the trees. As we walked into the clearing, I could make out two police cars parked beside one another in the front yard, and the porch light was just bright enough to reveal blackish, runny splatters on the door and wood siding.

"Oh man, there was blood all over the porch and the door's broken."

It took Amulii a moment to understand, but as it sank in, his ears flattened against the sides of his head as they usually did when he worried or was upset.

"She must think you are killed." We looked at each other, and Amulii grimaced. "This my fault."

"It's okay," I whispered, reaching up to give him a scratch on the head. Even though he wasn't a dog, he still had a giant wolf-like head, and I couldn't help myself. "It was really cool getting to know you. I might see you in a week, maybe two. It all depends on how well tonight goes."

"Can see you if I human?"

"Give it a week. This'll need some time to simmer."

I walked toward the house, but his rough, clawed hand caught mine, pulling me back. He opened his mouth as if to say something but stopped.

"What's wrong?"

He glanced at my chest for a moment. "It . . . nothing. Will see you in a week."

Amulii forced a smile, loosening his grip until his hand slipped away. It was sad to leave him, especially since it was obvious he didn't want me to go. I waved goodbye and made the walk of shame to the front door.

I tiptoed inside just in time to catch the final act of Mom's hysterics in front of two male cops. The weather strip under the broken door ended it with a flatulent sound as it rubbed across the smooth wood underneath. The room fell silent as she and two very annoyed police officers turned away from the dining room table and stared at me.

Both men appeared to be in their late twenties, though the dimness of the room made it hard to see their faces with enough detail. One was clean-shaven, with black hair, wearing a light blue police jacket and pants. The other had a trimmed brown beard and wore the same uniform with the addition of a gold-striped hat.

"I can explain," I said, struggling to push the broken door shut.

Mom tossed the phone on the dining room table and hurried across the room, sobbing as she crushed me in her arms.

"Thank goodness you're okay," she said, examining my face and hands before pulling away from me. Her face crumpled into a scowl. "You are never leaving this house again."

"What happened here?" the cop in the hat asked, as both men approached the front door. "Looks like someone really wanted to get in."

"Yeah, I did. I locked myself out, and a friend helped me break in"

The other cop eyed the security chain that dangled from a bent slit; it still had four screws attached. He cocked an eyebrow. "You chained the door, and managed to locked yourself out?"

"I chained the door last night," I said, trying to remain as calm as I could while also coming up with a convincing story. "I walked out the back door this morning, and it's easy to accidentally twist the lock. That must have been what happened, and I was lucky someone was hiking by to help me."

"And the blood?" Mom asked. "What the hell was all that?"

"He, uh, hunted a hare and had to set it down on the table. It was still bleeding." Her face went from pallid to an angry shade of red. "Everything's fine. I swear."

"Well ma'am, it looks like the case of the missing son has solved itself," the officer in the hat said, a bit of sarcasm in his voice. He placed a hand on my shoulder and shook his head. "Good luck."

The crooked door groaned shut as he and his partner stepped outside.

"Before you get too upset, I made a friend. I know how much you wanted me to go out and meet people," I said, trying in vain to shift some blame back to her. For as long as I was old enough to argue, that had never ended in my favor, but it didn't stop me from trying.

"I got 'too upset' hours ago." She stomped toward the dining room, grabbing the cordless phone before tossing it on the couch beside me. "What does that say?"

"I wuv you," I said, trying to lighten the mood as my voice shot up in pitch. It worked when I was younger, but this situation may have crossed a few hard lines. I also wasn't as cute anymore. When I grabbed the receiver, it read sixty-seven missed calls.

"Stop being a smartass. I nearly got a speeding ticket from one of the cops that just walked out. I had to explain that my son might be dead because he won't answer the goddamn phone. I must have sounded insane."

"Well . . . " I mumbled under my breath, clicking my tongue.

"Keep pushing, Alex. You were already on thin ice yesterday."

As she continued yelling, my mind wandered to thoughts of Amulii. What did maw'chas do most of the time? Was he hunting or about to curl up on his bed for the evening? Does he sleep curled up like a wolf does? I bet that's kind of cute. Maybe I should have taken him up on his offer and slept over.

"Alexander," she shouted, snapping me out of my daydream. "Are you seriously ignoring me right now?"

"No."

"I had to leave the conference early as well, which was rather important by the way. All I could think was the worst." She snatched a washcloth out of the sink and threw it at me. "Then, when I get here, there's blood everywhere."

She placed a hand on her forehead and lowered her voice. "I thought what anyone would seeing that."

She wasn't that far off the mark, but I couldn't tell her a werewolf *accidentally* broke into the house holding a bloody animal.

"Clean the door, and you're scrubbing that porch tomorrow. You're grounded indefinitely."

"What the hell do you mean, 'indefinitely'?"

Mom snatched the phone away, her face inches from mine. "I don't know. Maybe when you're fifty and I'm dead."

The argument was over. Dad would need to talk some sense into her when he returned, but that could easily backfire. I'd still be grounded, but with the added misery of being stuck in a war zone.

No—I couldn't get Dad involved. Hurricane Sally had to lose intensity eventually. Perhaps I could talk her into a more reasonable punishment in a few days.

CHAPTER FIVE

THE SOUNDS OF NIGHT

"So much for keeping in touch," I muttered, laying my tablet on the desk next to a half-finished calculus assignment before crawling onto the sturdy wooden awning outside of my window. I must have sent ten emails and left double that in voice messages, but Mike was a pro at the silent treatment whenever we'd argue.

We hadn't parted on good terms when I left Calgary. He was already upset that I was moving, and I admit, my shitty attitude didn't help matters. When I unintentionally blew him off my last day in the city, it was the last crack that shattered ten years of friendship.

"Hey, Alex." The hair on my arms stood on end when I heard Amulii's hushed human voice from below.

We hadn't seen each other since the night I got in trouble. It hadn't been a week, yet he was all I seemed to think about.

"You don't have to whisper. No one's here," I said, crawling to the edge of the awning while squinting at the unruly cotoneaster hedges that grew along the outer walls of the cabin. Since Amulii was a predator who hunted for his meals, he was disturbingly adept at staying hidden.

The shrub near the far corner snapped and rustled as he popped up from behind. He grinned and shook a few leaves from his messy hair. He had on the same tight, filthy shirt he wore when I first met him at the lake.

"How long have you been waiting there?"

"Not long," he said while stalking across the yard, his eyes darting toward the woods as he got closer. "I had to see you. Was very dull. You said a week, but I sneaky."

"You can come in if you want, but if my mom shows up, you gotta get the hell out."

I scooted toward the open window, but before I could make it, he jumped over the edge of the awning, landing on the surface. Him jumping several meters in the air was so unexpected I fell back into my bedroom and hung upside down against the wall, my legs still outside.

He reached through the window to grab my arm, but I allowed myself to fall to the floor. Amulii snorted laughter before climbing after me.

His strange howl-like chuckle was funnier than my clumsiness. We were both in fits as I struggled to pull myself off the floor. Amulii's timing was perfect. In between fighting with my parents, my best friend ignoring me, and being grounded, a friendly face was what I needed.

"I'm so glad you're here; you have no idea," I said, plopping down on my bed before leaning against the headboard. "I've been craving some human contact lately."

His eyes lit up as he scrambled onto the bed, removing his dingy shirt before tossing it to the floor. I couldn't tell what was happening until he was on top of me.

"Whoa. What are you doing?"

Amulii froze, his face inches from mine.

"You said you craving this. Cannot stay human for long while mating but can try."

As I examined his bare upper body, I noticed there were a few similarities he shared with his werewolf form, most notably the thick hair that covered his sturdy chest, narrowing into a trail that passed his belly button.

"Hold on, jeez. That's not what I meant." I stared wide-eyed at him for a moment. "Are you always this horny?"

"Oh." His eager smile shifted in the opposite direction. When he sniffed the air, I knew what was happening. "Your body is—"

"Stop it. Don't finish that sentence." I yelled, pushing up against him. "And get off me."

He fell to my side and continued his awkward staring. Amulii had the body of a human, and I'd let my guard down. His ignorant, beast-like behavior snapped me back to reality.

"Okay." A huge, shit-eating grin dominated his face. I got hot with embarrassment because I knew what he was thinking.

I hated the fact that he *knew*.

"So," I said, forcing a stream of air through my lips like a boiling kettle. "What have you been up to lately?"

Amulii drew his lips to a line and grabbed his discarded shirt from the floor, draping it over his lap, his right foot tapping the air impatiently.

"Talking boring compared to other thing."

"Oh, come on. I just met you."

"Hmm," Amulii muttered.

We lay on the bed next to each other in a bout of unpleasant silence before I finally said something.

"Thanks for coming to visit me," I said.

"It nothing to thank for. Very exciting. I not know people, not have friends. Had to come see Alex again."

"Yeah, it sucks not having friends."

Amulii narrowed his eyes. "What . . . human friends suck on?"

The serious tone of that question had me holding my gut so as to not laugh myself sick. "It's—" I couldn't breathe. "It means it's not good."

"Ah," Amulii grunted. "Not what I thinking at all. Thinking weird things." He snorted before joining in the laughter.

"You've got me as a friend," I said, finally calming down enough to speak clearer. "You really don't have anyone else?"

His expression darkened. "No. I hiding from humans now, most times."

I thought of Liam carrying that rifle, warning me about the very creature lying docile in the bed next to me. What kind of heartless people would try to kill someone who just wanted a friend?

"Those men with the guns," I said, placing my hand on top of his, "keep away from them. They know about you."

He smiled again and nodded. "I will."

///

It was past midnight, and I stood in the yard, admiring the waxing moon. I hadn't been able to sleep well since Amulii's last visit. A week had dragged by without him visiting, and all I did during that time was worry.

He got the wrong idea about what I wanted, and while he seemed fine afterward, I wondered if that annoyed him. Despite being a werewolf, he was still a guy. He wanted sex and I didn't give it to him. I hoped he wasn't like that. It seemed out of character for him, but I'd only gotten to know him for a couple days.

Maybe something bad happened to him. What if the hunters got him? There were so many unknowns, and all of them were terrible conclusions to jump to. I would rather him be mad at me than mounted on some redneck's wall.

A dry breeze tickled the chill bumps along my bare arms as I basked in the gentle, pale glow. Evelyn Peak's imposing silhouette in the distance lorded over the natural skyline. Nights like these made me wish I could grow wings and fly over everything.

There were no noises aside from the hissing of wind through pine needles. The forest's edge cast a line of shadow that sucked away the pale luminescence, creating an abyss I could almost fall into.

"Night is beautiful, and I see you enjoying it."

His deep but gentle voice sent a fresh surge of excitement through me. Though it was slight, there was a low growl in his tone, and I knew he wasn't human. Had he been watching me the entire time?

Glowing yellow eyes dotted the beastly shadow that towered over me. If I didn't know him, the sight would have given me nightmares, but I was relieved. He'd come back, which put to rest all the insecurities and worries that kept me from getting a full night's sleep for days.

"Yeah, it is," I said, smiling at him. "Where the hell have you been? I've been really worried."

"I had . . . encounter with humans and needed hiding. I smelled you and had to come see."

There was a slight slurring of his words, and from what I could see of his silhouette, his body slouched forward.

"How did you smell me from so far?"

"You not bathed. It easy to pick up in the wind," he said, his eyes illuminating his monstrous hand pointing a clawed finger at his snout. He was right, though it embarrassed me. I hadn't been outside in a while, so I didn't bother taking a shower for a few days. "That is the scent that is most alluring about you."

Chills ran the length of my back like someone was unzipping me. To have a werewolf's monstrous voice court me from the shadows was unsettling, but strangely exhilarating.

I pointed up toward my open bedroom window. "Think you could fit through that as a werewolf? It's cold out here."

Amulii nodded, and I led him to the ladder. When I heard more furious sniffing from behind, the excitement I felt a few moments earlier shifted to nervousness. Having him in my bedroom in this form seemed kind of dangerous.

Nothing about his attraction to me made sense, considering he often avoided human contact. What was it about me he liked? It couldn't only be the way I smelled, which still grossed me out.

My parents' room was downstairs on the opposite end of the house, so they probably wouldn't hear us talking if we whispered. It was a tight squeeze, even for my oversized bedroom window, and his movements were unusually sluggish, but before I knew it, I had a monster in my bedroom. I pulled on the lamp cord, and the light revealed what he'd been hiding from me outside.

"Oh my God. What happened to you?" I ran to the bathroom to grab a towel. Blood trickled from his right arm in a steady, pulsing stream. The wound was blistered and also oozing pus in places. Fur had fallen out around the hole, almost as if the bullet scalded him when it pierced the skin. "Don't you have crystal things to heal this stuff?"

"It not as bad as it could be. I not feel it much, and we heal fast. It will be gone by morning, but I need you . . ." He paused, catching his breath. This was a deep wound, and it was obvious he was trying hard to mask the pain. ". . . to do something."

The towel went from white to burgundy as it sopped up what must have been a liter of blood from the fur on his arm and chest. When I'd remove it, the wound would gush each time he tensed. Blood was my biggest weakness, and I wasn't sure what would take me out first: the nausea or the lightheadedness.

"Anything. What do you need me to do?"

"My fingers too big and claws not long enough to reach. Your fingers small enough to get poison metal out. Please." It was heartbreaking watching him struggle to keep calm.

Adrenaline kept me upright each time I'd feel faint. He would die unless I did something, and I'd need to concentrate on the task and not the gore. Swallowing the bile that swished its way into my throat, I reached for Amulii's upper arm. It was thicker than my leg.

"This is gonna hurt, are you gonna be okay?"

"I will," he reassured, giving me a soft smile and a slight dog-like whine.

Taking three breaths, I carefully widened the gushing wound with my fingers to get a better look. Amulii growled as thick, pungent fluid erupted like tiny, yellow geysers.

Don't throw up. Don't throw up.

"What the hell?" I slipped a finger into the bloody hole which went deep. There were shards shattered everywhere, and my mind raced to the next course of action.

As I slid the blood-covered digit back out, he bared his clenched teeth and whined again. I knew where the fragments were, and I could get them out with tweezers. In all the panic, I forgot about the first aid kit in my wilderness bag.

"I can get something that'll work. Can you hang in there?"

Amulii's grimace relaxed into another forced grin.

"Of course. It is nothing. I leave it in your hands." A deep, ragged breath punctuated every brief sentence.

I grabbed the kit from my bag, dumping its contents out on the desk. Grabbing tweezers, gauze, disinfectant, and my headlamp, I ran back over to him, trying to keep my footsteps light so my parents wouldn't wake up.

"How long have you been walking around like this?" I asked, securing the lamp around my head before turning it on so I could better see the bullet hole.

"Four days. What is in my arm makes me not heal. My blood not clotting, crystals not working. I eat to stay alive."

"Why didn't you come to me sooner? I would have helped."

"Humans always following. I would not lead them here. I needing time to lose them, but I would come to you when it safe. Would never put you in danger." Amulii lost so much blood that his head began dipping forward, his eyes partially closed. "Feel weak, so please . . ."

I worked the tweezers into the wound, feeling less sick the more dire the situation got. One by one, I pulled out fragments of what looked like silver. No wonder the bullet shattered so badly on impact.

When I pulled out the final shard, the bleeding trickled to a stop, and the wound sealed shut so fast I thought I was hallucinating. As the blisters receded, thick fur replaced the scar and bald spot on his arm. Did that really just happen?

Blood pooled on the floor, trickling between the gaps in the panels leading under the bed. Some of it got on my comforter, and I'd need to wash it, or Mom would freak.

As the adrenaline faded, the fetid stench from the injury punched my nose, but when Amulii wrapped his arms around me, none of it mattered.

"Thank you," he said as he held me against him.

I returned his embrace with my own, my head resting against the soft mane on his chest. As I pulled away, his fur had sponged blood all over my arms, soaking my shirt and trickling onto the elastic of my pajama pants. By some miracle, he was still breathing, and I hadn't passed out.

"I'm just glad you're okay." I shot him a glare. "I told you to stay away from those guys."

He remained silent, dropping to my mattress as his knees buckled. Seconds later, his eyes rolled upward as he fell back.

"Amulii."

I rushed to his side and placed two fingers under his jaw, trying to feel for a pulse. After a few seconds, I found a vein that thudded steadily under his fur, and I knew he was okay, for now.

After cleaning blood off my floor and taking a quick shower, I stopped to look at the slumbering creature taking up most of my bed. He rattled the windows as he snored, and a long, thin tongue dangled from the side of his open maw, drenching my comforter in drool. Most people would have found the sight of him repulsive, but that was the furthest thought from my mind. I scooted against the giant creature and raked my trembling fingers through the silky outer coat along his stomach.

After a minute or so of petting him, I pressed an ear against the thick mane on his chest. My head rose and fell in a steady rhythm as I listened to his strong heartbeat.

Amulii still smelled like blood, though it had dried, but his usual scent burned through, overpowering everything. The steady motion of his breath, the soft fur under my face, and the comforting smell together made it hard to keep my eyes open.

Shaking myself awake, I pulled from his warmth. A flutter worked its way from my stomach to my chest, culminating in an unusual heat in the center. My fingers were still shaky as I moved the crystal necklace out of the way and massaged the area. The odd feeling passed, but the emotions didn't.

"What's wrong with me?" I whispered, creeping toward the edge of the mattress so as to not wake him. After stumbling to my feet, I tiptoed through the door, closing it enough to dampen the loud snoring. The floorboards groaned as I took one step at a time, each seeming to get louder as I descended into the dark silence of the dining area. I glanced across the living room, and there was just enough light beaming in through the windows to see my parents' door wide open.

This was the one time I was thankful to be small and light as my feet slid quietly across the smooth wooden floors. I grabbed the brass knob and slowly pulled the door closed, turning it so there wouldn't be the usual click.

Though the dim moonlight lit my path back through the living room toward the kitchen, it was harder to see. I could make out an end table near the couch, and if I had walked any faster, I would have run into it, knees first. There were no windows in the dining room for light, but I could have sworn there was a shadow on one of the chairs.

I finally made it to the kitchen and opened the refrigerator door. The light made me squint for a few seconds before plates of leftovers sharpened into view. Grilled chicken, smoked brisket, pulled pork—it was a carnivore's fantasy. A meal fit for a starving werewolf, though with Amulii's size, I started to wonder if even this wasn't enough.

I grabbed the plates one-by-one and set them on the counter.

"What are you doing?"

My heart skipped as I jumped backward at the sound of my father's voice. The shadow at the dining room table stood and walked into the light of the fridge revealing his puzzled face.

"Dad," I said, my hushed tone pitching upward with surprise. "I—I was hungry."

He glanced at the counter, which must have had about ten pounds of food sitting on it, before crossing his arms.

"You're gonna eat all that?"

"I'm really hungry."

"Yeah." Dad wasn't buying it, but I had an idea.

"I want to bulk up," I said, my voice so low I may as well have been whispering. We didn't talk much, and when we did, he was usually yelling at me about something. "I want to build some muscle."

Dad cracked a half-smile, but the whites of his eyes still indicated suspicion. "'Bout damn time." He pointed upstairs. "So, I can expect you to finally start using that weight bench?"

"Uh, yeah," I muttered, lowering my eyes to the floor.

"Look at people when you talk to 'em," Dad said, a little louder, but catching himself as he looked toward the master bedroom door. My head snapped back up, and a familiar scent of whiskey stung my nose.

"What are *you* doing out here?"

"About to go back to bed," he said, turning away.

"Dad."

"Eat your food and go to bed," he said sharply. "And don't waste it." He wasn't drunk, but he'd done this before. It never turned out well. "Keep this between us."

///

After placing the barbeque buffet on my desk, I sat next to the maw'cha, giving him a shake.

"Amulii." I shoved him harder but couldn't move his bulk more than a few inches. Instead, I lowered my face next to his ears and tried calling his name a bit louder. "Amulii."

He snorted and opened his eyes. "Oh," he said, pushing himself into a sitting position before rubbing his forehead. "I not remember sleeping."

"I brought you something." I stood and tiptoed over to the desk, grabbing a plate of chicken before handing it to him. "It's probably not how you normally eat this, but it's food."

The look on Amulii's face was pure bliss when he saw the meal, and slobber trailed along his lower jaw. After rubbing his hands together, he grabbed the drumsticks and tossed them into his mouth, chewing bones and all before swallowing. It only took two more mouthfuls before the plate was empty. He inhaled every dish of smoked meat I handed him.

"You need to stay in your human form, and . . . maybe you should consider living here. I could hide you."

I didn't have a plan, and there wasn't a feasible way to keep him a secret from my parents. However, I didn't want him to go back out there again, at least not as a beast everyone would hunt as a trophy.

"I not mind, but I cannot," he said, smacking his jaws as he handed me another empty plate. "Hard for me staying human. I not feel good among your kind, especially the loud ones living here."

"Yeah, but you won't die. You'll be safe."

I knew he wasn't some lost pet that followed me home, but he was the first friend I'd made since moving. When I grabbed his rough, heavy hand, that odd warmth in my chest returned.

Everything about him confused me physically. I found the human part of him sexually alluring, but the werewolf was just as thrilling. Was I attracted to the beast as well? His sweet, caring disposition made every part of him shine to me. The only other person I felt this comfortable around was Mike, and I'd known him for years.

"You are special," Amulii said, getting more comfortable on my bed as he leaned against the headboard. "I right about you. You good human, Alex. None would help me like you did."

I thought for a moment about what I'd been wanting to ask him again. "Amulii, where are you from? And be honest this time."

I lay on the bed next to him, propping my head with a few pillows. He grabbed the crystal hanging from his neck, his expression distant—the same look he had last week in the kitchen.

"I from world that crosses once a year, during the long night. I not know why this happens, but it that way for many lives." He looked out the window toward the moon. "Old stories tell our worlds as great spirits, life givers." He glanced at me, his sharp smile glistening in the lamplight. "Lovers. They cursed and must travel same circle path but different ways. Other spirits very jealous of their love and forced your world into this existence and my world into other. They still travel same path, but meet only one day every year, and veil disappears. Where great spirits hold one another, connections form and some of my kind can travel between them."

If what he said about the two planets was real, it proved something theoretical physicists have been debating for decades. Maybe it all went beyond science, which the old me would have shrugged off as nonsense. Inviting a werewolf from another world into my bed made me a little more open to the supernatural, at least until I could explain it.

"One connection is on our spot, Spirit Island as humans call it. We know it as Segolia. It pulls some humans. They feel my world when it close. Your scent got my attention, but you are one of few humans who feel my world."

"There's nothing mystical about it," I said, shaking my head. "It's a popular tourist spot. I liked going there to see the sunsets. Lots of people like sunsets, Amulii. There's nothing special about that."

He took my hand in his, and warmth spread through me, my face burning. Slivers of discomfort pricked at the back of my mind, but I wouldn't pull away this time. Instead, my fingers slid between his, clasping his rough, padded palms as they dwarfed my own.

"Have you ever felt . . . pulling you not understand? You always stopping at the connection before going to our spot. This not happen once, but each time."

It was hard to find a proper response because there was something to what he said. He was right about me stopping at the same place each time, but that was only because I wanted to get a better view of the mountains. He looked back out the window and said nothing else.

I noticed something about Amulii tonight. His English was slightly less fragmented than it was last week, and he spoke faster as if he were more comfortable with the language.

"So, you're from a different world. I guess that makes about as much sense as everything else so far. You've never told me why you're here or what you're looking for."

Moments passed as I waited for a response, but he remained silent as if he hadn't heard me. He'd been through enough the last few days, and I didn't want to press him too hard. If it was something he wanted to tell me, he would—at least, I hope he would.

"Alex," he whispered, turning toward me again. "Spend time with me. We go for long walks and sleep under stars. We talk, and we can enjoy food. Does this sound good . . . for friendship?"

That thrill from earlier manifested as bumps that covered my skin. It sounded wonderful, and it would be nice to get to know him better.

"Well, sure. Of course we can, but you need to understand that I won't be here forever. Next year I'm going to college in the city, and I won't be able to see you at all unless you visit."

He grimaced for only a second, but it was enough time for me to notice. "We . . . have connection now. I am not upset."

"What does that mean? I'm sure you can't sniff me out when I'm in Calgary."

He pointed to the necklace I wore under my shirt. Ever since he'd tied it around my neck, I couldn't bring myself to take it off.

"This thing?"

"Yes. I find you wherever you are." He rubbed his crystal with his thumb again. "You are only human to have it. I never allow another to touch."

His tone went from normal to angry in an instant as he glared at the night sky again. The distance returned when he squeezed his crystal. Mine got warmer as he whispered something unintelligible to himself.

"I not . . . know."

"What?" I asked, interrupting his train of thought.

Amulii shook his head, startled when I spoke, like he had forgotten I was in the room with him.

"Nothing," he said, stroking my head. "I lose myself to thinking sometimes."

I woke up, surprised to feel a giant furry arm wrapped snug around my waist. As I turned, my nose grazed his wet snout, and thin, canine lips were a hair away from touching mine. He'd never left my room last night, and we'd fallen asleep together. Amulii's body pressed against me, replacing the chill in the room with intense heat.

I lay there for a while, watching him sleep. I couldn't help but chuckle softly at the way he drooled. Then panic ruined the moment when I heard the familiar creaking of footsteps on old wooden stairs.

CHAPTER SIX

WEREWOLF IN THE CLOSET

I shot up from the pillows, climbing on top of the slumbering were-wolf to shake him awake. "Amulii," I whispered, loud enough to get his attention, but soft enough that Mom wouldn't hear.

He was difficult to wake. I grabbed the fur on his chest with both hands and frantically tugged. He groaned before shifting position in the bed away from me, falling back to sleep.

My worst nightmare was about to come true if my mother barged through the door and saw us together. While rolling over, I misjudged the distance and fell to the floor with a crash that shook the upstairs.

The bed rocked as the heavy werewolf crawled to the side.

"That sounded painful," Amulii said, peeking over the edge, his eyes half-open and pointed ears lazily drooping downward. "Are you okay?"

"I'm fine." I crawled across the floor, pinching the lock as two shadows fanned the light under the crack of the door. "Get in the closet," I said in a loud, hushed voice. Scrambling to my feet, I panned the room to make sure there wasn't anything suspicious or blood-covered lying in the open.

Amulii smacked his jaws after another yawn and blinked twice. As he came to and heard my mother outside the door, he jumped out of bed, landing on his pawed feet with a thud. He pulled open the window and began to crawl through, but I dashed over and grabbed his arm, pulling him back inside.

"Are you nuts? What if my dad's out there?"

The doorknob rattled as Mom tried to turn it.

"Alex, are you okay? I heard something fall." She gave the door a few hard knocks. "Why is this locked?"

"I'm fine. Could you give me some privacy?" I shouted, pulling Amulii toward the door of the walk-in closet. "Get in there and don't make any noise."

Amulii crammed himself into the small room, using his massive paws to kick away the dirty clothes that lay in a pile on the floor. In my haste, I caught his tail in the door, and he yelped, pulling the appendage inside before growling at me.

"Damn, sorry." The pale glow of his annoyed glare was the last thing I saw before closing the door all the way. "Just stay in there until I can get rid of her."

"Is there somebody else in there?" There was a light brushing sound against the door where she pressed her ear. "What the hell is going on?"

"No." I pulled a clean T-shirt over my head. "Is the house on fire or something?"

After counting backward from ten in my head, I was calm enough to unlock the door and back away. It swung open and Mom gave me a suspicious glare as she stepped into the room.

"There's no one here, goddamn. What's your issue?"

"Watch your language. I'm not going to tell you again."

"Or what?" I prodded, rolling my eyes. "You're gonna super-duper ground me?"

"One of these days when I'm dead, you'll wish you talked to me better than you do."

My heart pounded when Mom wrinkled her nose after sniffing the air. The room reeked of Amulii, and so did I. His pungent odor had rubbed off on me while I slept against him, and a clean shirt wasn't helping. I caught sight of a blood-soaked sock in the middle of the floor next to the bed.

"Oh, spare me the guilt trip."

She clicked her tongue. "Like father, like son."

She knew that got under my skin. "Well, this shouldn't bother you, then. You're still married to the guy. You're the one that dragged me out here so you can save this dumpster fire of a marriage." I crossed my arms. "By the way, how's that working out? Was it worth screwing up my senior year so you guys could keep screeching at each other without worrying about disturbing the neighbors now?"

I kicked the sock under the bed while she wasn't looking.

"I know you're angry about all this, but it's better than being another broken family." She shifted her gaze toward the closet. "I remember how nasty my parents' divorce was, and they never even tried to work on their marriage."

I threw back my head and groaned. "We're already broken, Mom. We've been that way for years. 'Saving the family' is starting to sound like a running joke that isn't funny anymore." I was so annoyed that I'd forgotten about Amulii. "Stop me if you've heard this one: How many counselors does it take to save a shitty marriage?" I gritted my teeth. "And how many shrinks does it take to fix the kid you guys screwed up?"

"Oh stop being melodramatic."

I swallowed down the urge to start screaming at her.

"You guys left me alone in a booby hatch for kids when I was nine years old. I barely remember anything because I was so doped up on Prozac."

It wasn't the first time I'd brought it up in an argument, and it was still a sore spot for both of us. A light thump from the closet snapped me back to the potential disaster waiting for us if she opened that door. When she turned to look, I raised my voice.

"You've been on my case since we moved here, which by the way, thanks for the late-night text message instead of talking to me first. You punish me when I finally decide to do something around here I like, and then you berate me for treating you like shit, when being a shitty person is pretty much all I've been taught by example." The words seemed to slip from my mouth without me realizing it.

My temper cooled when I saw her tear up. This was something I'd been holding in for weeks, but I didn't expect to unload all of it right here. Still, it worked to divert her attention back to me. "Hold on, I didn't mean to say that." I stretched my arms out and leaned in. "I'm sorry."

It was hard to talk to her about how I was feeling without ending up on a therapist's couch. I also couldn't talk to Dad, because he had about as much emotional intelligence as a bag of dried concrete.

She gave me a sniff. With every inhale, I thought her nose would fold up into her face. "It's hard to admit when we fail at something, whether it's marriage or parenting. Hopefully, when you find someone and have kids of your own, you'll have learned what not to do."

"I hope you're not expecting me to breed, because our genetic line dies with me."

My eyes shifted to the side as she surveyed the room again. "What the hell is that smell? It's coming from you and the whole bedroom," she said, pushing me away. "You need to start wearing more deodorant. Is that a dog?"

"Oh," I said, nervously reaching for a story she'd buy. "You caught me. I found a dog outside the house last night, but I let him back out." She let out a sharp gasp when her eyes shifted to the dark stains on my comforter.

"What is that?"

"Uh, he was hurt, but I put some bandages on him. He looked good enough. I think."

"Is it still alive?" She folded back the comforter to find the stain seeped all the way to the mattress protector. "Oh my God. Alex, what the hell? First the blood on the porch, now this?"

It was shocking to see in the daylight, and I started to feel light-headed. The horror spreading across her face meant I had precious little time to get this misunderstanding taken care of.

"Now hold on, this isn't what you think."

An anime wall scroll fell to the ground after a crash from within the closet rattled the room. There was no way to divert her attention from something that loud. I tried to block her path as she stormed toward the noise.

"You lied to me."

"Wait a second. Let me explain," I said, trying to keep her from getting to the closet. "He's friendly. Don't freak out, okay?"

She pushed me aside and opened the door. I squeezed my eyes shut and held my breath, waiting for the scream.

"I am sorry, Alex told me to wait in here, but I trip."

My eyes snapped open when I heard his human voice. The relief was short-lived as Amulii stood in front of us in all his naked glory. He covered his crotch with one of my T-shirts and held a pair of my boxer shorts in the other hand. His pants were lying crumpled beneath him. Covering himself with my shirt, I could understand, but why was he holding my dirty boxers?

"Jesus Christ," I muttered, my face getting hot as I looked away.

If I weren't so mortified, this would have really gotten me going. This was the second time I'd seen Amulii without a shirt as a human, but now there was so much more. Thick, black hair trailed further, stopping above a black patch of pubes peeking from the shirt.

"Damn it, Alex," she whispered, pushing me to the side as she ran to my door, locking it before turning back. "Can you at least wait until after the divorce to do shit like this?"

"Okay, this looks bad, but it's not *that*." Oh, who was I kidding? Amulii stood naked in my closet, and I wasn't skilled enough to come up with another story she'd buy. "He, uh . . . helped me with the dog last night." God, what gross choice of words.

"I don't care if you're gay, but don't have sex in this house. Did you guys at least use protection?" She turned to Amulii. "What's your name, and are you sleeping with my son?"

"Put your damn pants on," I whispered, pushing him back inside before shutting the closet door. "We're not sleeping together. We're just friends."

Her voice got louder. "There's a huge naked man in your closet." She paused, lowering her voice. "He's naked and in your closet. Do you think I fell off the turnip truck yesterday?"

We both watched as the door opened and Amulii emerged in buttonless, blood-covered pants he struggled to keep around his waist with one hand.

"I am sorry, I was changing when you came in. There was much blood, and my button came off and . . . Alex gave me some of his clothing, but it not fit. This was my fault. I brought the dog." Amulii's response was surprisingly astute, at least for him.

"Okay, but why were you hiding?"

"I hid him," I said as Amulii opened his mouth to speak. "Because I thought you'd get mad at me for having someone over while I'm grounded."

The tense muscles in her face relaxed.

"So, you're not doing anything?" It hadn't crossed my mind until then, but Amulii's physical appearance mimicked Dad's in a way. Aside from his height and body hair, everything else checked out. The blush on Mom's cheeks made it clear that she was thinking the same thing.

I wanted to jump out of the window headfirst when I realized it.

"No."

The humiliation could be enough to kill me if I let this continue. There was something dreadful about having sex talks with parents, especially when they involved me being launched out of the proverbial closet. It was a conversation my father never wanted to have, and my mother had no filter.

"Well, this is awkward." She reached out her hand to shake Amulii's. "I'm Sally. Who are you?"

He grabbed her hand with the one that wasn't clinging to torn, loose pants.

"Am—"

"Aaron," I interrupted.

"I was asking *him*." She crossed her arms and focused intently on the half-naked man.

"Aaron. Yes, my name. Aaron."

"How old are you?"

Surprisingly, that was something I never thought to ask. I was curious to hear his answer. He looked a few years older than me, so I assumed he was in his early twenties.

"I will be eighty in three months."

There was a crushing silence as Mom shot me a bewildered glance.

"This guy." I broke into nervous laughter, my elbow jabbing Amulii's right arm. "Always joking around."

Was he for real?

"He's twenty." I turned away from Mom and mouthed the word *please*.

He broke into loud, forced laughter. "Oh. Yes. I sometimes make jokes." Amulii spoke in a monotone as his body went rigid. He was unraveling the longer he stood there, and his English was starting to break.

"You have a bit of an accent, where are you from?"

"Amulii was about to leave; he's got to go to work soon."

"Amulii?"

Fuck. "I mean Aaron," I said, giving the man a push toward my door.

"Oh, okay, *Aaron*." She shot me a doubtful glance. "I'll show you out."

Mom knew, and there was no getting around that. Her glare shifted to an annoying smirk before turning toward the bedroom door. Amulii ran in the opposite direction, and I knew what he was about to do. It was too late to stop it from happening.

"Thank you," he shouted, before making a horizontal leap out of my open second-floor window like it was the most natural thing to do. Mom gasped and dashed across the room before leaning outside. I rubbed my temples before joining her.

"Work," he shouted as he charged through the yard, struggling to keep the pants around his waist. "Cannot be late." Amulii wasn't exaggerating when he told me how much he hated being around humans.

Mom looked at me, eyes gaping with disbelief. "What the hell just happened?" She poked her head back outside in time to see him jump the firepit, tripping over his pants as they fell around his ankles. "Oh my God." She chuckled and placed a hand over her mouth, her alabaster skin turning an interesting shade of pink.

The image of a ferocious werewolf disintegrated as his pert, hairy ass vanished into the forest.

"He's . . . special," I mumbled. She shook her head before pressing her lips together while trying not to laugh. My face felt like it had been sitting next to a furnace. "Don't judge me. There is literally no one else my age around here."

"I just don't get it. If he's your friend, what else would you have in common? He can barely speak English." She crossed her arms. "Mike, I can see, but that guy?" She tilted her head, pushing the wire-framed glasses she wore up her nose. "Actually, now that I think about Mike—"

"No, stop." I wanted to crawl into a hole.

"I don't care if you're gay, but I do care if you're having sex with this guy you hardly know."

"Stop. Please," I muttered, rubbing my index finger and thumb against the bridge of my brow.

"Are you two having sex?" she repeated. "He's not much older than you, so I won't freak out about that, but you will tell the truth or this is not going to end."

"No, goddammit. Just stop talking."

She leaned against the windowsill. "You're a terrible liar. Were you with him that night last week? Was he the one that broke the door?"

"Yes, and yes. We hung out after that," I replied with an exhausted huff. "*Only* hung out. You said you didn't want me to go out in the woods alone, and I found someone who knows the woods better than Dad does. We just lost track of time."

I crossed my arms and glared at her as she examined my face like the human lie detector she was. None of what I told her was technically a lie, except the dog earlier. Given what Amulii was, I supposed that was a half-truth.

"Alright." She looked back out the window, watching as Amulii's discarded pants danced through the yard in a strong, swirling gust. "He didn't have much of a personality, but when you look like that, I guess you don't need one."

I groaned and turned away.

///

The showerhead trickled to a stop as I turned the knob and stepped out of the tub. From the moment I woke up, my nerves had been straddling a threaded line between shot and moments of numb exhaustion. After Mom left the room, I sat on the bed, blankly looking out the window for a solid hour while waiting for the fallout to settle after this morning's shit show with Amulii.

I should have told her years ago, and I knew she'd be understanding, but when I thought about opening up about that part of myself, Dad's voice would take over. He knew already; it's why he hated me so much. It took him browsing through my internet history in middle school to change our relationship from mere indifference to downright loathing. After he punched me in the stomach, causing me to throw up, we never mentioned it again. It became yet another open wound to join the many others that continued to fester, never fully healing.

I grabbed the towel from the rack next to the tub and patted myself down before drying my hair. The teenager in the mirror drew my eyes and my disgust. Such a scrawny, pale body, but I had a bit of Dad's face. What did someone as gorgeous as Amulii find so attractive about me? It didn't take long for the usual body dysmorphia to kick in, and the more I looked at myself, the more I hated.

I ran a brush through my short, damp hair before grabbing a clean shirt and boxers hanging on the door hook. After putting them on, I walked into my closet to find a clean pair of pants and a jacket. Once dressed, I grabbed my wilderness bag and left the room.

I had to see him again. There were so many thoughts and feelings I didn't have time to explore, and I couldn't determine what I really felt for the man *or* the wolf. The fact that I found his werewolf form attractive made me wonder just how fucked up I was.

What bothered me more was the feeling in my chest when I was up against him. Then to wake up in his arms like that . . .

I had to stop overthinking this.

The steps creaked as I descended. Had they always been so loud? My parents sat at the dining room table, eating in silence, and as uncomfortable as this made me, at least they weren't fighting.

"You gonna eat something, or are you still full from last night?" Dad asked, thumbing through his phone messages.

Mom looked at him, squinting her eyes. "Last night?"

He set the phone down and glowered at me. "Yeah, our son wants to start working out. He ate all the leftovers in the fridge."

"Oh, he did?" A knowing grin stuck to her face like tacky wallpaper. "*You* ate all those leftovers, huh?"

"Yes," I muttered, shuffling under my backpack. "I'm heading out to walk all of it off."

Mom stood and crossed her arms. "Did you forget something?"

I let out a sigh before turning back toward the stairs. After all the chaos, I'd forgotten I was still grounded.

"Let him go," Dad said, his tone unusually pleasant. "He's been in this damn house too much."

She nodded before looking toward the open living room windows. A calm breeze from outside jostled the curtains, and the scent of pine filled the house. "Fine."

That was it? No objection; no arguing? Something had mellowed them, and I knew what that something probably was. Dad was hiding his midnight binge drinking, and Mom was still trying to determine if her son was a big homo. Somehow, this worked in my favor, and all I had to do was keep my mouth shut. That part was easy.

"Here," she said, walking toward the cherry wood hutch that lined the far wall of the room to grab her purse. She pulled out her wallet and held up a gold credit card. "In case you get hungry later."

"Your credit card? Really?"

"Yours," she replied. "You're almost old enough to get one yourself, so I put your name on this account as an authorized user. I was going to give it to you last week, but then you went and got yourself all grounded."

"Well, gee-willikers, Mom, it sure was swell of you to do that," I said, reaching for the card, but she jerked it away at the last second.

"Keep being a smart ass, and you can forget it." She offered the card again, and I grabbed it with a nod. "Don't go crazy either," she muttered, before sitting back down at the table. "This is a lesson in responsible spending. And don't stay out too late."

"I'll try not to, but you know how wild the nightlife is in Jasper," I said, turning toward the front door before hurrying through the living room. I jerked the crooked door open with both hands.

"Keep away from the lake." I nervously looked back at Dad who seemed more concerned than usual. "There were a lot of gunshots a few nights ago."

Thoughts of Amulii's bloody bullet wound brought me back to a darker reality.

"Okay," I said, nodding before stepping outside.

It was hard to leave the warmth of the grocery store to battle the fierce winds with several bags in my hands, but it was already after two o'clock and I wanted to have enough time with Amulii before it got too dark. The parking lot was almost empty, which was unusual for a Sunday afternoon. The park wasn't too far; I could see the forest a kilometer or so in the distance. Jasper may have been remote, but it was a typical overpriced resort town, tucked into a valley and surrounded by prominent snow caps and glacier-fed lakes. The buildings all had an artificial quaintness, simplistic but pretentious in a way I couldn't explain. Everything either had a wooden facade or was painted different shades of gray and forest green.

I jogged toward my ATV before slinging the bags onto the cargo rack. There was fifty dollars' worth of food to add to the couple hundred I spent on clothing, and none of it was for me. So much for responsible spending. After Amulii's wardrobe malfunction this morning, I needed to get him something that would not only fit but could expand when he shifted. The elastic cargo pants and triple extra-large shirts would hopefully fit him better than what he had.

I bought five of each in an assortment of colors. The shirts had *Jasper National Park* in large, bold print on the back with a wolf howling on the front, and the pants were dark gray to conceal most of the dirt and blood he would undoubtedly get on them.

"Alex," a familiar voice called out from behind. I turned to see Liam, smiling as he waved from the entrance of the clothing store I shopped at twenty minutes earlier. There were two other men walking alongside him. One appeared to be in his mid to late thirties, stocky build with black hair dusted gray. The other man was slightly younger, dark-skinned and thin with smooth dreadlocks. Both wore clean navy-blue uniforms I hadn't seen on any of the hunters before.

Liam was dirtier than the night he was interviewed, and the jacket he wore was ripped in multiple places, shredded cloth dangling from his arm and lower abdomen. He drew closer, and I saw that the tears looked more like claw marks. There was no rifle strapped to his shoulder this time; instead, he carried a bag of new clothes. "Long time, no see."

"Hey," I said, waving back. "Get in a fight with a bear or something?"

"Something like that." He chuckled, patting me on the shoulder before turning to the other men. "This is this kid I was talkin' about." After how tense our last encounter was, he seemed unusually chummy. "He's been keepin' his eye out."

"He's a little young, isn't he?" the man with the dreadlocks said. "You nearly got yourself killed doing stupid shit like that alone. Don't start convincing unarmed kids to go out there."

"I didn't convince anyone of nothin'. I just told him to be on the lookout if he does go out."

"Uh," I said, losing my train of thought. I didn't remember agreeing to do anything. "I was just about to head out to the woods." I hoped that would bring an end to this uncomfortable interaction, but all it did was draw more interest as the three of them gawked at me like I'd said something idiotic.

"With all that?" Liam asked, sniffing the air. "Is that chicken?" He peeked into the bag. "Five whole chickens . . ." He looked back at the other men. The tone of his voice was light-hearted, but there was a nuance of suspicion.

"The kid doesn't look like he could finish a leg," the older guy said with a laugh. The insult pissed me off, but I didn't react as they stepped closer.

"I, uh—you never know when you might need more food."

Liam's stare narrowed to suspicion. "You mentioned your dad's a ranger, didn't you?"

I nodded.

"And you're bringing all this food into bear country?"

My face got hot. It was a stupid oversight, and I shouldn't have mentioned anything. "Ah, you're right. I should drop these off at the house before going out there."

"You shouldn't be going out there at all," the darker man said, his tone sharp. "It's dangerous, and we've been trying to keep people away from the area."

"I'm not dumb. I've been going out to the lake a lot, you know." My voice betrayed slight annoyance as I hurried the conversation along.

Liam cocked an eyebrow, and the men gave each other wary glances. "You've been out there a lot?" He crossed his arms. "How often? We've been at that lake for days, and I haven't seen you in about a week."

"I was grounded. Why the hell are you giving me the third degree?" I hopped onto the seat of the ATV and took off my jacket. There was so much sweat that my shirt was soaked. I was about to start the engine when I felt him grab the leather strap around my neck.

"What's this?"

There was something in his face, an intensity that made me want to tear out of that parking lot. "A gift," I said, pulling the crystal out before draping it over my shirt. "A friend gave it to me."

The men stepped back, their eyes piercing me.

"Whoa," the older guy said. "Oh shit."

Liam looked as though he were about to vomit. "You look way younger than I thought you would. Guess you fuckers don't age, do you?"

"What are you talking about?"

"Shut the hell up, monster," he snapped, his voice shaky as he spoke. "Silver bullets don't do shit to you either, do they? No wonder no one could ever find you. I thought you only turned into a wolf when you weren't on two legs."

My mouth dropped open, and I could barely breathe. There was a distinct thudding in my ears when I realized the mistake I'd made. Amulii wore the same necklace.

"You don't recognize me, do you?" He looked down at the claw marks on his jacket. "Been chasing your ass for years, and now I know what you look like as human. Goddamn freak."

"Silver bullets—" So Liam was the one who shot Amulii.

"I should've aimed for your heart or head, but I won't make that mistake again." He dropped his bag and reached into his jacket to pull out a steel revolver before pointing it at me.

"Wait a minute, what the hell are you doing?" his younger companion asked, grabbing Liam's arm. The older man looked on, the color draining from his face.

"Somethin' that needs to be done." The pistol shook as his finger rested on the trigger.

"Don't do it, Liam. He's a kid, in broad daylight. There's no way your Dad'll be able to buy enough cops to look the other way after this."

Liam chewed on his lower lip and took a shaky breath through his nose before lowering the gun.

"I'm givin' you a warning, *Alex*—if that's your real name. I won't shoot you now, but the moment you shift," he spun the chamber of the gun before locking it back into place, "one of these is goin' straight into your brain."

"You're all fucking nuts." The words choked from my mouth.

"See you at the lake," Liam muttered, picking up his bag before turning away. The others followed him, the man with the dreads glancing back once more.

I started the ATV but missed the gear as my foot fumbled for purchase on the pedal. After stomping down on the shifter, I tore out of the parking lot toward the forest.

CHAPTER SEVEN

CONFLICTED

I put several kilometers between me and the town before squeez-ing the brakes and cutting the engine, my arms still shaking as I collapsed onto the handlebars. It felt as though each limb wanted to fly off of me in different directions. I leaned over the side of the ve-hicle and retched, but nothing came up except a bit of saliva.

If Liam had pulled that trigger. . .

Was this Amulii's fault? That look of hatred on his face, the shredded clothing, the way his voice pitched with raw emotion—I didn't want to think about what Amulii might have done to garner that much loathing. He was so sweet, but what if there was a darker side to him, hidden away? If he got hungry enough, would he eat a human? Would he eat me? Why hadn't I considered any of this during those days I longed to see him again?

Perhaps my craving for fantasy and companionship blinded me, but after what happened moments ago, the luster of a possible forbidden romance was as tarnished as that revolver pointed at my head. What if Amulii was falling in love with me and wouldn't let me go? Would he go berserk and kill my family so I'd always stay with him?

"Stop," I screamed, grabbing a fistful of hair, pulling it in frustration. My mind wouldn't obey; gore and gunshots were all I could think about as I started the ATV again and put it in gear.

Everything I did now seemed to draw unwanted attention. The loud muffled whir of the four-wheeler's engine ripped through the valley with Liam's hunters likely hearing it, homing in on my location.

See you at the lake.

They were all going to hound me now, but as I gave it more thought, this terrible situation might actually work in our favor. It could throw them off of Amulii's track. Liam said he'd only shoot me if I shifted, and since I wasn't what he thought I was, there was no problem.

Nearing the edge of the lake, I cut the engine, and the calming ambience of wind and bird calls overtook the loud ringing in my ears. I wasn't too far from Amulii's cave, but I needed a moment—maybe several moments. I cradled my head in my hands and tried to push away terrible thoughts. The panicked episode dissipated, but I had to keep reassuring myself that everything was going to be fine, despite knowing nothing.

I hopped to the ground, the soles of my feet scraping along stones as I paced the shore, debating what to do from here. This was stupid, right? I'd just met Amulii and was already buying him clothes and food, all the while considering a much deeper relationship. It was all happening too fast, and this reckless abandon wasn't like me at all.

Amulii was a black hole, and I was the little dwarf planet that wandered too close. Now that I straddled his event horizon, I could either fall in and never escape or get the hell away before it was too late.

Even if he was dangerous, I still liked him.

A faint melody hummed through the valley, halting my nervous meandering. The tune vibrated in the air, haunting everything it touched, pleasing my ears as it drew my attention to the direction of the cave.

Was that Amulii?

The ethereal tone wailed like a human voice calling through the mountains. Intense vibrato gave life to the song as it twirled and danced over the lake, overtaking the gusting winds. Not wanting to drown it out, I grabbed the bags from the cargo carrier and walked the rest of the way along the bank as if under a spell.

As I approached the source, I saw Amulii perched high on a ledge overlooking the area, his eyes burning yellow when he spotted me. Entranced, I watched his nimble fingers dance along the holes of his instrument as his upper body swayed in time with the dramatic shifts in tempo and expression.

Atop the woodwind, a thick, duckbill reed protruded. It was bulbous at the mouthpiece, narrowing into a more flute-like appearance toward the middle. Brightly colored paint swirled in unique patterns along the length of the alien instrument. Distinct shades of reds, blues, and yellows contrasted with its darker melody. Feathers and beads swayed from thin leather strips that wrapped tightly around the flared base.

He was still in human form, and I couldn't tear away from his performance. There was a heaviness inside of me as I dropped everything and sat cross-legged on soft, golden grass. He focused on me as he pinched his lips tighter around the reed, pitching the tune into a soprano register.

The song drifted lazily along a haunting, minor scale, adding more mystery to its origins. Music in his world seemed to follow the same rules as ours, but there was something different about the effect it had on me and everything around the lake. Rocks resonated at the same frequency, and the earth breathed as it trembled to life below.

The instrument wept through the elegy. It climaxed, and the last note's reverberation lingered several moments after the music ended.

Amulii paused and smiled before pulling the reed from his mouth, yellow eyes dimming to their normal color. The hooks were in me deep, and I'd learned something new about him. How could he be dangerous yet so beautiful?

He leaped from one outcrop to another, and I jumped to my feet in panic as he fell. When he neared the ground, he kicked off against the cliff, launching himself into a flip before landing like a cat on his feet.

"I not expecting you. I saw you walking, looking worried. I thought music would help. Your mother not *kill* you being out here?" he asked with a silly grin, grabbing a wooden case off of the ground. He placed the strange instrument inside before securing it with straps.

"Nah, she thinks we're having sex with each other, so she let me out. I'm not sure what the correlation is there, but I'll take what I can get."

We laughed, but Amulii stopped, his grin turning lecherous.

"I not object. I have bed, but it not as soft as yours."

My guts tightened. Amulii's lasciviousness made his intentions crystal clear. If he were human, and we knew each other better, I wouldn't have to think that much about it. In fact, I'd have probably already done it. My mind melted when I thought about us in bed together.

"Not happening," I said, trying to appear nonchalant as my heart fluttered away. He shook his head and pointed to his nose like he did the other day, and I looked away embarrassed. I always forgot Amulii could smell what I was feeling.

"What's that?" I pointed to the instrument case, changing the subject.

"Bashjiri. It harder to play as human, and few learn to make it play music in my world. Learning needed to talk to the elements."

"The elements?"

"Mmm . . ." he mumbled, glancing at the case. "Music very sacred to us. Needed to learn secrets of elements, especially if I to lead as my father did."

"Wait, you're a leader?"

"Not yet. My mother leader until I am acceptable. I not sure if I will be and leading not birthright, though being big and born to a leader helps. I earn my place through trials when ready."

"Why do you have to learn how to speak to elements or whatever?"

"Important practice." He looked around the valley for a moment. "It not work right in your world, but effect the earth. What your world lacks in magic, it make up for in spirit. I see them in forest many times during meditation."

"Are you saying you're a shaman?" Mom's skepticism possessed me, and he seemed surprised by my dismissiveness. We were atheists. Spirits, ghosts, gods; all of it was absurd ramblings of those that couldn't be bothered to think critically.

"Humans know shaman still? Your ancestors would practice, back when my people and yours were closer. The humans of the past had something that those today have lost."

"The only things they lost were stone tools and shorter lifespans," I scoffed, rolling my eyes at how preachy he sounded. "They were primitive. They didn't understand the world the way we do now, so they pretended spirits were real. We lost our ignorance—well, those of us with any sense at all."

As soon as the words left my mouth, Amulii snarled, and I wished I could take it back. The 'incident' I caused during my sophomore year on the debate team came flashing back in neon colors. I lost a few friends that day.

"You say I have no sense?"

"Well, I didn't—"

"You cannot explain everything." Amulii cut me off as he snapped. "Some things exist that are never figured out." He bared his teeth and spat on the ground. "One day, you will know."

That sounded threatening and was the first time he'd ever shown anger toward me. Typical. Religious topics often brought out the worst in people. He stormed toward the cave.

"Oh, come on, Amulii. You're upset that I don't share your beliefs?"

"No," he said, stopping as a loud breath hissed through his nose. "I disappointed. Hoped you different."

"Oh, for fuck's sake." I grabbed the bags off the ground before following him. "You can believe what you want to, but don't pout because I won't pretend to follow along with that crap."

"You very condescending with how little you know. If you not explain, then it not exist, yes?" He turned back to me. "Foolish way to think."

"Foolish? You—" I had to stop myself before this got worse. "Fine. Whatever."

We neared the cave's tall entrance, and stepped inside, the warmth of the strange crystals bringing some feeling back to my numb hands and face. Amulii crossed his arms and glared at me. "Some humans I met over the years said same as you."

That reminded me of something I had forgotten.

"Speaking of years." I followed him closer, setting the bags on the cave floor. "Are you really almost eighty?"

Amulii plopped down on his bedding and looked up at me. "Yes. I am very young. Maybe your age among my kind, maybe younger."

"Holy crap. How long do you guys live?"

He shrugged and rolled his eyes. "Until we die."

"You're pretty immature and petty for being so freaking old," I muttered, leaning against the sandstone wall. "If this is gonna be a big deal, let me know. I won't waste my time with you."

"I annoyed by your rudeness. These my peoples' beliefs. That is why I not give you answer you want. Why I waste moments explaining to someone who does not care what I say and insults me?"

He had a point. I slumped my shoulders in defeat and parked myself in front of him, sitting on the smooth floor.

"Look, I'm sorry," I muttered, keeping my eyes averted.

He sat still for a moment, then nodded.

"Okay," he whispered. "I accept that you are stupid, thinking y—"

My head jerked upward. "Now wait just a damn minute. That's not how you accept an apology."

It was unsettling watching a human with sharp teeth and pointy ears scowl. I crossed my arms and returned his glare with my own. Though he intimidated me, I held my ground, and the anger on his face faded to annoyance.

"We not develop like humans, but much slower. First fifteen to twenty years, have no awareness, like animals. There are two minds that grow, the wolf and maw'cha. This why I say I more your age.

"There also no set age we die. It could be tomorrow; it could be many, many lifetimes from now. Our bodies not aging the way you do. We die; many times by accident, sometimes in war." His eyes sunk as he paused. "Sometimes, we use more than we put back, and Great Spirit calls us."

"What does that mean?"

After a few seconds, the annoyed look on his face returned. "Something you not believe."

"Okay," I said, biting my lower lip. When I heard his stomach growl, I knew what would relax the atmosphere. "I brought food." The saying "a way to a man's heart . . ." was even more true for werewolves. His glower softened to a half-smile.

A bit of drool streamed from the corners of his mouth and dripped onto the rotisserie chicken I placed in his lap. It was still warm, despite the ride over in the chilly weather. Amulii tore apart the soggy paper bag, snapping off a drumstick before ripping into it.

Even in human form, the way he ate was gross, but after last night, I didn't mind sitting there, listening to him smack and slobber all over everything. It meant he could maintain human form, and I wouldn't have to worry about him being killed.

Hesitation caught my lips for a moment before I spoke. "I ran into the person who shot you." Amulii was mid-chew but stopped when I brought up the subject. "That necklace you're wearing—you need to take it off."

"What?"

"He knows to look for someone wearing that necklace, so take it off," I said, reaching around his neck to untie it, but he caught my wrist in his grease-covered hand. Amulii's eyes glowed as fur sprouted from his skin.

"No, Amulii," I yelled, pulling on his arm. "You need to stay human. Are you able to stop it?"

The fur receded, but Amulii's focus was distant as he let go of my hand and untied the chélanc. Swallowing what remained in his mouth, he set the chicken and necklace to the side, then stood and walked out of the den with his hands on his head. I jumped to my feet and ran after him.

"Amulii, come back to the cave," I called out after him, but he continued wandering, seemingly lost in thought until he stood at the edge of the lake. He knelt near the water, washing his hands and face but stopped to gaze at his distorted reflection. "Amulii?"

"I am the foolish one," he said, looking over his shoulder. "You are wearing chélanc like mine. He came after you, did he not?"

He put that together way faster than I thought he would. Every time I thought he was a naive, simple creature, he'd do or say something that made me realize he was a lot more intelligent than he'd first led me to believe.

"Yes, but that's fine. I'm not a werewolf, so he can waste his time following me instead of you. It works out."

His breathing grew rapid, and his eyes widened enough that I noticed how constricted his pupils were. He should have been relieved, but his reaction was anything but that.

"That human hid face and scent when wounding me. I needing know what he look like and where finding him."

"W-wait. Amulii, what are you thinking? I just told you everything will be okay."

"Tell me." His voice was a combination of human and beast, and his eyes burned bright as he struggled to maintain his form.

I shook my head.

"You're freaking me out. I already told you what we'll do, and we're gonna stick to it, you understand?"

He grabbed my upper arms tight, digging his fingers into me. He grew more furious and impatient the longer I kept quiet.

"Do not . . . protect human. He very dangerous. Tell me now." His voice roared, and I cringed, turning away. I didn't know who had materialized in front of me, but it wasn't the Amulii I thought I knew. Every speculation I had earlier returned.

"Let go of me." His grip loosened, but I couldn't get away. He stood there, waging what looked like an invisible battle with himself. "Are you a monster, Amulii? Is that what you want me to think?"

His eyes faded back to their original color and he took my hands in his. "He come after you. They all come. I need hunting them. Cannot let them hurt you."

"I don't understand why you're acting like this. They aren't gonna kill me, you dumbass." I pulled my hands back. "You're gonna make this a hundred times worse if you start killing people. If you think one idiot with a gun was dangerous, just wait until there's a whole damn army. You can't hunt all of them."

His eyes remained crazed as he shook his head. "I did something I should not have." He paused before seizing the crystal dangling over my chest. "You not understand." With a firm tug, the leather strap broke free. He threw it at a boulder with monstrous force, the jewel shattering into thousands of pieces before falling like red glitter to the sand. "Must stop this."

I felt a slight twinge in my chest as I stared at the broken remains of the symbol of friendship he'd given me. The symbolism was striking.

"What's going on, Amulii?"

He grabbed my long sleeve shirt and, with a jerking motion, split it down the middle, ripping it off of me before running his hands along my upper chest. There was no logic to his actions anymore.

"I—I can't do this." I took a step back, clutching my arms over my chest.

"I am sorry." His panicked demeanor didn't change.

"You've got five seconds to explain."

He took a step forward and reached for me, but I pulled away. "Please understand; maw'cha have powerful instinct to protect. I lost sense when thinking you in danger."

"I call bullshit on that." An exasperated groan left my lips. "How many times do I have to tell you that we'll be fine?" I closed my eyes and exhaled, giving consideration to what I would say next. "Well, we *were* gonna be fine. I think this was a wake-up call."

At first, Amulii appeared confused by what I was saying, but after a moment, he raised his brows in surprise. "No, please." He kneeled, looking up at me with watery eyes. "You are only friend I have here. I not want losing you."

Like an idiot, I fell hard for his act. He'd nearly assaulted me, but it hurt to see him like that.

Was I still circling, or had his gravity pulled me the rest of the way into him?

Placing my hands on his shoulders, I lowered to one knee and gave him a hug. Once my arms were around him, he relaxed, but I was still tense.

"The ride up here, I felt like I was talking myself off of a ledge. The more I thought about you, the more scared I got." I pulled back, and he lifted me to my feet. "I didn't want to come back, but I also needed to warn you. I don't want anything to happen to you."

"Then do not leave me." His big, glassy eyes wore the rest of me down. "It hurts." Amulii's voice trembled as he grabbed his chest. "I am very sorry I frighten you."

His earnest expression, the sincerity of his voice, the passion. His words were lassos tightening around me.

"I know you like me, but I need to know what your intentions are because ever since last night, I feel like you're hiding something."

"You know already," he said without giving it any thought. "I wanting you, Alex. More of you. I not be any clearer."

"Damn," I whispered. He wasn't coy with his answer this time. "Everything's wrong with this. You're over sixty years older than me, you're a different species, and I don't know enough about you. And after today, I don't know if I can trust you."

"Tell me what you want. I do anything if you stay."

"Stay human."

He shook his head, panting a bit as his anxiety worsened. "I not do that. Maw'cha what I am. It take too much not to be."

"You're human right now, and you said anything. Did you lie?"

He shook his head again. "I not lie, but how I hunt? How I stay warm without fur?"

"I'll make you a promise." If I ended up regretting what I was about to say, I'd have no one to blame but myself. "If you stay human, I'll get you everything you need, and I'll visit you every day. Okay?"

A huge grin showed off every unusually sharp tooth in his human mouth. It was idiotic to make that promise, but it was my chance to cool things between us and give me time to figure out where everything went from here. I couldn't be anything more than a friend to him, and he had to understand that, eventually. I also had to deal with those hunters, somehow.

"Fine," he said. "I honor you and stay human, but you must visit every day. I not care about the excuse. You need finding a way. I rely on you now." He paused for a moment, as if lost in thought. "I not wanting being alone anymore."

"Okay," I said, placing a hand on his shoulder. "I do like talking to you, but don't ever grab me like that again. I can't deal with you freaking out like that."

"I not do it again, but you need being truthful with me."

"What are you talking about?"

"You lie—very often. I catch you every time. I tell you I want more. You tell me you do not, but it is big lie. The smell of you drives me to mate, but I can do nothing about it. I know you not maw'cha, but you not understand the feeling. A potential mate saying they not want more, while their body invites." His breathing got heavier as he drew closer. "Like now."

"Hold on, wait a minute," I shouted, pushing him back, but that didn't stop him.

"No. No more minutes, no more weeks. Stop denying yourself."

Amulii wrapped an arm around my waist, his skin rough from the cold and excitement while still burning hot. He drew me the rest of the way into him, and I didn't resist. How could I? My left ear lay against his broad chest, his racing pulse matching tempo with mine.

"We both . . . desire," he whispered before catching his breath.

Despite everything that happened moments ago, I had fantasized about this nonstop since that day on the mountain. Amulii told me what he wanted to do, and while I was afraid to go too far, I wasn't about to refuse this. I tried to swallow, but I couldn't get anything down.

He traced my cheek, then caressed my chin, lifting it so our eyes could meet. Amulii's movements were familiar, and I knew what to expect this time. His shallow breaths were a steamy contrast to the chilly mountain air moments before fevered lips pressured mine to open. Anticipation faded to instinct as I closed my eyes and let him explore what he wanted.

When his tongue met mine, he had me.

The kiss was gentle at first, but it gave way to the rough and untamed. It wasn't Amulii that was forcing his tongue into me; I was doing it to him. Each time we broke away, he came back at me with more ferocity, provoking me to respond in kind.

We caressed, moaning as each continued to fight for dominance over the other's mouth. Amulii growled with each thrust of his tongue, losing control as his knees bent while his massive body pressed harder into my smaller frame. When I felt the fur on his arms, I had only moments to stop what was coming.

"Wait," I panted. "You're changing."

I pushed him away, but he caught my hand, yanking me back into place. Amulii forced himself through my lips again, now grinding his lower body into me. His chest and mouth quivered as bestial groans intensified. If this continued . . .

"Amulii." My scream startled him, and he froze before leaping backwards, his fur receding and sharp canines sinking back into his gums.

I licked my lips, which were wet from our tongue's multiple excursions and a bit of blood where a tooth grazed me. Our rapid breathing slowed now that we had put some distance between us.

If a kiss from him could offer that much pleasure, what would more of his body give me? Those thoughts were dangerous. Amulii had nearly transformed and was ready to take it further right there on the banks.

Oddly, the thought of him losing control excited me. My fears became fantasy, but I could never act on them. Amulii was big, even bigger as a werewolf, and I'd be helpless under him.

"That was—" he panted, catching his breath. "We good like this."

He stepped closer, more timid than before, seeming to keep himself in check. His face flushed through his bronzed skin, and he took a sharp breath as he leaned in again, wrapping his arms around me. We were both a bundle of nerves, pulsing with electricity.

I rested my head against his chest again and couldn't help but take in his scent. The odor I couldn't stand a week ago now made it harder for me to break away. When I felt a bulge against my abdomen, my eyes went wide as I glanced down.

"Holy . . ." I'd expected there'd be a size difference, but that caught me off guard.

"The lake water cold," he said, holding back what looked like a bit of embarrassment as he glanced at the water. "Join me?"

CHAPTER EIGHT

HALLOWEEN COMPROMISES

"You're not going to hide in your room this year," Mom scolded, supporting the wooden chair I was standing on. "It wouldn't kill you to be more social."

I taped a tacky paper ghost to the wall, trying to keep my balance. "Being bored to death is scientifically possible, Mom. If I have to listen to a bunch of middle-aged gastroenterologists bring up the fascinating subject of anal fissures again, I'm going to be looking for something to hang myself with." I glanced down at the streamers rolled up in packaging on the floor. "Maybe those will work if I use enough."

"You're such a riot. Where did you get that mouth?" She unrolled the orange and black ribbons before handing me the ends, and I had to stand on my toes before taping them to the ceiling. "Careful."

"Everyone that comes to these parties is at least two decades older than me. What do you want me to talk about?"

"Why don't you invite that guy you've been seeing?"

I dropped the roll of tape, catching her scrutinizing stare from the corner of my eye. "I'm not—"

"Oh come on. I haven't seen you all week, and you never bring him to the house." I hopped to the floor and looked out the window, trying to ignore her. "I'm not stupid, Alex. I just hope that you're being safe," she added. "Guess it's time to add condoms to the shopping list."

"Oh my God," I muttered under my breath.

There was nothing I could say that my face hadn't already. After that insane kiss, Amulii and I had a long conversation about how our relationship would work going forward—if it even could work. I'd kept my promise and visited him every day, and he'd convince me to stay for hours. Whenever I'd try to leave, he'd playfully pin me to the bed. There was a lot of chemistry between us, and most of the time we'd make out until we were both so horny that he'd start to shift. We'd be locked in an endless cycle of kissing and cooling until things got too hot. That would often be my cue to leave and let him finish what I'd started—by himself.

"Mom . . ." She gave me a librarian stare over her glasses and waited for my next lie. Maybe she'd always known I was gay, but Amulii made it more real for her. "We're not sleeping together. I swear."

"Well, now that you've just admitted you like the guy, tell me about him. Where does he live? Where's he from?"

At first, I was going to try to come up with another convincing lie, but that would have been unnecessary effort. The truth, it seemed, would actually set me free in this situation. "Okay," I said, trying to hide the smile pinching back my lips. "He's from another world, and he crosses into ours through a portal that opens up on the winter solstice." She rolled her eyes toward the ceiling, and I continued my onslaught of honesty. "He's also a huge werewolf that lives in a cave by the lake."

"You could have just said you don't feel like talking about him."

I wanted to take a bow, but the award should have gone to Amulii and his absurd existence.

"I don't feel like talking about him, and I don't think it's a good idea to invite him here with Dad around."

"How about this," Mom said, tossing a fake cobweb over the cube-shaped living room lamp sitting on the end table. "If you make an effort to talk to people tomorrow, I'll let you leave early to hang out with him. But you're to be home by ten." She shot me a glare. "And no unprotected sex."

"Deal."

"Not even oral." She couldn't help herself. "You both haven't done that, have you? You can still catch—"

"I think we're done here." I nearly tripped over my feet as I jogged toward the front door. If I had let her finish that sentence, my brain actually would have imploded.

///

After spending all morning and part of the afternoon helping Mom decorate the house, it was almost two by the time I could ride to the cave. Amulii was probably starving, and I knew he would give me an earful when I got there.

Mom never questioned the charges on the card, so I used it to keep a dependent werewolf alive. But for how long? The amount of food he ate was unbelievable. When I first visited, he made it clear I hadn't brought enough, so I had to ride back to town to get more.

Amulii kept his promise, as far as I knew, remaining in his human form while not wearing his chélanc. Either the hunters weren't around much lately, or they were very good at staying hidden. Whatever the reason, we never strayed far from the cave. Since that day Liam threatened to kill me, he seemed to fall off the planet. Maybe he lost interest after realizing he was wrong about me.

My body was clammy and hot today, the fatigue and aches that accompany a fever wearing me down. It was flu season, and if I hadn't made a promise to Amulii, I'd be back home in bed. The symptoms were strange: the fever and achy muscles made sense, but my chest itched and burned, and there were times I'd scratch until I broke skin. Perhaps I'd talk to Mom.

I parked the four-wheeler on the bank, grabbed the grocery bags from the cargo carrier and dragged myself to the den. Amulii wasn't around, so I sat the bags on his bedding and went outside. It was hard to keep my eyes open, and I contemplated having a nap before venturing back home.

"Alex," Amulii shouted with a snarl from the top of the cave entrance.

"Fuck." I spent several seconds clutching my chest before picking up a stick to throw it at him. "Stop doing that."

A slightly nasal chuckle accentuated his toothy smile, and he sniffed the air. "You peed a little." There was no hiding anything from him, even stuff that embarrassed me. When he finished laughing at my expense, he jumped off the cave entrance, landing inches away.

"I have not hunted in a while, so I needed to stalk something. And since you are so late . . ." He playfully growled, clasping my rear end as he leaned in and pressed his lips against mine.

It was always too much to resist. He knew how to get me going, and when he ravaged me like this, I couldn't think straight.

His tongue left a trail of fire along my neck, followed by gentle bites as he lifted me from the ground. I lost more of my self-control each time he did this, and he banked on it. Amulii was sea water lapping against my limestone. Given enough time, there wouldn't be much left holding him back. I had to be careful about that.

I'd forgotten we were standing out in the open, and I tensed when a familiar feeling pricked the goosebumps on my skin. Amulii pulled away.

"What is wrong?"

"We can't do this out here," I whispered as he lowered me to the ground, but his firm hold on my ass remained until I swatted him away. "Someone's gonna see us."

"So?" Amulii shot me another one of his bestial grins. He was so gorgeous, especially since I'd dressed him in clothes that fit. "We are human."

He was being unusually careless, which was my fault. I hadn't told him the extent of my encounter with Liam and the other hunters, or that he'd almost killed me. There was no way in hell I'd bring that up. While it was nice having a werewolf protector, he'd shown me just how overprotective he could be, and that scared me.

"Oh," I said, remembering the other reason I'd come up here. "Can I ask you something?"

"Do you often ask if you can ask someone something?"

Amulii had been rather cheeky lately, which seemed out of character for him. He had a much better grasp of English, and more of his personality broke through than before. His sarcasm and rhetorical questions irritated me sometimes, but it beat the badly translated instruction manual he was when we first met.

I was still impressed by how much he'd improved in such a short time.

"Hmm," I mumbled while walking into the cave. "Sometimes, people start a question with a question when they know the answer will probably be no."

"I cannot say no to you." He followed close, wrapping his arms around my waist before his heavy breaths lashed hot against the back of my neck. This would have been the overly sappy and romantic part of a movie that made me gag, but I fell hard for it in real life. "Whatever you want, I will do it," he whispered, carefully nibbling my earlobe.

"Oh, that's great. So, you won't mind coming over to my house for a Halloween party my parents are throwing?"

Amulii's overbearing presence evaporated as muffled footsteps scurried toward the exit.

"Absolutely not," he shouted from outside.

"Come on, please." I begged while following him to the lake. "My parents are forcing me to stay home and go to this thing, which means I won't be able to visit you."

He pretended not to hear as he effortlessly scaled the face of a small cliff toward a rocky outcrop, out of my view.

"There's gonna be a ton of food. Way more than anyone will eat." He lay on his stomach, and I saw the top part of his head as he peeked down from the edge. "Interest piqued, big guy?"

"What kind of food?"

"Brisket. It's your favorite."

"Hmm." As much as he didn't like other humans, he loved my dad's cooking whenever I brought it to him. "I will go if you do something for me."

"The food is the something," I shouted. After giving what Mom said more thought, it was either try to get Amulii to show up, or I'd have to talk to my parents' friends for hours.

If I had to somehow drag him kicking and screaming to this thing, I would.

"No, the food barely makes up for being around your family."

"We won't even be around them."

"If that is the case, then spend this so-called 'Halloween' at my cave."

He exasperated me to the point where I had to stop and close my eyes while rubbing my temples. It was an automatic response for the few occasions Amulii and I actually argued.

"You are getting angry again."

"Gee, what gave it away? Was it my scent, or the fact that if you were down here, I'd beat you over the head with a piece of driftwood?"

He jumped to the ground and walked over. When he reached for a hug, I pushed his arms away.

"Don't even think about it. Not everything in a relationship has to be a quid pro quo."

He paused for an uncomfortable moment. "What is that?"

"You can do something for me without expecting something in return."

Amulii stood still, averting eye contact with me while mumbling something angry in his language. When he slumped forward, I knew he would cave.

"Fine," he muttered.

I leaned in and gave him a hug. "Thank you. I know this makes you nervous, but you're doing me a huge favor."

"If I am doing such a huge favor, would you do me a small one?"

I huffed and shoved him away. "Just because you word it differently, doesn't make it any less scummy. What do you want, Amulii?"

He smiled and his eyes traveled downward. "You often leave things unfinished. Maybe I could . . ."

"Amulii, we've been through this."

"All I want is—"

"No," I interrupted. "It's only been what? A few weeks? I'm not ready for that." I looked away, thinking back to when he almost lost control at the lake. "And . . . I don't know if I ever will be."

"Why? I thought you were comfortable with me. You want more, I can tell every time."

"I just don't want to."

"Stop lying." His gentle hand slipped under my chin. "Tell me. I will understand. Maybe I can put your mind at ease."

It took a second before the words flew from my lips like a swarm of hornets.

"Because I'm scared, okay?" I knocked his hand away. "I'm fucking terrified of you." Amulii would be my first, and if sexual partners were levels in a video game, he would have been the final boss fight, not the tutorial. "You may be able to tell that I'm turned on, but you have no idea what's going through my head. When we really kissed the first time, you didn't stop when I did. You started to shift, and you couldn't control yourself. If I decide to do this with you, would you be able to stop if I told you to?"

"I do not understand. If we are mating, why would we stop?"

I let out a sigh and looked away. "You just answered my question." I went rigid with frustration, though I was more disappointed than anything else. "Forget I asked anything."

The last week had been wonderful, but all he wanted the whole time was to rut me like an animal. It was my fault. I knew what he was doing, and I led him on, thinking it harmless.

"Wait, please," he shouted, running after me. This sounded familiar. "Tell me what I said that was wrong." He grabbed my shoulder and pulled me close. "Please do not leave like this."

He was a big guy, but those sad eyes made it hard to stay angry. Was he feigning ignorance, or was he actually confused about this? Now that his English was better, it was harder to tell. I wanted to give him the benefit of the doubt, anyway.

"Amulii." My voice was a lot calmer than before. "I need you to understand something, okay? If, and this is a *huge* fucking if, I agree to sleep with you and I tell you to stop, you have to stop. You could end up killing me, and you wouldn't realize it. I'm not a . . . maw'cha like you. I'm a lot smaller. You'd have to be in control, and you'd need to stop when I tell you to."

His mouth hung open as though he hadn't considered that a possibility. Someone his size probably never had to worry about getting injured during sex, but after explaining it, I think he understood.

"When I am with you, I forget we are so different. Why did you not tell me that day? I did not realize you were so scared."

"I tried to; you just didn't hear me. Sometimes when you get that way, you don't hear anything. It's happened a few times, not just at the lake."

"I am sorry," Amulii choked out. He opened his mouth to speak but stopped and averted his eyes.

"What?"

"What if you could be a maw'cha? Would you want to be with me then?"

The blood in my face drained away when I remembered all the times he had bitten me during our rougher make-out sessions, sometimes drawing blood. I was jumping to conclusions. He wasn't even in werewolf form when he did that.

"If you're able to turn people into what you are, don't do it to me. It's hard enough to keep guys I like a secret. Why don't you just stay human?"

"I have told you, it does not work that way," he said, staring at the ground. "I think you would be happier as maw'cha."

"No," I said, my tone growing serious. "Don't do that to me."

"I . . ." he muttered, as he grasped for words, only to sigh as he gave up arguing. "I will not, though I can."

"How? Through biting?"

He squinted and tilted his head, like I had said something crazy. "No. That is awful. Why would you think that?"

"Uh . . . I just thought that's how werewolves passed along their disease."

"I am not diseased," he shouted. His nose wrinkled into a snarl as his brow creased. "How could you think that about me? Do I look diseased?"

"No," I said, trying to walk back my words. "I'm sorry. I'm thinking of werewolves in myths. How do you do it?"

"It does not matter. You do not want it." The more we spoke, the more frustrated he got. "Can we still be together? I do not care if it does not go anywhere, I just want to be with you, as close as I can get. There is no one else in this world I can be with, and maybe we can go a little further without going too far."

It made no sense for him to agree to go back to that, knowing he'd probably never make it any further. It wouldn't be long before we got bored doing the same thing every day. For now, we enjoyed being with each other, and I didn't see the harm in getting a little more out of what we did have.

"Yeah," I said, feeling my face flush. "And I'll think about the other thing." His face lit up. "*Think* about it. Don't get your hopes up."

The doorbell rang, and since Mom put me in charge of greeting each guest, I had to answer. Approaching my limit of wearisome affirmations that I had, in fact, grown over the years, I dragged myself to the front door. This felt more like community service than a party. I wasn't surprised to see yet another man in his forties or fifties caked in pale makeup, crooked fangs hanging awkwardly from his mouth.

"Alex," he said, eagerly extending his right hand. The glimmer of a gold Rolex adorning his wrist caught my attention. "Man, you've sure grown." The acrid scent of coffee on his breath assaulted my nose. He seemed familiar.

"So I've been told," I muttered, struggling to maintain the fake smile that had taken up temporary residence on my face since the first guest arrived.

"You don't remember me, do you?" He slipped out of a black shearling trench coat, revealing a slender, fit body, his Gucci loafers tickling the wooden floors as he stepped into the living room. "Your mom used to drop you off at my house when she'd have a long day in the OR."

"Dr. Mitchel?" I forgot his face, but I didn't forget his enormous house and Olympic-sized swimming pool. I also couldn't forget the traumatizing memories of being forced to wear dresses and makeup by his brat of a daughter. She was a couple years older than me, and I was just the right size to be one of the many dolls she got to play with every time my mother left me there. "How's Annie?"

"She's a sophomore in college now." He scanned me and shook his head. "Damn, the years fly by, don't they? Last I heard, you were in the running for valedictorian."

"I was, until Mom decided we just *had* to move."

"This is a little . . . out of the way, but I'm sure you can handle the self-study and online courses. You always were gifted. Your mom brags about you all the time."

"I wish she'd stop that," I muttered, looking out the window. "I do like the independence, and at least it's pretty around here. Ever been to Spirit Island?"

The doctor's face flatlined as he examined mine. "I have, a lot. It was a part of my job a few years ago. You don't go out there alone, do you?"

"Nah, I've got a friend I go with."

"Even with someone, it's not safe right now. There are some dangerous things out there."

That caught me off guard.

"Dangerous things? I haven't noticed anything," I said, trying to appear unfazed by the revelation.

"Just trust me on this. Don't go out there." His eyes lit up when Mom emerged from the kitchen, and his unusually giddy attention snapped to her. "Sally." When they started catching up on old times, I took the distraction as my chance to slip out the back door.

That was disturbing. No one in town seemed to take the hunters seriously, but Dr. Mitchel's words had a lot more weight to them. He was a geneticist, and a well-known one too. If he was involved with the hunters, this just got a lot scarier.

///

I sat under the awning for about twenty minutes, watching as the pine-covered hills turned gold while the sun lowered on the opposite side of the house. Dad and his obnoxious posse of hooting yokels gathered around picnic tables in the front yard. As uncomfortable as I was around Mom's guests, I'd take them over Dad's crowd any day. At least I was finally out of sight. My eyes kept shifting toward the edge of the forest every time a stiff breeze would rustle through bushes. If Amulii hadn't shown up by now, I doubted he'd make it at all. Who could blame him? I wasn't exactly a beacon of hope yesterday.

Maybe he was over me because I couldn't give him what he wanted. He still had his hooks in me good, and I wished things weren't so complicated. I didn't want to be a werewolf, but I still wanted to be with him.

The back door opened, and Mom wandered out in a glossy leather catsuit. When I first saw that costume, it was in an open box on the couch. There was no description on the packaging, and if not for the fact that Halloween was approaching, I'd have thought it was a type of fetish thing. Imagining either of my parents in one of those made me want to douse my eyes with kerosene and light them on fire. I hated my brain sometimes.

"You're isolating again," she said, sitting on the ground next to me. "Dr. Feinstein's here if you need to talk to him."

"You actually invited my therapist?"

"He's one of my colleagues, and he knows more about you than I do, apparently. You won't talk to me anymore. I always had my suspicions, but I wasn't completely sure you were gay until I saw that piece of eye candy in the closet."

With a drawn-out sigh, I leaned back against the house and surveyed the woods again.

"That piece of eye candy and I might not be working out, so . . ." I said, shaking my head. Mom was the last person I wanted to discuss this with, but it wasn't like I had any other friends. "I don't think he's coming."

"Honey, he's the first guy you've dated, at least as far as I know. No one ever gets it right the first time." She let out a bit of defeated laughter. "I mean, look at me. I didn't even get it right after marrying the fourth guy I thought I was serious with, and that was only because I got pregnant in medical school."

"We're not even serious." I couldn't stop lying. "I don't care what he does."

"Did you guys have a fight?"

"Kind of. He didn't want to come. He's not exactly a people person."

Mom laughed. "Gee, sounds like he's the perfect match." She tapped my shoulder and pointed to the handsome figure emerging from the trees. "Look at that. He's wearing clothes this time."

Smiling was a reflex as I watched him cautiously pad barefoot across the yard. This was a test I hadn't realized I'd given him, and he passed.

"Your dad used to look at me like that a long time ago." I hadn't noticed Mom shifting her attention back to me.

"Mom," I said, the embarrassment setting in again. "Let's not talk about this."

"Fine, I'll leave you two alone. He doesn't look like he's in a hurry to talk to me either." She groaned, her joints popping as she stood. Amulii took his time, but his hawk-like expression didn't change as his eyes went from me to my mother. "Don't do anything in front of your father, though. That's not a fight I want to have tonight, but we will need to all talk about this at some point. You're not an adult yet, and I want to know more about this guy."

As the back door clicked shut, Amulii zipped across the yard. After his embarrassing first meeting, avoiding my mom made perfect sense.

"You made it," I said as he sat next to me, crossing his legs. His hair was still a little wet, but at least he was bathing regularly now. "Just so you know, we can't kiss or anything because my dad will freak out."

"I do not care," he said, his full, warm lips pecking my cheek. "We will not do it around him, but I am hungry and cranky."

"We call that being *hangry*," I said, kissing him back. "When you didn't show up, I thought it was over."

He gripped my hand, sliding his fingers in between mine. "I thought about it, and if I knew there was no chance, I would not be here." Serious deliberation replaced Amulii's usual carefree demeanor. "I have traveled between worlds for over a quarter of my lifetime, and I have been through many disappointments. You are the first that has shown any promise. If you think I cannot wait, you do not know me well. I am a skilled hunter, and I have patience. You will be mine one day, I know it. But I will wait and be yours first."

We were both getting tired. He hated that I never admitted how I felt about him, and I was sick of pretending I was fine keeping him at an arm's length. It was all I could think about in bed last night, and at the very least, his persistence deserved heart-felt honesty.

Smoked meat and spices swirled along a gentle breeze, tantalizing our noses. When his stomach roared, I remembered I wasn't able to feed him today. He needed to eat first, and we'd talk about all of this in the privacy of his cave.

"Stay here, I'm gonna get you food," I said, hopping to my feet. "I'll be right back."

Forgetting about the conservative convention in my front yard, I bounded toward the smoker like the love-sick teenager I was. Tonight, I would tell Amulii everything. I'd give a name to what I felt, and it would soar confidently from my lips to his ears. Maybe we could work out something better.

It was too soon to toss around the L word; I didn't have to go *that* far. The thought of baring my soul was frightening, but if there was the slightest possibility that we could make it work, he needed to know. We also needed to get to know each other a lot better.

"This is my boy, Alex." Dad's voice shocked me out of my reverie. There was no clear pathway to the food without running into either my parents or other guests that wanted nothing more than to stop and chat.

Slumping forward, I forced a smile before turning around. Dad was wearing a Zorro costume, and he'd been chatting with some guy in a surprisingly realistic werewolf mask. It kind of looked like Amulii.

"Hi," I said. "Nice mask."

"Hey Alex." That voice. I wanted to throw up when I heard it. "Haven't seen you in a while. Well, we haven't seen each other, anyway. I knew you'd like this costume." Liam removed the mask and flashed a grin. He was clean and shaved today.

I had a feeling he'd been trailing me to my house, as I thought he would, but what was he doing here? I thought once he found out I was a normal teenager, he'd leave me alone, but now he was playing weird mind games.

"You two met?" Dad asked.

"Yeah," I muttered. "This is one of the hunters that's been threatening people." I glared at Liam and crossed my arms, confident that my dad hated the hunters as much as I did. If this didn't get him thrown out of our yard, I didn't know what would.

"I know." Dad sighed as he grabbed a large metal spatula before opening the grill. That was an unexpectedly meek reaction.

"I'm sorry about last week," Liam said, strolling over to put his hand on my shoulder, like we were best buds. I flinched at his touch. All I could see was that weapon pointed at me. "I had to see if you were tellin' the truth."

"You almost shot me, you crazy fucking hick," I said, my frustration boiling over. "Dad, he pointed a gun at me."

"It wasn't loaded," Liam said, giving me a pat. "I had no intention of shootin' you." He seemed too collected, not at all the face of insanity I saw that day. There was no way any of that was an act. "I was taking my precautions."

"Don't be pointing guns at my kid. I don't care if they aren't loaded," Dad said as he flipped the burgers over the dim glowing charcoal. "You guys really believe in that bullshit, don't you?"

"It ain't bullshit, Robert." Liam stared at me, his eyes widening. "Your son can tell you that."

"You still think I'm a fucking werewolf?" I looked at Dad, who chuckled once but didn't interject. What was wrong with him?

"Nah, I know *you* ain't the werewolf, kid." His eyes shifted toward the side of the house. "But you know a lot more than you're lettin' on."

Amulii barreled toward me, eyes wild and angry. I'd been terrified for the last three minutes, and it was enough time for the wind to carry my scent to him. He wasn't his usual timid self as he took his place by my side before crossing his arms.

BREAKING ORBIT

"Dad, this is, uh, Aaron," I said, my eyes locking with Amulii's as I silently pleaded. "He's a . . . friend of mine."

Liam snorted, but said nothing as he pulled out a smartphone, his fingers sliding across the screen.

Dad took in Amulii's height and shifted his eyes to the side. "First time I've seen you around here."

"I have seen you," Amulii muttered, his deep voice biting at my ears. "I have heard you too. The entire forest has."

His response added weight to the tension already pressing me into the ground. I never asked him how much time he'd spent outside of my house stalking me before we met, but his words made it clear he understood my family's issues better than I thought he did.

"You got a problem with me?" Dad inched closer, his voice taking on a more aggressive tone.

Amulii smiled, which seemed to make Dad shrink even more. "I have many problems with you and the way you treat your son."

Dad scowled at me, causing me to flinch. Amulii may have thought he was helping, but all he did was make everything so much worse.

"What, you badmouth your parents to anyone that'll listen now?"

"No, I—"

Amulii cut me off. "He has never mentioned you once. There is no reason to waste time speaking of people with no significance."

"You should probably get the fuck off my property," Dad hissed. "Cause I'm about to lose my temper."

"Gladly." Amulii took my hand. "Come."

What was he doing?

"Go home," I whispered, jerking away. "We'll talk about this later."

"Uh, before you go," Liam said, his stride cautious as he approached. "I want to ask you something." He locked up, glowering at Amulii. Was he shaking? "What are your intentions with the boy?"

"That is none of your concern," he growled. "I am not in the mood for stupid questions."

"You wanna turn him or eat him, don't you? You wanna turn him into what you are." Liam's glare shifted to dad. "I know what this monster wants, Robert. Keep your kid away from him."

"I don't believe in your bullshit, Liam, but I ain't letting my kid hang out with this creepy fucker."

"Hang out?" The hunter raised both eyebrows. "Is that what you think they've been doin'?" Liam tapped the screen of his phone once more and handed it to Dad. "Nah, that beast wants to do more to your son than hang out with him."

Tinges of red flushed Dad's tanned face in the dim light. I didn't have to see the picture to know what was in it. There was a faint chatter of grinding teeth as Dad swallowed his disgust, handing the phone back to the hunter.

"I warned you." Dad kicked over the grill, embers and food scattering across the ground. Everyone outside went silent. "I warned you when you were in middle school."

"What the hell are you doing?" Mom scrambled out of the house, Dr. Mitchel following her.

"I'm 'bout to kick this motherfucker's ass." Dad removed his jacket before throwing it to the ground. "What the fuck is some grown-ass man doing with his tongue in my boy's mouth?"

There was a brief flash of light out of the corner of my eye, and I saw the hunter and Dr. Mitchel discussing something while a camera focused on the drama unfolding.

Dad stormed up to an unusually calm Amulii and grabbed his shirt, their glares locking. I held my breath, hoping Amulii would keep whatever calm he had left.

"Are you fuckin' him too?"

Amulii said nothing as another grin inched up his face, and Dad's attention shifted as he let go of the man. He was so manically belligerent that what came next was a complete surprise.

All I saw were a few specks of light before my vision dimmed and ears rang. When I fell to the ground, disoriented, the dull pain on my face just below my right eye intensified. It wasn't the first time Dad had hit me, but it was the first time he'd ever hit me that hard.

"Robert," Mom screamed, running over to help me off the ground.

"You don't listen to anybody." He glared at Mom. "This is your fault. I told you how he'd end up."

"I have had enough of this," Amulii muttered, snatching Dad's throat with lightning-fast reflexes. He slammed Dad against the side of the house before lifting him a half a meter off the ground.

"Amulii, stop." The swelling on the side of my face made it hard to talk. I thought if I could tear his focus from my dad long enough, I'd be able to calm the beast in him. He stared back at me as Dad choked and sputtered, desperately digging his fingernails into Amulii's arm to break free from his inhuman grip. My assumption was wrong.

"Hmm . . ." he muttered, turning back toward the man he held like a doll. "Not so strong, are you?"

"Let him go," Mom shouted, running toward them before Dr. Mitchel grabbed her arm and pulled her back.

Every guest watched in disbelief as Amulii lost even more control. Ignoring the pain, I wobbled to my feet and grabbed his arm.

"Please," I said, keeping my voice low and calm. I snatched his chin and forced him to face me. "Calm down."

His fury softened into the familiar as he looked into my eyes. Dad dropped to the ground as Amulii let him go.

"I . . . lost control." He shook his head. "Again."

"It's okay," I said, grabbing his arms. "You need to get out of here."

He leaned in to kiss me on the cheek, which sent Dad into another rampage. He leaped to his feet and dashed between us, pushing us apart.

"Stay away from my kid." Leading with his shaky fist, he reared back and struck Amulii's lower jaw with a loud crunch. Amulii barely flinched on impact and maintained his human form despite the rage returning in his now glowing yellow eyes. Dad screamed as he doubled over, clutching his shattered hand. Amulii knelt next to him, grabbing a fistful of his hair so that he could hold his gaze. The amber glow lit Dad's face, revealing the terror and pain.

"I stopped for your son because I love him. I will do anything for him." Amulii gripped harder, eliciting humbled grunts from the man he now dominated. "I want you to look into my eyes. I want you to see a maw'cha's fury, so you never forget your place again."

Mom and some of the guests ran at Amulii, but Dr. Mitchel dashed in front of them.

"Don't go near him," he shouted back at me, but it was too late.

I wrapped my arm around Amulii's neck when I saw his descending canines primed to rip into my father's jugular. He let go of Dad and stood up, knocking me to the ground. As he focused on my face, contempt melted into a bewildered haze. A gasp escaped his lips, and he fixated on the thin layer of fur covering his hands.

"No. I . . . I did not . . ."

Dr. Mitchel remained frozen in place as he stared in amazement, but the hunter crossed his arms, having known all along. Part of me wanted to see Amulii rip him to pieces for ruining everything, but I had to shrug away those thoughts.

Panicked gossiping gripped the crowd as they gawked at Amulii before their judgmental stares shifted to me. I was the freak that had fallen in love with a monster. Running was all I could think to do. I was angry, scared, heartbroken, and it was all my fault. It was stupid to bring my werewolf boyfriend to this party.

I should have known from last week he was unstable, but everything was so normal lately, it passed from my mind. Why was I so careless? This may have been bad, but it finally sunk in, and no amount of him begging would change it. Amulii was too dangerous.

He grabbed my hand and tugged, but I jerked away and ran in the opposite direction toward the woods. There were no blissful feelings anymore when he touched me.

The forest swallowed the ground moonlight couldn't reach, and aspens that I'd once thought were beautiful now clawed at the sky with their spindly, bare branches. I stopped and clutched my stomach, panting as my back fell against the trunk of a pine, the world spinning. Amulii was a shadow, not making a sound as he trailed close.

"I told you I did not want to go."

"Stop it," I yelled, pushing him away from me. "You messed everything up." He was unprepared for my reaction and nearly stumbled as I pushed him again. "I could have handled myself."

"These are instincts. I smelled your fear, and I would have done anything to protect you."

"He's my dad. It's not like he was gonna kill me."

He grabbed my right wrist with one hand while his thumb brushed my swollen eye.

"He struck you hard. I could smell the blood from your nose. That man—"

"That man hit me once and stopped. You didn't stop." I winced as my thoughts shifted to his teeth near Dad's neck. "You almost killed him." I wrenched my wrist from his grip. "Get the fuck away from me."

"Do not talk to me like this." Giant hands now squeezed my arms. "I will protect you. I protect what I love, what is mine."

When he said it, I watched him cringe, and his grip loosened.

"Don't say that shit to me after this." I took in a sharp breath and shook my head. "And don't call me yours."

He let go, and I tore away.

"I should have never," he muttered, clenching his teeth before going silent.

"What? Should have never what? Stalked me? Followed me to my house? Pretended to be a friendly werewolf, so I'd let you fuck me? I should have listened to Liam. I should have paid attention to the warning signs, but I really liked you."

My heart broke as I remembered what I wanted to say to him earlier. I had to choke everything down or the grief would overwhelm me.

"I didn't just like you. Maybe I loved you. I was going to tell you that tonight." The pain in my chest got worse. "Ever since that day you got shot, when I woke up in your arms, all I could think about for days was hoping I'd get to wake up like that again."

His eyes lit up.

"Then we can make this work. No human has ever told me they loved me. I have confessed many times, but—"

"You don't understand," I interrupted. "I *loved* you. I had hoped tonight I could finally feel like everything would be okay for once, but I can't now."

"Alex." He tried to reach for my shoulder, but I jerked away. "I love you. Please give me another chance. Be my mate," he whispered, his voice cracking as tears welled in those sparkling topaz eyes that seemed much less wild than they were earlier. As much as it tortured me, I had to show some backbone and not fall for this again.

"I can't," I said, grimacing. "This is hard for me. It's like I'm ripping out my heart to save myself and my family from you." Amulii tried to speak, but I shouted over him. "I don't love you. You're lucky I don't hate you after what you did."

His dim eyes glimmered as ethereal light reflected in them. He never hid his softer emotions from me, which only made this much harder.

"You don't belong here. This was never gonna work. It's only a matter of time before something terrible happens to both of us." He looked at the ground. "I don't want them to hunt you down."

"Maybe death is what I would prefer," he snarled, wiping his eyes with the back of his arm.

"Over me? That's a little melodramatic, don't you think? We've barely known each other for three weeks."

"It is not that," he shouted. "So much time wasted. So much searching to find what I was looking for, only to have someone who truly mattered reject me." I jumped as his fist slammed against a thick tree trunk which cracked under the force. "I am done here. My father was foolish for thinking humans were worth this much pain."

His revelation answered the question I'd asked when we first met.

"It was me," I whispered. "That thing you were looking for that you couldn't go home without. Wasn't it?"

The whirlwind of anger and sadness flushed from his face when the veil of ignorance lifted from mine. The more I thought about it, the more furious I got.

"You were going to make me go with you, weren't you? Your plan was to spirit me away to your world. Did you think I'd leave my family and my life behind for *you*?"

He shook his head. "You would not, but I had to hold on to some hope that you would choose me in the end. I would have waited. I have waited this long; I would wait decades more."

"Go home," I said, turning my back to him. The gravity that once pulled me from a safe orbit instead flung me deep into space, far away from him. "Stay with your own kind and stop wasting your life here."

I walked away, but he remained. As I crossed the threshold of shadows into the moonlight, everything I held inside rained onto the pale grass as I pushed onward. This was my first break up, and it hollowed me.

Not wanting to go back home, I wandered the hillside overlooking our property. Everyone knew my secret now. Maybe it was for the best, but I wanted to come out on my own terms, not because some creepy redneck took pictures of me with my boyfriend.

The ambience of wind-rustled leaves gave me a little serenity as I sat on the ground, contemplating for several minutes while watching the guests in the distance leave one-by-one. I didn't want to go back home, but there was nowhere else for me to ride out this storm like I had in Calgary. I'd have given anything to be at Mike's house, bitching about my life while eating my weight in pizza rolls as we watched awful movies. What was my life going to be like going forward?

At least I'd be off to college soon, and maybe I'd make new friends. Maybe I'd find someone else who made me feel the passion that Amulii did.

As lonely as I was, I still had my mom. Amulii didn't have anyone, but that was his choice. Why was I still thinking about him? I had to stop feeling guilty.

Dad's truck zipped down the driveway, slipping along the gravel as it disappeared into the trees. Our tentative relationship was already hanging by threads, and now I wondered if he'd ever speak to me again. If he did, the only words I'd want him to string together would be a detailed apology to me and Mom.

The lights were on in the house, so I knew Mom was still there. She went from being the last person I ever wanted to talk to about all of this, to being the only one. My hands and feet slid across the crunchy, dead grass as I pushed myself to my feet, and like a zombie, ambled emotionless toward the cabin, having cried myself dry.

My left eye had swollen shut, so it was harder to see the narrow gravel path to the front door. Dad had never hit me like that before, and I doubted he felt any remorse judging from his hateful glare when he stood over me. It was hard to gain the acceptance of a man who always demanded more than was possible.

The porch steps creaked as I sauntered to the door and tiptoed through the house toward the kitchen. I didn't want to disturb Mom. Forty guests may have witnessed the end of her marriage tonight. She loved Dad for whatever reason, but I couldn't see this continuing, and I was more overjoyed than dismayed. All I wanted was to go back home—to my *real* home.

Grabbing a bag of frozen peas from the freezer, I dragged myself upstairs to my room and shut the door. My hand hovered over the light switch, but the dull throb spreading from my eye to my head made me reconsider turning it on. The bright moonlight cast shadows in the window's shape on my bed, and even though there were new sheets and blankets, I still imagined Amulii lying there, snoring when he passed out after I'd saved him.

I couldn't believe fell in love with a beast that night.

Love at first sight was complete bullshit, but this was pretty damn close. Would I ever feel that way about anyone else? Would I ever connect with someone the way I did with him?

I wish he'd never followed me home.

After carefully placing the bag of peas under my pillowcase, I rested my head against it. Amulii's faint, musky odor diffused through the new fabric. Somehow it became a drug I couldn't sleep without. This was his pillow, and I kept it close every night.

Thinking about it now, every time Amulii rubbed against me and I'd get a good whiff, my brain would short-circuit. The hold he still had on me after everything he did was unnatural.

I flung the pillow across the room and grabbed my other one. Healing meant cutting every part of him from my life. Maybe if I couldn't see or smell him anymore, I could move on.

A howl shattered my serenity, and a heavy sob tore from my throat. It was such a lonely and heartbreaking sound, and he wanted me to hear it. After several mournful cries from the wild, it stopped, and suffocating silence wrapped tight around me once more.

The wood floors outside of my room groaned, and footsteps stopped at the door. There were about ten seconds of deliberation, and I knew Mom had been struggling to come to terms with this terrifying new reality.

This was beyond my therapist, for sure.

She knocked after what felt like hours of her standing there. Between the heartbreak and the persistent fever, I was too exhausted to raise my voice. She cracked the door and peered inside.

"Are you awake?"

"Don't turn on the light, please. My head hurts," I mumbled, speech slurred as half of my face remained buried in plush down. The bed dipped as she sat next to me, stroking my back.

"Are you okay?" I wasn't the only one who'd been crying. Her voice broke apart as she spoke.

"No."

"Do you need to go to the hospital?"

"That's not what I'm talking about."

She stopped rubbing my back. "How did your dad find out?"

"Someone was spying on us in the woods. Apparently, he snapped a couple of pictures and showed Dad."

Mom paused, considering her next words. "What is he?" she asked, her voice barely a whisper. After what she'd witnessed tonight, I couldn't blame her for being afraid.

"He calls himself a maw'cha, which is a type of werewolf, I guess." Every muscle in my body stiffened as I turned toward her. "He's not from this world. He'll be going back home when the portal opens." I paused. "Yeah, I know how incredibly stupid this all sounds."

"I thought you were pulling my leg yesterday. This is for real?"

I nodded. "I don't know what I was thinking. I was so desperate for someone to talk to, but he became much more than a friend. Even though I knew what he was, I still wanted to be with him. Maybe I'm just messed up in the head, like usual."

For the first time, Mom didn't overreact. Maybe she was too stunned to say anything after I admitted to being attracted to a monster. Words that I'd been wanting to say to another human being for weeks continued pouring from my lips.

"The morning you walked in, that wasn't a dog you smelled. It was him. The hunter that outed me to Dad shot him that night, and I saved his life. We were both so tired that we fell asleep together and didn't realize it. He was able to change back to his human form, but when he did, his pants fell off. That's why he was naked. I didn't even know I loved him then; he was just a good friend."

"After what I saw tonight . . . promise me you won't go near him again."

"It's already over between us, Mom." I choked up again, rubbing tears from my swollen eye. "And it hurts."

"Wow, you really liked him, didn't you?"

"A lot." Every time I thought I was done crying, the tears would fall again. "I didn't want to admit it for a while, but I kind of loved him. A part of me still loves him." Mom pulled me in for a hug. "You only saw the worst in him tonight, and the awkward dumbass he was that day."

I pulled away from her and sniffed, wiping runny nostrils on my sleeve. "You didn't see the person I saw. He was insightful, spiritual, caring, emotional. I didn't expect to fall for him. I didn't want to, but man—we'd talk for hours, and he'd say the sweetest things to me. And when we kissed," I closed my eyes, imagining the heat of his tongue, "nothing could compare to that. He made me feel loved and safe. I can't really explain it."

Mom smiled and kissed my forehead.

"I know what that's like. Why do you think it's so hard for me to leave your dad? He was sweet—we'd talk about everything, and I'd feel the butterflies when we kissed each other. It blinded me to the little parts of his personality that I overlooked. I thought if we loved each other, that would change."

She let out a weak sigh and shook her head. "But it doesn't change. People don't change like that, and you can't fix someone who doesn't see the problem to begin with. Before I knew it, I had a child and eighteen years had passed, and what I thought was a small part of who he was ended up being all he was."

She pushed herself off the bed, her face flushed with concern.

"It might not feel like it now, but you're lucky you learned this lesson early and had enough sense to walk away. I wish I'd have been that smart, but then I wouldn't have had you. I know I get on your case a lot, but you were the best thing to come out of this. I wouldn't change a thing. My special little boy grew up to be someone I'm proud of every day."

I needed to hear that. I was okay being her little boy tonight. Thinking about adulthood scared me now, and there'd be many more sad moments like this that I'd probably face alone. For now, I was thankful to have her here.

"Good night. I love you," she said as she turned back to shut the door. "We'll talk more tomorrow, if you want."

"I love you too—and thanks Mom."

CHAPTER TEN

BETRAYED BY THE MOON

"Thirty-nine degrees." Mom scrutinized the thermometer before turning her attention back to me as I lay in bed. "If this gets any higher, I'm taking you to the clinic. You shouldn't have slept with the window open last night."

I glanced at the sill and the floor beneath, the wood still damp from the nasty weather outside. It was a late first snow, and I wondered if Amulii was warm enough in his den.

"I'm fine, I just want to sleep," I muttered, my sweat-drenched body half under the blankets. If I stayed covered, I'd get too hot; if I took the covers off, I froze.

She sat at the foot of my bed and put a hand on my leg. "You wanna talk? I understand if you aren't feeling up to it."

It was around two in the afternoon, and I'd been slipping in and out of consciousness since last night. The breakup was still fresh, but

I wasn't crying every half hour either. I sat upright, pulling the covers to my chest.

"I don't know why I'm like this. We barely knew each other, but it feels like I lost an arm." Grabbing a damp washcloth from the nightstand, I sopped the sweat from my face and laughed. "I don't know. Maybe I was desperate to cling to the first werewolf that showed me any affection."

I let out a chuckle, but Mom didn't find that funny.

"Honey, this is scary. We know nothing about what he is. He could carry diseases, or he might try to come after you now." Her face stiffened. "You might be sick because of him." There wasn't much to refute. Every point she made was valid. "What does he look like? As a werewolf?"

"Like a buff eight- or nine-foot-tall wolf that stands on two legs." I paused to gauge her reaction, but she didn't appear to believe me. "I don't know how else to describe him; that's what he is. And I don't think he'll come after me. He seemed pretty hurt."

"Well, he hurt your father," she replied. As traumatic as it was last night, thinking about it this morning made me laugh. "It's not funny."

"He's not dead, and I'm glad someone put him in his place. He knows what it's like to be on the receiving end for once." After running the washcloth across my face, I handed it to her. "Can you wet this for me?"

She grabbed it and walked into the bathroom. "He needs surgery on his hand," she said, her voice muffled by the running water.

"Well, that was a self-inflicted injury. Amulii didn't do anything to him, I mean, aside from nearly choking him to death."

"Why are you defending a monster?" she asked, tossing the washcloth at my face.

"Why are you defending one?" I retorted, folding the cool fabric before pressing it to my forehead. "Amulii wasn't the first one to do anything. Dad threw the first punch—at me. Remember? Amulii thought he was protecting me."

"Please don't go back to him," Mom said. "Promise me."

"I'm not going back. You just need to understand that Amulii wasn't the only one in the wrong here."

"I know." She removed the rag and pressed her lips against my forehead. "That's why we're going through with the divorce. Your dad's going to be gone for two days, and I was going to leave for Calgary tomorrow to meet him to get the papers finalized. But with you sick like this—"

"Please, just get this over with so we can get the hell out of here. Don't worry about me." Few teenagers would have said those words with such excitement, but I'd been rooting for the end of this terrible ordeal for a while. Perhaps I'd finally get to enjoy the few months I had left until adulthood. "As long as we can get back to Calgary, I don't care."

Mom looked at me before heading out into the hall. "Oh, we are so done with this place. This wasn't one of my better ideas," she said, an aura of melancholy darkening her features. "I guess I screwed this one up."

"No, you learned. Isn't that what you told me?"

"When did you get so smart?"

"Smart? I fell in love with an actual werewolf," I said, trying to lighten her mood.

She smiled. "Get some sleep, and call me if this gets worse, okay?"

"I will."

///

No longer sweating, I peeled my dry eyelids open. The rag on my head was stiff, and if not for the possibility of death by dehydration, I'd have stayed in bed. My feet slid along the floor as I dragged myself to the bathroom. I dampened the rag in the sink before filling my water bottle. An itchy rash set the skin of my chest ablaze, and I'd been subconsciously scratching at it through my shirt all day. When I looked into the mirror, what I saw left me horrified. There was a raised black mark centered on my sternum.

///

Heat flared from my chest, tearing me from a dreamless sleep on my sweat-soaked mattress. I rolled to my feet, but it was hard to breathe.

I needed an ambulance.

Disoriented, I fumbled for the phone on my desk, but as the room became a spinning carnival ride, I hit the floor hard. As I rolled to my back, the intensity of the full moon burned my skin, bathing my body in a crimson hue. The physical world resembled a dark room as everything the beams touched turned to blood. Was this a nightmare?

Another wave of serrated pain put to rest any doubt that I was conscious. What I thought was moonlight oozed like bloody mucus from the walls, creeping across the floor to where I lay. What was happening to me?

There was an unnatural pounding in my chest, and a ruby-tinted glow there caught my eye. The once black mark now burned crimson, the same color as the crystal Amulii had shattered. Glowing, diseased veins snaked outward from the mark, like lava seeping into every limb.

I screamed, choking on agony, turning into one giant charley horse as every muscle knotted before tearing. The glow severed my nerves, and every limb surged with static electricity.

Prickly, itchy waves pulsed through me. The bloody light of the room made it hard to see, but there was something on my arms. It was a dark dusting at first, like I'd been rolling around in the sand. My skin itched as the dust thickened before shooting upward into tufts of brown fur.

"Amulii," I screamed, as the numbness vanished and the pain returned.

Still images sprang to life behind my eyes as though my conscious mind wanted to clobber me with weeks of subtle hinting that I'd willfully ignored.

It is . . . chélanc, a uh, symbol of friendship . . .

Another memory appeared of Amulii by the lake the day I told him about the hunter. The crystal shattered when he threw it.

What if you could be maw'cha? Would you want to be with me then?

I have to stop this.

There was a reason a sliver of distrust always lingered no matter how close we got, but it was too late. I ignored every warning, and now it was time to face the consequences of my stupidity. Another deepening shriek rattled the windows as hooked claws ripped through fragile fingernails, tearing them away with a bloody crack.

Sounds of pops filled the room as my spine snapped and twisted. The violent transformation extended my vertebrae in both directions. I was getting taller, and a thickening bone pushed between my rump, then lowered to my leg. Time no longer flowed in seconds and minutes. It was like hours had passed as the torture continued.

"No more, please." My voice gurgled as I screamed. I'd heard once in a religious debate that "there are no atheists in the foxhole," and I begged to any deity I imagined would listen. God, Buddha, Vishnu, even Satan—I didn't care. If the pain would end, the devil could have everything.

Blood filled my mouth as a thousand tiny fingers inside of me wrenched my face. Teeth loosened, then detached at the roots, nearly choking me as I swallowed one. Turning onto my furry stomach, I opened my jaws and let them fall to the floor in a thick, bloody soup as much larger teeth pushed from my bloody gums.

As my skull expanded, there was a moment where the pressure inside my throat and nose made it impossible to breathe. New muscles throbbed along the top and sides of my head and pulled my ears upward.

The pressure subsided, and I gasped.

Blood poured into my sinuses and into the back of my throat before dripping onto the floor as I hacked it up. It was all I could smell or taste. My once thick human tongue turned to taffy, flattened as the foul magic stretched it until it hung away from my mouth. I squeezed my eyes shut as a snout finished forming.

When Amulii shifted, there was no way he felt this. Gore sloshed around me as limbs flailed, and hot urine soaked my lower half as I writhed, rolling onto my back again.

The last part of my transformation was the worst. The skin on my penis ripped as bone and thicker muscle jammed into it. While I couldn't see what was happening, I could feel every excruciating stretch as it grew longer, thicker, and less human. My feet were also changing, like Amulii's did, lengthening, my heels becoming a part of my leg as the front of my feet and toes roughened to pads. Claws ripped through my toenails, eliciting one last monstrous scream.

And then, nothing.

It was over.

Sprawled along the floor, I lay there crying, panting, disbelieving. This couldn't be happening. Within seconds, I went from exhaustion to a jolt of energy that drove me to run. As the pain of the transformation vanished, an intense pang of hunger replaced it. My stomach roared, and the desire to fill it with anything was all I thought about.

Shaky paw-like feet held me up, and I had to face what I'd become for the first time. The floor creaked and groaned under the heft of my massive body as my claws tapped a monster's gait. I stood in front of the mirror and flipped the light switch. My eyes were so sensitive, it was as though I'd turned on the sun. After letting out a sharp whine, I turned them off and was able to see much clearer.

A brown maw'cha stared back at me with teary eyes, which flashed an intense sky blue, adding a hint of strange beauty to the beast. My human hair had fallen out, replaced by thick fur of similar color. Light brown fur covered every inch of me, and a darker, silky mane draped me from my neck, trailing from chest to groin.

Not a single part of my body resembled who I once was.

I flicked a claw against my right ear, and it twitched. My ears turned in different directions, amplifying creaking cabin noises coming from all over as the winds howled outside. I didn't control them; they just followed whatever noises they heard.

My new muscles were enormous, and I had grown at least a foot and a half taller, maybe more. Pointed ears pressed against my head as I thought about Amulii. I balled my clawed hands into fists and bared my teeth. How could he do this to me?

The entire time we were together, he knew what he had done by giving me that necklace. His freak-out at the lake made perfect sense. He knew I would turn into this, and every hunter would be after me when that happened. This was his plan all along. He never intended to wait to take me back to his world. He wanted insurance.

Ire raged in me, and this house was no longer my home. Amulii destroyed my future and erased my humanity with one *friendly* gesture.

A whimper shuddered from my nose, but my voice wasn't the same. When I tried to speak, I couldn't control my tongue.

"Aaam-sh . . ." Clear spittle sprayed the mirror and dripped from my mouth. Wolf-like tongues and lips were so different that I couldn't form words. Amulii could talk, but why couldn't I?

The boiling noises from my stomach signaled that I needed to eat— now. Blood dominated everything, and as the voice inside commanded me to kill, I became what I feared. I needed to consume. I would eat anything I saw: human, animal, anything.

This new body understood survival and would do what it could to ensure that. What if my parents had been home? My mother flashed into my thoughts for a moment before all I could see was violence.

My claws raked the floors as I dashed out of my room, losing my balance in the process. Being taller and standing on my toes meant I had to shift my posture forward when I ran. I was quick to adapt, and short-term memory faded in and out. One second, I was kissing the floor, and the next, I was slipping down the stairs before the refrigerator appeared. I jerked it open and ripped into plastic wrap and containers as handfuls of anything edible slid down my gullet.

Every leftover from the party went from the fridge to my maw, but the more I ate, the hungrier I grew. Losing patience, I tilted the refrigerator, dumping everything to the floor. Now on all fours, I continued to inhale the unfulfilling meat. I needed every calorie, but nothing sated my appetite as it all vanished into an even angrier stomach. I felt a call, a powerful pull, as the once screaming voice in my head whispered what to do. The house was no longer welcoming; the walls were too close.

Bolting from the cabin, I froze, taking in a world that I knew was the same, but seemed so alien. My enhanced vision sliced through the darkness, and with the aid of the full moon, it may as well have been midday. The landscape was more vibrant and alive than ever before, and I took in every color and smell.

The air was icy against my wet nose but came with a scent, one that was bizarre at first but soon became an uncontrolled orchestra of different instruments playing in harmonic dissonance. As they clashed, a new part of my brain picked them apart one by one.

Before I knew it, my feet were pounding the ground as I took off toward the mountains. The snowy, moonlit landscape raced toward me. Violent winds whipped me as I skimmed the ground, but I wasn't cold.

The rush of pleasure pounding through me as I sprinted toward the moon couldn't be described in human words. The motherly orb in the sky welcomed me like a lost, orphaned child. Millions of sensations pummeled me as my brain struggled to keep up with them.

Different colors faded into my vision as if they were jagged trails moving away from me in countless directions. I instinctively knew what this was: two senses working in tandem, creating an augmented reality of sorts. I held my hand over my nose, and as expected, the trails vanished.

Incredible.

The pulsing sensations through my muscles were akin to the best orgasms I'd ever experienced. The pleasure didn't last as the trails and scents overwhelmed me like billions of people screaming conversations at once. There was no one trail I could follow; it was everywhere, and I could no longer separate them. More scents appeared on top of others, and I had to shut down or my head would explode.

I roared in frustration but knew how to handle the stress. As if by instinct, my head pointed to the sky, and I arched my back. A shrill howl pierced the night, echoing into the mountains. It was high in pitch and warbly at first, then got deeper and cleaner. My first howl. There was an odd sense of pride that came with it. It was pure ecstasy, and I wanted to do it again. Distant wolves in the wilderness heard me and joined in, making me smile.

Stress drained from my muzzle as more howls filled the surrounding area with both dread and excitement. After the baying subsided, I fell to my knees again in relief. Steady side-to-side movement came from behind as I wagged my new tail, which was trapped beneath the tight, bloodstained pajama pants that were at one point really loose. Needing to be free, I tore them away. A wave of sadness hit again, and I fell forward on my clawed hands and cried out, my fists pounding the snow.

I couldn't control my emotions. Sadness, anger, excitement, and sexual arousal hit me all at once. They felt the same because I couldn't understand the animal sensations that came with them. Pleasure gushed through my arteries, but my mind suffered. Was the wild my new home, all alone? The voice inside understood.

Can't be alone.

I'd felt nothing like it before. As a human, I enjoyed being by myself, but now it was like slowly dying.

Have to find Amulii . . . need him.

My nose pointed to the trees ahead, at the figure concealed by shadow. His scent was different now; still intoxicating but there was something deeper. As I drew near, I could sense he knew I hated him. He was afraid, and the voice shifted from wanting his company to wanting him dead. His comforting musk became a fetid odor.

That infuriating scent drove my hunter's instinct crazy. The emotion was as offensive as decomposing roadkill on a humid summer afternoon, and I raged as it assaulted my nose. I was losing my ability to reason.

My head snapped toward the shifting yellow trail that hovered like dense vapor above the ground, and I bared my teeth. Saliva poured in thick strands from maw to chest. He'd pay for this.

Beastly snarls shook my throat as I bolted toward the trees, letting my nose take the lead. His unblinking eyes were calm, and he braced himself as I leaped into the air, focusing all I had into one deadly attack. His movements became fluid as he evaded.

Fear faded from him, and the familiar, alluring scent returned. What was he doing? The thought of his manipulation angered me more, and I jumped on him. He grabbed my arms, pinning me to the ground. I expected fury, but his ears fell to the sides of his head as a high-pitched whine left his nose.

Sadness smelled different. It was sweeter, subtler, not as strong as fear. At first, I wanted to join in the sadness, but then the voice screamed that he was the enemy.

My frenzy peaked, and I bucked him away before grabbing handfuls of fur, pinning him as he sank into the snow. He was so much bigger than me, even though I was a werewolf now. Was I strong enough to overpower him?

Opening wide, I went for his neck, but he raised an arm to take the brunt of my bite. The tang of iron filled my mouth. It was revolting, but I clamped harder as tears fell from my eyes. I jerked my head from side to side to tear flesh from bone. I wanted him to suffer, but he didn't retaliate or even make a noise.

He pushed his arm deeper into my mouth, locking my jaw before rolling me over and positioning himself on top of me again.

"Alex." Hearing him say my name made me want to throw up. "You need to come with me. You cannot be alone like this."

For a moment, I didn't want to let go, but Amulii understood the feelings I didn't. I opened my mouth and released his arm, retching before spitting out the remaining blood that had pooled under my tongue. There was something about the taste of maw'cha blood that went beyond disgusting. An evolutionary trait, perhaps?

"Say something to me."

I growled at him. *"I hate you. I fucking hate you."*

"I know what you are thinking, and there is nothing I can do to reverse it or take it back." He let out another painful whine. "You were not supposed to be this feral."

There was no more struggle left, and though my attack had little effect, the emotional pain of watching someone he loved suffer was its own punishment.

"You will be okay. I will take care of you now." With a shake in his voice, he let go of my arms and stood, the gruesome injury I'd inflicted on him earlier already healing. He scanned me with his glowing eyes before focusing on my face. My pants were gone, and the monster standing there liked me much better that way. I could smell it on him. The familiar scent of his grew stronger, and I finally understood why. This was the arousal he spoke of when we first met.

"Let us go back to the cave. I have a fresh kill and a bed."

"If you touch me, I'll rip your dick off and feed it to you."

He sprinted ahead, and I jumped to my feet to follow, my pace easily matching his for the first time. The slope we bounded up was familiar. It was the same mountain we traversed on our first outing together, only now, my new paws and powerful legs made quick work of the steep terrain. Super strength surged through every muscle, and I felt like the strongest thing in the world. But I was powerless at the same time.

What was I going to do now?

We approached the cave entrance where a warm carcass lay before us, chunks of meat already missing. Amulii must have started eating but stopped when he heard me howling. When I saw the dead animal, everything left of my humanity pleaded not to give in to what I wanted. Turning away, I padded toward the cave, my stomach complaining as wolf-like instincts declared war.

"No," Amulii said. "Eat."

Who was he to demand I do anything? I scratched at the snow with my new paws, kicking it at him. As I entered the warmth of his den, he grabbed the nape of my neck, pulling the loose skin taut.

"I will not let you sleep until you eat this. I do not care if I have to force the meat down your throat. I will not lose you to hunger."

I froze as the skin around my nape tightened more, and he led me back to the deer whose scent was like a buffet of everything I loved as a human.

The beast inside me screamed. *"Eeeeat iiiiit."*

The skin fell loose as he let go, and after a second, I regained control before raking my claws at him. Not fast enough. He was better at being a werewolf than I was, but I couldn't let him dominate me like that.

He avoided my claws and teeth again and grabbed me by the nape, forcing me to my knees. There was a sad, distant look on his face as he knelt next to me. Slippery noises perked my ears as he thrust two of his massive fingers into the carcass before smearing the blood across my nose. A blue glow emanated from my eyes, shimmering in the animal's bloody fur as instinct became harder to control. He nudged my snout deeper into the gore. I wanted to tear into it, but the human voice . . .

"Please. You need to eat. You cannot shift back to human when you are hungry."

As he released me, I could feel him stroking my back, prodding me with friendly encouragement. The battle continued in my mind, but the outcome had already been determined the moment I shifted. I trembled as I made a last attempt to hold back from what the wolf so desperately needed.

"Come on now."

He tried scooting closer unnoticed, still petting my back. When I snarled, he jumped away. I closed my eyes, still deliberating while keeping Amulii at a distance.

As the human in me died, I mourned the loss by pressing my face against exposed organs. I licked the blood, trying to ease my way into it.

There was no more holding back.

All I heard were crunches and wet noises as I tore the body apart to sate my repulsive appetite.

"Very good," Amulii said, but his voice seemed far away.

Canines sheared muscle and bone like a new set of knives. My sharp molars barely tenderized the toughest parts, while I swallowed everything else whole. This was what I was now.

My stomach bulged, full of fur, bone, and guts, and I wanted to throw up as the human seized back control of my thoughts. I cried over the exposed skeleton, whose every bone was picked clean. By me.

I felt a hand on my back and snapped like a wild dog. It had become an automatic reaction as my body and mind worked together to reject all of him. The werewolf next to me was more of a person than I was now.

"I do not know what you want me to do. You need me. I made a mistake. I am sorry," Amulii said, his voice full of the same tired regret he acted out each time he fucked up, only this time, I wasn't sure I'd ever forgive him. My teary eyes never left the ground as I continued to grieve for the life I'd lost. Dad hated me already, but would Mom hate me now too?

"That day on the mountain, I thought I could force you to be with me. When you broke your ankle, it scared me. To be human is to be fragile, to die young. I know now I had no right to force this on you."

I felt a void as my eyes leaked. There were no whimpers or sobs. Amulii did to my soul what I had done to that deer.

"All I can do is protect you. I can never truly make amends for this." His deep voice pitched with sincerity, but it was all too late.

A wave of exhaustion overwhelmed me as I collapsed onto the snow. Amulii caressed my face in his lap, and I had no energy left to drive him away. Tomorrow I'd get to see the aftermath in daylight. Tonight, I had no choice but to trust that Amulii would take care of me.

CHAPTER ELEVEN

THE VOICE

An orange-lit, rocky ceiling sharpened into view as I blinked away the sleep from my eyes. A wintery gust stung at any bare skin not covered by the blanket hastily draped over my lower half. Everything had a richer, deeper scent than I was used to. The overbearing muskiness of Amulii's cave told me a thousand things about him, but most of it made no sense.

"Good morning," a deep voice whispered from my side, startling me. I rolled off the fur bedding before snapping upright against the wall. "You are okay, do not worry."

"No I'm not okay," I shouted. Amulii's eyes wandered lower. "Don't fucking look at me." I snatched the blanket, draping it over myself.

Amulii's ears lay flat against his head. "I do not know what to do." He scooted across the bed, getting closer, but I shifted toward the cave entrance.

"And you think I do?" I shivered, not just from the cold, but from anger. "Fix this. Make me normal again."

He shook his head. "There is no way to undo it, but I can teach you how to live as maw'cha now." His ears perked upright, and the tail that once lay close to his legs patted the floor. "I could teach you all about—"

"Why are you happy about this?" I yelled. "Oh, I get it. You got what you wanted."

"Alex, please understand."

"Shut up. Just shut up." Tears ran down my face as I thought about the agony of last night. "You're awful. I can't believe I was so stupid to trust you." I rubbed my eyes and looked back at him. "What am I gonna do now? I've gotta get back home."

After crossing my arms, I slid my fingers over my hairy, rigid midsection. My eyes widened as I glanced down at my now broad chest and swollen abdominal muscles, and it became apparent the change altered everything, including my human body. I pulled the blanket away to glimpse the thick brown hair that trailed down my chest.

How would I explain this?

"You cannot. Home is here now," he said, jumping to his feet. His paws tapped across the floor before he knelt in front of me, his rough fingers brushing my damp cheek. "It is too dangerous for a new maw'cha to be around humans, and those hunters may still be out there."

"Don't touch me," I said in a low tone, pushing him away with as much contempt as I could visibly muster. He leaned close, his bared canines inches from my face. "W-what, are you gonna bite me or something?"

"I do not want to force you to stay, but I will if I must. You are my responsibility now."

Amulii's heavy gaze crushed my resistance as I turned away from him. "Teach me how to control this so I can get back to my life."

"I still love you, Alex." He heaved a disappointed sigh before standing.

I covered my ears. "Goddammit, stop. You don't get to say that after all of this."

He leaned over me and grabbed my forearms, forcing my hands away. "I did this because I fell in love with you. We are perfect for each other, even more so now."

"Loved me—" A bestial roar I didn't expect tore through the cave as I pushed him hard against the ground. "You think because I'm younger than you that this sappy bullshit is gonna work on me again?" I balled my fists as he pushed himself back to his feet. "I ended this the night you showed me what you really were." I looked down at my hands which still had dried blood on them from last night. "And now this."

He bashed his heavy fist against the cavern wall, the impact causing a couple warming crystals to rattle. "You ended it because you were scared of me. Now that you are maw'cha, what do you have to fear? We fit now." Letting out a low growl, he walked toward the mouth of the cavern without turning back. "I am glad you turned. Being human makes you insufferable."

"I hate you." I lobbed a jagged stone at his head, and he ducked before it hit. "I hope the hunters don't miss anything vital this time." Hearing myself say that made me cringe. It could be me in the crosshairs now.

"Hate me all you want, that will not change my feelings. I will take care of you, regardless." He looked over his shoulder, revealing wet fur around his eyes. "I am getting you food. I will be back." His voice cracked as it got lower. "Do *not* leave."

His ears folded down as he vanished around the rocks.

I stood, searching the cave for the new clothes I had bought him. The bag sat against the wall next to the entrance, so I let the blanket fall and made a mad rush to grab it.

"You're not gonna do this to me," I said to myself, locking my jaw tight. "I'm such a goddamn idiot."

After throwing on an oversized pair of pants and a dark green T-shirt, I took off toward home.

///

Ten minutes. That's how long it took me to run from Maligne Lake to the cabin while barefoot in the snow. The new pants already had holes where they rubbed together between my legs. If my thighs were any thicker, they would have caught fire. I was desperate to get away from that cave, from Amulii.

The cabin's warped front door groaned as it swung back and forth in the breeze, the weatherstrip catching the frame before it could slam shut. Hopefully wild animals hadn't made the cabin their new home. When I thought about cornering a helpless critter inside, my stomach went crazy.

"Oh God." I held my head, trying to rid myself of the bloodlust that swelled, turning my vision red and hazy. How much energy had I used? A flashback from last night replayed second by horrifying second, the trauma fresh. "No . . . I can't turn. Stop."

Taking several deep breaths, a tranquil feeling passed over me as I stepped the rest of the way inside. There were leftovers in the fridge that would hopefully sate the wolf, at least long enough for me to buy some food.

It was colder inside, despite the heat being on. My heart sank when I saw the refrigerator door held open by empty shelves hanging out at odd angles. Broken dishes, grease, and barbeque sauce covered the floor like a mosaic portrait of whatever desperation gripped me last night.

I didn't remember doing any of this.

Despite my hunger, I had to clean the mess werewolf me left behind. When I knelt to sweep the broken plates into the dustpan, a powerful odor choked me. While different in nuance, it was like Amulii.

Was that stink coming from me?

Time wasn't on my side, but I needed to shower. If Amulii appeared, I'd fight him. Though I stood little chance of winning, he wouldn't take me back, at least while I was still alive or conscious.

After cleaning, I rushed to the bathroom, the mirror catching my attention as I locked eyes with a full-grown man. My face had aged almost five years into someone I barely recognized, though nuances of my previous physical traits showed through. That coupled with the slightly pointed ears and sharper teeth made me kind of freaky-looking, but really attractive. The features I now possessed, the bulky physique and strong, masculine face, were what I'd always wanted, but they weren't worth the price I unwillingly paid.

I tore away from the mirror and made the bath water as hot as I could stand it. Eager to be clean, I undressed before easing myself into the steamy veil of water. As stress and filth flowed down the drain, I had a moment to reflect for the first time since the shift.

I was human now, but could I stay that way? Was being a werewolf something I could hide like my sexuality? The thought of being forced out of one closet only to run right back into another made me want to scream. I couldn't live like that again. It was hard enough keeping mundane secrets, but this could have deadly consequences if it ever got out.

What if instinct took over? Being gay never made me want to sink my teeth into human flesh. What if I couldn't be around anyone anymore? Years of prepping to get into a college of my choice, to have a shot at a successful life, could vanish in one uncontrollable fit of rage or hunger.

Dirty suds circled the drain, and as I ran the soapy washcloth lower, I gasped. The physical change I underwent meant *everything* had increased in size. It was a minor consolation, but at least there was another upside.

With all the stress I was under, a delightful thought crept into my head. Amulii would be here any minute, but that concern was light years away from what I wanted to do at the moment.

Leaning forward, I braced myself against the wall, letting fantasy overtake despair as I gave the limp mass of flesh a squeeze. It took little effort to bring it to full mast in my hand. The dick didn't feel like mine at all as I jerked a stranger off in the shower. A few moments of pleasure were all I wanted as I thrust unevenly into two conditioner-slick hands. A loud, bestial groan echoed from the tiled walls as a roomful of men surrounded me in the fantasy. It didn't take long to bring myself closer to release as I stroked faster. That was when Amulii barged into my thoughts, grabbing me by the back of the neck, and bending me over a bed. He was in *that* form, rutting me as he snarled into my ear. What the fuck was happening? A growl rumbled from my throat, and my eyes snapped open.

"Oh shit," I shouted, punching a crack in the shower wall as brown fur burst from my arms. "No." Sliding down the slick tiles, my ass hit the tub as I rocked back and forth, trying to stop what was coming. "Please . . ."

A mantra of refusal combined with deep breathing seemed to work. When the tingling stopped, I opened my eyes to see the fur had receded. Masturbation, it seemed, was out of the question.

Would I ever be able to have sex without turning?

If it meant I would never feel that kind of pain again, I'd become a damn monk. The negatives of being a werewolf far outweighed any of the positives. What good was having a body like this if I couldn't be with anyone?

After standing and turning the knob to cut the water, I got out, wrapping myself in a towel as I walked into the bedroom. I locked up after stepping on bony fragments. A gory scene lay under my feet as I jumped back; sticky dried blood, teeth, and human hair littered the floor. There was also a powerful scent of urine where I had pissed all over myself.

I had to get out of there or relive the trauma from last night.

The dresser drawer squealed as I pulled it open to grab a pair of underwear. It didn't dawn on me until the tight fabric tore halfway up my thicker legs that nothing I owned would fit me anymore. The only oversized article of clothing I owned was the pair of pajama pants that were likely buried under snow out in the woods.

After removing the ruined boxers and kicking them under the bed, I ran back to the bathroom to grab the stench-covered clothing I discarded on the floor earlier. There wasn't time to go through Dad's clothes to find something that fit. I lay the clothing on the bed and doused it with as much body spray as I could stand, my now sensitive nose bearing the brunt. I now understood why Amulii didn't like this smell when he'd first met me.

A shrill tone made me jump as the phone rang, and I looked down at the receiver to see Mom's number glow blue on the caller ID. I pressed the call button and held the receiver between my ear and shoulder as I grabbed the dirty pants and slid them on.

"Hey Mom," I said while trying to fake a nasal voice and a convincing cough.

"You sound awful."

"I'm feeling a little better. My fever's down."

The phone went silent for an uncomfortable moment as I waited for her response. As I donned the oversized shirt, my nose crinkled, and I gagged as werewolf stink mixed with the now caustic-smelling deodorant.

"What's wrong with your voice?"

I noticed it earlier when I was arguing with Amulii. My voice had gotten deeper. Thankfully, it was a phone call, and I was "sick."

"My throat hurts. Can you pick up some lozenges when you come back tomorrow?"

"Yeah . . ." I picked up on the growing suspicion in her voice. "I'm glad you're feeling better because you had me worried." She didn't know what kind of nightmare awaited when she returned, and I didn't know how I was going to break it to her. "I'll be home tomorrow afternoon, okay, sweetie?"

"Okay." The crooked front door skidded open downstairs, and rapid footsteps thudded toward my room. "I need to go to the bathroom, love you." I hung up, tossing the phone on the bed before opening my window and climbing through. A large, sandpapery hand wrapped around my ankle before I could get all the way onto the awning.

"Have you lost your mind?" he growled, yanking me back inside before lifting me to my feet, his snout inches from my face. "I told you not to leave. Follow me back home."

"This *is* my home." The more I struggled, the stronger his hold as he pushed my back to the wall. "I'm not going back out there."

"I do not want to do this, but—" When he raised his fist, I knew what was coming. This was serious; he was actually going to knock me out. "When you wake up, there will be food. You will heal very fast." Amulii shuddered as my knee cracked against his groin. The high-pitched whines he made as he crumpled to the ground made *my* balls hurt.

"Ugh . . ." he groaned. "Alex . . ."

"Don't worry, you will heal *very* fast," I said, mocking his tone earlier. I gave the pathetic creature one last glare before grabbing the credit card off the desk.

The ATV raced along the side of the road as the steep-angled wooden buildings of downtown Jasper appeared. Amulii wouldn't stop until he caught me, and I wasn't sure how much time that ball-busting move would buy. Where would I go now?

Going back home was out of the question. My stomach stirred awake as I caught the scent of barbeque on the wind. I'd only been downtown a few times, and most of that time was spent in one or two places getting food and clothes for Amulii. I still wasn't familiar with all the restaurants and stores in the area. It was hard to focus on following the scent of food when car exhaust kept overwhelming my now sensitive nose.

I drove down one of the side roads and saw a rustic brown building with forked wooden support beams holding up the roof of an outdoor eating area. The four-wheeler had barely rolled to a stop before I jumped to the ground and dashed toward the entrance.

All I craved was rare meat; in fact, I would have taken anything raw if it meant I wouldn't have to wait for it to cook. The closer I got to the door, the worse I felt.

If I ate soon, I'd be okay. Amulii said he could stay human for as long as he wanted if he kept himself fed.

The warm, delicious air inside tantalized my nostrils as I stepped through the door. The entryway was typical of more upscale barbeque joints: lots of glass, polished wooden floors, and walls leading to a lobby with a waterfall and koi pond, of all things. The best barbeque often came from mom-and-pop restaurants that had run-down appearances, but Jasper didn't have any of those, as far as I knew.

"Welcome to Texas Dan's." A young waitress pulled my attention from the over-the-top décor as she grabbed a menu from a basket nailed to a wooden beam. There were wagon wheels, animal heads, and butter churns throughout the building, but there were also enormous screens everywhere, each with a different sport displayed over a long black granite bar. It was as though the restaurant couldn't decide what it wanted to be. "How many today?" she asked.

When I opened my mouth, saliva dribbled onto my chin. My face burned as the woman shot me a sideways glance. Hopefully no one else saw that. "One please."

She looked at my feet and shook her head.

"There's a strict policy about wearing shoes inside."

All the things I had carefully considered before becoming a werewolf mattered less as I lost my ability to multitask. The only thing I could focus on was my hunger. Shoes never crossed my mind, and they probably wouldn't have fit my huge feet anyway. Was I getting dumber?

"I, uh . . ." Thoughts of tearing into her sent a fresh rush of panic through me. I had to come up with some excuse, or this wouldn't turn out well for either of us. "I got lost in the mountains and my shoes are floating down the river somewhere. I haven't eaten in a few days."

A shocked expression replaced the scornful look she gave me earlier. "Are you okay? Do you need me to call someone?"

"No, I just need to eat. I know the way home."

"Sure," she said. "Follow me. I'll get you the corner booth in the far back."

The wolf calmed as I followed her to the table, taking a path through rows of tall booths that kept me and my bare feet out of sight of the other people eating.

"I can get you something quick for an appetizer, if you want. What's your name?"

"Uh, Alex. And just meat—a lot of it. I don't care what kind. As rare as I can get it." I paused for a moment as I thought about what I craved. "Is there any way to get it raw?"

Did that just come out of my mouth?

The horror she exuded brought me back from the brink. I let out a nervous chuckle.

"Just kidding. I'm so hungry I can't wait for anything to cook." She gave me an uneasy smile. "I'll uh, have three racks of ribs and water," I said, trying to keep my voice low. The waitress gave me another wary glance.

"I-I'll get right on that." She almost ran into another waiter walking by as she backed away.

My forehead hit the table, and I released the breath I had been holding in. This was a test to see if Amulii was right, or if I could still function as a human being. So far, it wasn't looking good. Though I appeared normal, below the surface the monster was becoming harder to handle.

The table shook as someone slid into the seat, and I snapped to attention. Amulii was human, dressed in one of the forest green wolf shirts and camouflage cargo pants I got him. He glared as he positioned himself uncomfortably into the bench across the table.

A slight shudder ran through me as I broke eye contact, but I could still feel his angry eyes boring holes in my head.

"What the hell are you doing here?" I whispered, my voice barely audible over loud chatter and clanking pans from the kitchen close by. "Leave me alone."

"Saving you from yourself. I am in pain, and I am pissed, Alex." His low, seething voice made me want to jump through the oversized window panes. "Humans surround us. This is dangerous and you do not listen."

"If you're that uncomfortable, then leave. I'm enjoying myself," I said, my heart racing. Amulii easily saw through the façade as a rough smile cracked his gritty countenance.

"You know you do not belong anymore. Come back with me."

"Another one?" the server asked. The clank of an icy glass on the table cut the tension. "Sorry, I didn't see you come in, sir."

"He was just leaving."

Amulii's brow furrowed as he crossed his arms, never turning away from me. "I think I will stay."

"Whatever," I mumbled, surveying the steadily filling parking lot through the window. "Do what you want."

"What can I get you to drink, sir?"

"I do not understand your question. Do humans not drink water?"

I cringed and let out a nervous laugh so as to soften the weirdness of his statement. "He'll have water."

"Riiight. I'll be right back," she said.

Amulii watched as she left before cutting back into me.

"Why are *you* here?" he asked, snatching the glass of water in front of me before chugging it.

"I'm hungry."

He slammed the now empty glass on the table.

"There is food at the den," he shouted. The restaurant fell quiet.

"Keep your voice down." I sank into the seat and covered my face.

"You should not be here." Amulii whispered. "You put everyone here at risk. Why can you not understand?"

"I don't want to go back with you," I said while swirling the pooled ring of condensation with my finger where the glass had been. "I just want to go home."

A smooth, southern voice sliced through the garbled conversations in the restaurant.

"The usual booth, sweetheart."

A low growl swelled in Amulii's throat as he turned to the window. I went rigid as what little calm I had left evaporated.

"Of all the places—"

"We have to leave, now," he said, sliding to the end of the bench.

"You go first. He won't recognize me like this." I pointed to the back door. "Slip out that way."

"Come with—"

"I have to eat. I waited too long." My hushed voice gave way to panic as my hands trembled. Though I'd been trying to hide it from him, the hunger had been pummeling my mind with gore since I got there. "I'll join you when I'm done. Get out before he sees you."

"Hurry." Amulii hurled one last glare in my direction before limping out the back door, still bow-legged from earlier.

It wasn't a moment too soon as the server led Liam past my table to the next booth over. He slithered into the seat with his back facing me. I didn't lift my head enough to get a good look at his face, but he wore normal clothing today. In fact, he was dressed as though he'd be off to a board meeting soon, in a slim-fitting casual black blazer and white button-down shirt. The ensemble came together with black dress pants and a pair of fancy leather derby shoes. If I hadn't resented the man so much, or ever heard him speak, I'd have thought he was quite the catch.

"Hey, your ribs'll be out shortly," the server said, sliding another glass of ice water across the table in front of me. "Where's your friend?"

"It's just me." I tried to smile, despite wanting to run away screaming from this deepening nightmare. "Sorry about this."

"It's okay," she said, trying to hide either annoyance or pity.

She returned my smile with her own and a little something extra. A sweet scent enveloped my nose, and every receptor knew exactly what it was. It was easy to see how Amulii had figured me out so fast. Wild thoughts returned as the voice in my head snarled something unintelligible. As she hurried to her next table, I grabbed at my hair, pulling hard to push the beast back where it belonged.

I am starving. I should eat the hunter.

I closed my eyes and tried to shake the thought away. The voice had become so loud that it drowned out all other noises in the restaurant. A large metal platter clacked and slid against the table, giving me a moment of relief.

"Three racks of ribs, and I tried to get them rare, but the chef wouldn't do it. Food safety reasons. They could only do medium rare."

"That's fine," I said sharply, ripping into half a greasy slab. "Thanks."

"You're welcome." She tossed me another flirty grin as I chomped into the meat.

Thinking about anything other than eating seemed like a waste as I fell into a strange trance. My sharper teeth easily stripped the meat from the bones, and savory rubbed spices covered my face in greasy layers as more went into my mouth. I wanted to slow down, but every time I'd reach for a napkin, I'd snap off another rib.

"You sure are a loud eater," Liam muttered, facing me. He appeared annoyed before his expression changed to curiosity. "You look familiar. Have I met you?"

"No, sorry," I said with my mouth full, tearing into another strip of meat. The hunter grimaced at me before turning back to his table.

The server approached with another glass of water.

"How are the ribs, Alex?"

A bone dropped to the platter with a clang as she said my name. I'd forgotten I'd used it when she'd seated me.

"Alex." Liam turned toward me, inspecting me again. "Alex . . . I knew your eyes looked familiar."

"You must have me confused with someone else." I swallowed the last piece of meat before tearing open a wet-nap packet to wipe my face and hands. "Could I get a to-go box?"

"Sure." She glanced nervously at the hunter.

"Hmm, sorry. I'm a little on edge lately." He turned back around as the heater kicked on, the vent blowing over me. "Wait a minute," the hunter said, standing before sniffing the air. "That smell . . ." He climbed into my booth, crinkling his nose. "That stench. You smell just like him." He shook his head as he glared at me. "Cologne ain't gonna hide that. I remember that nasty fuckin' stink well."

My throat went dry.

Kill. Kill. Tear out his throat.

"Stop," I shouted, grabbing my hair again. "Leave me alone."

"Your eyes are glowin', Alex," he said, trying to catch his breath. "God damn, what'd he do to you? Your ears and teeth are just like his. You're a monster now, aren't ya? I told you to be careful out there. Now we gotta take you back with us." He reached into his pocket and grabbed his phone.

"Shut up," I growled, my voice a mixture of beast and man as I slammed my fist on the table, cracking it. The restaurant fell silent again. I clenched his shirt, ripping his buttons as I pulled him close. "I . . . never . . . go . . ."

It was happening. The monster I feared demanded freedom as it carpeted my arms in fur.

"Calm down. We're not gonna hurt you." He sat his phone on the table. "We just wanna help."

The tingling spread across my neck and down my back. As the wolf clawed to the surface, the human inside faded, but not before the transformation ground to a halt as I spent what little willpower remained.

"He turn . . . me. You . . . made Dad hate me." The rushing river of blood pulsing through his jugular was all I could hear. "Maybe . . . a bite . . ."

"No, beast. Get back." The hunter tried to push me away, but my face inched closer. "Someone call the cops!"

Screams. That was all I heard around me, but I couldn't break my hold on him.

Eat. Him.

A firm hand clamped the back of my neck and squeezed, pulling my dripping teeth away from my potential meal. Another arm wrapped around my chest, jerking me backward as the heels of my bare feet dragged against the smooth floor. Amulii whisked me through the exit before I could fully shift.

"You said if I ate—"

"It is okay now. Please, we must go back." He tightened his embrace, and the demanding voice vanished. What was happening to me? Hopelessness smothered any flame of rebellion as my forehead rested against his chest.

"Okay," I said, sobbing into his shirt. "I have to get my four-wheeler."

"Leave it." The whine of distant sirens grew louder. "We run now."

CHAPTER TWELVE

FREE FALLING

The far corner of the cave iced over as I sat there shivering, knees pressed against my chest. Amulii was sitting cross-legged on his bedding, staring at me.

He'd open his mouth to speak, eyes wider than before, then pause and hunch over when I'd look away. These were the moments I hated most, and the silence did little to help matters. The incident at the restaurant brought to light what I feared most about myself now.

A dull pang in my stomach was quiet at first, but soon reverberated through the cavern in loud, angry rumbles.

"You are hungry." Amulii stretched both arms before standing.

"I just ate."

Amulii tilted his head to the side. "Please stay this time. I will get more food."

"I don't want anything from you, especially that." I crossed my arms over my raised knees, muffling frustrated groans as I buried my face in them. "My parents will be home tomorrow. I'll eat then."

"Do you plan on eating your parents?"

"Why the fuck would you say something like that?"

"Because that is exactly what will happen," he snapped. "Why do you still deny what you are? You have eyes." Amulii stomped over to me before getting on one knee. He caressed my chin, lifting my head to meet his gaze. "This is hard for you, but you are not human anymore. That will not change."

"As long as I eat, I can stay this way. You said that—remember?"

"I did not mean indefinitely," he shouted, jerking my head as he let go. "Your body will make the shift to your true form, and it will be beyond your control. You need proper food, not human food. That is why you are hungry again."

"Bullshit. I fed you human food for a whole week, and you were fine."

"I was malnourished." He sat next to me, but tensed up as he spoke. "I was starving, no matter how much I ate. The cuts of meat you brought do not have all the nutrients to keep the hunger away. We need entrails, organs, blood, skin, and we need it raw." He paused as his body slouched forward. "I had to hunt."

"You mean you broke a promise." Manic laughter shook my aching stomach. "Not even surprised. You lied to me about everything else, so why not?"

"Would you rather me starve over a stupid promise?"

"Promises aren't stupid, and you could have seasoned what I got you with that pun'chei for nutrients. I'm not stupid." I shoved an elbow into his ribs. "And don't sit so close to me."

He scooted away and hissed through his teeth before pushing himself to a stand. "I have to save that. It is very important, and we may need it soon."

"Then you should have just told me the truth. It's not like I wouldn't have understood."

"Really? Is that one of your *jokes*?" Amulii sneered, removing his shirt and pants, tossing them against the wall as his bones popped and muscles stretched. "You barely understand me when I tell you to stay, and it is not because you are stupid." His breathy voice lowered as his head morphed and neck broadened. The transformation happened much faster than last time. "It is because you think you know more than you do. If I had not been there today, you would have killed everyone."

"You—"

"Stop talking," he interrupted, snapping his canine jaws near my face as he knelt in front of me, fully shifted. A splash of spittle made me turn my head away, only to have him force my attention back, his rough hand gripping my jaw tight. "I only told you what you wanted to hear because it was easier that way. We were having fun and getting close. Why would I want to ruin the moment? It was harmless."

"This is not harmless. Look at me. Look what you did. I'm a monster." I tried pulling away but froze as he tightened his grip.

"Do you think I am a monster?" Amulii's snarl softened, his teeth disappearing behind thin, blackened lips. "Is that what you thought that night when you saved me?"

I said nothing as I pulled away, his hand losing its grip on my chin. His snout wrinkled, lips pulling back to bare his teeth once more.

"I am done apologizing with meaningless words. I will hunt, and you will eat. That is the end of this talk." Amulii released me before standing. He trudged toward the mouth of the den, and I jumped to my feet, following him.

"Please don't make me do it." He ignored me and continued walking. "Please." I begged this time, grabbing his hand, hoping to garner some sympathy. I knew what would happen if I ate a carcass.

The animal inside ached to free itself at the first scent of blood. "If you care about me at all, don't make me go through that again."

"Stop." My pleas didn't even soften his scowl. "You will eat, and you will live."

"I'd rather die." Flashes of screams, blood, and agony from last night had me hyperventilating. It was hard to fathom choosing death, but that was a pain I never wanted to experience again. "Just kill me."

"I will not listen to this." He grabbed my arms and squeezed. "Never talk about wanting to die. To be maw'cha and live this life is a gift. You may not appreciate it now, but you will." Amulii didn't understand. Didn't he experience any pain at all?

He pushed me away before sniffing the air. After catching a scent, he darted outside, leaving me to stumble sick back to my corner. Muffled sobs choked from my mouth, and I lifted the blanket over my head before curling into the fetal position on the floor.

Amulii's footsteps rapped out a warning as he rushed into the den. I was still curled up in the blanket, my face covered.

"Come. Food is outside," he said, nudging my leg with his pawed foot.

"No."

"I was not asking."

Amulii's tone belied any patience he'd once had. It was as though what I felt never mattered to him. I'd have given anything for the caring, sweet person he was a week ago.

But was he really that person? The more I remembered of our time together, the more self-serving Amulii's attitude seemed. That nightmare I'd had when I passed out in this den for the first time may have been a premonition.

His furry, muscled arm brushed against my skin as he sat next to me. I jolted upward before scooting further into the corner, still refusing to look at him.

"Fine," he muttered, shuffling closer. "Let us talk then. Take the blanket off."

After a few moments of hesitation, the blanket fell from my head and I glimpsed his burning, yellow eyes. "I can't do it. I c—"

Amulii smothered my face in wet warmth, and the next breath I drew shot a metallic scent like an arrow straight into my brain. I wiped the blood away with my shirt, but the scent remained. No matter how hard I tried to shake it, the transformation wouldn't stop this time as thoughts of ripping through flesh subjugated all others.

"Why?" I wailed as fur erupted from my skin.

"Because I love you, and I do not want you to die. It is okay," Amulii whispered, drawing me close as my human groans of discomfort lowered to bestial growls. A dull throb pulsed through me as muscles bulged and bones cracked, tearing through my shirt. The pain wasn't an iota of what I felt the first time. The transformation was over before I could think.

"That was not so bad. Why were you so afraid?" he asked, giving me a sympathetic grin before his arms loosened. His expressions were softer for the first time since we'd gotten back to the cave. "Come. I have prepared a lovely meal."

As upset as I was, I couldn't help but grunt out a relieved laugh at the irony of his statement.

"It is good to see you smile in this form. I know you do not want to hear me say it, but you are a . . . " He paused and swallowed the drool seeping from his mouth as his voice got breathier. "Beautiful maw'cha. None of my people have blue eyes like yours."

I growled, wanting to tear into him, but my ability to speak vanished like it did last night. Jumping onto my pawed feet, I stumbled toward the exit, nearly falling forward before Amulii caught me. Walking on my padded toes tripped me a second time as I kept trying to step heel first with no heel.

"You still cannot speak?"

I shook my head.

"Try to say my name," he said, nudging my arm. There was a looseness in my mouth as I tried to move my stubborn new tongue. It was as though the muscles in my face were no longer designed for speaking human words. I shook my head. "Try, please."

I let go of a whine that sounded hilariously sad. "Amroooo . . ." This was embarrassing. The floppy, reluctant muscle slipped to the side of my mouth as I tried to enunciate slower. "Amrooor—" I yelped when a stray tooth bit down on it. A thin layer of blood coated my mouth as I put a clawed hand to my face. Biting my tongue as a human hurt, but as a maw'cha it was dangerous.

"Good," he snorted, trying to hold back a laugh. He wasn't taking my frustration seriously at all. Was this a joke to him? "That will heal fast. You will speak again in a little time." A hiss escaped me as I turned around, but a low, nasally chuckle grabbed my attention. "It is rather peaceful not listening to you complain."

My knee jerked upward, just missing the large fur-covered scrotum that hung uncovered between the other werewolf's legs. He flinched and jumped backwards, shielding the sensitive area with his hands.

"We need rules," he snarled, grabbing my arms. "Do not ever kick me there again." Amulii spun me toward the cave mouth and shoved me outside as he followed close behind. "We heal fast, but *that* still hurts."

"Gooooood." My tone was deep and drawn out as I stepped into the sunlight. When we approached the opening between the crags, I gnarled my claws and pointed a finger at his crotch. Though I couldn't see my own expression, I hoped the rage roaring to the surface would be a stark enough warning. But instead, his tail fanned up an amorous scent.

"If you want, I can teach you how to use that new tongue of yours in better ways." The sharp-fanged smirk that slithered up his broad muzzle pushed me over the edge. I swung at his face, the tips of my claws slicing into Amulii's nose. After shaking his head in surprise, he put his hands up. "I am sorry," he said, dabbing the blood with his fingers.

I wasn't in the mood for jokes, especially that one. Everything scared me now, and I couldn't even tell him how I was feeling. Despite turning into a massive killing machine, I was nothing more than a small, frightened teenage boy on the inside.

Amulii's stroked the back of my neck as he pointed at the moose carcass, which lay in stained, pale red snow, steam rising into the air where he had ripped it open. "Let us eat now, and we will work things out as they come. When you can talk again, how about you set some rules for me?"

After gorging myself sick on a bloody carcass again, disgust and nausea set heavy in my gut. My stomach bulged, overloaded with as much as I could fit into it. It was too painful to move after I collapsed onto Amulii's bed. Barely able to keep my eyes open, I examined the black maw'cha lying next to me, dead asleep.

Being together like that brought back feelings I didn't want. I still loved him, despite everything he'd done to me, though I didn't know why. Even after I broke it off that night, if I hadn't been sick, I would have run right back into his arms like the idiot I was. None of what I felt for him made much sense. How could I still have these feelings?

His chest heaved as deep snores rattled the crystals on the walls. Looking at him made me think about what I'd become, and the emotions that dominated my new existence returned: anger, fear, self-loathing, and confusion.

He was so broken that night we went our separate ways—so angry and beaten. Now that the circumstances had changed in his favor, I knew he would stop at nothing to see his investment in turning me pay off.

God, I was actually turning into my mother.

The night Amulii opened up to me for the first time, I couldn't help but fall for that friendly voice and those gorgeous eyes. Again, I wondered how much of that was a façade. What kind of relationship would we have going forward now? Could I ever trust him again?

If it wasn't Amulii, who would it be? No one would ever love me like this, and I'd never be able to trust myself around anyone. Maybe there was another freak like me in the world who would fall for a werewolf, but would I have to wait twenty, thirty, fifty years to find him? The snoring monster drenching my arm in drool was likely the only shot I had now.

Maybe it wasn't love. Maybe it was desperation.

I was a prisoner of the wild now, and I had two wardens: the werewolf inside, and the werewolf by my side. Loneliness scared me more than anything.

If Amulii had been truthful and more understanding, we'd likely be at a different point in our relationship. Maybe I would have fallen so hard for him after years of being together that I'd have made the choice he wanted. But that would have been my decision to make. He stole that from me.

As I pondered further, every blink of my weighty eyelids lasted longer until I couldn't hold them open anymore.

My legs moved on their own as the world around me faded into the dreamscape. It felt so real as ice and snow nipped the souls of my bare feet.

I have to go back. They'll catch me.

A small, human voice tried to reason as I pushed onward toward a familiar destination. At that moment, I lived only for pleasure. To sink rows of my sharpened teeth into warm, fleshy necks. I wasn't sure why this dream was so bloodthirsty, but with each step, I gave more of myself to that desire.

The thought of sating my appetite with wild game wasn't enough. I had to have something riskier—something that screamed to God before it died.

The fullness from earlier had vanished. Amulii was right about this worthless human form taking so much more than it gave. With my nose trained on Jasper, I inhaled the intoxicating aromas wafting on the wind, but it wasn't the smoky barbecue joints this time that enticed me.

My pace slowed when my cold feet landed on rough, sun-touched asphalt. It wouldn't take much to hunt a human. They were slow and clumsy. Wearing the skin of one for the moment gave me the element of surprise.

A patrol vehicle approached, and the cop's eyes met mine as he sped past. It was at that moment the numbness faded and I woke from the dream.

"What the fuck am I doing?"

The fragmented human thoughts that surfaced sliced through the fog in my mind.

This isn't a dream, you idiot.

The single whoop of a siren stopped me in my tracks. This was the worst-case scenario, and I wasn't in any way prepared to get myself out of it.

A car door slammed shut, and I faced the officer cautiously walking toward me. I recognized the man. He was one of the cops that showed up at the house the night Mom called them. There was no way he'd recognize me like this. When he unlatched the buttoned leather strap holding his handcuffs, my face went cold and everything in sight tapered to a point.

"Sir, I'm gonna have to ask you to put your hands behind your back."

"Why?" I took a step back, which prompted his other hand to flinch toward his weapon.

"You meet the description of a person of interest, so I need to bring you in for questioning," he said while circling behind.

Icy cuffs zipped tight around my wrist, causing me to twitch. Something about this didn't seem right. Could he just arrest me like this? I debated fleeing the scene—it wasn't like he'd catch me—but something more sinister than fear kept me locked in place.

"I need you to cooperate, okay?" The officer tugged at the other arm, securing both behind my back. That was when a familiar scent caught me off guard, strangling the human inside. The sight of me terrified him, but why? I was human.

It was getting harder to rationalize as I struggled against a much stronger fight or flight response than I'd ever experienced. If I ran, I'd never be able to return without being a wanted fugitive, but the result of me being locked in a cell with other humans while hungry would be catastrophic. I could eat him, bones and all. I could get away with it. Who would stop me?

The voice returned, and the disorienting miasma rolled in once more.

"I can't do this . . . I can't." I growled, still fighting with myself, not noticing the officer reaching for his gun.

"You—you have the right to remain silent," he said, pulling me by the arm toward the patrol car.

EAT HIM.

"No," I bellowed, jerking away. The cuff chain snapped like a plastic toy as I raised both fists in front of me. Neither of us moved. The cop's confusion turned to horror as he examined the broken chain that hung from my wrists. Still fixated, he lifted the shaky gun and pointed it at my chest.

"S-stay where you are. Don't move," he shouted, reaching for the radio on his shoulder. "Officer Baker reque—" That was all he could get out before I lunged at him. I barely felt the firearm discharge into my abdomen, but the sound almost deafened me.

I roared, grabbing the weapon, bending it useless with one hand. There was no pain from the wound as rage pounded in my ears. In an instant, he hit the ground with me on top. As the officer writhed like prey underneath, instinct overtook any rational thought I had left.

The prickly sensation was back, and there was no stopping the transformation. The man shrieked as I burst through the shirt I wore. Changing form left me even more famished, and the man's screams and struggles affected me differently than when I was human. This was not a person anymore. This was a meal.

Take a bite.

Don't.

The voices in my head engaged in another show-down for my sanity. As more fear assaulted my nose, the predator demanded blood—now. My tongue traced along pointed teeth as I leaned over, my maw wide enough to swallow his head. Torrents of thick saliva roped onto the officer's face and neck as I prepared to clamp down on his windpipe.

"Please, God," he shouted, tears streaming down his cheeks, his eyes squeezed shut. "God help me."

That was the sound I craved, but an unseen force slowed my progress. I moaned, struggling to hold back.

He's not food.

I glanced at the band hugging the officer's ring finger.

He's someone's husband. Maybe someone's father. This is not my prey.

The human inside got a foothold as a flood of compassion bought me enough time to think. I stopped inches from his neck before backing away. The amount of energy it took to hold my position was staggering. Though I could barely speak, I had to try and warn him.

"Dooo nnnnnot rrrrrrrun." The sound of drawn-out, breathy words rumbling from my hideous mouth was chilling. If he ran, he was dead. My legs primed to give chase, and I wouldn't stop either. Inside, I wept as I understood this was the new norm going forward.

Monster.

"Ssst . . . ssstaaay . . . th . . . therrrre." My speech improved, but I was shaking, trying to slow my panting. Every word sounded like a threat. "I . . . do . . . nnnnot . . . wannnnt kill you. Sssstay." I held my hands up as I backed away.

A strong odor of ammonia pulled at my sensitive nostrils. He was moments from death and must have lost control of his bladder. The scent, thankfully, made him less appetizing.

I had just enough coherence to remember the dash camera recorded everything, and if I couldn't take my rage out on the cop, I could destroy his vehicle. The door tore away from the frame easily with my freakish strength, and I began shredding everything with thick, bladed claws. Tearing into the plastic dash before moving to the seats, I released more of my hungered rage. The steering wheel snapped as I pulled it free, tossing it out of the car before pulling the seat up, bending and snapping its metal frame. In only a few minutes, every car door, wire, and seat lay in a heap of jagged scrap on the grass next to the vehicle's skeleton. The man hadn't moved, remaining on the ground as I instructed, whimpering and shaking.

I could hear a car approaching in the distance.

"I . . . ssssorrry," I whine out, tears falling from my eyes as I squeezed them shut.

We have to run now.

Anguished howling exploded from my hungry maw as I charged through the trees. The misty world of scents whipped past me as I became even more disoriented. Piece by piece, my clothes fell to the ground in tatters as I tore them away.

I howled louder, hoping Amulii would hear me. He was always close, but I couldn't smell him anywhere. I was all alone with this terrible voice. Thick haze blanketed more of my conscious thoughts as the wolf feasted on my humanity. If I lost now, people would die.

There was a limit to how much longer I could remain in the light. Silence choked my ears as though I had dived head-first into a swimming pool. All I heard was my breath and the human voice wasting away to hopelessness.

I don't want to live like this.

The voice echoed those words in a wistful tone. The fog lifted again, and I understood what had to happen. Clarity wouldn't last, and there was no time for further deliberation. If I gave it more thought, I'd never go through with it.

Scattered feelings narrowed to intense focus as I approached the mountain. If the wolf regained control, survival mode would kick in. It was the opposite of what I wanted. If I died, I'd be free. Free from the beast, the hunters, the police—from Amulii.

But there was so much I hadn't done yet, that I hadn't seen or experienced. I didn't want to go through with this, but thoughts of possibly killing my parents or anyone else drove my reluctant feet faster up the grade.

As a beast, I made quick work of the sheer cliffs and outcrops. The fall needed to be hundreds of meters with no ledges for safe jumping. It was then I saw it: a long protrusion of rock, jutting tens of meters from the slanted, icy cliff face. My way out.

I slid to a stop near the ledge and looked down, letting out one last desperate howl for Amulii.

My chest heaved as the human inside began to sink into the mire, and an intense primal drive to live began to take hold. There was no more time to wait for salvation, but I was frozen.

I . . . I can't . . .

Before I could finish the thought, the solid ground under my feet vanished. The world around me slowed, and I was weightless. My eyes glimpsed the majesty of the mountains before they closed for the last time.

Brief visions of my mother played like a silent film and all the good times I had with Mike faded away. It was then Amulii's scent caught my nose, bringing me back to the fate I had chosen. I was only seventeen. Why? Why did I do this?

At last, gravity won as it pulled me down. Deafening wind roared around my ears as the ground fast approached. A single tear vanished from my eye.

CHAPTER THIRTEEN

HEALING

*T*here was nothing.

Somehow, I was conscious, though the only sure thing was the blackness that wrapped around me like ink. It became all of who I was. All I felt was cold and heavy. There were fragments of things I knew but did not know. There was enough to question existence, but not enough to comprehend it.

"Owne kai ku'hun foru'van."

Many voices spoke at once, coming into existence before dissipating. The words seemed familiar, but were nothing I knew at that moment. They called me again beyond the void, beckoning with a soothing inflection.

"Ac'hela," a lone voice silenced the others, reverberating against invisible walls. It had a deep resonance, and warmth soon overtook the cold as it spoke more. "Alex."

That last word had no meaning. A tiny orb of light flitted about before elongating into a blazing, white spear, threading heat through my chest like a needle.

"Alex."

That time, I understood. It was my name. Thoughts and words poured into me faster than I could keep up. Some of who I was, my language and personality, began to fill me.

Two yellow eyes, barely visible at first, opened into stars, slicing through the black before casting light on my physical appearance. Golden fur covered me, glimmering like a small sea of ethereal strands of short silk, and when I moved, the fur disappeared, revealing pale-blue translucent skin.

A force pulled me toward the distance, away from the stars. I didn't understand what it was, but I knew it was where I needed to go.

Something stronger tugged me in the other direction, and I looked back at an outline of a wolf-like face whose maw opened, inhaling me. As I crossed a threshold of fangs, all light vanished once more.

"Ac'hela, Alex." The voice was now directionless, as though it were coming from inside of me.

"Hello?" I said, but the sound didn't come from my mouth.

"I did not foresee this."

A flood of orbs flickered around the void, each one turning into hot, white lances as they riddled me with holes of light, not leaving an inch of essence untouched. There was a thunderclap of pain as I smashed into rocks. I tried to breathe, but instead, choked on blood.

Every memory hit me at once. The life I had, Amulii . . . the cliff.

"I didn't have a choice."

Endless gems sparkled across the abyss before merging into one.

"You are a newer soul, a mere infant drawing its first breath out of the womb. This was your second life, and you will live countless more, though you will never remember them if you return to the circle. You say

you had no choice, but you cannot see unless you open your eyes to all possibilities."

The single star intensified, pulling my soul into a material realm. A pair of brawny arms wrapped around my waist as I fell against a handsome man. His touch chased away the loneliness of death. Another crash of thunder and his face morphed into a beast's.

"This is Amulii's second life as well, and you have known each other once before."

The world around me faded back to a single point.

"What are you talking about?"

"There is much you should have done in your life, all of which will never be realized if you return to the circle."

"That doesn't answer my question," I shouted at nothing. "And what is the circle?"

"You cannot see the answer as you are now. We are on the precipice of oblivion, and your body still draws breath. Mortals are rarely given another chance, and what I am about to do goes against rules that govern all existence. But I have seen what awaits Earth and Terr'volk. It is the same destruction that I saw in your pasts. We have come full-circle again."

The being's voice sounded fearful, his words coming faster than before.

"What does any of this have to do with me?"

"Light is fading. Time is not what we have in this realm."

A swirling cloud of light appeared before me; beyond it lay my bloody maw'cha body.

"Your future is beyond any of us. Once I break this rule, you will not exist to Them anymore. I am sorry, but this may be a blessing."

None of what he said made any sense, but there was a dread that overtook me as he spoke. Something was coming at us from the darkness.

"Your body will not last much longer without a soul, and it is taking all I have to keep this moment frozen."

"I can't go back to that life."

Two yellow eyes blinked into existence again, cutting the void before an immense body materialized through the hazy purple and red radiance of a nebula. He was an outline of a maw'cha, and blacker than anything I'd ever seen. The spirit warped space around him and no light reflected.

Though I couldn't see a face, aside from the glow of his eyes, I experienced the joy and pain of his emotions. The shade reached for me.

"This is not your darkest hour, and my son is not your enemy. I knew what I would give up to bring him into existence, to see our people and yours saved. The two of you will face many trials in life, but there will be times of joy that drowns out the sorrow. I have watched you, and you did not choose death in those last moments."

"Your son?"

His hand grabbed mine, but there was no sensation, just a sense of force. The swirling light in front of me heaved, drawing me deeper into it until all I could see was white.

"This meeting was one I do not feel deserving of. I am Vol'drik. Tell my son the prayer. Tell him I am proud, and I always watch over him. Forgive him. He is like I was. His mind is cloaked in blood, and he will never see the truth without you. I pray that when he does, he will forgive me . . . for everything he does not yet know."

The voice faded, and light surrounded me as the sensation of falling became stronger until sharp rocks crushed my ribs. There was no more room in my lungs to breathe, and a high-pitched whir sounded.

". . . ex." A muffled voice broke through the muddy silence. A head lay against my chest, but my eyes wouldn't open. Arms scooped me from the sharp ground, and icy air burned my lungs as I wheezed.

". . . lex . . . ex . . ." As more of the voice became audible, a shock tore through me. It was slight at first but worsened as the seconds continued.

"Alex, please come back."

My eyes snapped open as I gasped. Every breath was another glowing hot blade plunging deep into my chest. Amulii's hand rested against my abdomen as his blurry visage hovered over me.

"Be calm. You are okay now." His voice shook in a slightly nasal tone, and a wet warmth pressed against my lips. "I—I am right here."

Patches of memories stitched themselves together into a quilt of torment. I remembered being weightless and looking out across the valley before being drawn into an endless void.

"I . . . died." My raspy voice was barely audible through the coughs as a warm taste of iron splattered into my mouth. When everything merged into focus, there was a yellow glow from all around, and Amulii's potent scent filled my nostrils. "Amulii . . ."

I could say his name. This canine mouth formed words with no effort.

"Shh . . ." Tearful remorse burdened his features in place of the stony expression he wore earlier. "I will not let you die."

I managed a slight smile as vivid pictures of the afterlife, of Amulii's father clung fragilely to my memories. The mystery of what happens after we die was always answered by faith, but never by experience. I knew what awaited all of us now when the time came.

My wistful gaze remained fixated on the black maw'cha as he stroked my head.

Forgive him.

Despite the pain, there was something euphoric about being given a second chance. Problems didn't go away, and trust didn't magically return. But there was genuine compassion as my head rested in his lap. Amulii's touch wasn't revolting anymore; it was comforting.

"I did die though." My voice croaked as I tried to speak. "I jumped. I felt like . . . that was . . . the only way." Every shallow breath between words skewered my chest, but as the seconds passed, the pain dulled to more of a boot heel bearing weight.

Amulii shut his eyes and drew a strained breath, trying to maintain his usual equanimity. He said nothing as he hoisted my limp body into his arms, rocking me from side to side.

I didn't understand; if we were the same now, why was I the one that turned into an uncontrollable monster? My shaky hands latched onto Amulii's arm.

"I'm scared." The joy didn't last as hopelessness returned worse than before. The reason I threw myself from that cliff still lurked inside, waiting.

"I am awful for what I have done to you. I neglected your feelings though I knew you were scared. I thought you would understand, but the truth is, I do not fully understand what is happening to you."

Amulii stopped moving before leaning forward, resting his forehead against mine. "I will no longer tell you not to be scared. But I will hold you close to me when you are. You will not have to go through this alone, and I will give you whatever you need."

"Monsters," still having trouble breathing, I dwelled on the moment my teeth were inches away from that cop's neck, "are too dangerous to live."

Amulii grasped me tighter. "You are not a monster. Is this why you jumped?"

The person he held in his arms shattered and whined like an injured dog. My words were almost unintelligible as I wept. "I can't stop myself."

His long, clawed fingers raked through the thick mane trailing my chest. "I was overwhelmed, and I needed to find answers near Segolia. You were sleeping so peacefully that I did not want to wake you. When I returned from my meditation, you were gone. I followed your scent, and then heard the howl as you fell."

"It all felt like a nightmare," I whispered. "It didn't even feel real until I almost killed—"

"It is okay," Amulii interrupted. "I will not be so careless this time." The hand stroking my chest traveled down to my abdomen. "I am drying meat, but I set some aside for you, if you want."

I shook my head. "I'm not hungry."

"I will not force you, but I will grab some in case you change your mind." Amulii balled the blanket into a pillow, placing it under my head as he pulled away.

When he disappeared beyond the rocks, that familiar feeling crept up from the void.

I will not let my guard down again.

"Amulii." My voice cracked in terror as I screamed his name louder, and the thick, malevolent cloud dissipated as he rushed back into the den.

"What is wrong?" he shouted before falling to his knees beside me. "What is it?"

"It—it's gone." I shook as I clutched the fur on my chest. "The voice came back."

Confused by what was happening, he leaned away and held the crystal against his chest, then walked to the cave entrance. "I am going to go outside. Tell me if it comes back."

He walked through the cave mouth and disappeared around the corner. The presence began to slither around my mind, constricting my thoughts. "It's back."

He entered again, this time removing his chélanc. "I think I understand." He fastened the crystal around my neck with a tight knot. "Again, let me know if it returns."

He followed a similar path out of the cave, but nothing happened. A few more tense seconds passed before I exhaled in relief.

Amulii strolled back inside with a handful of dripping entrails he laid on the table. After sitting cross-legged on the bedding, he pulled me back into his arms, cautiously placing a bloody finger on my lips. I chomped at it. "Careful. These are mine," he said with a slight laugh.

The taste of blood brought back intense hunger, and I craved the organs on the table next to my face. "I . . . I can eat now." I lapped at his fingers and hand with my dog-like tongue. There was a saltiness to the blood, likely Amulii's sweat. When I first met him, his hands were disgusting to me, but this had an air of normalcy I hadn't expected.

After snatching a wobbling hunk of flesh, he tore it in half. "I know these are not your favorite, but they are nutrient rich for healing fast," he whispered, dropping a morsel of the pungent meat from a safe distance into my mouth. "I am going to tell you something that I feel you should know, though you may hate me more."

Part of me didn't want him to say anything else. Every time I got comfortable around Amulii, he'd reveal something even more terrible about himself.

"These crystals were crafted by a sect of shamans in my world." Amulii brushed a finger along the piece of jewelry against my chest. "This and the chélanc I gave you were made using my blood. I wear one, and the human I choose wears the other. The longer the crystal stays with the human, the closer the bond becomes."

"What bond?"

"The bond between the crystals and the wearers. Think of it as becoming . . . attuned. The longer you wear it, the more our souls intertwine. I can find you anywhere, but it also—" He paused and looked off to the side. "—keeps you close to me. The chélanc you wear now has a small part of your human essence trapped within it. This may be what is keeping you from hearing the voices, though I do not know why that is."

He dropped another piece of meat into my mouth and I gnawed a few times before swallowing. "What about the one you broke?"

"Its purpose—" He paused again, and I started to get a familiar, uneasy feeling. "Its purpose was to infuse you with my blood. That was what caused you to change. When I broke it, I wanted to believe that I had stopped the inevitable, but deep down I knew it was too late the moment I put it around your neck."

What he said didn't surprise me. I'd surmised as much the first night I transformed, but what was that earlier hesitation? "Why? Why did you do that?"

Amulii let go of another shivering breath as his claws fidgeted with the fur on my chest. "I . . . was lonely." His eyes met mine again. "When I say it out loud, it is selfish. I was desperate for your affection. I thought, if you were like me, we could be together for life. All humans rejected me, and I was alone for so long. When I saw you, I saw my opportunity to test the chélanc, and I would deal with the consequences of that decision later."

There wasn't a reason to get angry anymore, but the sadness of the betrayal still hurt, and I didn't know how to process it. There was no way he'd loved me then. I thought back to when we'd first met, and he'd struggled with the decision, reaching into his pocket only to pull out an empty hand.

"Can you leave me alone for a while? I need to sleep," I said, turning toward the wall as my vision blurred with tears.

Gentle hands lifted me as though I were antique china. After laying me in bed, Amulii tucked me in and rested his hand on my chest. Though I didn't look at his face, I knew what he was feeling from the sweet scent of sadness and his trembling touch.

"There is not much I can say to ease your thoughts but dying is not the way. Let me try to fix you. Give me a chance to do whatever it takes to make this right. I will not give up. All I ask of you is to do the same."

Dim light trickled into the cave as I came to. Being unconscious and near death took away all concepts of time. Had it been a day or a week? Judging from the muscle cramps and intense thirst, I'd have wagered a couple days at least. My painful injuries had become little more than mild bruises.

Fur and claws filled my vision as I raised a hand to my face. I was still in this form. Why hadn't I changed back?

The sounds of shuffling and clanking rocks echoed from outside, making me wonder what Amulii was up to now. My stomach growled as the scent of something familiar filled the cave. Despite the cramps, I sat up and looked around.

"Dad's brisket. When did he . . . ?"

"It is good to see you awake," Amulii said as he wiped sand and clay onto his pants, making his way inside. He shuffled through the bags in the corner before dropping one on my lap with my canteen filled with water. "A gift for you."

"My canteen. How did you get this? How long was I asleep?"

"Your father, and four days," he said, sitting on a rickety stool near me. "He is not what I thought he was. He is very complex and has been teaching me many things. I am building what he calls a smoker, which I can use to dry meat faster." His tail wagged with enthusiasm.

I had never been more confused. "What's happening right now?" After a quick downward glance at the aluminum foil poking through plastic, I tore open the bag before shoving my hand inside.

"I am doing what I promised," he said, lowering his head. "Taking responsibility." He pointed downward. "And I am wearing pants. See? I put them on before visiting your parents. Your father was there first. You should have seen his face when he saw me."

"You didn't shift back?" Handfuls of partially chewed meat slid down my eager throat. I missed the taste of seasoned food, but like Amulii had warned, it wasn't filling. "Surprised you didn't give him a heart attack."

"He peed a little. I can see where you get that from." It was funny until he brought that up. "Considering our last encounter, it was better to be in my real form. I explained to him what happened to you, and he was scared. I did not know that your father cared for you so deeply. I had misunderstood. This has all been a humbling experience."

I smiled at him, his sincerity making me feel lighter. "He—he actually talked to you? *My* dad?"

I shoved a claw into my arm. Somehow, I had fallen asleep and woken up in another reality.

"I get this feeling around him, like I have known him before. It is very hard to explain. We have been talking a lot about you, and he has many regrets. I felt that."

Nothing he was saying clicked. Since when did Dad do male bonding with a gay werewolf?

"How's my mother?" I asked, picking at the twine that held one of the healing crystals to my arm.

"Do not loosen that," he said, ears drooping to the sides of his head. "She does not like me. In fact, she is loud and physical when she is angry. Maw'cha or human, mothers are savage when defending their young, no matter who they are up against. She behaved differently when I told her I would bring you by as soon as you are better."

"I can't let them see me like this."

Before now, I had always subconsciously shifted back before waking up. Why was I stuck?

"Your body cannot go through the change for a while after sustaining such injuries. They have already seen me and are accustomed to it. I am sure your parents will be fine seeing you like this."

"You're making an awful lot of assumptions right now," I muttered, polishing off the rest of the meat in the bag, my lap soaked in drool and grease. "I still don't understand why Dad's hanging out with you."

"People can surprise, and I am learning that myself. Plus, your dad seems obsessed with strength, and he shared his love of wolves. His appearance is similar to how humans were described by my father."

That made sense, considering his Native American roots. My dad never opened up about what he loved to his own family, let alone strangers. He loved dogs, and he had ceramic wolves decorating the den at our old home in Calgary. Memories of our German shepherd, Hardtack, surfaced. Dad adored that dog. When Hardtack died, he didn't take it well. It was three days before he came back home after burying the remains. If only he cared about me like that.

"Since I am strong, and I look like a wolf, he seems to like me. In fact, it is strange, I think he prefers maw'cha form to human. That is a first." Amulii grinned at me. "Perhaps it runs in the family. We do not talk about much, but he is teaching me different ways to prepare meat." His eyes widened and tail wagged as the topic seemed to excite him more. "I did not know that humans pounded meat just as we do. I often pound my meat before drying, but your father's method gives his a unique flavor I am trying to emulate." I was struggling to hold back laughter and failing miserably. He cocked his head. "Why are you looking at me like that?"

"Please don't tell me you're falling in love with my dad too." I tossed the empty plastic bag toward the corner and curled under the blanket as my head hit the mattress.

Amulii laughed. "It is nothing like that." He lay next to me, stroking my back like he usually did. "You should be well enough tomorrow. It will be good for you to get out of this cave. Most of the hunters are gone. They always leave during this time of the year."

"I nearly killed a cop." That came out of nowhere as my emotions went blank. Amulii stayed silent for a moment before picking clanking pieces of metal up off the ground. He laid the broken cuffs in front of my face.

"I know. I saw these around your wrists. Your father told me all about 'cops' and told me that they asked questions, but it was not anything serious. You did not kill him, and that is all that matters."

"I was so close. I would have eaten him. I would have eaten a person." He scooted closer. His arm wrapped around my chest and chin rested atop my head. The full-body embrace was enough to calm me. "If he ran, I would've chased him. I was barely able to warn him not to run."

"Stop," Amulii said, his voice calm. "The human is alive. It is over. Let it fade from your mind."

"Okay." My head settled against the notch of his neck. We lay there like that until the episode passed. Thinking back on how awful I thought silence between us was, this didn't bother me.

"Alex," Amulii said, tapping my chest with a claw.

"Yeah?"

His arm tightened around me.

"Do not jump off of any more cliffs, okay? Your body is tough, but crystals can only do so much. You died in my arms, and it was a pain I had not felt in many years." He paused, his fingers now combing the fur on my chest. "But you came back. You did not want to die. It may seem like you do not have a choice now, but *now* is not years from now. This is only the present, and none of the bad times last. I do not want to be without you, okay?" He nuzzled the top of my head with his snout and sniffed. "You still smell so good."

"You're gross," I muttered as I thought about soaking my grimy body in a tub of scalding water. I peered back at him, smiling as I remembered something important. "I, uh . . . saw your dad. You know, when I died."

He smiled and nodded, though I could sense his skepticism. No one would know that look better than me.

"You did? What did he have to say?"

A name growled low through my thoughts in the spirit's voice. "He said his name was Vol'drik . . ." Amulii jolted at my words and sat up. "Owne Kai, uh . . . something. It was weird and I can't pronounce it. He said he's proud of you and he always watches over you too." A slight shudder shook the bedding. "Are you okay?"

"You really saw him," he said, wiping his eyes with the back of his arm. "There are times I miss him so much it hurts. It is not normal for maw'cha to lose a parent so early in life. I am glad you got to meet him. He was a good . . . dad, as you call them."

"He told me a lot of things I didn't understand." The spirit's words were swirling storm clouds in my head. I remembered being frightened by what he said, but I didn't know why. Vol'drik wanted me to be with his son, to forgive him. That was quite the opposite of my dad.

"My father often recited the old prayer. Ancient and passed down through the ages." He gazed at the ceiling. "Owne kai ku'hun foru'van. It's the only phrase from that language that survives."

"What does it mean?" I asked, having trouble keeping my eyes open.

"No one knows. In teachings, when the eternals and elements were young, they spoke this language, and the only one to ever hear them was the first shaman. It is only a story though, as no one knows who said it first. My people believe the words are good fortune."

"Amulii . . ."

"Yes?"

"Thank you for bringing me back." Not wanting to go to bed on such a serious note, I faced him, glaring. "But if I ever catch you and my dad making out, I'm going right back off that cliff."

The next morning, I woke up still in Amulii's arms. One of his legs hung over mine, and his chin rested on the mattress over my head. Thick fur still covered me, despite hoping I'd wake up human for today's visit.

After struggling to shift positions, I wondered if I'd be strong enough to make the trek back home. The pain was gone, but I was weak. Considering how awful my injuries were, making a full recovery in only five days was nothing short of miraculous.

"How did you sleep?" Amulii asked. His loud yawn was contagious as I followed it up with my own.

"I wasn't too uncomfortable."

"Well, at least you are sleeping. Maybe we should ask your parents if we can have your bedding."

"Hell. No."

As far as my parents knew, their son was not being spooned to sleep by a wolf man. I could take a few guesses at what Dad would say, and none of it was pleasant.

"You might sleep better. I do not know how to make my bed any softer for you."

"It's fine, okay?"

There was no way I'd tell him it was the best night's sleep I'd had in a long time. I knew this side of Amulii well enough by now. If he got a hint of how I really felt, he'd try to push me further. The wounds he'd inflicted were still too fresh, and I didn't want to fight with him.

I began undoing the twine that held the crystals in place, groaning as I bent to reach my legs.

"Do not push yourself too much," he said, standing to make sure I kept my balance as he clawed through knotted strings in areas I couldn't reach.

After we finished, I slipped on a pair of pants, threading my tail through a pre-torn hole in the back. I scrambled through the clothing to find a shirt but stopped when I remembered I'd destroyed the last one.

"Shit. No more shirts."

"It would not fit you anyway, have you forgotten? Pants are fine. Let your parents see you as you are now."

"I have a really bad feeling about this."

"That is because you overthink everything. Even if it does not turn out well now, it does not mean it will always be that way." He gripped my shoulders before turning me around. "Remember?"

"Yeah, okay."

///

After thirty agonizing minutes, we approached the cabin. It didn't take that long because I was sore or weak—that went away five minutes into the hike after a long drink from the lake. I faked it so I'd have more time to prepare.

We climbed the wobbling porch steps, and I stopped to close my eyes, taking in a deep breath. An audible swallow left my throat as my large, sharp index finger pressed the doorbell.

"Wait, you press that when you want to get attention? I have been hitting the door, as I thought was customary."

"And you're sure my dad likes you?"

The rubber weather strip gripped the waxy floors as the front door creaked halfway inward. Dad peeked through the gap with an unblinking expression I'd never seen on his face before. He hesitated to open the door all the way, and the scents of anxiety and fear came off him in waves.

"Alex."

CHAPTER FOURTEEN

WAYWARD WOLVES

Amulii and I froze as Dad looked me over with a dumbfounded expression on his face.

Helicopter blades chuffed in the distance, getting louder, and he threw the door the rest of the way open. "Get in here," he shouted. Amulii and I glanced at one another and then back at him. "Alright. Stand there like idiots then." We scrambled inside, nearly tripping over each other as Dad pushed the door shut behind us. The chopper roared over the house, hovering for a moment before veering off at top speed toward the lake. "Goddamn," he whispered, peeking through the closed curtain of the front window.

Amulii crept behind Dad, leaning over him as he tried to glimpse whatever was out there. "What is happening?"

Dad jumped, yelping in surprise. "How the fuck are you so big and so damn quiet?" He pushed the lumbering werewolf away before eyeing me again. "That's really Alex?"

"Good to see you as always," I grunted, plodding toward the dining room. "Where's Mom?"

Nothing about this place felt like home anymore, but when had it ever? Family portraits adorned the walls, the forced smiles in each one masking years of unhappiness. They were printed memories of something that had never existed. We were always broken, but now—this could be the moment that finally destroyed us for good.

"Come here . . . son," Dad said, his voice masking his jumbled emotions as he offered wobbling arms in a semi-welcoming motion. A small blue cast covered his right hand, bruised and swollen fingers peeking from the top. That was a gesture I'd never seen him make toward me.

"What?" I glowered with suspicion and crossed my arms. I didn't mean to come across as intimidating, but after seeing his unusually timid reaction, I was rather pleased with myself.

Amulii shoved me forward. "I sense what you feel, Alex. But you have come here to heal."

As strong and threatening as I thought I was, the closer I got to the man, the greater the force of gravity pulling my posture down. "You're not gonna hit me again, are you?" I asked, baring my teeth. "Because I don't think that's such a good idea right now."

Dad said nothing. Though I didn't like him, I could sympathize. The scrawny teenage boy he punched in the face the other day was now a seven-foot beast that could break him in half. I'd be scared too.

"Tell him, Robert. Tell him what you told me."

Dad had always been a stone and only expressed two emotions: anger and indifference. The look he gave me at that moment was neither.

"I'm sorry," he choked out, his hesitant arms still spread wide enough to embrace someone much larger than he was. After several seconds of awkward "*almost hugs*," he sighed and stepped closer. "Fuck it." He could only get halfway around my chest before pulling me in for the first time since I was a toddler. My dad was this burly, intimidating presence in my life, but looking down at him was a strange new perspective.

"Dad?" I reached around him, returning the uneasy hug. What should have been a touching moment turned uncomfortable and stiff the longer it went on. We released each other and backed away.

"I told your mom to wait in the bedroom until I got to see you." He looked me over once more. "This is gonna kill her." His brows crumpled as he shot Amulii a glare. "You're a real goddamn son of a bitch. I can't believe you did this." The other werewolf slumped his shoulders forward as his ears fell against his head.

He circled around before running his left hand through the fur on my head, scratching a sensitive area behind my ears. This was how he used to pet Hardtack, and the rough strokes of his hand made me feel even less human. He sighed. "When I told you to man up, I thought staying human was implied."

"That's real fucking funny," I muttered, pulling my head away from his hand. "Are you going to lecture me about how if I wasn't a faggot, none of this would have happened? Congratulations. You were right."

"Don't be puttin' words in my mouth."

"Why not? I've been hearing those words all my life." We both paused when my parents' bedroom door creaked open. "Mom?" I tried to make my voice sound higher, but only managed a bass grunt.

She dragged her slippers across the hardwood floors and her tear-stained face went from surprise to disgust. I started to feel lightheaded. That was a look I expected from Dad, but not her.

"That's not Alex. That . . . *animal* is not Alex."

"This might be bad," Amulii whispered.

I stepped forward and held my monstrous arms out, but she shielded her face and stepped away from me.

It was devastating, and I thought I'd retch from the pain. I wasn't her son anymore. Not a single thing resembled the person she'd given birth to. Reality was much crueler than the many negative scenarios I'd played in my head on the walk here.

"I can't do this." She wiped her eyes and returned to the bedroom.

Her reaction made no sense. The look of affection she often gave me was now gnarled, twisted into revulsion. So this was why Dad apologized; he knew this was coming. How was I to go on when the one person who always had my back abandoned me when I needed her most?

"She'll come around eventually, so don't get all soft," Dad said, clearing his throat before giving me a pat on the back. Everything inside of me shattered, but it wasn't sadness that grabbed hold and shook me. No—this was disappointment and a decade's worth of rage.

"I never expected much from either of you after everything you've put me through my entire life." I snarled and winced, my voice lowering while I stared at the ground. Dad backed away. "At one point, I needed you, and you weren't there. Now I need Mom, but it's the same fucking thing. Everything's conditional for you people, right?" I roared, slamming my fist through the cabin wall. "You're both fucking horrible."

My voice cracked into a dog-like whine as I squeezed my eyes shut. "I hate you."

Amulii placed his hand on my shoulder, and it only infuriated me more. My father hated that I was gay. My mother hated that I was a monster, and Amulii—

I bared my teeth, pushing the other werewolf away. "You didn't even like me as a human. You all fucked me up." Everything poured out of me as I pointed a clawed finger at Amulii. "You destroyed my future." I glanced at my father. "You destroyed my childhood." The bedroom door behind Dad slipped into focus and I put another fist through the wall. "And she hates me now." I rested my forehead against the ruined wall and lost myself to pain. "None of you cared when it mattered, and you all played a hand in this. But somehow, I'm the one that has to keep living like everything's fine. Wait a lifetime for everyone to 'come around' to accepting me. Maybe I need to die again so she'll care about me now."

Striking a wooden beam next to me, I wailed as more boiled to the surface. "I hate all of this." My claws dug into the wood, peeling it away in thin, curled strips.

Two different hands came to rest on my back.

"I have apologized, but you need to allow me to live up to my words." Amulii said, his wet nose pressed against my cheek. "You will get through this, and I will never abandon you. Your mother did not abandon you either, and she does not hate you. She is scared, and I know it is all my fault." He tugged at my arm, turning me toward him. "I would give anything, even my own life, if I could undo what I did."

My father patted me on the back a couple times before turning away. "I'm not good with this stuff, and I'm not making excuses for myself. I'm a shitty dad, and shitty dads run in this family."

That was about as much as I could expect from him. It would never be enough, not from where I stood. They all took pieces of my life, and it collapsed like Jenga blocks before I got a turn to play.

"You've always been angry, keeping everything you felt locked in your bedroom, but I thought that was just you bein' a pissy teenager." He turned back to me, the solid, muted expression he wore turning to flimsy sentiment. It didn't seem like much, but for Dad, I suppose it was. "That anger you're holdin' onto . . . mixing with whatever you've turned into is dangerous. You almost killed someone, and I know it's not your fault."

The muted tv was tuned to the local news and showed a prerecorded shot of our house. Dad walked over to the window and looked out again. "Something happened yesterday. The police aren't the only ones lookin' for your asses. They've got helicopters, black vans, and men in uniform with rifles—scary government-type shit. I should have known this would get outta hand, I just didn't expect it to hit my house." He looked at Amulii. "They're after my son and you. There's a whole army out there."

I wasn't sure why I was shocked. What I'd almost done to Liam and that police officer wasn't going to go away like it had never happened. The hunters weren't gone; they were just regrouping. From now on, I existed solely for the purpose of being hunted down, killed, or worse.

"I still keep tabs on police activity around here. All they had was eyewitness accounts from the officer you attacked, but the police car you destroyed kinda fucked all this up. They still didn't have proof it was you until they found your pants with your credit card in the pocket. They were able to put the eyewitness testimony from the restaurant together and now they know who to come looking for."

My rough hands went clammy. The actions of that day had little consequence since I'd have been dead soon. I was careful when I tore the video evidence from the car, but my mind wasn't right when I was running through the woods.

"Your mother knows what you did. She saw the pictures of claw and teeth marks on the car, and the police questioned both of us. So, she's going to have a hard time accepting what you are now. Thankfully, you didn't hurt that cop, but you scared him so bad he left the force."

We all stopped breathing as another helicopter passed overhead before fading off toward the east.

"They're gonna focus everything on this area, with our house being the epicenter. They're gonna find you unless you two get the hell outta Jasper. And I mean far."

"I have seen the strange vehicles near my den. I expected this, preparing for days to get Alex away," Amulii said. "That is why I brought him to say goodbye."

"Wait, what?" I said, shaking my head. "No. I just got back home."

"You don't belong here," Dad snapped. "I know this wasn't your fault, but I'm kickin' you out for your own good."

"I will take him deep into the mountains. You have my word that I will protect him."

"Wait a damn minute," I cried out.

"You need to be careful, too. You're all he's got now." They both ignored me, and I understood I didn't have a say in this anymore. "Take care of my boy."

Dad cleared his throat as his shimmering brown eyes locked with mine. There was a finality to his stare that scared me more than anything. I was the domesticated wild animal no one could keep anymore. "Listen to him. I taught you a lot about the wilderness, but he can teach you shit and protect you in ways I can't. Maybe when all this blows over, we'll see you again, but don't you fuckin' come back here."

Everything happened faster than I could process. Amulii grabbed my hand and gave me a slight nudge toward the door.

"Come, we have a long way to go." He looked back at my dad. "We will meet again, Robert."

Dad gave me one more hug, but it took him longer to release his hold. There was no time to cope, no time to get used to what I was, and now it was already time for me to leave. I couldn't live the rest of my life in the wild away from everything familiar. This was all I knew.

"I don't say it as often as I should, but I love you," he choked out, letting me go as Amulii pulled my arm, dragging me down the steps and across the yard.

As I got further from the house, I kept glancing back at my dad as he and the cabin shrank into the distance before disappearing when we crossed into the forest. In seventeen years, he'd never said those words to me. As soon as he was out of sight, I lost it.

"I fucked up," I cried out, slowing my steps. "I don't wanna leave."

Amulii snapped his head toward me. "You will not do this now. No more thinking about what you should have done. It is pointless, and I should know." He grabbed my hand and pulled me along at his pace.

"We are maw'cha, and we adapt, always looking forward. This is one of many lessons."

At first, I thought he was scolding me, but as his brows softened and a smile graced his thin, black lips, I relaxed. Amulii would need to be my rock for a while, and he was right. I couldn't look back if we were going to survive.

///

We stopped by the cave, grabbing essential items but leaving the rest. I gathered what pants we had left in a plastic bag before folding our blanket over the top. My wilderness bag was still at home, and I felt naked going deeper into the forest without it. It would do us no good though. Why would we need flashlights and first aid kits when we could see in the dark and injuries healed in seconds?

Amulii sifted through his things, tossing some crystals to the floor while keeping others.

"You're not bringing all of them?" I asked as he dropped the last pale healing crystal that had covered me earlier that morning.

"There is no more in these. They do not last indefinitely, only giving us enough, and then the power in them fades away. I cannot recharge them in this world." He paused and held up a dimly glowing bag. "I have more, but we need to be careful and use them only in emergencies. We cannot afford to be reckless."

I nodded, grabbing the leather sacks of food Amulii had preserved. He shoved old books into the last leather satchel and stood upright with his entire life now on his back. We looked at each other before turning briefly toward the now dark and lifeless cavern.

"We will find another. Everything will be okay." We shuffled outside, and he pointed down to Spirit Island before we made our way northwest, descending the slope toward the sprawling lakeshore. "We do not have long to wait until Segolia opens. We will be safe then."

"You really are gonna take me away, aren't you?" My head sank to my chest as my thoughts grew lonelier. Moving to Jasper meant leaving my old life behind for isolation. Leaving Jasper for the wilderness topped that, but to live on a different planet entirely . . .

Amulii's ears folded against his head, and he did something I didn't expect. He stopped in front of me and got on one knee, holding my hand in his.

"It is so much to expect of you. Too much. To leave all you know behind to follow me, but this world does not hold the answers we need. The shamans can fix you, and it is not as if the portal stays closed." His eyes sparkled with his confident smile, and he rose to his feet, nuzzling my neck. "We will come back. I am not heartless."

"You promise? I know how much you don't do those."

Amulii nodded.

"That was me being selfish, and this is not that. You are of two worlds now, and you will always have a connection with this one. Every year we could come back for a day and visit."

"Only a day?"

"If the shamans can fix you and if things settle down over here, I will think about staying the year." At least he was discussing the possibility instead of dismissing my feelings. "I think you will change your way of thinking in my world. Life will be better for you among your own kind, and I can give you anything you want. You will not want to stay here for longer than is necessary."

It was strange thinking of the maw'cha as my own kind. Would they even accept me in his world?

"You sound pretty sure that everything is going to work out when we get over there, but you don't know that. You don't even know what's wrong with me."

Amulii gave me one of his annoyed, side-eyed glances.

"Just have some hope, Alex. Do not always think the worst." He grumbled and shook his head. "I need to break you of that."

"I haven't been wrong, have I?"

"Point taken. But still, let me worry about things for once. I can take care of you, raise you as maw'cha in our ways."

"You sound more like a parent than a lover."

When I realized what spilled out of my mouth, it was too late. He'd heard my sarcastic mumbling as though I'd shouted a marriage proposal from the mountain tops.

He stopped and grinned, his tail wagging so fast it nearly propelled him forward. "Lover?"

"I didn't mean it like that."

He continued walking, but that annoying grin never left his face. We were going to be alone together for a while, deep in the woods. It seemed like the inevitable next step to someone who thought of sex nonstop, but now that I was like him, I understood that drive and those feelings. A teenager's libido was nothing compared to this.

Our new circumstances allowed us to hit the reset button, only now there was less trust and a lot more emotional baggage. It was us and no one else. Amulii still had so much to teach me about what I was, but I had to remember who I was—or at least, who I used to be.

Every day I was in maw'cha form, my mind adjusted to it. Walking on these strange foot-paws rather than feet wasn't as awkward anymore. The thick fur that blanketed my skin was plusher and warmer than the best jacket I owned. Recognizing what every scent was gave me an edge over the human I used to be. It was all so normal that it scared me.

Hunger signaled my maw'cha brain to hunt, but I didn't know how. This new body was a powerhouse, and depending on how active I was, I could probably burn through a thousand or so of calories an hour. I was glad Amulii had the foresight to make jerky for us.

After grabbing a pouch, I shook it over my mouth, delicious strips of dried meat dropping onto my tongue. The irresistible taste was unforgettable as I chewed. It was spiced with the same herb that made me violently ill last time.

"I might get sick, but I can't stop eating."

Amulii laughed and reached over to grab a handful for himself.

"I doubt it. Your stomach can handle it now."

We trekked west all day, and the sun lowered behind the range. As wild as Jasper's wilderness was, it was still civilization. Where we ended up was about as far from that as we could get. There were no signs of human activity, no smoke, no helicopters. Human feet likely never touched these unspoiled sections of the forest.

It was beautiful, but knowing we were the only people for tens of kilometers weighed heavy on my mind. The fear of isolation made me want to cling to Amulii more, and I wondered if he felt the same way.

"This is a good place to stop for now," Amulii said, dropping his bags to the ground. Thick evergreens concealed our location, and a fast-moving glacial stream sloshed further down the hill. Both of us raced to the banks and lapped greedily at the noisy water, having only eaten salty dried meat all day with little to drink.

My tongue knew what to do, and it did it efficiently as icy water splashed into my mouth and down my throat. When I first drank from the lake as a werewolf, I tried to suck water through my lips like a human. I ended up inhaling everything through my snout. It burned, and I hacked up water for a while after.

It took several minutes of drinking before the intense thirst subsided. After pushing away from the stream, I followed Amulii back to camp. The air was bitter, but aside from my sensitive, wet nose, the temperature didn't bother the rest of me.

The warming crystals that once decorated the walls of our cave now lay in a circle on the ground around us. They were a lot more convenient than fire, providing constant warmth and light with no need to keep gathering fuel. The silky dead grasses under the pines would be our bedding this evening since the snows had temporarily melted.

It was twilight, and the sun was little more than a burned mango hue along the jagged outlines of the alpine terrain. Everything to the west was a black silhouette against the glowing background. We lay together under the blanket, admiring the sky through a clearing in the canopy. There were more stars than I'd ever seen before.

Pine and earth overpowered all other scents, and faint scurries of nocturnal creatures rustled along fallen leaves as they foraged for food. A memory of something Amulii said lingered in my thoughts as the moments passed.

Spend time with me. We can go for long walks and sleep under the stars.

I couldn't have imagined being in this situation a couple weeks ago.

"How are you feeling?" he asked, grabbing my hand under the covers. "Your words back at the house have been repeating to me. I always thought of myself as a good person that would hurt no one. There was so much that I could give, all of it, all of myself. I only wanted that. I never wanted to hurt anyone, especially you."

"I'm okay now," I whispered, giving him a reassuring smile. "Everything was happening so fast. I got angry and the words just poured out. Whenever I get like that, a walk really helps, and we've been walking all day."

There was truth to what I said. The further we got from conflict, the better I felt, and my loneliness dissolved with him so close. We had food, water, and warmth. As long as I felt secure, my mind stayed away from the dark places.

"Did you know that my mom was going to do that?"

"Yes. She said something similar when she arrived, and I met her while talking with your father. I needed you to experience that so we could work through it and move forward. Your father is strong, and I think he will help your mother move on as well."

He made it sound like I had died, which made sense, I guess. The Alex they knew and raised had disappeared. Dad was finally showing affection, but it took me losing my mind while being inches from death for that to happen.

Amulii's gaze softened more as he squeezed my hand. "Tell me what you feel."

"I may as well be dead." Amulii started to say something, but I cut him off. "I know you're gonna tell me what I want to hear, and I appreciate it. This is gonna take a while."

Amulii pointed up to the stars.

"The sky is different here than in my world. When I was little, my father and I were very close to each other, and we would sleep under the sky often. He had his responsibilities to my people, but he was always there for me. He was a good father."

His mood lightened to child-like wonder as he recollected.

"He taught me everything about life, leading, and being a shaman, though I never really caught on to his lessons. He even taught me how to play the bashjiri. I was his only son, as few of my people have more than one child. Many can never become parents. My mother loved my father so much. She had loved him since the day they met, thousands of years ago, here in this world."

"She was human?" I asked.

His eyes glistened as he nodded. "They had a strong bond that lasted much longer than any other. Bonds between maw'cha last only a century or two before both move on. When they are between males and females, they are temporary unless their mating produces a pup, then they stay bonded for much longer." He stroked my head.

"Bonds between two males or two females are different. There is a strong need for these relationships, as they keep the balance and take away loneliness, and all participate at some point in their lives. Many find their opposite mate, but there are those like me who want life-long mates of the same gender.

"It is different with humans, according to my father. My parents' bond lasted for ages, though they could not bear offspring. Maw'cha that take up human mates stay mated for life, regardless of their ability to breed. No one knows why that is.

"Humans were much different than they are now. A few of my people that could traverse Segolia—my father included—lived among them for a time, and the natives here revered them. The maw'cha helped the humans live and taught them the way of the shaman, but no one had mated with a human before.

"My father was drawn to a young woman fetching water from the lake you call Maligne. To be chosen by a maw'cha, especially a leader, was cause for reverence among the humans, but his people disapproved. He and my mother became one after a night together. She was still human then but would change soon after.

"No one had expected it to happen. That was when my father discovered the connection we shared with humans and that blood or seed would cause the change. Since her transformation, their bond became revered by maw'cha as well. It was strong, and she adapted quickly to her new life.

"When my father told me about how he met my mother, he encouraged me to do the same. He was not the only maw'cha to mate with a human, and though they are rare, humans that were changed have been brought through Segolia.

"I wanted a bond that would last like my parents', while being mated with a male. I was not expecting to be drawn to you, but when it happened, it was all I could think about. You are the first male human chosen this way, and the first changed through blood."

There were more like me in his world, humans that had undergone what I did. This was a lot to process, and part of me wanted to bring up what his father had said in the afterlife. But it was hard to remember, like a dream I'd forgotten moments after waking.

"How did he die?"

Amulii paused and closed his eyes.

"He used up more than he put back, and it was time for him to go."

"You said that before. What does it mean?"

He sighed and folded his hands over his stomach. "He had a pup when he was not meant to have one. My mother could not bear, so they lived for thousands of years together longing for offspring, but neither wanted to leave the bond. As I mentioned, not every bond produces pups, and it is the Great Spirit's design. It is why we can live for so long and never worry there will be more mouths to feed than the land can provide. When that happens, we use up more than we can put back. The world cannot survive that way, so balance has to be restored.

"The Great Spirit's blessings can be manifested through ritual, but a price must be paid. Whatever the blessing, there must be an equivalent exchange. The price for my mother to bear a son meant my father's lifeforce would be transferred to me when I became an adult. He would grow weaker as the years passed and would die, but it was a death he welcomed knowing that I would get to experience life as he once did."

A faint memory of the spirit's words whispered in my mind.

I knew what I would give up to bring him into existence . . .

For Amulii to live, Vol'drik had to die. That had to be a heavy burden to pass along to a child, and I wondered why he'd go through such an extreme. It didn't make any sense to me.

"I'm sorry you lost your dad."

"I mourned a lot when he died, and I felt like fate had taken a bite of my soul. There was an emptiness in me. I had always sensed his presence in my life, though. When you told me that prayer, it was something I needed to hear. Even the most spiritual lose faith once in a while." He reached for my hand and lifted it to his chest. "I knew when I first met you that you would not believe, but now you do. To see the beyond—that is a gift I wish I had been given."

"Amulii," I whispered, leaning in to kiss him on the cheek. Hearing him in that moment gave meaning to his actions, as cruel as they seemed at the time. There was comfort between us once more. "Even though it turned out like this, I'm glad I got to know you."

A smile stretched along his maw, and his eyes peered deep into my own, our hands still locked together. I drifted into dreams as what lay dormant awoke and clawed to the center. He found his way to my heart again.

Amulii's thoughts, feelings, the way he cared for those he loved—they weren't alien or beast-like. They weren't even different. They were the essence of what I thought was unique to humanity.

CHAPTER FIFTEEN

THE FIRST HUNT

Light shuffling jostled me awake as chickadees laughed their morning songs, but everything remained dark under our thick blanket. As dense fur tickled my nose, I grew increasingly aware of my position. During the chill of the night, I must have rolled on top of Amulii for warmth, wrapping my arms around his double-coated torso.

He was awake but tense, trying not to disturb me further. The spicy aroma between us was somewhat pleasing, and Amulii's words when we first met clicked as I lay there with my nose still buried in his chest.

I liked your scent.

At first, I thought he was purring beneath me, but I soon realized it was his rapid heartbeat. Not only did I smell good to him, he also woke up with me sprawled over his body. I knew what was going through his mind, and the longer I remained in that position while awake, the more uncomfortable it was.

I rolled over and peeked out from under the covers, shaking away a surprisingly large amount of snow that had accumulated on top of us during the night. I squinted and a sliver of sunlight penetrated my sensitive vision, revealing a landscape of blinding white. Being able to sleep like the dead outside made me oblivious to the changing weather.

"Good morning," Amulii said, a dreamy expression plastered on his face.

"Morning." I yawned, rubbing the sleep from my eyes. The glistening white mounds around us were about three feet high, enough to bury us if we didn't have those crystals. "Damn. I didn't even notice it snowed."

"I did not notice it either. We must have slept quite well." His grin widened until I could see most of his teeth. "It was a pleasant surprise—"

"It's pretty out here," I interrupted, jumping to my feet while stretching. "It doesn't feel that cold though."

At some point, I had to confront what I was feeling because last night we'd made a real connection for the first time. His story opened my eyes to who he was and the similarities between our species. We hadn't fought in days, and I was really liking this.

Amulii stood, shaking out the damp blanket before folding it neatly into a bag. "Having fur keeps our body temperatures steady. I love my fur, but there is one thing about being human that I miss." He shot me a look that made my face burn. "The feeling of a lover's skin against your own as they lay on top of you."

"Well, when you find a lover, make sure to stay human."

My dismissiveness did little to dissuade him. "That is only one downside, though." I rolled my eyes and turned away as he continued reaching for romantic things to say. Amulii's footsteps crunched louder through the snow as he approached from behind, his husky voice a whisper as his breath tickled my ear. "If a lover chose me, I would make him writhe in pleasure for hours."

A chill went down my spine as Amulii's arms slid around my waist, his teeth gently grazing my neck.

"I . . . I hear guys that talk a big game aren't really that good in bed." It was hard to be flippant when everything about my body language screamed the opposite.

"Do you want to see if I am being truthful?"

My stomach gurgled as hunger broke the tension between us. Amulii pulled away and pointed to the west, the playfulness in his tone fading instantly.

"This morning, I will take you hunting with me."

My ears flattened against my head. I knew this was inevitable, but I needed a few days to adjust to this.

I'd be hunting defenseless animals as an animal, and that prospect brought about horrible memories. Remembering the bloodlust I felt the day I attacked that police officer, coupled with seeing the bloody gashes on the necks of game Amulii brought back to the cave, made me fear how brutal we were when instinct took hold. The thought made me both hungry and sick.

There was no way the human part of mind would be able to cope with that.

"I don't know. Maybe it's too soon," I muttered, holding my arms tight against my chest.

"It is never too soon to learn how to survive, especially out here. If something were to happen, and I became unable to hunt or worse, you need to know how to survive."

My stomach groaned again, and I squeezed my arms tighter, trying to muffle the sound. "Maybe next time."

"Follow, Alex." There it was, that indifferent tone he'd used days ago when I hadn't wanted to shift. Why couldn't he understand the fragile mental state I was in?

"Why are you like this? I told you I'm not ready, so respect that." My stomach wouldn't shut up, and a slight rage built the longer we stood there. "I'm always so hungry. Does this ever go away?"

"Did you not need to eat as human?" His sharp, sarcastic reply marked his irritation. Amulii crossed his arms, baring his teeth; the intensity of his scowl made me angrier.

"This is ridiculous. You think this is better than being human? I want everything to go back to normal."

"There is no going 'back to normal.' This is your normal. You are maw'cha, and you *will* be an exceptional one, but you also need to eat."

"I lose control and want to eat people without this stupid necklace. I reek all the time, and I have to stay out here in the middle of nowhere because I'm being hunted down." I kicked a pile of snow at him. "Yeah, real exceptional. I'm having an *exceptional* time."

"It is going to be that kind of morning with you, I see." He kicked a pile of snow back at me, hitting my face. A snarl parted my lips as I brushed the powder from my head. "We are three beings in one, and it is our burden to bear. Our bodies use more energy to maintain any form we are in, so we need to consume more to stay alive. Most of my kind can go up to two weeks without eating. According to my father, those of us with human blood can only last a week before we go into survival mode, and after that, we become unable to move."

"If we can't move, how the hell do we hunt?"

Amulii snorted. "By that point, we will have starved to death, so no hunting will be necessary. I hope you understand now why I have been serious about this with you."

This was terrible. Humans could go weeks without food, and they would survive. What would we do if food became scarce? It was almost winter out here. The thought terrified me.

"Yeah, real hilarious." My voice shook. "You—how could you sentence me to a life of this?"

"I did not *sentence* you to anything. You are far superior." He grabbed my snout, tilting my head up. "We will always have food if you stop being so stubborn." He jerked his hand away and shook his head. "What you think is so terrible can be used to your advantage."

I ground my teeth, still trembling. "I want to go back to being human, like before. How do I shift back?"

His only reply was a loud huff as he continued walking toward the woods. When I didn't move, he turned back and pointed to the ground in front of him.

"Follow."

"Not until you tell me."

Amulii balled his fists, the hackles on the back of his neck sticking out straight like porcupine quills. Instinct sent a stern warning to my brain, and my body felt a bit heavier.

"If you are going to use energy maintaining a form, it had better be maw'cha. I will not teach you to be useless out here."

"You're kind of a dick, aren't you?" I leaned against the broad trunk of a tree. "You pretend to be all sweet and understanding, and then you say shit like this. If you think humans are useless, why the hell have you been chasing them? Why didn't you go back to your *superior* race and find a *superior* mate, or whatever?"

A terrible thought crossed my mind. As we bickered, I couldn't help but notice *again* how similar our relationship was to my parents'. Perhaps this was karma getting me back for all those times I called Mom stupid for staying with Dad.

"We are done discussing. I said no, and I will not change my mind. Move on from this, Alex."

"Teach me. You said you'd take responsibility, so teach me how to turn human. Isn't that also a good survival mechanism to have?"

"I told you it was useless, and I have had enough." Amulii's eyes glowed a darker color, as if blood drenched his vision. The bizarre feeling from earlier began to pull at me again, and uncontrollable shaking weakened my legs as I struggled to make eye contact. "No."

I couldn't speak or move. When I'd try to muster a sliver of rebellion, gravity pulled harder.

"What the hell?" I whispered, clutching the fur on my chest as it became harder to catch my breath.

He continued staring me down.

I bared my teeth and lunged toward him but fell on shaky hands and knees before collapsing onto my stomach. Muscles relaxed, disobeying any order I gave them.

Slow, crunchy footsteps shuffled to my side before he knelt, gently raking his claws through the mane on my back.

"If you took a moment to really think, you would know."

I shook my head, struggling to hold it up.

"You are a pup that relies on me to survive, and you think you can stand on equal footing? Though you will not admit it, you look to me for leadership. Once you accept your place, you will stand. Until then, stay on the ground and throw your tantrum until you feel better."

"I hate you so much," I muttered, letting my head fall onto the snow as I gave up. "I guess I really am a stupid animal like you."

"We are not animals." Amulii stayed where he was, still stroking my back as I lay there. "I am sorry if this seems cruel, but I need to break you of bad human habits before we go to my world. You must learn to give those above you respect. Everyone must do it, even me. It is how we thrive."

"You're not above me," I yelled, trying to buck his hand from my back. "That's not how a relationship works."

"Oh, you want a relationship now? I thought you wanted to keep pretending that our feelings mean nothing—again. You are better at lying to yourself than me."

"I can't believe what a condescending ass you are." A roar shook me as I pounded my fists into the snow. "Goddammit. Why are you doing this to me?" After a few more minutes of silence, my head hit the snow again as I relented.

"I am not doing anything to you," he said with a mocking laugh. He was getting sick satisfaction from this, and all I could do was grimace while my tears fell to the frozen ground.

"We may be intelligent, but we still must obey our baser instincts. We can control them a little, but some we cannot—some we should not. We are the way we are for a reason. We learn to live with our weaknesses, because they are also our strengths. It is harder for you because you were not born what I am. You must learn quickly and as an adult." He chuckled again. "Though I would hardly call you an adult given the way you behave."

"Oh shut up. You're just as bad. You're the one that didn't think things through. This is all *your* fault, or have you already forgotten your apology?" My stomach growled again. "I don't want instincts. I don't want to be an animal."

"We are not—" Amulii raised his voice before pausing to take a breath, letting it fall back to normal. "As a human, did you not have instincts?"

"No," I muttered, now able to flip onto my back. His hand fell to my stomach.

"That is not what I have seen." He smiled. "You never noticed them because you were born with human instincts."

He continued, proudly wearing smugness as his hand traveled up to my chest.

"Humans turn red when they are embarrassed or aroused, which signals to other humans how they feel. They use facial expressions the way we use our ears and tails. They have primal, irrational fears. You did not think about a lot of the things you did, because you are compelled to do them. It is how humans survived long enough to become what they are now. It is the same with us. There are things we do that we do not control, and it all serves a purpose."

"Humans don't do *this*. We don't lose control of our bodies."

"You do not?" Amulii asked. "Have you ever been so frightened that you cannot move? I have seen this happen to humans when they see me, but it does not happen to maw'cha when we are afraid. Humans are either too scared they cannot move, or they scream." He laughed as he thought of something else. "Or they urinate on themselves. You seem to think that maw'cha instinct makes us animals, but when you peel back the layers of humans, there is an animal underneath all that undeserved arrogance."

He made me feel so stupid sometimes—well, most of the time lately. I liked it better when he was simple.

I sat up and sighed, now able to look him in the eyes while knowing at that moment, he was right. God, just thinking that pissed me off. I was the child, and he was the adult.

It was a disturbing feeling, especially since he wanted to sleep with me. I often forgot how old Amulii actually was, but then something like this would remind me of our vast age gap. I had the body of a full-grown adult maw'cha, but I was still a baby to them. There were decades of experience he had that I could never catch up with.

"What am I to you?" I asked.

"Right now?" He shrugged. "I do not know. We are not friends. We go beyond that." He put his hand on the left side of my chest. "One day, I hope to be your mate; that has always been my goal. I will do whatever it takes, but with the way you behave sometimes, I cannot think of you like that."

"Then don't. I ended things between us that night at the party anyway." I was losing eye contact with him again. "Did you ever understand how I felt?"

"This is about survival. We'll deal with your feelings when we have that luxury. Your father tasked me with this, so let me do what I need to."

"Are you my new dad now?"

"Leader." Amulii's sharp response reverberated through the cold silence of the wilderness. There was a look of disgust on his face. "'Dad' is never what I want to hear come out of your mouth to describe me. I want to teach you everything about being what you are and then I want to be your mate. Not your parent."

"Okay," I muttered with a glare. "Dad."

"Stop." He was calm as he rose to his feet before stepping along the banks of the stream.

I stood and ran after him. "Should I obey because that's how my tiny animal brain works now?"

"Alex." My mind tumbled as I slumped forward, pissing me off more. The threatening way he spoke made my chest hurt.

"There's the instinct again. Guess I'll lay on the ground like a dog. You want me to fit in with your people, right?" I paused and swallowed hard. "With all the other dogs."

In a flash of red, claws ripped across my face as he threw me to the ground, the full weight of his body pressing me into the snowdrift. He bared his teeth, snapping his jaws, and I turned away, squeezing my eyes shut. As expected, I couldn't move.

His violent outburst turned to cold shock.

"Alex, I—" He crawled off of me before stumbling to his feet. "Are you—"

"I'm done." I snatched the crystal on my chest, ripping it away. Everything seemed to happen in a blur as I struggled to think clearly.

Amulii tackled me again as I pulled back my arm to throw it. "Stop. Are you insane?" he shouted, forcing the hand that held the crystal to the ground. "Do not—" He calmed his voice. "Please, do not do this."

We brought out the worst in each other. Amulii had never attacked me before, even when I tried to kill him the night I transformed. Now, we understood enough about each other to push all the wrong buttons.

"Do you want someone to fight with? If I take this off, I can fight you fair like I did that night."

"I hate this about you," he snapped, squeezing my fingers around the crystal as he pulled me against him. "You have done so many foolish things lately, and I can forgive them all because I have done worse. But if you do this—" He paused for a moment as I struggled to free myself from his grasp. There was a slight tremble to his voice. "I might have to kill you."

I froze, and as breath left my lungs, it was hard to take in another. "You'd kill me because I'll stand up to you?"

"No," he said, his forehead pressing against mine. "Because it would be a mercy. The chélanc is all that keeps you whole. You are playing with your life right now—both of our lives. If I have to kill you, it will kill me inside." He released my hand and dropped to all fours.

"I admit that I lost control, and I am as stupid as you. That was not a leader that struck you." He pressed his head into the snow before collapsing onto his stomach as I did earlier. "I am sorry, Alex. I will stay here until you tell me to get up. Just please put the chélanc around your neck."

"All of this sucks," I said, fastening the broken leather strap in a tight knot. As he lay there in submission, I felt compelled to pet him like he did me. "I've seen abusive relationships, and I know how they start. I told myself I'd never let that happen to me, but here I am."

"That is not what this is." Amulii shouted, keeping his head against the ground. "Why do you keep trying to find this true nature of mine that only exists in your head? Why did you keep pushing me, insulting me and my people when I asked you to stop?"

"Because . . ." I stumbled over my words as I thought about Amulii's smugness from earlier. "When I was on the ground, you laughed at me. It was your way of shutting me up, so you didn't have to acknowledge that I'm in pain. You're the one that insulted me first by calling me useless. Don't you see the hypocrisy here?"

Amulii's once puffed-up, prideful demeanor deflated as he continued to lie there, his head sinking further into the snow.

"I need to know that if we argue, you won't take advantage of instinct and beat the shit out of me while I can't do anything. Not being able to move is scary. I don't want to feel like that again."

"I would never do that. I will also never strike you again; that is not who I am. But it is only natural to be angry at you sometimes, and you need to learn your place with me."

"I'm not playing into these roles." I lifted my hand from his back. "If I ever hear you say that to me again, we're gonna fight. I mean it."

"If I can be under you right now, and tell you that you have won, can you give me respect and follow me?" His sad eyes glanced up at my face, chunks of snow on his nose melting before falling to the ground. "You have won. I am hungry and do not want to fight anymore today. I also do not want to teach you how to be human. Learn yourself. I will not stop you, but respect my wishes."

"Fine," I muttered. My stomach groaned as the once dull pangs sharpened to pain.

"This is what hunger does. If we had full stomachs, this would not have happened."

I wobbled to my feet, dusting my ripped, snow-dampened pants. Amulii remained on the ground. This was what hangry was like as a maw'cha, and it was kind of scary.

"What are you doing?"

"Do you want me to get up now?"

My eyes rolled as I heaved an annoyed sigh. It was a pointless display, and I didn't want either of us to feel like we had to grovel for respect.

"I didn't want you down there to begin with, dumbass."

///

A herd of elk grazed meters upwind at the base of a small hill with patches of brown grass peeking through the snow. The area had fewer trees and being out in the open like this made it harder to hide. I crouched, hunting instinct beginning to dominate higher functions. Amulii did the same as we padded through the snow with ninja-like stealth. The hunger was so painful that I wanted to run as fast as I could toward the scent.

"I know what you are thinking, but do not," Amulii whispered, gently squeezing the nape of my neck to calm me. "We need to study them, find the weakest, and only kill that. It is easy to lose focus of your target in the confusion and excitement when they scatter. Keep your nose straight and pay attention to the surrounding terrain."

I kept my voice low as one of the massive creatures raised its head and scanned the area. "What's so hard about that? Aren't we faster? Can't we just kill them?"

"Not them, one. Only one. We could kill all of them easily, but that is not the point of this lesson. Killing is easy. Controlling the instinct to keep killing is difficult. You will feel something when you bite down the first time. Right now, you think you will hate it, but that is not what will happen. If you are not mindful, you will lose control and kill more than you can eat."

My eyes never left the herd, and I swallowed mouthfuls of saliva, some of it pouring from the sides of my maw in preparation of the meal I'd soon eat. Back at camp, I hadn't wanted to hunt, but now I needed to ease the pain in my gut.

"Hunting is not just about eating. It builds trust and companionship. It is about learning control and becoming comfortable with what is inside of you. You learn the dance of life and death. The wolf hunts to survive and strengthen the pack.

"They rarely kill more than they need, but sometimes they will frenzy. There is nothing worse than killing too much now and not being able to eat later because there is nothing left. Does that make sense?"

I nodded. Logically, I understood what he was saying, but the wolf was howling in my mind.

"Alright. Find your target, the weakest of the herd. An elder if you can. Do not kill the strong because they will breed and make more food for us." He pointed to the animals. "There are three old elk in the herd; you can tell by how they chew. Their teeth are worn, so it takes longer for them to eat. Look at the antlers—they have more tines the older they are."

"They all look the same to me," I whispered.

"Focus on the male, second to the right. It is enough meat for both of us. Focus on him only. Do not turn away for any reason. Do not let your eyes get distracted by something closer."

"Okay." I squinted at the old bull elk he pointed to earlier. He was clear in my vision, but everything around him faded to black.

"Now, do not let the land fade from view, but let everything else disappear. Tell me when you can only see the male and the land, nothing else."

Everything stayed the same, and the harder I focused, the more of the herd phased back into view. When my gut made more audible demands, my concentration broke.

"Goddammit."

"Keep trying. I know you are hungry, but you must do this."

After several minutes, the terrain returned, and everything got fuzzy. It was then the image of the bull in front of me sharpened, and without thinking, I lowered to the ground on all fours as if to lunge.

I growled, unable to form words as I inched forward; my leg muscles flexed, ready to bolt toward my prey. All I could hear was my steady heartbeat.

"Go," he commanded.

That was all I remembered as the trees whipped by, and I leaped across the clearing. The herd scattered, and for a moment, I lost my target. A cow bounded in front of me in the opposite direction and I followed it.

"To the left," Amulii shouted from where I was moments ago. "Not that one."

My nose pointed left, and my pawed feet slid into the snow as I shifted position, balancing myself with my hand as dropped to all fours. The bull was in my sight again, and my powerful legs launched me forward like pistons in an engine. Another bull ran next to the target, and my eyes began to shift.

"Stay focused," came a growled voice closer behind this time. "You have this. Go for the neck. Avoid those hooves."

My legs pumped faster and before I knew it, I was airborne. Time seemed to slow to a crawl as I soared meters from the ground. How was I so high? The buck came at me fast as I fell on top of it, my arms wrapping tight around its neck.

"Your jaws," Amulii shouted. "Use them."

Red stained my eyesight, and a shrill cry faded as my jaws clamped, crushing the animal's neck. It was quick, but I wasn't finished. My ears pointed toward crunching snow and all attention shifted to a cow as it scrambled to the safety of the trees.

I have to chase it.

I have to chase it . . .

. . . have to chase it . . .

Something fast and heavy slammed into me, and my face hit the snow. As I lay there, my thoughts slowed to normal, Amulii maintaining a firm grasp on my tingling upper body.

"You did it. Your first hunt." He leaned in, touching the top of my head with his lips as he panted. "I am so proud of you, Alex." There was excitement in his voice as he rolled me over, pinning me as I tried to stand. His praise and thoughtful look sent a wave of encouragement through me. My eyes locked with his, and his jagged grin brought out the smile I had locked away. When I licked at the blood dripping from my muzzle, guilt overwhelmed me.

That old elk didn't want to die, and now that the hunt had ended, its choked, suffering screams were all I could hear. Tears welled, blurring the vision of Amulii's face. He leaned in, and his forehead rested against mine.

"Now you understand. You called yourself an animal earlier, but this is what makes us different. That feeling never goes away, but it gets easier. One must die so that the other can live. It is both beautiful and cruel, as my father used to say. It is an awful thing to be the creature that takes life to survive, but if we did not, balance could not exist, and everything would suffer. I teach this to you now, as my father did me.

"We must have respect for those that unwillingly nurture us. If you remember this feeling the next time you hunt, you will not stray. You will only take what you need. That is what it means to be maw'cha. That was also what it meant to be human long ago."

CHAPTER SIXTEEN

TIME'S UP

A haunting tune spread through the valley, sounding a bit more uplifting than when I first heard it at the lake. A hefty buck hung lifeless over my shoulders as the melody helped unlock an invisible path through the snow back to camp, freeing up my nose to scout for any other prey in the area.

Over the last two days, I'd insisted on hunting by myself. Amulii and I butted heads often enough that frequent breaks from one another greatly improved our relationship. Killing animals was the last thing I ever expected to be my forte, but it came as naturally now as breathing.

It allowed me to use a part of my brain I hadn't in a while. Though it wasn't nearly as challenging as, say, chess, hunting offered a unique opportunity for strategy. When prey got harder to catch, I'd figure out alternative ways to use anything to my advantage. The alpine wilderness forced me to be as cunning and resilient as I could.

It was harder to breathe whenever we climbed higher into the mountains, and my legs sometimes buckled under my weight, let alone my weight combined with the heavy kill I carried. As physically adept as maw'cha were, the higher elevations humbled us. That coupled with trudging through knee-high snow meant I had to be creative.

No matter how frustrating the situation, I wouldn't come back to camp empty-handed. I knew Amulii could easily survive out here; he'd been doing it for a while. But after our big fight, the last thing I wanted was to depend on him all the time.

Despite still missing the comforts of human civilization, I started to enjoy this way of life. Perhaps allowing myself to be a beast was a way of coping without falling deeper into depression. All I had to do was think about the hunt and let all the troubles fade to the back of my mind.

Amulii was content remaining at camp. So much of his energy went into caring for me this past week that he hadn't taken much time for himself. Though he tried to hide it as we traveled, I could sense the anxiety he unknowingly gave off. Since I'd taken over the hunting, he'd been meditating more during our breaks and playing his bashjiri for me at night. We were enjoying ourselves as much as we could out here in extreme isolation. Thankfully the weather had been calm.

"Lunch is here," I called to him, letting the buck fall from my shoulders.

"This one took you longer than usual. I was getting worried." Amulii set his instrument to the side and rushed over, locking his arms around me. Sometime between our fight and now, modest affection became the usual thing between us.

"Everything's harder to find up here. Why do we have to be so high?"

"I have a feeling." He sniffed the air, his head facing toward the tree line. "It is likely nothing to worry about, but we are safer the higher we are."

"We've gotta be more than a hundred kilometers from Jasper by now. I don't even know how they would get out here without a helicopter, and we'd hear that." This wasn't the first time Amulii had brought this up, and some of that paranoia was rubbing off on me. "That meditation isn't working very well, is it?"

"It is. I am much calmer than when we started our journey." He glanced at the carcass. "I am very pleased that you have become so skilled, so fast. I said you were exceptional, did I not?"

My face heated as his hands slipped further down my back, crossing a boundary I'd set for him a while ago. "Amulii," I whispered, giving him a shove.

"Fine," he muttered, letting go as he pulled away. "I will wear you down, one day."

"Maybe one day, but not today."

///

"This is getting hopeless," I said, my eyes wandering to the ominous clouds beyond the valley. "How do you even know there's a cave around here?"

Amulii opened his hand, revealing a green baseball-sized marble that gleamed as he shuffled it around in his padded palm.

"It heightens the senses and enables one to see the layout of the land with their feet."

"Holy crap, for real? That's amazing. Can I try it?"

"Of course," he said, dropping the weighty sphere into my hand. My fingers closed in around it as I waited to feel something.

"So . . . what now?"

"For you? Nothing. It takes years of study to learn how to use these tools." He rubbed my head. "If it is something you desire to learn, I can teach you when we get to Terr'volk."

That name sounded familiar. "Terr'volk? I thought your world's name was Segolia?"

He let out a light chuckle as I handed the sphere back. We continued our trek over the rough, snow-covered slopes.

"Segolia is the gateway. Terr'volk is my world, similar to how your world is called Canada."

"Actually, it's Earth."

"Oh," Amulii said, slapping his forehead with the base of his palm. "I always forget that."

Every day I learned things that would have already come up in a normal relationship. When we first met, we should've been getting to know each other better. If only Amulii hadn't been so secretive.

"I don't like the looks of that." I pointed to the billowing wall of cumulonimbus obscuring the range in a dense, gray veil.

"We are almost there. How is your hunger?"

"Manageable. I'm more worried about not being able to see where I'm going. If we slip here—"

"I can feel the terrain. If you lose vision, just grab my tail and hold on."

The winds picked up as we ascended a path only Amulii could see. It didn't take long for the clouds to roll in around us, and I grabbed hold of Amulii's tail as he instructed. Having already fallen off of one cliff, the last thing I wanted was to plunge into a hidden, icy ravine.

Visibility dropped to less than a meter, but as Amulii's tail wagged, I knew he had found something.

"We are here," he said, stopping to drop his bags. There was nothing, only white, as I stared at the cliff face.

"Where is it?"

"The snow is thick up there. We need to dig, but the entrance is not too far."

"Are you kidding me?" I dropped our bags to the ground. "You'd better be right about this." I scooped a few clumps of snow away, but Amulii was already halfway into a hole. It hadn't occurred to me to dig like a dog, and once I did, I made quick work of the mound.

As I scooped the loose powder away, some of it fell back into the hole. I couldn't see anything as I dug, the snow more compact the deeper I went. I was so focused on what I was doing that I didn't notice the snow giving way. The thin wall of ice ahead shattered, and I fell headfirst onto the stone floor.

"Ow. Shit."

Amulii shook with laughter as he helped me stand. "I knew it was coming, but it was too late to warn you."

The larger werewolf pulled a warming crystal from the leather satchel that hung from his shoulder. As he held it high, orange light flooded the shallow depths. It was roomier than the last one, and there appeared to be sheets of ice near the back. I grabbed one of the crystals and examined the area closer. It was a shallow pond of glacial melt, completely frozen over. Perhaps once the cave warmed, we'd have a ready source of drinking water without having to melt snow.

"Let's get our bags," I said, turning back to the entrance before kicking through the knee-high mound that remained. We'd need to finish clearing, but with a blizzard on the way, I wondered how much good it would do.

"It is good for the spirit to have a place to call home, at least for a little while."

A gust of wind knocked me back as I exited. "Damn. It's dangerous up here."

"Yes, but it will keep us from the danger that might be following. Let us hurry back inside," Amulii said, supporting me from behind as he gathered the rest of our belongings.

After we placed crystals throughout our new den, I shook out the blanket and spread it along the floor in the back corner, next to the frozen pond.

"It's not exactly a bed, but I guess it'll have to do." I tossed a sly grin at Amulii. "You don't mind if I lay on top of you again, do you? You make a good mattress."

After some light laughter, we sat on the blanket, our backs resting against the wall. Warmth spread quickly through the cave, and before long it was as cozy as our old one.

"I know this is still a raw wound for you, but it is good to not be alone anymore." He glimpsed at me before facing his lap. "It is still no excuse for what I did, but I cannot help but be happy. Does this make me selfish knowing you are not happy?"

He hit on something that had been dwelling in the back of my mind. I felt like he was the only one reaping the benefits of all of this, and I was just along for the ride.

"A little," I mumbled, trying to think of a way to explain. "But I'm okay. It's why I've been hunting so much. It takes my mind off of everything."

"This will not be our life forever." Amulii placed his hand on mine. "I wish I could console you better, but that is beyond my control. I cannot force you to be happy as you are now, just like I cannot force you to love me."

Now that we were relaxed, it was as good a time as any to tell him. "You don't have to force me to love you. I already do."

His ears stood straight. "I have been so consumed in my thoughts; I had not noticed."

"I'm coming around to forgiving you, and a part of me will always resent what you did. But I do still love you for some idiotic reason." His eyes glimmered in the light as he beamed.

Amulii longed to hear those words, and I knew what that was like, in a platonic way, while waiting for Dad to come around. We both desired validation, love, and acceptance. Thinking about it that way allowed me to feel a bit more empathy toward him.

"I was worried. We have been close these last few days, but there has also been an emotional distance between us."

"That's because I still don't know what to do. We need to do this the right way, though. I want to know everything about you. I want to know that you can be my best friend, and that I can trust you with anything—before we get closer." We were already close, and this was mostly me stalling for time. Even as a werewolf, the thought of intimacy with him frightened me. "I'm still not sure how I feel about it though."

"That is fair, but—" He paused, catching his words. "The reason I have been pushing so hard—" Something else caught his tongue as he fell silent.

My eyes narrowed with suspicion. This was familiar. "What?"

"It is not important, at least not yet." He looked up at me before his gaze fell back to the ground. "Have you been feeling okay lately? Nothing strange?"

Reluctantly, I let his strange behavior go without pressing him further. "Everything feels strange, Amulii. I spent almost eighteen years of my life as a human and what? A little over a week as a maw'cha? It's getting better, but there's a lot to get used to."

"That was not quite what I meant." He paused again, and his constant waffling demeanor had me more worried. He was keeping something else from me.

"What is it? Tell me."

"Nothing to worry about."

"Amulii."

"Do not worry. I just want so badly to have a mate."

It wasn't like Amulii to be so coy talking about sex, especially sex with me. He'd been beating me over the head with it since I met him. Once again, I let it go.

I gave him a gentle pat on the back. "Well, you've waited this long. No one's ever died from a case of blue balls."

He cocked his head to the side. "Blue . . . balls?"

"Never mind."

///

You can't get rid of me.

My eyes snapped open. Hunger pangs tore me awake this time, wreaking havoc on my dreams, and at some point during the night, I rolled from the blanket onto the rocky floor. When Amulii asked if I was hungry yesterday, I wasn't completely honest. My stomach ached, but I thought I could hold out for another day considering the storm that had blown in. I didn't want to risk our safety if I didn't need to.

A sharp sniffle came from the corner as Amulii resumed snoring, still fast asleep. A bomb could detonate, and he'd probably nap right through it. I'd give anything to sleep like that all the time.

The pond hadn't thawed yet, so I stumbled to my feet with a groan before grabbing an orange crystal from the wall. Between the altitude and lack of sleep, I felt heavier as I dragged myself to the cave's mouth, the roof of which was lined with sharp icicles from the snow that had melted due to the warmth, only to be refrozen again.

Maybe drinking some water would help calm my stomach.

I laid the crystal on the ground and watched it melt the snow into a pool of tepid water. Scooping up a mouthful, I lapped at every drop. No matter how much I drank, it didn't ease the pain.

The blizzard howled outside, and I stood, listening at the entrance. Despite the cold, the whistling wind that sang through the cavern mesmerized me as the gale raged. A faint scent, alien at first, but then very, *very* familiar drew me further from the cave and into the storm.

Hungry. A dark voice from within whispered, making my fur stand straight.

Careful with my footing, leaning into the wind, I stepped further from safety and warmth to the edge of a small cliff. Though the snow was blinding, I could see just enough of the soft ground tens of meters below me. Driven by a need stronger than my will, I leaped from the edge, landing deftly on my hands and feet before taking off toward what I desired.

I didn't care how far I'd gone or how long I'd been out. There was a human scent on the wind, and as it got more potent, I could picture the man it belonged to.

How nice of food to come to me for a change.

I let loose a howl, louder and more furious than nature could match with her winds. It was a game now. He was at a disadvantage out here, which made me wonder if he had some sort of a death wish. How had he tracked us all the way here? It didn't matter to my groaning stomach.

Another howl pierced the night in the distance, and I kicked myself for allowing pride to override my common sense. Amulii knew now, and he would be along soon enough. If I wanted dinner, I'd need to be faster than him.

Challenge accepted.

There were many human scents which alarmed me at first, but they were further away. There were dogs close by that barked out alarm the closer I got. Their once aggressive tones became whines once they smelled what was coming, and they abandoned their master as they fled. I'd always loved dogs. They were smart enough to run, unlike the man who had wandered over one hundred kilometers to his demise.

The hunter was twenty, no, fifteen meters away, now twenty again. He ran from me, his scent reeking of fear.

The glow of a single taillight ahead pierced the haze as a black snowmobile with a cargo sled hitched to it roared to a start, sliding across the terrain and ice as the engine revved in a panic. He was blind in the blizzard, but I wasn't. What I couldn't see, I could smell and hear.

I loved what I was now. This was so much fun.

An azure glow in the white that surrounded us gave me away as my eyes burned with light. Only able to see the tree ahead at the last moment, he pivoted before slamming into another next to it. A grin parted my lips as I slowed, savoring the sensual terror that poured into my nostrils in pulses as the force of the collision threw him to the ground. A sound of scurrying through snow caught my ear, and then I heard a click.

"Come over here, fucker. I got some silver for you."

"How are you gonna shoot something you can't see?" I whispered in his ear before darting away as he turned, firing into nothing. The sound pierced my sensitive ears, and the stench of gunpowder blinded me for a moment before his pungent stench and scent trail returned.

The human was ten meters in front of me, now five, as I dashed behind him, raking my claws through the back of his jacket. He screamed and fired again as I darted away. The fear—him knowing this was his last night on earth—dripped through me, hot and slick. If this were sex, I'd have come a while ago.

Remembering my new hunting techniques, my eyes locked on the red, misty line of odor, letting everything but the terrain fade from view. This time, instead of the quick death I normally granted my prey, I'd control myself enough to rip every limb from his writhing body before he died.

He stood no chance as I pounced from the shadows, slamming into him with a muffled thud and a snarl before pinning him to the ground. The rifle flew from his hands, landing inches out of reach. When he saw me, his face went from horror to something else.

"Hey Liam. Long time no see."

"Alex," he said, his whispered voice interrupted by a hard swallow as I gripped his neck. "I thought you were the other one. I don't wanna kill ya. We got—" He choked as I squeezed harder. "We got doctors that can help ya. They're close by."

"Doctors? All the way out here?" I guess since I was so young, he thought I was stupid. "You're a monster now. Just like he is." My voice faded to breathless whispers, and I took in more of his irresistible aroma of dread. "That'sss what you told me . . . rrrememmmberrrr?" Drool sputtered from my mouth as it got harder to speak.

"Please, I know you're still in there. Let me go. I'll leave, promise." Another lie. When I saw him cast a quick glance at his weapon in the snow next to him, I knew it was an act. He had come here to kill us both, but he couldn't hunt the better hunter. "Come on, did he make ya a monster like him, or is there still a person in there?"

I could feel his every movement. His hand clasped the butt of the gun, but I slammed the naughty limb into the snow, gripping it with my claws until I could smell blood.

I leaned in close and whispered in his ear. "I love being a moooonsterrrrrr." I ran a claw across his cheek, slicing the soft flesh. I moaned while licking the mixture of blood and tears from the man's face.

I moved to the side, and rows of jagged teeth surrounded his arm.

"No. No, Alex," he screamed. The more he struggled, the more I wanted.

With a satisfying crunch, my jaws clamped shut. Shrill screams sent waves of wet heat to my groin as I ground it rough against him. Jerking my head from side to side, I heard it—a snap, then a ripping of fabric and tendons.

The hunter's muscles spasmed before hanging limp in my mouth. He couldn't stop screaming, and I thought he'd pass out.

Enjoy this. Savor this.

There was so much pleasure. The blood, the fear, the screams—it all brought me to a quivering brink.

I grinned and leaned in for another arm, but something hard hit me. I went airborne for a few seconds and had the wind knocked out of me when I slammed into a tree trunk. Amulii lifted the injured human from the ground to a standing position. The hunter yelped, holding the bleeding nub where his arm once was.

"Run, you idiot," Amulii shouted at the human, turning to brace for what I'd do next.

"No." I growled, kicking against the trunk of the pine as I lunged toward my escaping prey. Amulii tackled me, pushing my upper body into the snowdrift.

"Alex," he yelled, anguish in his tone. "Please come back."

He pressed a hand to my chest, but I continued to struggle. Red clouded my vision as I snapped my jaws, blood-tinged spit flying everywhere.

"Amruuuu," I snarled, unable to speak again. It all felt like a vivid dream, and I had no control over the rage.

"I cannot do this," he cried. "I cannot keep my promise."

There was an overwhelming need to escape, and the presence inside knew my life was in danger. Survival mode kicked in as I pushed with everything I had to get away.

"I did not have enough time with you. This is not fair." He leaned in close, his teeth primed near my neck. "I am so sorry." As his jaws opened, the entity that had blinded me vanished.

"Am—Amulii?"

He let out a gasp and laid his head against my chest.

"Oh, thank the spirits," he whispered, trembling violently as tears froze to his face. "Thank all the spirits."

"I don't feel right," I choked out, grabbing the necklace. "Something . . . something's wrong with me." My voice was back, but it was still hard to speak.

"You are okay now."

As Amulii lifted me from the ground, I glanced in horror at the severed arm that lay pale in the cherry-colored snow. Liam had escaped with his life, but for how long? A heady, metallic scent hung heavy in the air, and I knew he wasn't long for this world. What had I done?

There were more humans on the wind and sounds of whirring engines closing in on our location. Amulii hurried me away from the gruesome scene.

I had almost eaten another person—again. I retched uncontrollably as I remembered my arousal at the scent of his torture. Everything about the wolf's disgusting desires revolted me now. The intent to devour him alive as he screamed was still clear in my head. That was what disturbed me most. I'd been aware of what I was doing, and I'd wanted to keep doing it.

As we ascended to the cave, I glimpsed Amulii's distant expression. It was a look I'd never seen until now. He shook the snow from his fur as we entered before falling to his knees in front of me.

"That was . . . so wrong. Everything I believed . . ." His quavering tone was unusual for him. I felt nauseous again. "The elders told me blood magic was dangerous. I thought I could let you go at your own pace, but we are running out of time."

"Am I going to die?" Panic set in as Amulii went quiet. "Amulii. Am I going to die?"

"No, you need not die, but—"

"But what? What's happening to me? I want the fucking truth."

"There is a reason I have seemed impatient, always trying to arouse your interest in me as a mate." There was an unfamiliar scent wafting from him. "Blood is not a safe way to change a human, and though our circumstances are different now, a bond will calm your mind."

I backed into the wall and slid to the floor, pulling the blanket over me.

"Are you lying again? I'm tired of your lying. I can't believe after what I just did, you're trying to scare me into letting you do that."

"That is not my intention. I never wanted to force any of this, which is why I said nothing. I thought we had more time, but since I broke your chélanc, the window is closing."

Gritting my teeth, I pressed my knees to my chest—a habit I'd developed to cope with anxiety. "What do I need to do? Just have sex with you?"

"It is so much more. Make the full bond with me," he said, his eyes stern and locked onto mine. "Be my mate. I cannot make any promises because there are too many unknowns, but I think this will quiet what is raging inside of you."

I wrapped my arms tighter around my legs as I rocked.

"What the hell's a full bond?"

"It happens when we are locked together for however long it takes to finish. During that time, our souls are at their most vulnerable. That is when our spirits touch, and we become bonded mates. But we both must be willing."

"Locked together? What?"

"Alex," he whispered, kneeling next to me as he placed a hand on my knee. "In the time you have been maw'cha, have you not explored yourself? All of yourself."

"What the hell are you talking about?"

He looked down at my crotch and I began to understand what he meant.

"Seriously? Even if I wanted to, when the hell would I have had the time?" Whenever I'd take a piss, I'd noticed my disgusting, dog-like appendage. It still grossed me out. "I wear pants, so I don't have to look at it."

"Hmm," he said, trying to cheer me up with a reassuring smile. "You should try that before we do anything. I know human anatomy well, and you are definitely not aware. When we bond, it will be an unpleasant surprise if you are not ready for it."

"Damn it, Amulii." Even sex sounded stressful when he described it. I was sick of all the "unpleasant surprises." "So, we have to be in this form to make the bond?"

"We are not able to stay human during this, so yes."

I glanced down at his thighs. He was wearing pants, but I knew what was under them. In human form, his size was intimidating, but as maw'cha, I couldn't even fathom it.

"I don't want to lose control like that again. I guess a few minutes of that is better than the alternative."

"A few minutes?" he asked, seemingly surprised by that.

A chill ran through me.

"Oh no—"

"Alex, I have an entire day planned. You have never experienced it before, so there is a lot we need to do. And even then—" He set his hand on my shoulder. "The act itself will take significantly longer than a few minutes. That is why you need to be prepared."

I'd never had sex, but I understood how it all worked. How different could this be?

"There is more that you should know. Once the bond happens, it is done. We will be soul-locked, unable to leave each other for a long time, maybe life. That is an instinct more powerful than the rest, or so I have heard. I have never made a full bond, so I do not know how this will feel."

"You're making it sound like I have other options." Every time Amulii made another awful revelation, I'd start to resent him again. "Just don't hurt me anymore. Don't make this hurt."

Amulii grimaced as his ears fell. "This was not how I wanted our bond to be. It should be something sacred and desired by both, not something done out of necessity. I swear, I am not what you seem to think I am, and I would not have suggested it if I knew of any other way. And I will not hurt you."

"How long has it been? A month and a half? I've only been a maw'cha for part of that, and I'm not even eighteen yet. All of this is wrong. We're taking leaps when we should be crawling. I'm not ready for a lifetime commitment." My already labored breathing grew heavier. "I've never even been with anyone else."

He nodded, standing to stretch his legs before reaching down to grab my hand. "I know. All I can do is promise that I will try to be everything you want in a mate. I have a lifetime to make this up to you."

"I thought promises were stupid," I muttered, letting go of his hand.

"I—" A hiss of air escaped his nose. "*I* was stupid. I still am stupid. The promise I made to your father, and the promises I make to you going forward, I will not break while I am alive."

"Do you promise not to hurt me?"

"I will never hurt you again. I will make the day of our bond the best day of your life. You will see that there is no reason to fear being with me. I will take as much time as you need, and I will stop if you tell me."

Having felt how hard it was to control even the most basic urges, I had my doubts about that. "If we're gonna do this, then do you have a last name?"

"Hoc'áne. That is my family name, passed from my father."

"Ho-kah-nay," I repeated. "It's not bad."

"It can be yours as well."

We were about to do something I would have never dreamed of doing at this age. This sounded a lot like marriage.

"Maybe. I—I don't know. Let's just get through this part first."

CHAPTER SEVENTEEN

THE BOND

I'll belong to him. That's what the bond does, right?

I flinched as I fell from a cliff in yet another vivid night terror. It was a gruesome level-up from the drowning dreams that preceded it throughout the night. After every nightmare, I could feel the claws of whatever lurked inside of me raking through my thoughts.

I cast a sideways glance at the snoring maw'cha next to me and understood the other cause of the dreams. Instincts were powerful, and I had no control over them. However, once the bond happened, I wouldn't be able to leave Amulii.

Though he seemed sincere last night, his track record for honesty wasn't exactly spotless. He never told the whole truth when it mattered; instead, he spoon-fed me bits and pieces because it was easier to deal with me that way. What if this bond made me mindlessly subservient, and he could do whatever he wanted, no matter how awful? After

I lost control of my body during our fight earlier this week, I had compelling reasons to fear instincts like that. Anyone would.

What really depressed me were my options. I could either be his bonded mate for life or die. There was also a chance none of this would work, but at least I'd have gotten to experience sex—or whatever the hell this weird shit was Amulii had in store for me. I silently chuckled at what little consolation that gave.

Would he be gentle and slow, or would he be rough and fast? I didn't want my first time to feel like I was being torn apart. Amulii could lose control, and then what? It would set the tone for our relationship going forward. If he was a monster in bed, what could I do after it was done?

Amulii stopped snoring as I continued to watch him sleep. Was he dreaming about what he would do to me? This was something he'd been wanting since I met him. I'd hoped we'd be human our first time, but the more I examined his massive body, the more I wanted to run away screaming. He was ready, but he wasn't the one that would feel pain. I was.

That's what he said, right? He'd be the one fucking me, not the other way around, though I hardly understood why that mattered. In order for this to work, we needed to make a full bond. I didn't know what I was doing, so this was probably for the best.

He snorted, blinking as he woke. He sat up and looked at me softly, his large, gentle hand falling to my chest. He'd been doing that most of the night, so we weren't going to be very well rested for this. He stirred and got out of bed earlier, and I wondered what he was doing.

"I'm still fine," I said, throwing a tired thumbs up in the air. "I still feel . . . normal, if you call this normal."

His tail wagged as he leaned against the smooth cavern wall.

"I have something prepared for you."

"O-okay." It was hard to speak, being as nervous as I was. Were we going to start already? "I'm kind of hungry."

"When we are done, I will be the one to bring back our feast. You do not need to worry about hunting today. Let me handle everything."

He stood, reaching for my hand, and I grabbed onto it, allowing him to pull me to my feet.

"It stopped snowing," I said, clearing my throat as I pointed outside. The dawn sun was a red-orange glow behind the mountains, and there wasn't a cloud in the sky; there also weren't any signs or smells of hunters on the wind. It was painfully frigid, but the snow was like a fresh coat of paint, giving the land a smooth, shimmering appearance.

"I hope it worked," he said, walking toward the opening, shivering. "It is very cold out there, so this part might not be as good." He left the cave, signaling me to follow.

We meandered along the mountain trail, our breaths shallow and quick as ice clung to our nostrils. The breeze was light, but at subzero temperatures, it may as well have been hundreds of thumb tacks pushing into my nose and eyes. Steam rose from a small pond near the frozen river below.

"A bath," I shouted, running the rest of the way down the mountain. "Finally." The pool wasn't very large, just wide enough to fit both of us, and not too shallow that we couldn't stay submerged. I didn't care if it was cold out; I stank so bad that I needed to wash. Two points of orange light at the bottom caught my eye. "Did you do this?"

"Yes, last night while you slept. I hoped it would work, and it looks like it did. They will lose their charge faster, but we still have enough. And this day is too important not to use them."

Overjoyed, I wrapped my arms around him before dipping a paw into the water. It wasn't my usual scalding hot, but it was warm enough. Amulii followed behind, tugging at my pants before I could go further.

"Lose these," he said, with a grunt. I'd forgotten all about them. Though I understood what would happen later on, I was still nervous about not wearing anything in front of him. I locked up, my hands trembling as I unbuttoned my pants. "Do not be scared. We will not do anything now."

His gentle hands clung to my hips as he kneeled and slid my pants around my ankles, pausing midway at my groin before looking up at me with a half-cocked smile. If werewolves could blush, I'd have been a lobster. My hands fell to my front, covering the fuzzy sheath that hid my strange anatomy.

Amulii stood, removing his pants before wading into the pond first, lying flat in the deeper part of the pool. He reached up and grabbed my hand, playfully pulling me on top of him. We both moaned as we sank deeper into the warm water, and I turned to sit in his lap.

The tip of what felt like a bone pressed against a very sensitive part below. I struggled to stand, but Amulii cupped my rear end and pulled me up against his chest, allowing that area proper distance for now.

"I tried to do what you told me last night, but I wasn't feeling in the mood. I left it alone. I still don't like looking at it."

Amulii sat his chin on top of my head.

"It is different, and I remember the disgust when I saw my human parts for the first time, all exposed and hanging down. I will ease you into all of that. Right now, we will get clean and relaxed." He rubbed his hands down the length of my chest and abdomen, sometimes dipping lower. "This is our first bond, and it is the most amazing. Though I have never fully bonded with anyone, I have had quite a few encounters. I will guide you through."

That wasn't unexpected. I knew from the way he spoke that Amulii had experience. After almost eighty years, one would, right?

"The first step is to make sure we are washed and comfortable. I know how much you like to be clean, so I wanted to do what I could. Plus, for what I am going to do to you, it is better to be clean."

That piqued my interest. Perhaps it would be a pleasant surprise. Given our claws and long, sharp teeth, I couldn't imagine maw'cha being very good at foreplay. In fact, just thinking about it sounded risky.

I lay on top of him, responding positively to his touches, closing my eyes as he ran his fingers through the mane on my chest under the water. It was relaxing resting against him as he stroked a gentle rhythm from my sternum to my stomach, our bodies an almost perfect fit.

We stayed in the makeshift hot spring until the sun climbed higher and the crystals died. I didn't want to move from that position, but the water was getting cold. Amulii shuffled out from underneath, and I followed.

The once clear spring now resembled a cloudy soup of unmentionable grime that had collected in our fur from the journey. We now had less of a mangy appearance and smelled better too.

"How are you feeling? Any changes?" he asked as we shook the excess water from our outer coats.

"No, I feel the same." I grabbed my pants but didn't put them back on. They smelled horrible, and I contemplated burying them. I followed Amulii back to the cave, almost falling into several snowdrifts. My mind was elsewhere, and I wasn't concentrating on the path we made in the knee-high snow. By the time we reached the entrance, tiny icicles had formed on the tips of our wet fur.

Usually, our outer coats were waterproof, but being submerged for so long negated that. I shook again, this time knocking the ice away. It was good to be back in the warmth of our den.

Amulii sat on the blanket, his yearning expression beckoning me over. I took a calming breath and plopped in front of him, my eyes wandering downward to see if he was ready to make a move, but nothing was out of the ordinary. He kept his promise, moving slowly while making me more comfortable.

"We have kissed many times as humans, but this will be the first time as maw'cha. We might not have larger lips anymore, but we have bigger tongues. For humans, the lips are the most sensitive, for maw'cha, it is the tongue."

He leaned in and slid a finger under my chin, tilting my head to meet his lustful gaze.

"Instead of our lips touching first, it will be our tongues. You go first. Just explore around my mouth at your pace, and I will meet you."

Licking his mouth wasn't anything new. We often cleaned each other's bloody muzzles after meals, but this was different. It was strange starting a kiss this way. When I leaned in as instructed, I closed my eyes and got a taste of his wet nostrils by mistake. He jolted back in surprise before laughing.

"Oops." It was my awkward first kiss all over again.

"It is fine, you can lick whatever you want, but try my mouth this time." His warm smile and light humor broke some of the tension, but my stomach was still in knots. Letting out a forced laugh, I kept my eyes open this time as I tried again.

My long, thin muscle circled his lips, carefully maneuvering through his canines before coming to rest against rough taste buds. Our lips, while they weren't as soft, locked a little way around the front. Unlike a human kiss, a long muzzle meant we couldn't use our entire mouths. Our tongues were flexible though, wrapping around one another with so many more nerve endings that it surprised me. The feeling was indescribable, and the taste of his mouth made me crave more. It may have been different, but it was just as pleasurable as when we were human.

We both pulled away, and I took in a deep breath after what seemed like minutes of holding it during the kiss. I glanced down at what lay thick, blood-red, and wet against my thigh. It was startling to see that thing come out of me, and I felt rather ashamed of it, despite Amulii having the same appearance.

"Lay back. There is more I can do that you will enjoy." His voice was throaty but had a tenderness about it which made my heart skip. I did as he said and lay on my back, but I wasn't in place for more than a second before a soaking heat enveloped my now overly sensitive dick.

"Oh, fuck," I moaned out, jolting as my claws ripped at the fabric of the blanket. There was much more intensity than I thought there would be. His tongue was soft enough for it not to hurt but textured enough to stimulate every nerve along the shaft. There was no glans on it in this form, but I discovered that there was no need for it. My entire length buzzed under his dexterous lapping and curling.

Worries melted away as wild sensations rippled through my writhing body with every slide. Thick saliva roped around the base, dripping along my fuzzy taint as it soaked that and everything lower.

Like humans, Maw'cha could do this easily, even with sharp teeth uncomfortably close. My grunts became quavering moans as his lips sealed, the tip of my cock sliding down the back of his throat as he carefully sucked. How was he doing this without injuring me?

A strong pulse erupted from my loins as I came quickly. Grabbing fistfuls of Amulii's fur, I stopped the movement of his head as I continued to squirm and jerk, letting out quiet whimpers. The orgasm wouldn't stop, and Amulii didn't keep his tongue still for long. I howled and thrust deeper, unloading more of what I had been holding onto for weeks.

I'd never come that hard before, nor in such copious amounts. It didn't take me half as long to get there as it did to finish. Amulii knew how to get me off fast, and all the attention paid to every detail made me long for more of him. He let out a choking sound, and I let him go.

My back hit the blanket as my ragged breathing slowed back to normal. Both legs turned to jelly as I continued to tremble. I wasn't sure I'd ever be able to stand again after that.

He leaned in, and his tongue slid against mine, the taste of what he greedily choked down still lingering thick in his mouth. The flavor wasn't at all bad, but anything at that moment would have tasted delicious to me. Our mouths separated, and his long, eager tongue began another journey down my body. Was he going to do this again?

"Wait," I said, still catching my breath. "Give me some time. Damn."

"Do not worry. You will love this." Amulii grinned, his pointed canines glistening with saliva. "Close your eyes, and trust me."

After a moment of hesitation, I did as he said and squeezed my eyes shut. When Amulii propositioned me weeks ago, if I'd known it would feel like this, I wouldn't have been so uptight. It wasn't just passion he elicited from me. He was patient and considerate, even at my most vulnerable as I stretched before him while he explored areas no one else had ever touched.

Hot breath tickled my neck as gentle kisses trailed to my shoulders. Something was strange about the feeling of his lips. My eyes snapped all the way open, and what I saw excited me more. He was in human form.

"I said I would make this amazing for you," he whispered, gently biting the side of my neck. Even as a human, he was big; he was almost the same height that I was in werewolf form. His bronze muscles glistened with sweat as he posed like Adonis against the rays of morning sunlight pouring into the cave.

"Oh fuck me." Where did that come from? Things I was normally too embarrassed to say, I wanted to scream. He made me drop my inhibitions. Amulii stripped them from me one by one with every stroke of his tongue. The parts of my body that made me feel ashamed, he couldn't keep away from.

Amulii grinned, growling low as he put a hand to his mouth, spitting into it. Parts of my lower body that he'd feasted on earlier were already soaked; anymore was overkill. He lubed his thick, angry cock, his foreskin making slick noises before one of his fingers pressed against what was now so eager to feel it.

He rubbed all along the outside before gently sliding a digit in. I squinted and snarled as my jaw locked, but he persisted, pushing it deeper. It was then I understood why he turned human. Any claw near that area would have been devastating.

I whined louder as he pulled it out. "Don't stop," I moaned, gripping the blanket tighter.

Another finger stealthily slipped in alongside the first, and I winced at the pain stabbing the inner ring.

"Are you okay?" He stopped, and I bared my teeth, trying to push through the discomfort. I thought I was ready, but these were just fingers, nothing compared to the stiff monster that pulsed eagerly between his thighs.

My muscles relaxed as the pain subsided. "Yeah, keep going."

The two fingers pushed and stretched me further before a third joined the fun. There was no more pain, just a strange fullness. The sounds alone coming from my lower half was enough to get me hard again. He pulled out but did nothing more, and I opened my eyes to glimpse what was happening.

While on his knees, a devilish half-grin crept along Amulii's rugged face.

"I want you to command me to fuck you, like you did earlier," he said, gliding the slippery tip of his massive dick in circles, teasing the entrance that wanted desperately to be filled again. This was the second time I'd heard him use that word, and it turned me on even more. "Scream it for me."

His forceful, almost malevolent sexual banter had a surprising effect. I loved it. As his features darkened, his personality shifted from cautious to insanely dominant, and the strong, intoxicating scent he emitted would have made me do anything he asked.

I'd never been more ready, nor had I wanted as much as I did then.

"F-fuck me." The words trembled out in breathy pulses.

"Beg," he grunted, as he surrendered to more of the animal. Amulii's fingers and tongue teased me, not only loosening my most sensitive parts, but loosening my lips as well. There was no denying him now, as a different hunger emerged that went well beyond basic instinct.

He struggled to remain human, but unlike me, never lost an ounce of control—not at all what I'd imagined. His amber eyes flashed yellow, but with a commanding breath, he forced the wolf to heel.

Fingers weren't enough. The bestial glare he shot made him the hottest man in the world to me. Why was I so afraid? Even if it hurt, I had to have him. All of him. Human, maw'cha—everything.

"Please," I whimpered, quivering uncontrollably. "Fuck me, Amulii."

"Tell me that you are mine." He applied pressure to the tip and slipped inside, stretching me tighter than before. I felt pain. Or was it pleasure? It was all muddled together now, and I wanted more.

"I—" My voice cracked, and I gasped before gazing nervously into his eyes. "I'm yours."

He paused again, pulling it out before sawing the cleft of my ass underneath. The wet noises, the feeling of his glans against every nerve ending tortured me.

"And I am yours, Alex. I will always be yours."

His eyes glowed as he worked his way into my depths. It was agonizing at first, and I felt like there wasn't an end to it. He was slow and shallow, going in and out. With each thrust, he'd go deeper until he rammed everything into me.

"Ugh, nnn-fuck," I cried out, growling as the stabbing pain shot through me, but it didn't last. My legs wrapped around his hips, stopping him as he tried to pull back out. "Wait." My painful grimace became a grin. He returned the expression and began rocking his hips when I loosened my grip.

Dull aches pulsed around the invader. Amulii was so deep that he punched through another hidden entrance inside. He lay against me, thrusting his hips forward and then back in a rounded motion, grinding himself against the sensitive areas inside of me I never knew existed.

I couldn't believe he held his human form under such pressure, but I knew it couldn't last. Fur covered his body, and his face stretched as his human moans became roars. The transformation was faster than I could prepare for, and my insides tightened around what was getting even larger. A shriek left my mouth, and I pushed my hand against his abdomen.

"Fuck. Stop." Did he plan on doing this to me when I was human? There was no way I would have survived this.

He froze, giving me time to adjust to his new size. His actions put to rest any fear of him losing control as he pulled halfway out to kiss me. As we locked eyes, it wasn't only animal lust staring back. There was so much more than that.

I gave him a nod, and he pushed back into me, thrusting faster than before. Thick, fur-covered hips slammed violently against my lower body, the glow of our eyes reflecting on each other's faces.

We turned to beasts as his teeth sunk into my shoulder and my claws raked into his back, every violent act shooting a scent of blood to our noses. The pain was irresistible, and I wanted him to bite me harder. I now craved the wild, the rough—the pain. There was no way to form the words I wanted to scream out, and everything I once feared I now couldn't get enough of.

The cave reverberated with sounds of monstrous lovemaking, which would have horrified anyone daring to get close enough to hear. Wet squelching and muffled thuds increased in volume, matching the furious snarls and growling. I was going to come again. When I thought he couldn't thrust any faster, he'd speed up.

His loud panting and unsteady rhythm threw me off. Amulii was close as well. He slowed, pushing into me with all of his weight, and something pressed against my wrecked opening that I hadn't expected.

The entire length slid inside, and a swollen, fist-sized bulge at the base of his alien cock popped into place, making me yelp in surprise. He tried to pull back out but ended up dragging me with him. I gritted my teeth and whined low as it swelled. It throbbed erratically, stimulating me more from within as a warm tightness spread through my core.

Our eyes never stopped glowing, and his stare was intense as he leaned in, our tongues meeting once more. The wet heat of our mouths combined with powerful pulses forced me to another climax, soaking the fur between us in one last torrent of relief.

An overwhelming bliss washed away any trace of resentment. The only word to describe the feeling as I gripped the back of his neck was . . . power. There was a power inside of me that gave me a sense of wholeness, like I was no longer trapped between two states of being.

The bond wasn't what I'd feared it would be, and I'd never been so satisfied. It went beyond the physical as Amulii said it would, well beyond. He must have felt it too as we lay there, him on top of me, as something deeper touched for the first time. Amulii accomplished what he set out to do, but his weary smile wasn't one of conquest.

The intense feeling Amulii warned me of began to blanket my mind. Everything was about to change between us.

CHAPTER EIGHTEEN

A MATE'S CONFESSION

I woke up calmer after sleeping the rest of the day and all through the night. We were both exhausted, not just from the sex, but from all the uncertainty over the last week.

The bond had an unusual effect on both of us. Before we fell asleep, I could hear light sniffles coming from Amulii as he faced away. He was always so emotional, but something about the way he cried in secret seemed off-kilter. When I asked if he was okay, he wiped his face and assured me everything was fine.

Despite my suspicions, it was nice to wake up with my arms draped over his chest, and my muzzle resting on top of his. Our legs intertwined, trapping the heat between our bodies as we lay on the heavy blanket, now ripped and stained from yesterday.

I combed through the mane on his head as he slept and smiled, remembering how he made me feel yesterday. It was the first time in a while that he'd done something new to me without being a complete jerk.

I studied him, still wanting to satisfy a lingering primal desire from yesterday. His scent, the warmth of our position, sent shots of heat to all the right places. Now that I had done it, I wanted to keep doing it again and again. I hovered for a moment, ready to wake him with my tongue, but I paused and thought about what was happening to me. Everything from now on would have me second-guessing. Was this the bond, or was I just horny? What he did to me felt good, and I wanted to keep feeling that way.

A little spit snaked from my jaws as I leaned in, wanting to get a taste of his mouth, but my stomach roared with other needs. I let out a heavy sigh as I stopped myself again. We'd need energy, and I was in a hunting mood. I didn't want to leave without telling him first, just in case he got worried and came after me.

I straddled his hips and leaned in to kiss him. He slipped his tongue into my mouth and reached around me, gripping my ass below the tail. I broke away and laughed as his claw brushed the area. I didn't know I was ticklish there.

"I'm going hunting," I said, leaning in to nibble his neck. It was hard to maintain control. Neither sex nor the bond would be a panacea for what we had, but at least the sex was damn incredible. We had a foundation to build a relationship, but we'd have to see if it would be strong enough to deal with whatever we had to face going forward. The hunters were still out there somewhere, and there was also the small matter of me having to go to a different planet through a portal.

"I believe I was the one that promised you the feast." We were kissing again, and I nearly lost track of what I had planned on doing. Every time one of us would speak, the other would pounce. I had to get away from him.

"I wanna get out of this cave, plus I like hunting."

"Then I will go with you," he said, pulling me closer while his hips rocked underneath.

"No. I'd like to eat at some point today, not scare all the animals away because we can't stop fucking each other."

"I did not think you would be this receptive," he said, breaking away before sitting up with me still in his lap. "I am not complaining, though. I love this."

"Well, isn't this what the bond does?"

He shook his head. "The bond just keeps a pair together, nothing more. What we feel now is emotion, not instinct." Amulii put his right hand on my leg, running it along my inner thigh.

"How do you know that? You've never done it before. You said so."

"I have had many other mates in my world. Most of them were male, so I learned some things. I also learned I preferred males to females." He gave me one of his suggestive grins again. "The first male I was with wasn't as lucky. I hurt him, and I felt terrible, but I was more careful with the next one. I was so young, about fifty or so, not fully grown. Most maw'cha at that age are just starting to feel the drive for sex. It is not old enough for a bond."

Fifty seemed an odd age to be considered "so young," but he did tell me that maw'cha don't mature as fast as humans do. Perhaps those were his teenage years.

"I'm thankful the first guy took one for the team then," I laughed out, scooting off his lap to sit next to him. "You said they were your mates. How do you have mates without bonding?"

"Hmm." He paused. "We did not make a full bond. It was casual because I felt nothing more than friendship for them. My people mate with as many others as they please. However, there must be enough between the two for a bond to happen."

"I still don't understand what that means exactly. You had sex with them, but you weren't bonded, but we had sex, and we are. What's the difference? Just a feeling?"

"Oh." His ears shot up, and he nodded. "No, what we did, what locked us together, and what we experienced after—that was a full bond. I had always pulled away during that moment.

"With that first male, I had an accident, and I was stuck inside him. It was terrible. I remembered the fear between us, as neither wanted anything more. When we lay waiting, there was no connection, no soul touch. After that, I understood what my father had told me about mating and the bond. We needed a deeper connection. You and I have that, which is why I am relieved to know your feelings for me are real and that the bond took."

Being stuck together had scared me at first because I wasn't expecting it. After a few minutes, when raw passion subsided, we'd looked into each other's eyes, not saying a word. Then something weird had happened that I still had a hard time believing wasn't a dream.

"When we were like that, I could have sworn I was in your body looking down at myself. It was hazy though, and I don't know if it really happened."

"It did, and I was told that everyone's experience is different. Maw'cha have more than sex when they bond. It is the ultimate display of empathy, going as far as experiencing moments through the other's perspective, as we did. I felt everything you did, and even saw . . . memories." He paused before a light shudder shook his body.

"You cried last night," I said, pulling his attention back to my face. "What happened?"

"I did no such thing." He laughed it off, but his watery eyes betrayed him. "I just had something in my nose."

"You were crying, Amulii. Obviously, our experiences were different. The only thing I could do was see through your eyes and feel what you felt."

"Listen, I—" Both of our stomachs growled at the same time. "Are you sure you do not want me to hunt?"

He nuzzled the side of my neck as he changed the subject.

"No. And I'm not letting it go. When I get back, we're talking, okay?"

He nodded, his eyes shifting to the side. "Of course," he whispered. "Do you . . . regret yesterday?"

"I don't know yet. That's up to you. I don't have much of a say, right?"

He still didn't look at me as he spoke. "That is not true. Perhaps it came across as something I did not intend. What we did does not mean one holds power over another. This is something—never mind."

He struggled to hold back whatever upset him, and I pushed away before trudging toward the cave entrance.

"I don't know what's going on with you, but we have to be honest with each other now." He sat slumped over, ears off to the side. "No more secrets, okay?"

Suddenly, I felt like I was the one leading *him*. Whether he admitted it or not, the bond affected us in different ways. I could feel it. Somehow, he got softer, and I could stand a little higher than I did before.

I didn't want to leave things so serious between us.

"When I get back, and after we eat, do you wanna do more of what we did yesterday?"

His ears perked and tail went crazy. "Of course." The sad, uncertain expression he wore seconds earlier became one of elation. Typical horny Amulii. "That is not something you have to ask me."

"Well, I think I should, because I wanna do to you what you did to me."

His ears fell again.

"I have never let anyone—"

"Well," I interrupted, licking a sharp, top canine. "You know how to prepare for it."

///

Animal odors that had been prominent in the forest vanished, replaced by the faint but pervasive scent of humans and gasoline. Prey wouldn't stick around, and I needed to go deeper into the valley. Every few hundred meters I'd rub my neck against the trunks of trees as Amulii taught me, while trekking through deep snow. It was one area that produced our unique scent, that and urine. If it started snowing again and visibility was poor, I'd need to sniff my way back.

I thought about Liam and hoped he was still alive. How long could one survive with a severed arm, freezing while bleeding out?

I knew he'd been hunting us, but I hadn't tried to kill him in self-defense. There'd been an intent, a burning desire to consume his flesh. I'd pursued a human solely for the pleasure of killing. I hoped he'd survived, if only because it meant I wouldn't be the monster I feared.

The weak scent of something else took me from the trail, and it was one I remembered from that night. Dogs. That was how they'd tracked us so easily. Though the hunters who were here moved on yesterday, the smell of canine urine mixed with human blood told a vivid tale.

I followed the smells and came upon snowmobile tracks which soon turned to human footprints. The more I sniffed, the more Liam's strong scent trail stood out from the rest. He had made it that far, and there were four others with him.

Five sets of human prints went to four as I came upon a body-shaped depression with a red tinge to it. Two divots created by dragged legs made a long trail, punctuated by splatters of blood.

He'd gotten himself to the safety of the other hunters before collapsing, and he'd done all of this several hours after I attacked him. I only knew this because there was no snow covering any of the evidence. The storm had calmed early in the morning, hours after our encounter.

As I continued my investigation, two landing skid marks revealed what I feared. The altitude in this area wasn't high enough to keep helicopters away, but maybe our cave was. They must have medevaced him, but the other hunters remained behind. Though the scents were old, being there was risky, and I didn't want to follow the tracks further.

They knew we were here now, and they'd be back. There was nowhere we could go without them following. We were in some of the most unforgiving terrain, and they managed to push through it, coming within a few kilometers our den. How had they not tracked us to our exact location? Granted, the harsh weather helped, but for how long?

I turned and noticed my deep paw prints. Compared to a human's footprints, they were massive. No animal could make tracks like that. Any hunter that saw those would know exactly what made them. I was too hungry to waste energy covering the evidence, and I wasn't sure it would have mattered anyway.

///

Desperation set in after two more hours of smelling no game. Survival mode kicked in, calming my fear as my mind went blank. Everything I did from that point on focused on energy conservation.

Catching the scent of something delicious, I closed my eyes and crouched, lightening my steps. Instinct took me from survival mode back into a hunting stance, allowing my brain to focus on strategy.

Up ahead was a doe and its fawn. The fawn was too small to make a proper meal for both of us, and I would need to kill the mother. I remembered what Amulii told me about leaving the young to die.

The fawn would face a slow and lonely death, and I couldn't let that happen. As cruel as it was, I would need to kill both, starting with the baby. It wouldn't go to waste. Hunger made me callous, and deep down, that made me sad, but human empathy would be my death out here. This was about doing whatever I could to keep us alive.

My eyes focused on the fawn first, and after that, all I could see was red. In seconds, the two deer lay before me, still and lifeless. Another of Amulii's lessons was giving thanks to those that unwillingly nourished us. I leaned in, touching the fawn with my forehead, whispering the words he taught me.

"Gokai, ale'c'héa il meri't."

His language rolled well off of my new tongue once I spoke it enough. The words gave thanks and comfort to the spirits of the deceased as they ascended to the circle to begin life again.

The circle—I remembered Voldrik saying something about that. I didn't believe any of this stuff before, but after everything I'd been through, I was hyperaware of my blossoming spirituality. The maw'cha belief system made more sense than any dominant human religion. It was much easier for me to follow something that connected me to everything, rather than making me feel above it all.

According to Amulii, his species had a much stronger connection to a "god" than anyone in this world did. Their deity supposedly made things happen, and it was much easier to believe in a great spirit that didn't require his followers to fear it in order to be loved. Maybe I'd romanticized their faith more than I should have, and there was a chance I'd be just as disappointed with it when I got to his world.

I slung the doe's body over my shoulders and carried the fawn in my mouth as I made my way back to the cave. Amulii and I would eat well tonight, and the meal should last a week if we kept physical activity to a minimum. After seeing how scarce food was, sex was out of the question, at least until the urge got too strong.

When I entered the cave, I noticed Amulii scribbling something in one of his leather-backed tomes using a sharpened piece of charcoal. This wasn't the first time I'd caught him writing in that book. He set it off to the side and smiled at me as I let the fawn drop from my maw, setting the mother beside it.

"You have gotten so good at this," he said in a bit of a breathy tone as he walked over to greet me. "You were gone for a while, and I knew you would figure out that food is even harder to come by now. Finding us such a bounty up here makes me so proud."

It was silly, but hearing him praise me like that did wonders for my growing confidence in who I was now. My lower body shifted slightly as my tail swung from side to side. The honeymoon phase wouldn't last forever, but I'd enjoy these moments of sweetness when they came.

///

We lay together on the blanket, our stomachs distended from our desperate binge earlier. Being so hungry caused us to overeat, which often incapacitated us for hours.

I glanced at him before licking the blood from his mouth. "I never thought I'd be doing any of this stuff a month ago. I'm used to it now, but I still have a hard time believing sometimes. I kind of expect to wake up." Amulii belched into my face, changing the mood of the moment. "You're such a fucking pig." I yelled, covering my nose.

Amulii grinned. "It is like this for me as well. Getting a human mate was more of a challenge than my father made it out to be."

His words kind of rubbed me the wrong way, and I turned toward the wall. "I hope you're not proud of that. That *challenge* really fucked me up."

He shuffled over quickly and touched my arm.

"I did not mean it in that way," Amulii whispered, his claws brushing the fur on my arm. "This has been a harsh lesson for me. There have been a lot of harsh lessons for me over the years."

I turned and looked into his eyes, seriousness returning to my face. "There's something I want to talk to you about."

Amulii's ears fell as he moved away from me, as if he were expecting this.

"I saw some things out on the hunt that have me worried."

"Is this about the humans?"

I nodded. "That hunter I attacked might still be alive, but they know we're here."

"I smelled them that night on the wind, and I have been thinking about heading further north, away from here. But they keep following us." He reached for the green sphere he used to find our new den. "This has many uses, not only for finding our way. It also keeps us hidden as long as we are in the cave. It is the only way I have lived here for so long without them finding me."

"There's a reason they keep finding us," I said, recollecting the scene earlier. "There were more footprints in the snow around the area toward the east, and they have tracking dogs."

His nose wrinkled upward. "I have seen these dogs many times at the lake before I met you. They betray their ancestry and do whatever humans demand of them. They are stupid but wise not to come near me," he said, a bit of disgust dripping from his tone. "The once-proud wolf, proud no longer."

"Yeah, dogs do what they're told, but a lot of people love them." I smiled as a memory came back. "I've had a few over the years, and we treated them like family. My dad spoiled the last one we had until the day he died. He was a retired military dog, so of course Dad took a liking to him."

"I did not know there was such trust between man and animal. My people do not keep such companions, as many animals know not to come near. I have always wondered what it would be like to have such a creature, but there is always that fear I would eventually get hungry and . . . well, you know."

"Damn," I said, getting a dose of reality again. It was sad to think I'd never be able to have pets around. "I forgot about that."

An arctic breeze whistled through the cave, and I rolled toward Amulii, wrapping myself with the edge of the blanket. The larger maw'cha began to drift asleep, but I shook him.

"C'mon, I'm not done talking about this," I said, my eyes darting to the entrance. "Something's not right about these people. I know for a fact this didn't start with me."

There was a second of surprise on his face that disappeared shortly after.

"Segolia will open to us soon. Winter is harsh in the mountains, and that should keep them away. As dangerous as it is to remain, it may be worse to leave."

"You're that hunter's target. Why?"

Amulii yawned, turning away from me. "I am tired, and I do not feel like talking anymore about it."

"That's not the way this is gonna work," I said, poking him in the back with the claw on my pointer finger. He winced each time I tapped him.

"Please," he growled.

"Amulii, we talk now, and this shit's serious. I want to know what the hell's going on." He said nothing as his muscles tensed. "Amulii."

"Okay," he huffed, shaking his head. "I suppose I cannot make you think any less of me than you already do."

"I don't—"

He held up a hand to stop me. "It is not like I do not deserve it." He grunted before resting his hand on my abdomen. "It was ten years ago, back when I had just come through Segolia to study humans—"

"Hold on," I interrupted. "I've gotta know. You said you've met humans over the years, but when you met me, you hardly understood English."

"That is because back in that time, I did not speak your language, and I would not learn for years. I have only befriended a few humans over that time, and I was slow to learn—I must speak with humans often to learn quickly. I learned a lot over the years, but not enough to speak and understand well, until I met you."

"You went from barely understanding me to fluent English in, like, two weeks."

"Remember, the chélanc you wore then connected us. I could learn very fast once it was around your neck." He smiled for a moment, but that didn't last. "Are you sure you want to hear this?"

"Amulii . . ."

His shoulders rose and fell as he let out another heavy sigh. "I had come back from a swim in the lake. I smelled humans and realized they had been in my cave going through my belongings. I knew one of them had taken very important items from me. Things humans should not touch. It was a feeling of violation."

I raised an eyebrow. "Yeah, I know a thing or two about that."

His ears fell to the sides and his eyes shifted. "I tracked the human. He was a young male with black hair and a beard. I will never forget his face as long as I live because my conscience will not let me. I was so angry that I ran out of the trees and grabbed him.

"He panicked and screamed, and I felt a burn from my guts where he stabbed me with a small knife. All it did was enrage me more, and—" He struggled to stay composed, his eyes glossing over as he recollected. "I remember my jaws around his throat, and a very young human on a hill saw everything. He must have told the others."

"Oh my God." I held a hand to my mouth as I tried to process what he told me. "Why did you kill him? He wasn't even a threat to someone like you."

"I . . ." Amulii trailed off.

"You're thinking of a lie right now, aren't you?"

"No." He shook his head. "No, I am not. It is just hard for me to remember. I was not in control of myself."

"You lost control and killed someone because they stole something from you? I don't believe it—and that's saying something considering all the horrible shit you've done. If you're telling the truth, then you're a cold-blooded killer."

"Please, Alex. It was a moment I could barely recall, and it happened so fast. After doing it, I was sick. You understand what it is like to lose yourself being what we are."

"I—" Bile burned my throat as I swallowed it back down. "I guess."

"I remember loud noises and blue and red flashes like we saw that first night at your home. They searched for me but went away after a few months. Then months later, the hunters began coming. There were few at first, but then more would come. Sensing my life was in danger, I spent a few years back home.

"While in my world, the shamans taught me how to hide where I lived from human sight and gifted me with the orb. I knew I would need to be cautious, but I needed to accomplish what I sat out to do. I had a feeling the humans would be back. That is when I saw that one human, Liam as you called him, always chasing."

My blood ran cold as I thought back on every interaction I had with Liam. The way he looked out at the lake when we met. When he threatened me that day at the store, there was pure hatred in his eyes. There was more to everything than him just hunting a trophy.

You don't recognize me, do you? Been chasing your ass for years, and now I know what you really look like.

He mentioned his brother used to take him for hikes around the lake. Liam really did mistake me for Amulii back in that parking lot, and if those other guys hadn't been there, he would have killed me.

"Amulii." My voice shook as I spoke. "You killed his brother. He was that small human on the hill."

The larger maw'cha's ears fell and his eyes closed in contemplation. We were both killers, and there was no waiting for this to go away. They were going to hunt us to the ends of the earth if it came to that.

"I tore his arm off." Amulii squeezed my shoulder and tried to calm me down. "I wonder how many of his friends are going to be coming after us now. They followed us this far, and a little weather won't stop them. They know exactly where we are, and they're never gonna stop coming."

CHAPTER NINETEEN

GROWING PAINS

It may have only been a month, but it felt like years—years of re-calling the comforts of civilization all while being stuck in a cave surrounded by people that wanted us dead. Amulii meditated in the corner, and I stood by the cave entrance, watching another black heli-copter fly low over the valley.

Hunter activity in our area got worse by the week, and it wasn't uncommon to see multicolored tents lined along the slopes with snowmobiles dragging sleds of supplies and weapons. Black choppers often circled the mountain, dropping more supplies while the weather cooperated.

A couple weeks ago, I'd observed a pair of hunters hiking up our slope and saw for myself what Amulii mentioned a few weeks ago. While their dogs could track our scent, there was a limit to how close they would get, often whining before pulling away from their owners. Every animal in the forest knew to avoid us, even the bears that weren't hibernating.

A giant male grizzly made the mistake of wandering too close to get away from all the commotion in the valley, and being as hungry as we were, Amulii wasted no time. I was hesitant because the bear was larger than both of us combined, but it took only seconds before he severed its spine, dragging it back for us to eat.

I'd been in this body for almost two months, and it still amazed me to think we were so deadly that even half-ton carnivores didn't stand a chance.

Humans, on the other hand, were much more dangerous.

They knew we were close, and we had to take extra care not to lead them back to our cave. Though the dogs wouldn't get near, if we didn't cover our tracks, the hunters would find us, magic or no. Surviving out here was hard enough, but those extra precautions made even taking a shit a harrowing, time-consuming ordeal.

"Are you done yet?" I stood and padded toward the concentrating maw'cha. He didn't move, still deep in whatever trance he was in. I kind of wished I was able to do that. "Hey." I gave his shoulder a light shake, and he jolted before looking up at me.

"What is the matter?" He asked, leaning back against the stony wall.

"I'm going insane." I sat next to him and leaned against his shoulder. "I don't know how you're so calm. I'm bored out of my mind."

"How about we mate?"

"That's all we ever do. We've already done it five times today, and it's not even noon yet. How the hell do you have anything left?"

Amulii growled out a chuckle as he smiled at me. "Then we will talk. Tomorrow is the big day."

This had been our routine for weeks. Since the humans showed up, we had to hunt every few days at night, traveling over the mountain the long way to the valley on the other side so the dogs couldn't sniff us out. We slept the rest of the night and into the day while having as much sex as we could in between for any kind of entertainment. As fun as it was, it was getting stale.

"What's special about tomorrow?" I asked, pulling the blanket over us as another blast of wind blew in from outside. The cave faced northeast, and it wasn't well shielded like the one at Maligne Lake. I was glad we had fur, but I hated knocking snotsicles off my snout all the time.

"Segolia opens soon, and we will need to head back to the lake."

"Really? That's awesome," I said, not able to contain the painful grin on my face. I was so overjoyed we were leaving this hell that I almost forgot what was going to happen when we got there. The smile faded.

Amulii talked his world up a lot, telling me how great it was. It could have been a utopia, but I'd still be sad about leaving my family and friends. Before the bond, I was against leaving with him, but now I couldn't picture the two of us apart for very long.

We'd been in close quarters every day though, and little things like his snorty breathing started irritating me. Still, I was glad he was there, and I loved him more as time went on, especially when we talked. We hadn't really argued, and I didn't want to make waves every time he said or did something that I didn't agree with.

We never changed positions during sex, and every time I'd bring it up, he'd shut me down or come up with an excuse. I understood we were stressed, but I wasn't sure how much longer I'd keep quiet. When he took our roles outside of the cave and applied them to everyday situations, it became a little disturbing.

During hunts, he'd keep ahead of me, doing everything himself while I stood there for moral support—if he let me go at all. When we walked anywhere, he'd push me back behind him. Yes, he was worried about me, and there were a lot of humans around, but I was strong enough now that we'd need to start handling things together.

"How many days will it take?" I asked.

"Seven. It is a five-day journey back, and I am giving us time to evade when we can."

"Do we really have to leave? If we just turn human and—"

"Alex." He grabbed my hand, raising it to his lips. "We have to go. You know this."

I hung my head and sighed. "Yeah, I know."

It was difficult to accept, and I missed Mom. It still hurt remembering how she'd looked at me like I was something disgusting, and I knew it'd be worse if she saw me now. I was a mangy mess, stinking of dried blood, and God knows what else—all of it caked into my matted fur. We hadn't been able to leave the den long enough to bathe, and we didn't want to use the water in the cavern pond for anything other than drinking.

Mom had no clue what Amulii's intentions were from the start, which would probably make her hate him even more. I wanted to turn human and ask Amulii if I could see her before we left, but I'd never learned how. I'd grown so accustomed to being maw'cha that I couldn't even remember what having human features was like.

"I know this will make you sad, but I want you to be safe. The shamans need to heal your mind." He smiled and wrapped his arm around my back before pulling me into him. "Everything will work out once we are home."

Home. Would anywhere ever feel like that again?

///

"Are you ready?" asked Amulii, his back loaded with crystals, food, and the books he'd been writing in. I also had heavy bags of supplies on my back, and our tattered, rank-smelling blanket draped around my neck. Despite the setbacks, we'd managed to stock up on enough food for at least half the trip.

"I was ready a month ago. Let's get the hell out of here." We would have laughed if the mood were cheerier. We were under a lot of pressure and too tired to be making such a long trip on foot.

We trekked around the mountain as we usually did while hunting, steering clear of any infrared goggles trained on our location. It was pitch-black on the western slope, despite the moon being out, and a faint orange outline on the horizon appeared where the sun would soon rise.

The thin air was so frigid that every stiff joint in my body screamed, and even with my thick fur, the chill on my face froze the condensation around my nose and eyes. Every breath I took as we ascended felt like aggressive hedgehogs rolling over in my lungs.

"When we get to my world, I have so much planned for us. Since our bond, we have rarely had good times. We will not have to hide anymore." Amulii looked back at me. "Are you still upset?"

"This is hard for me." I sped up and walked next to him, but he pushed me back. "Stop doing that," I growled, forcing my place at his side again.

"We have been through this. It is dangerous, and I would have a better chance at fending off the hunters."

"If you're worried that there's danger ahead, I'll be able to spot it just as fast as you can."

"I . . . Alex." He hesitated, his voice dropping to a whisper. "This is not the way things are done. I was not going to bring this up until later, but in my world, there is an etiquette for bonded mates."

And there it was. I knew there was more to his behavior than just fearing for my safety—if that was even a concern in the first place.

"We're not in your world yet. And even if we were, what does that have to do with me walking next to you? We're together, and I want to walk with you."

"That is not the point. There is always a balance in a bond. A leader and the—"

"Not this again. This is the hang-up in bed, isn't it? I never agreed to something so stupid. I was only doing what you told me because I had no clue." My pace quickened as I stomped harder into the snow. "I'm not that person anymore. So, stop treating me like I am." I bared my teeth and flexed my muscles. "Look at me. I'm huge."

"You are still smaller than me. I know we have been getting along lately, but this is where I stand firm. What confidence will my people have if someone who is to lead them lets his smaller mate step on equal footing?"

I stayed focused on the path ahead, biting my lower lip so hard I drew blood. After taking a calming breath, I turned and met his eyes. His ears drooped to the sides of his head.

He knew this was wrong.

"Please do not be angry. This is the way things are, and I cannot change them."

"Why would you want to change it? It obviously only benefits you."

"It benefits both of us," he said, the tone of his voice bordering on impatience.

"It doesn't. It just makes me dependent on you. And what kind of shitty leader can't change a dumb rule?" I glanced sideways at the now furious maw'cha as his ears lay flat against his head. "You know this is pointless, right? You also know I'm not going to let you have your way here."

"Maybe once we have established ourselves, I will feel more comfortable having you stand beside me. Until then, you are under me, as our society dictates."

"No, I'm not," I replied in the teasing, sing-songy tone I knew annoyed him.

"You are being unreasonable," Amulii growled out. "You would not do this one thing for me? How selfish." When he said it, I saw an immediate flash of regret.

Despite being so pissed off, I was calmer than usual. "I can already tell by your face that you know exactly where this is about to go. We've had this discussion before and guess what's different now?" I paused, standing up straight, my arms spread out. "I'm not on the ground."

"We are not yet equals. You must learn a lot more before that. Yes, you can stand up to me, but we have roles as mates now."

"Keep that up and there won't be much mating anymore," I said, sliding ahead of him as we descended. A smile crossed my face when I thought of something. If Amulii was going to be this insufferable, I was prepared to meet him halfway. I stopped and turned to him. "You know what? Fine."

"Thank you." Amulii eyed me suspiciously as he slid ahead.

"On one condition."

He huffed and balled his fists, his body going rigid.

"I'll put on a show in public. I'll play along with this stupid role and do whatever you want. But, when we're in bed, the roles change."

"You are really trying me today," he snarled. His eyes hadn't glowed like that since our last big fight. I shrugged and walked ahead. He felt strongly about his ridiculous demand, and I needed to handle the argument with more delicacy than in the past.

"Hey, it's your choice. You can get your way if I have mine." I dashed ahead of him again.

"Not everything has to be a . . . *quid pro quo*, was it?" he sneered, trying to mimic my voice from that day. I knew he'd throw this back in my face. "You can do something for me without expecting something in return, remember?"

"Oh boy, things have sure as hell changed, haven't they? Since we're bringing up things we said in the past, I believe you mentioned something about spending your life atoning for what you've done." I was trying to keep things light-hearted, but I was also starting to get angry. "So, atone. Preferably, on all fours with your ass in the air and me behind you."

He quickened his pace until he was beside me but didn't stop glaring. It had no effect on me anymore, which quashed his anger, and a breathy groan of defeat graced my ears.

"I will . . ." he grunted, trying to find the words. I raised a brow. "Fine. If you want your way, have it." His face simmered as he now kept his gaze ahead. I couldn't believe he didn't put up more of a fight. Maybe the bond mellowed him out more than I thought, or maybe he was trying to compromise, in his own hardheaded way.

Something didn't sit right the more I thought about his ridiculous relationship rules. What kind of messed up, old-timey culture was I about to step into?

"Oh, I'll have my way, alright—" He yelped in surprise when I grabbed a handful of his rear end and squeezed, digging my claws in slightly. "—with that ass."

"That is not funny." He bared his teeth.

Placing a hand on his shoulder, I leaned in, kissing him lightly on the side of the head.

"Come on, Amulii. Loosen up." I snorted. "But don't get too loose."

A reluctant grin and gruff chuckle gave him away as he shook his head. "That was kind of funny," he muttered, shoving me lightly to the side. "But I do not know whether I should think that was clever or be embarrassed for you."

We made good time as we neared Maligne Lake earlier than expected. Amulii and I took the safest route, staying at high altitudes, at one point jumping from tree to tree to throw off any dogs that were tracking us. We avoided clearings, keeping an ear for the few helicopters that flew nearby.

Through two days of heavy snow, we kept warm at night by curling up together, our faces buried in each other's fur. When it came to sleeping outside, we stayed comfortable no matter where we were.

Our shabby blanket kept most of the snow off of us and our fur kept us from freezing.

By late afternoon on day six, we made it back to our old cave. Amulii's bedding and all the makeshift furniture had remained untouched, covered by a thin layer of rough frost. Depleted crystals that lay scattered along the floor brought back a flood of terrible memories. I hadn't felt that kind of hopelessness since the night I attacked Liam.

There'd been a shift in my attitude since the day we'd run from this place. It was gradual, but everything I'd been through up to now had put me in a much clearer state of mind. I'd grown to appreciate the life I shared with Amulii, who didn't turn out to be the abusive monster I'd expected. Despite our arguments, I had to give him credit; he was much more patient now, trying his best.

Learning to compromise was something we both had difficulty doing, but Amulii often surprised me. The dominant and submissive concept was going to ruin things, but deep down I think he understood it wouldn't work with us.

"It will be pleasant to sleep in a bed tonight," he said, dropping his bags before shoving the green sphere he held into a similar-sized hole in the wall near the entrance. Though I couldn't see it happening, the cave would disappear from sight, concealing us. He then collapsed onto the pile of fur, a cloud of dust billowing out from the impact.

"Agreed." I followed suit, sliding forward, not wanting to move. I'd been holding off talking about something important until we were more comfortable. Amulii might refuse, and I wouldn't blame him. Even I was hesitant about the idea with all the human scents strong around the lake.

"Can I ask you something?"

A puff of air hissed through his nostrils.

"Oh no. The last time you asked me if you could ask me something, I nearly killed your father."

I had forgotten about that conversation.

"Well, this question is kind of similar, and if you say no, I'll understand."

He turned and smiled, his wet nose touching mine.

"You want to see your parents before we leave."

My apprehension faded away with those words. He knew what I was thinking, and perhaps it had been on his mind as well.

"Why do you think we arrived early? I would not deprive you of a goodbye. I understand how hard it is to be away from family, but I do not expect this meeting to go better than the last one." He licked my nose, and I laughed, wiping the slobber away. I both loved and hated when he did that. "But regardless of how this goes, you will always have me."

Muffled thuds from my tail rose from the stone floor. If Mom knew that tomorrow would be the last time she'd see me for a year, she might come around.

"Thank you," I said, returning the nose lick, eliciting snorted laughter from Amulii. "I'm glad you're my . . . mate." I grimaced. "I really hate that word."

"Why?"

"I don't know, it just sounds weird to me." At one point, I kept referring to us as a bonded pair, but I'd have too many AP chemistry flashbacks. "What are mates in your language?"

"On'she." When he'd shift back into his native tongue, his voice would drop to something more guttural. "You would be my on'she. On'shii for mates. When added to a name or a word, ii changes the meaning from single to plural. My name, for example, means many spirits."

"Damn, I forgot. I've got to learn more of your language." Amulii spoke fluently in English now, and I got so used to his accent that I often forgot he wasn't a native speaker. There was no way for me to communicate with anyone in his world except him.

"Do not worry about that. Compared to this confusing language, ours is simple. With shaman teaching, it will not take long to learn it."

"I don't know if I trust magic after everything that's happened."

"Once you see and understand it, you will come to appreciate and respect the wonders it can do."

Before dawn, we hiked a familiar difficult route, taking the slopes to avoid humans that were surly patrolling the easier forest path. When we approached the cabin, I saw Mom's white Mercedes and Dad's forest green pickup truck parked in front.

"I never thought I'd be so scared to see my own parents," I whispered, reaching for the doorbell.

"Perhaps it will go better this time."

Amulii wrapped his arm around my waist in time for Dad to open the door. His eyes were half-open and there was a fabric imprint from his pillow on his right cheek. As our presence registered, his face brightened.

"What the hell?" he shouted excitedly. "Get your hairy asses in here before you're seen." He opened the door all the way to let us in and forced it closed after we entered. "I thought I told you guys not to come back. They're everywhere out there."

"This is our last day in this world for a while. I wanted Alex to spend some time and say goodbye."

"What do you mean 'last day'?" Dad asked, putting his arm around my neck before pulling me into an embrace, dry heaving as he pushed me away. "Holy Christ, you guys reek." He gagged again as he got another whiff. "Damn."

"That's usually what happens when you're out in the wild with no way to bathe," I said, my face flushing hot beneath my fur. I hadn't thought about how bad we stank, and the lake was too frozen to wash up before coming here. It was too risky for that anyway. "We have to go to Amulii's world. It'll be safer for all of us if we left."

"This is gonna kill your mother."

"Well, what would she prefer? Me dead?" I looked toward their bedroom door, which was cracked open. She was talking to someone, though her voice was barely audible, even for my sensitive hearing. "How is she? Is she going to be okay enough to say goodbye?"

Dad took in the sight of me and shook his head. "Alex . . ." He let out an exasperated sigh. "Where the fuck are you guys' pants?"

"I knew I forgot something." I walked into the hallway and grabbed two beach towels from the linen closet, throwing one at Amulii. "Wrap this around your waist."

"Why?" he asked, letting the towel fall to the floor.

Dad bent over and snatched it up, shoving it into Amulii's abdomen. "Just humor me and put it on. It's hard enough she thinks he's an animal now, and you guys show up stinkin' and dirty with no clothes on."

He was right, but he also hinted that Mom was still messed up. Maybe I had grown too wild to see her again.

"I forgot," I said, securing the towel. "I guess I've gotten used to being an animal."

"We are not animals, and do not say that again." Amulii snapped as he shot a glare at my father. "In my world, we do not stink, and we are not forced to live away from society. Yes, we rarely wear clothing, but that does not mean we are animals."

"Amulii, please." He was angry, but I couldn't blame him. Once again, we unintentionally insulted him and his people. In fact, I insulted myself. All the confidence I thought I had vanished now that I was back here.

"It's okay," Dad said, facing the floor. "I'm sorry. I know you guys aren't, but it's a hard sell to his mother. You turned our boy into something we didn't even know existed. I've come to terms with that, and—" He looked up again, his face turning a weird shade of pink beneath the tan. "And the other thing."

"The other thing?" Amulii asked, not picking up on his subtlety.

"The bond," I whispered through mostly sealed lips.

"Oh yes, I remember you were not happy that I chose your son as a mate. It is good that you have accepted that."

"I haven't *accepted* anything. I'm just not gonna object to it anymore because there's not a damn thing I can do about it."

The tension was awful. I thought Amulii and Dad liked each other, but they spoke candidly, with mild resentment in their voices.

"It was never in your control to begin with. We have talked about this. I have told you male or female means little regarding mates in my world. I was angry at you the first time I realized where Alex's denial came from. I thought you hated him."

Flustered, Dad struggled to find words.

"I don't . . . hate Alex. I just didn't want that future for him. It's hard to be like that in this world, or it used to be."

"Hmm," Amulii mumbled. "It is odd to hear that. That is not the way things are where I am from. So be happy that my world is better for him." The touch of his lips jolted my wandering mind back to the room, and I had a hard time reciprocating the gesture in this house. "We have already bonded and have mated many times." My jaw dropped as Amulii went there so casually. "Maybe a hundred t—"

"Amulii, stop, please," I interrupted, rubbing my forehead. It was brief, but I caught a glimpse of the horror on Dad's face. I felt almost bad for him having to visualize that.

Amulii laughed as he examined the two of us.

"Humans," he snorted. "Why are you so ashamed of the very act that brought you into the world? To be with someone in such a way is celebrated, not shameful. Our people do it in public if they are feeling amorous enough."

"Just so we're clear, we will never do that," I muttered, shoving him away as I enunciated the next word slower. "E-ver."

"Alex?" Mom's voice caught my attention as she slowly emerged from the bedroom.

"Mom." My voice got higher as I tried to sound less intimidating. She ran across the room, and I struggled to maintain eye contact. "Sorry, I stink, and I don't have any clothes—and I look like this."

"It's okay," she said, hesitant to embrace me at first. When she saw Amulii, her smile turned to disgust. "What the hell are you doing here?"

"Sally, you know he's been watching over Alex, making sure he's okay."

"This is not okay," she shouted, pointing at me.

"Mom, you gotta let it go. There's no way to go back. I'm the one it happened to, so if I can accept it, you can."

She wiped her eyes and shook her head.

"You should have run. You should have run the hell away from him when you saw what he was."

"It was too late then," Amulii said. "I had already given him the mark. You are fine to hate me, but do not blame him. He has had a hard enough time."

"Don't *you* lecture me. How could you do this? How could you take advantage of him, play with his emotions, and then not even tell him what you did? What an awful monster you are."

Amulii slouched forward, ears pressed against his head as he faced her scorn.

"Hmm," he said. "I have been waiting for you to say this to me. Now I do not feel as bad for what I am about to say to you."

"Amulii." I wanted to stop him from making matters worse, but there was no holding him back.

"Whether or not you accept it, I am now your son as well. Alex and I are like you and Robert."

"Whatever you did to him doesn't mean you're married." she shouted, but Amulii continued.

"The difference is, what we have is better than the bitterness I often heard from this house. What we did goes much further." He slipped his arm around me. "When I take Alex to my world, there will be a celebration, and he will take my name."

Leave it to Amulii to force my mother head-first into a conversation I was going to have with her in private with a lot more tact.

"What the hell are you talking about?"

"They're leavin'," Dad said as Amulii opened his mouth to speak. "Alex can't live in this world anymore. There are people after him that want to kill him."

"They're not trying to kill him. They want to help him," Mom said, as my gaze snapped to her. Those words were like a rockslide of betrayal. "You can't take my son." She grabbed two handfuls of fur from Amulii's mane and pulled. "Change him back."

He shook his head, and his posture got lower the louder she shouted.

"I have told you already; what is done cannot be undone. I am sorry."

"You lying bastard." She reached up and slapped him across the face over and over until I grabbed her arms.

"Mom, stop," I said, her tiny wrists shaking in my hands. I wanted to question what she meant earlier, but I had to calm her down first. "I'm ready for this. It's not like I'm going away forever. I'll be back."

We all jumped as the doorbell rang, and Dad rushed over to the window. When he opened the curtain, I saw the reflection of flashing lights on his face.

None of this made sense. We were so careful.

CHAPTER TWENTY

RELUCTANT ROAD TRIP

"We need to run." Amulii grabbed my hand.

"Calm down," I said, trying to keep my own urge to run under control. "Where the hell are we gonna go?"

He turned to Dad. "How did they find us?"

With arms crossed, I glanced at Mom, remembering the quiet conversation she had in her room earlier. "Yeah, I wonder how they knew we were here."

"Sweetheart," she whispered before another ring of the doorbell startled her. "They can help you. Dr. Mitchel—"

"Sally, I swear to God," Dad whispered through gritted teeth. "You haven't got a damn clue what's goin' on out there. They've all got semi-automatic weapons pointed directly at this house. They didn't come here to make Alex all better."

The doorbell rang again; this time a loud pounding on the door followed it.

"Shit." This was the first time I'd ever seen Dad panic. Sure, he'd get angry all the time, but seeing the pale fear on his face sent my stomach into freefall. "Take Amulii upstairs and grab your bag. Get your phone and wallet too." He grabbed my mother's hand as she reached for the door. "They will kill him. I saw the guns."

She hesitated, and pulled away.

Dad pointed to a pair of pants next to the couch he'd been sleeping on before grabbing a pen and sticky note. "Get the debit card from my wallet. This is my pin number." After scribbling, he pressed the paper into my rough hand. "We've got about twenty grand in this account."

"What am I gonna do with this? Shove it into a tree and wait for cash to pop out?"

The pounding on the door got louder.

"Robert, Sally, it's Officer Vanderwater. You guys okay in there?"

"I just woke up, gimme a minute," he shouted at the door. "This is for just in case." He pointed to the stairs. "Go on."

After grabbing the card, I took Amulii's hand, pulling him along. Our clawed feet tapped along the wooden floor in sync as we ran up the stairs. Once in the bedroom, I rifled through my belongings and grabbed anything I thought we'd need, shoving all of it into my bag. Amulii was silent. The distant look in his eyes and the scent of fear made me even more sick to my stomach.

"You need to take a breath or something," I said, reaching over to rub his back. "We're gonna be okay."

"We will not. We need to get to Segolia."

Our eyes darted to the window, toward metallic clicking sounds outside.

"We have to go the opposite way. They're gonna catch us if we go back to the lake."

He grabbed my hand and squeezed.

"We cannot miss this, Alex." We heard the front door shut, but nothing else. "We cannot evade capture for an entire year. A month was exhausting enough."

"Guys, come on down," Dad shouted.

"If we go back there, they're gonna kill us." Amulii followed me toward the hall as I let the towel fall from my hips before kicking it away. "You need to trust me."

It was weird watching Amulii crumble like that. He was always level-headed when it came to survival, but the tone of his voice wasn't that of someone rational.

"Alex, I cannot–" He paused for a moment, catching his breath before swallowing hard. "You should not—"

"You don't have to be the leader all the time. I've learned a hell of a lot from you." I stopped and turned to him at the top of the stairs. "Lean on me now, like I did with you."

"The police are gone, but that doesn't matter," Dad said, glancing back out the window. "Damn, that's a lotta guns. I think they have the house surrounded."

Mom was in tears again as she rushed over to the staircase.

"Change him back," she yelled, slamming her hand against the railing.

"Stop it, Mom." My growled response surprised her as I cautiously descended the stairs, nearly slipping as the pads of my canine feet lost their grip. "This is your fault, so stop yelling at him. Why did you call those assholes?"

"Listen to yourself." She placed a hand on my chest. "He's kept you out there for so long, you think you're an animal like him."

"We're not animals, and we're not monsters," I whispered. "I've accepted it, and I'm still Alex." I grabbed her hand from my chest and held it for a second before letting go. "I'm still me, I just look different."

"The old Alex didn't attack police officers or try to kill people in restaurants."

I opened my mouth, trying to think of how to respond to that. She had a point.

"That is not who he is," Amulii chimed in, his voice softer. "We have made the bond, and his mind is at peace for now."

"Shut your mouth." She was breathless as her words poured out. "You took advantage of a teenage boy. Whatever you did, you may as well have raped him."

With that, he couldn't look her in the eye anymore. She turned back to me.

"What about your future? Are you willing to give up everything?" she asked, shooting another scowl at Amulii. "For that?"

"Again, he cannot be changed back. This future you want for him is no longer possible. His place is with me," Amulii spat back, his voice increasing in frustration. "We are family."

"They're going to catch you and skin you alive, and I hope I get to watch them do it," she said through her teeth, tears pouring from her eyes as she stormed back to the bedroom. "You're not taking my son. I'll make sure of that." She slammed the door behind her.

There was something about my mother that made her as dangerous as those hunters. She loved me, but *she* had to be the one in control. The future I thought I wanted—that was what she wanted. Everything I had ever done in my life had to have her approval, but it wasn't something she beat over my head.

No, Mom was more manipulative than that. I always thought Dad was the only one, but listening to her go off the rails and admit to calling those people put the events of my life into clearer perspective.

"Not exactly the goodbye I wanted," I muttered. "We need to figure out how to get out of here."

Eager woofing from dogs in the distance snatched our focus. Those same clicks and spring noises we heard earlier rang out from different directions around the cabin. I wasn't sure if they were loading guns or setting traps. If we jumped from the window, we had to be careful to study our route of escape first.

Clawed hands gripped me and shook my shoulders.

"We have to run."

"Stop, please." My inflection was gentle as I pressed my palm to his chest, trying to sound as confident as I could while trying not to fall apart. I looked back at Dad. "Will they be able to get a warrant or something?"

"Warrants don't matter. The cops are gone, but those other people are still out there on our property. They didn't seem to care about that."

All three of us stood in near silence, save for the nervous tapping of Amulii's pawed feet. Light beamed in through slits in the curtains now that the sun had come up. If we left now, we wouldn't have the cover of darkness, but with every minute we waited, the enemy was more prepared.

Not only did I have Amulii's safety to consider, I also had to think of my parents. They didn't have rapid healing like we did if the enemy forced their way inside and sprayed bullets everywhere. The only choice we had was to make a break for it, but we had to be smart.

"I have an idea. It's not great, but it's all I can really think of. They have guns pointed at the front and back doors, but—" I ran toward the windows on each side of the house, opening the curtains enough to peek out. There were several men in dark blue uniforms shoving more traps into the snow outside. "Maybe if we jumped out of one of the second-floor windows, we might get further before they notice us. They've got traps everywhere out there, but they aren't really hiding them." I shook my head. "They must think we're stupid."

"That could work to our advantage," Amulii said, also peeking out of a side window. "They are placing them randomly, thinking we will run in a straight line."

"Amulii, come here." I ran up the stairs to the guest bedroom window, which pointed southwest. Dad followed close. "That's the direction we need to go. The trees are closer, and we need to head the opposite way of Maligne."

"What about Segolia?" Every time he brought up the portal, he lost more of his composure.

"Let it go," I shouted, clasping his arms. "It's not happening. We need to go south, and then we'll see from there. There's no way they can be everywhere, and if we do manage to escape, the wilderness might not be the best place to hide anymore. That's where they expect us to run."

Amulii shook his head, knowing what I was going to suggest.

"Now you are being foolish." Amulii growled out. "In the wild, we can keep running. If we go into places full of humans, someone will see us."

"Nobody's gonna give a damn if you're human too," Dad joined in, lowering his voice. "I think it's the only shot you guys have, but you can't stay in one little town for long. Try to get to Calgary, rent a motel, and stay inside as much as you can."

"Edmonton's closer."

"It's also to the east. You may as well take your chance at the lake, since you'd be heading back in that direction."

"Oh yeah," I whispered, feeling a little silly having brought that up.

"We are to do that for an entire year?" Amulii grew more desperate as Dad and I continued to discuss the plan he despised. "Living among humans in close quarters? Absolutely not. We are going to Segolia. End of discussion," Amulii said, tilting his head while pointing an ear to the ceiling. "What is that noise?"

"Well, that's not good," I said, inching the curtain back, revealing several black drones with cameras attached overhead. "They trapped us out there last time, and I'm not going back to that. We're going to the city."

"Keep your voice down. I don't want your mother knowing where you guys are going."

"We are not going to a . . . city. We are running for the portal." No matter what I said, or how much sense I made, he wasn't listening. My back was to the wall, and I shuddered at what instinct told me to do. I had to bank on this working. It took a couple months, but now I understood more about maw'cha behavior.

"No, we're not." I let out a deep, throaty growl as my hackles rose. There was a glint of reddish-blue from my eyes reflecting in Amulii's glassy stare.

Instead of being pulled downward, I stood my ground as Amulii's neck fur stuck straight out. Perhaps I was wrong because he wasn't backing down either; in fact, he looked like he would attack me. My father backed away as we both snarled at one another, and as I got into a lunging position, his knees finally buckled. Amulii fell on all fours and struggled to stand. When instinct pulled him all the way to the floor, I knelt next to him.

I couldn't believe it worked.

"You told me that you're the leader, and I can't go against you. Well, right now, you aren't that. You're scared, and you're gonna get us killed." Amulii faced me with a look of bewilderment. "You're gonna follow me now. I'm the leader."

He took in a sniff of air as he pulled himself to his knees. His ears hung low and his tail hid between his legs, while I stood over him.

"Hmm," he mumbled, looking back up at me. "This does not feel very good. I am not accustomed to this."

"I'm not going to be an asshole about it like you were. We've gotta work together. You can't do everything yourself, and I can't either." I sighed, inching closer to him. "Remember this when we go to your world." I leaned in to meet his lips, forgetting about my father watching us in the doorway. "We're . . . on'shii now, right?"

I may have butchered that word, but he understood what I meant.

"You remembered," he said, his soft smile widening to a pearly grin. "I am sorry I made you feel this way." He leaned in toward my mouth with ten times the passion and a lot more tongue than before.

Dad cleared his throat, which ripped us out of the moment. My face flushed with embarrassment when I saw him cover his mouth, feverishly rubbing the side of his face with a fidgety thumb.

"Uh, yeah," I mumbled before standing. Everything about my body language was more assertive, even as I reached down to help Amulii off the floor as he had done for me so many times in the past. "I've got my bag and your money." I gave Amulii a nudge toward my dad. "The only thing we never got was your approval. I'm not gonna get it from Mom, so you're the only one. There's a chance we'll never see each other again, and I'd like to have something good to remember."

Dad lowered his hand and hesitated for a few seconds before slowly extending it toward my mate. Amulii eagerly reached for it and grinned, his tail wagging.

"This is fucked up, but fine. I like Amulii, and I love you, Alex. If this makes you happy—" He groaned, looking away from us. "I guess I'll be happy for you."

Amulii and I pulled him into a tight embrace, which he desperately tried to break free from.

"Alright, that's enough," he coughed out, gagging a little. "Fuck, you guys smell so bad." He pulled away and walked into the hall, crinkling his nose. "When you get to a town, try to find some place to bathe, or you're gonna attract unwanted attention."

I'd gotten so nose-blind to our stench, I barely noticed it anymore. No wonder the dogs didn't have trouble tracking us.

"I love you too, Dad," I laughed, looking out the window to see if there was anyone below. I was careful, but the old metal latches clanked as I opened it. I popped the screen out, snatching it in midair before it fell, pulling it inside and closing the curtains quickly as I waited for the drones to fly off again.

The forest was close, and if we pushed our speed to the limit, we could take cover in the trees before they trained every weapon at us. Once we had evergreens to hide behind, it would be easier to stay out of sight. I still wasn't sure what we would do about the helicopter circling the area—or the drones. We only had to run two kilometers west to get to the road and then across the frozen Athabasca River.

There was a chance that we'd need to use lethal force, but it was a last resort. Reaching into my bag, I grabbed a bottle of bear spray.

"This might be worthless, but what the hell."

I pointed toward the hastily covered lines in the snow through a slight parting in the curtains. Being up on the second floor gave us an aerial view of where the hunters placed the traps. We could either run around or jump over them.

"There aren't many traps. They probably put most of them near the exits."

"I saw two humans behind trees over there." He pointed to the western edge of the forest. "They probably do not know how fast we are at full sprint. They will not have time to react."

"Let's try not to kill anyone." Remembering how overcome I was with bloodlust after ripping Liam's arm off, I wondered if there was a possibility of that happening again.

"If it comes down to them or us, I will choose us."

"I know," I whispered, giving Dad one last glance before getting into position to jump. "Are you ready?"

"Mm-hmm."

The world went silent and still as I closed my eyes and counted to ten in my mind. When I gained a moment of calm, I leaped from the window as far as I could, landing on my hands and feet in the snow. There was a crunchy thud behind me as Amulii hit the ground.

"They're out," a man shouted from the forest's edge in front of us. Another next to him peeked from around the brush.

"They're out, they're out." More voices echoed around us. The men to our front weren't able to get their rifles aimed before we were upon them. Bear spray coated their eyes, and one collapsed as Amulii took the gun and backhanded him against the trunk of a pine. He didn't know how to hold a gun, and it made me nervous watching him handle it.

"Gimme that," I shouted, reaching for the weapon. I was both disappointed and relieved to see it was a tranq rifle. It didn't have any use to me, but it gave me more insight into their plans. Capture was their goal, not killing. I tossed the weapon and looked at Amulii. "Never mind."

The snow was thicker in this area, and we had a much harder time running through it. We knew the humans could never catch us on foot, but they didn't need to. My ears pointed in the direction of snowmobiles far in the distance behind us and approaching drones above the canopy.

Chuffing helicopter propellers pulsed a muffled cadence in my ears, and I knew we had little time to evade it. I had a flashback of activist videos showing Alaskan wolf hunts. They had the advantage in the sky, and we wouldn't be able to outrun it.

"Shit," I hissed under my rapid breath as two darts whizzed past us. Amulii was calmer than I thought he would be. As the chopper hovered low, just above the trees, he nodded and disappeared, leaping straight into the air before vaulting up against a tall pine. "What are you doing?" I shouted up at him.

There was no way I was going to stop and stare as more darts flew by my head, but I had to look back to see where Amulii went. He soared skillfully through the air, grabbing onto the landing skid of the low helicopter before swinging himself into the open door. One of the men lost his balance and fell, landing headfirst in the snow. My ears picked up the sickening sound of his neck snapping.

I knew from my experience hunting that we could jump high, but not that high. Amulii could launch himself from the tree to the hunters above and make it look effortless. Another man rained down, crashing through tree branches before landing unconscious in front of me. I jumped over his body and kept running.

So much for not killing anyone, but I wouldn't cry about it. We were at war with an unknown brigade of mercenaries who were not only organized but had a lot more resources at their disposal.

Amulii landed on the ground to my left, and I ran to check on him. The chopper veered off with a nose-down tilt, out of sight.

"Holy shit," I shouted as he bounded over to meet me. The hunters were too far for the darts to hit us with any accuracy. They were slow enough that I could hear them whiz through the air, giving me enough time to move out of the way.

"I do not know what came over me. I saw an opportunity, and before I knew it, I was in the air." Adrenaline kept us going at top speed, but we ducked as the helicopter hit the ground behind us, propellers sheering away as shrapnel flew in every direction, some landing close to us. The body of the vehicle fell into the dense trees, catching fire in a small explosion as the fuel tank ruptured. "Hmm . . ." He seemed surprised. "I guess there are things I do not even know about myself."

The drones above sounded like swarms of bees as they kept pace with us, and the whirring of snowmobile engines got louder.

"Alex, we can run faster on four legs," Amulii said as he grabbed my hand. The terrain sloped, leading down to the highway out of Jasper. Beyond that, the river and a new wilderness we hadn't yet explored.

"I don't know how to do that," I shouted as we ran toward the road only to see a lone green truck speeding toward us. It couldn't have been more perfectly timed.

"Another human wants to die today," Amulii growled, getting into the pouncing position with his sharp claws at the ready. The way he said it made me pause. He was delighted at the prospect of killing again.

"That's Dad."

His ears shot up as his aggressive stance shifted to excitement, his tail wagging as the truck screeched to a halt. I opened the back door and pushed a hesitant Amulii inside before hopping into the front seat. We were fortunate the vehicle had an extended cab and tinted windows; otherwise, we'd have a hell of a time fitting into it and staying out of sight.

"I didn't know you were gonna do this," I said before being thrown back in the seat as Dad gunned the engine, fishtailing the truck.

"They all left to chase you guys down, so I took my chances with the road, hoping I'd get here in time. Plus, I remembered you guys can't exactly go shopping for clothes naked." His eyes were wide as he turned to me. "I saw fire. What the hell was that?"

"Just Amulii jumping into a helicopter."

"Christ," he said, looking back at the proud maw'cha. "I won't piss you off again."

"Even if you did, I would not kill you." My father glimpsed Amulii in the rearview mirror. "Though you are much younger than me, my relationship with your son makes me your son too."

Dad squinted and looked back at Amulii. "What the hell do you mean you're older than me?" As the truck veered off the road, I grabbed the steering wheel, turning it sharply to the center.

"Dad," I shouted, "you're gonna kill us."

"I am older in years only. I will be eighty soon. That would be very old to humans, but to my kind, I have only just become an adult."

"You're a real motherfucker, you know that?" Dad yelled. "What the hell is an eighty-year-old . . . *maw-paw* doin' with a seventeen-year-old boy?" He glared at Amulii through the rearview mirror. "If I weren't sure you'd rip me in half, I'd kick your ass."

"It is *maw'cha*, and you are trying to equate human values with my kind. Your son is basically an adult, and he is rather intelligent. It is not as though we have nothing in common."

I knew how Amulii justified the age difference between us, and the more we were around each other, the more his youth and immaturity showed. What a nightmare to be a maw'cha parent having to raise a wild animal for the first two decades and a toddler for decades after that. But since they lived so long, sixty years of childhood and adolescence might have seemed like less time to them. I wondered what Amulii looked like as a child. Perhaps I'd get to see some maw'cha children if we made it to his world.

Amulii put a hand on Dad's shoulder, causing him to flinch. "You are stuck with me now . . . father. You would make a good maw'cha."

"Hell no." Dad laughed nervously. "That's way more trouble than it's worth, and I already smell bad enough as a human."

I watched their interaction with one another; both were relaxed and casual. This must have been what Amulii was talking about. I would have never believed it if I hadn't seen it with my own eyes. Amulii never got along with other humans, and Dad never got along with anyone. But they had something in common that allowed them to become friends.

"I wonder if the drones are still following us," I said, rolling down the window to stick my head out. There was nothing but gray sky. Hating myself for thinking it, I opened my mouth and let my tongue flop around in the wind.

"Hardtack used to do that," Dad said. It was only a second, but he saw me do it. Embarrassed, I inched my head back inside, rolling up the window while keeping my eyes straight ahead.

"I know what that looked like, but it wasn't. The wind just caught my mouth, and don't compare me to a dog."

Dad laughed. "You reminded me of the way he'd stick his head out the window and get slobber everywhere." He reached into the glove box and pulled out an old fast-food napkin. "But he was just a dog, so clean your damn mess off the door. This is a new truck. It's gonna be hard enough getting the smell out of the seats."

Dad was taking all of this so much better than Mom. I wished that, for once, they would get along with each other and my mom with Amulii. I wiped the door and threw the napkin in the small trash bag hanging near the middle console.

We continued down the highway, and I wondered how far he'd be able to take us. This would be the first time in years that Dad and I were on a road trip together. When I was younger, I dreaded going anywhere with him because there was always a discomfort that lasted the whole trip, even when music was playing. I didn't feel that way this time.

"Where are we going? Banff?"

"Canmore," he said, keeping his eyes straight ahead. "It's closer, and I have a friend who owns resorts in the area. Gonna see if he has anything available." He snapped his fingers and pointed to the glove compartment again. "Grab a pen and a napkin and write down yours and Amulii's sizes so I can get you guys some clothes before we get there. After that, you both better turn human."

"Are you gonna teach me now?" I asked, turning my head to look at Amulii. "Because I still don't know how to do it."

He scowled, shifting his eyes to the side. He couldn't possibly think we would go into town looking like this.

"Fine," he muttered. "I guess I have no choice."

CHAPTER TWENTY-ONE

CLARITY

"I'm impressed," Dad said, sitting on the edge of one of the two full-sized beds. The lodge interior looked a lot like our cabin living room, only it was one open area with a bathroom in the back and a large flatscreen television on the wall facing the beds. Pictures of Banff's slanted peaks decorated the faux wood walls, and antique Tiffany lamps on matching oak nightstands gave the room a subdued orange hue. "How did you get him under control like that back at the house?"

"Instinct." I rubbed my now clean, human hands together and cupped them against my mouth for warmth. The heat didn't work, and there was no propane for the gas fireplace. It was the only reason we got the place at all, considering how booked everything was for the holidays.

When we arrived in Canmore, Dad left us in the truck to buy food and clothes, parking behind the buildings so no one would see two werewolves in his truck. Amulii used that time to teach me how to shift back, which was more arduous than I'd assumed it would be, and I didn't succeed until hours after we got into our room. Since it was snowing out, visibility was poor and there weren't many people walking around. Amulii and I used that cover to our advantage as we prowled across the icy parking lot to the front door.

Amulii was in the shower, and I wanted to be in there to show him how to wash properly with soap. However, after hearing the blizzard warnings on the news, I thought it best for Dad to stay with us, and it wouldn't have been appropriate for me to do that with him right outside the door. Plus, I couldn't risk shifting back in case Amulii wanted to have fun in the tub.

"Amulii thought because he was bigger than me, he was automatically the leader and the—well, how do I put this?" Though Dad and I were growing closer, a few hours of conversation didn't erase years of mental and physical abuse. It was still hard to talk about my relationship, even if he had accepted it.

"Yeah, I think I know," he said, putting his hand up to stop me from stumbling through my words. "He doesn't force anything on you, right?"

"No, Dad." I grimaced and looked toward the bathroom. "He'd never do that. Let's talk about something else."

"Gladly," he said, uneasy laughter shaking from him. "So, uh, what does it feel like to be what you are now?"

I pursed my lips, trying to think of a way to explain. "At first, it was a nightmare I couldn't wake up from," I said, gradually looking back at his curious face. "But not so much anymore. When I was human, I could only experience the world through five senses, but when I transformed, everything changed. Every sense is so strong now that it feels like there are brand new ones. I can see smells and smell emotions and feel sound. It's really strange but cool."

He nodded, but I knew he couldn't fully understand. It was like explaining my sexuality to him; unless he knew what it was like on a personal level, he'd never get it. We sat in silence for a little while before I opened my mouth to ask him the question that had been festering in my mind the entire trip.

"You didn't seem to give a shit about me before now. Why is it that when I'm a werewolf, you tell me you love me?" Dad put a hand to his chin, fidgeting with his beard as I spoke.

"I don't love you *now* just because you're different than you were. You're my son. You were just more your mama's type because we had nothin' in common. When I saw you that day, I didn't believe it was you until I looked at your eyes. After I saw what you did to that car, I knew that you were gonna need my help sooner or later. Then Amulii told me about the cliff and that was when I realized I almost lost my kid."

We were having the heart-to-heart I'd wanted for years, and as he spoke, the walls he'd spent decades building collapsed one after the other.

"I didn't start caring about you because of what you are now. I always have, but maybe I cared too much about the wrong shit. I was worried about you growin' up different and how hard your life was gonna be because of it, so I wanted to make sure you were tough enough to handle it." He cleared his throat. "Your granddaddy didn't die an alcoholic like I told you. He died of AIDS."

The tension melted away as my brain caught up to what he was saying. I'd never known my grandfather; Dad and Nana had never brought him up. There were no pictures, no memories, nothing. It was as though he'd disappeared from existence.

"He left your nana and me when I was nine. He walked out the door with another man after they fought, and I never saw him again." He paused, continuing to swallow any hint of what he'd always considered unbecoming of a grown man. "I didn't know he died until

I was in high school, and I didn't really care either. Mom worked her fingers to the bone to provide for me, and I worked through school but never got to graduate. I got my GED and went straight into the Marines at eighteen. I resented that man my whole life."

Whenever Dad played "The Ballad of Ira Hayes," that was the only image I had of my grandfather: a war veteran who died an alcoholic. It was a different picture now that Dad was being truthful for once.

"Does Mom know?"

He shook his head.

"Nope, and it ain't her business, either. It's your legacy, though, because his blood runs through your veins like it does mine. I never learned much about my heritage 'cause Nana's as white as they come, but I should have learned on my own and passed it to you. I had many opportunities, but I didn't care." He stood up and sat next to me on the bed, putting his arm around my shoulders. "I was wrong, and I admit that. I was scared you'd end up like him."

That was when he broke. Try as he might to hold back again, the floodgates opened when he kissed me on the head. "You're all we've got, and it looks like I'm still gonna lose you anyway, but at least you won't die of some disease. That's why I was kind of relieved when I saw you weren't human anymore, but the cliff thing scared the shit out of me. I still can't believe we all drove you to want to kill yourself."

"Dad . . ." The words I wanted to say wouldn't form. This entire time I thought he was just a terrible bigot. My world kept turning upside down with every secret let loose, be it from Amulii or my father.

It didn't excuse his ignorance or the way he treated me, but there was a tenderness as I looked at him. He was showing genuine emotion for the first time. Both of my parents loved me and knowing that lifted the weight I'd been carrying around for years.

"HIV's not a death sentence anymore, and I know how to be safe. Mom's a doctor, after all. She's drilled it into my head enough. Why didn't you tell me this?"

He wiped his eyes on his sleeves and sniffed a few times as the stoic look returned to his face.

"Because I didn't want to remember. When I saw that picture of you and Amulii on that guy's phone, the pain came back, and I didn't know what to do with it."

Amulii emerged from the bathroom, soaking wet and buck naked.

"Speaking of pictures I wish I could get out of my head," Dad shouted, pretending to be upset so he'd have an opportunity to regain his composure. "I had to see his balls earlier, and now I get to see the whole fuckin' package."

Amulii smiled as he grabbed the towel he'd forgotten to take into the bathroom earlier.

"I am human now. Why does this still embarrass you?" he asked, vigorously rubbing his hair dry before moving lower. "Do you not possess the parts that make you male as well?"

"What the fuck did you just say to me?" Dad looked back at him and stood, puffing his chest out like he always did to look intimidating.

Amulii was, of course, unfazed. Instead, he kept teasing my father while not bothering to cover any part of himself. Dad's face was red from either embarrassment or rage knowing he couldn't do anything about it.

"I am just confused. If you are male, then you have seen one before, yes?"

"It's about decency, you fuckin' animal," Dad said, shaking his head.

I smiled and shrugged. Typical Amulii. When I'd get angry or embarrassed about something, he'd throw it back in my face, asking rhetorical questions that made it worse.

He looked down at himself and snickered before grabbing a pair of shorts from one of the bags Dad gave him.

"It is unfortunate to be a human male when it is so cold."

///

I awoke early the next morning to Dad putting his shoes on before gathering his things. He always got up before the sun, and when we lived in the city, he'd wake me at the same time on the weekends to do chores and yard work.

"Not gonna stick around for breakfast?" I whispered, sitting up carefully to avoid waking Amulii. He was snoring and had turned back into a maw'cha during the night. He probably got too cold and couldn't sleep without his fur. I did like the extra warmth while lying against him.

"I gotta get the hell away from that God-awful noise he's making," Dad whispered back. Amulii snorted and shifted position. His tongue drenched the pillow as it hung out of the side of his mouth. "I barely slept. How the hell have you not smothered him in his sleep?"

I let loose a sharp laugh, giving the noisy, slumbering beast in my bed a quick glance.

"I guess I got used to it. I don't even notice it much anymore," I whispered as a funny memory popped into my head. "Remember that smoke alarm that chirped all the time when we lived in Yakima? He's kind of like that."

"Heh." He let out a quiet chuckle. "Almost forgot about that thing. None of your mom's colleagues stayed over for very long because of it. That was enough incentive to leave the thing alone than to change the battery."

"Did you try to call Mom again?"

"Yeah, but she's not answering the home phone, and her cell phone is out of service, so I know she's still at the house." After tying his laces, he stood and stretched. "I don't know what we're gonna do now. We've put off the divorce because of all that's happening, and she barely gets out of bed. I don't want to leave her by herself, but I'm pissed off that she called those people."

"Was I the reason you guys fought all the time?" Since he was opening up and being honest, I thought I'd try to get more out of him.

"Alex, this stuff was happening before you were even born. Your Mom and I have a weird-ass marriage, and to be honest, I'm surprised it's lasted as long as it has. In fact, you're probably the only reason we're still together. I still love her, but we're miserable."

"Why don't you actually sit down and talk to her like you did with me? Not gonna lie, before you told me all this, I hated your guts. Now you're finally a human being." I laughed through my nose as the irony hit me. "Now that I'm not going to be around anymore, why don't you try to make it work?"

Dad shook his head and gave me one of his signature shitty looks.

"What's a seventeen-year-old kid know about marriage?"

"See this asshole sleeping behind me?" I said softly, pointing at Amulii. "He's kind of like you. He loses his temper, he has outdated opinions and beliefs, and we argue and fight all the time. The difference between what we have and what you guys have is we're talking more and trying to understand each other. We don't have much choice. We're gonna be together for a long time, so we have to make it work or be miserable like you and Mom."

He reached over and rubbed my head playfully before grabbing his keys.

"I'll try something." He walked toward the door and looked back at me. "You need to take care of *him* now. He's not gonna know what the hell to do out here, and I saw how scared he was. But I think you guys are gonna be fine if you stick to the plan. Try to get to Calgary and lie low and call us now and then, so we know you're okay. Get a burner phone if you can and keep yours off unless it's an emergency. I don't know how much these fuckers have control of."

He paused, and I could tell he didn't want to leave me there. But we both knew those hunters would eventually track his truck if he continued to chauffeur us across Alberta.

I stood and tiptoed across the room to give him one last hug before he walked out.

"Thanks, Dad. You really saved our asses."

"Don't lose that card," he said, returning my embrace. "I love you, son." Moments later, I watched him drive away in the snow. When I was pulled into the wilderness by Amulii, I felt like I was being kidnapped. Now that we'd been dropped off in a strange town hundreds of kilometers away, I felt like an adult. It was a crushing, lonely feeling, not at all the freedom I had expected when I was younger.

Two furry arms wrapped around my chest from behind and pulled me into a fuzzy warmth. I shut the door before anyone saw and looked back at him, tears trailing my cheeks. There was so much to process, but it was nice having someone to help me through it.

"You are cold. Come back to bed, and I will keep you warm."

"Are you still mad at me?" I asked, following him back across the room. My bare, human feet ached against the freezing wood floors. I wished I could shift back to maw'cha just to avoid the discomfort, but until I could make a smoother shift, I couldn't risk it.

Amulii forced a silly canine grin before diving under the downy blankets, causing the bed to make a cracking sound under his weight. I joined him, playing the little spoon again as he wrapped his arms and legs around me.

"Not with you," he whispered, his cold, wet nose touching the nape of my neck. "I am angry at this world. I do not want to be here anymore, especially now."

"I had to get us away from there."

"I understand that, and I am sorry about yesterday. I was not thinking clearly." He gave me light, repeated sniffs, and I could feel him stiffen as he ground his hips against me. "After you took control, I had a hard time accepting it. This morning, though, if you want to take control in another way, I will be okay with it."

He chose now of all times to give me an offer I had a hard time refusing. It wasn't as though I found our usual sex boring because he always made it enjoyable, often making sure I'd have at least a couple mind-blowing climaxes before he finished. I'd learned a lot about what got him going through our many lengthy sessions of foreplay, and I wondered if I could give him the same careful attention with me on top.

"We can't do it right now. It takes too long for me to go back to being human, and we're gonna have to leave soon."

"Practice is the only way you are going to learn," Amulii said, slowly inching his fingers down the front of my pants. "We are nice and clean now, and I am offering myself to you." His voice lowered as he cupped my groin. "You do not want to say no to that, do you?"

Within seconds of him touching me, I shifted into my maw'cha form, ripping away my torn clothes before throwing him back into the mattress. Amulii grinned moments before my tongue was in his mouth. His submissiveness made me feel a bit odd, but he seemed to enjoy it, at least for the moment.

"Beg for it," I growled, baring my teeth. It didn't sound nearly as sexy coming from me as it did him. My tongue traced his neck before my canines closed around fur and flesh. It was hard enough to hurt, but soft enough to not draw blood. Just the way he liked it.

I'd wanted to say that to him for a while though, and he was eager to play along. He rolled over and presented his raised tail to me.

"I do not need to," he said, turning back while flashing his eyebrows.

Later that morning, after a breakfast of cold raw roast, I shifted back into human form. It didn't take as long as the first time but still required a couple hours of frustrating concentration. We couldn't keep shifting like this with the little food we had left. I needed to stock up before we made the long trek to Calgary.

Once we were there, I'd need to find a butcher and see if I could get the parts they would normally throw away. If I couldn't satisfy our nutritional needs, survival mode would kick in for both of us. Two hungry, desperate werewolves in a city full of humans and pets was a disaster waiting to happen.

We showered separately. After our last bout of lovemaking, Amulii seemed content, but I was embarrassed. It took about three minutes before accidentally going all the way in, locking us together as I finished. My new anatomy was going to take some getting used to, and I'd certainly expected to last longer than that. Hopefully, it was something else that would get better with practice.

I had a hard time gauging him afterward because he didn't say much. He had a goofy look on his face when we got out of bed, and I kept getting the feeling that my poor performance had been unfairly judged.

We dressed in winter clothes, and I helped Amulii put on his new shoes. It was about eighty kilometers to the city, but even as humans, long-distance sprints weren't an issue. The snow would be, though, and I'd need to purchase a tent to keep us dry when we set up camp.

I grabbed my clothes and backpack, and we walked out into the freezing, blustery wind.

///

We traveled east, away from the roads, after running into a few men and women in blue uniforms. It was only common sense that they'd look in the direction Dad's truck went. There were only a few groups of them, mainly focusing their infrared instruments and drones on the wooded areas around town.

I wondered how many of them knew what we looked like in our human forms. They were looking for beasts, not two young men walking by. To our relief, they never gave us a second glance. That made Amulii more confident.

He carried our tent on his back, and I upgraded my small wilderness bag to a hiking pack. It was large enough to hold everything else we needed.

As uncomfortable as the cold weather was with no fur, it was nice to walk around and blend in with other humans for once. We even held hands as we made our way out of the small resort town, passing a few couples struggling against the wind while we strolled along unimpeded. I felt a sense of pride having a man like him next to me.

We traveled for over thirty kilometers, not saying much as the gale continued to howl around us. We were lucky to have the speed and stamina of the wolf in this form. The city skyline appeared as tiny dots of color in the distance, flickering through the haze of falling snow, and I decided we'd gone far enough for today.

Pitching a tent in a blizzard was much more difficult than I thought it would be, but with Amulii's help, we got it set up before crawling inside for the night. I pulled out the raw meat I bought from the store earlier, forgetting it would freeze by the time we ate.

"This is gonna be so gross," I said, holding the solid brick of steak to my mouth. My smaller canines had a tough time breaking through, but I could finally get a proper mouthful. Our noses were numb and the scent of blood was locked away in ice, thankfully preventing us from shifting as we ate. "Oh God," I muttered, disgusted when the slush-textured flesh melted into gristle between my teeth.

"Warming crystals would have come in handy here," Amulii said, disappointed as he chewed through bloody chunks of ice.

"At least tomorrow, we'll be warm and have decent food to eat."

Amulii took another bite and gave me a more serious stare.

"I am worried." He tossed the last piece of meat into his mouth, chewing while he spoke. "There was a reason why I was so desperate to get us to Segolia."

After struggling to tear off some frozen wet wipes, we cleaned our hands and mouths.

"It's about whatever's going on in my brain, right?"

He nodded. "I do not know if your condition is better, or if you will get worse. The longer it takes to get you to my world, the longer this goes unchecked. Right now, everything appears fine, and you have my chélanc and my bond to help. But this is all unknown to me."

I hadn't thought about that in weeks. The voice in my head vanished after the bond, and my mind had never been so clear. However, after Amulii said that, I thought back over the last few weeks. Had I noticed anything out of the ordinary? It was like running through an empty web and feeling imaginary spiders crawling all over my body. Once it was back in my mind, it was all I could focus on.

"I feel fine," I reassured, placing a hand on his shoulder. "But I'll tell you if something doesn't feel right, okay? Maybe we'll figure out something else if the voice comes back."

"I thought getting caught by the hunters would be the worst fate for me, but now, the worst thing I could ever go through is losing you. We have to be careful, and I will teach you meditation to quiet your mind."

Hearing Amulii's voice was reassuring, though he didn't sugarcoat what could go wrong. Did I make the right decision, or should we have taken our chances at Maligne?

Whatever consequences we faced going forward, it would be on me now.

CHAPTER TWENTY-TWO

OLD FLAME

The curtains were drawn, and the motel room had an ingrained dreariness, lit only by the glow of an older CRT television. It wasn't the prettiest place, but it was cheap, and we could stay indefinitely without the owners asking too many questions.

Amulii sat on the king-sized bed, his back against the headboard as he stared at the screen. His glazed-over eyes reflected the cartoon he couldn't tear himself away from. It was the only thing he cared to do lately.

We'd been in Calgary for over a month, and we weren't adjusting well. I thought coming back to my home city would make me happier, but I felt as miserable as he did. We'd only gone outside a few times, and when we did, the bustling metropolis was a direct assault on every heightened sense.

I sauntered over green shag carpeting and sat on one of the ugly yellow vinyl chairs that surrounded a table near the window. The room was stuck five decades in the past, which made everything even more drab, if a little unsettling.

Maw'cha got depressed like humans, and since we hadn't been physically active while eating a deficient diet, we were losing interest in everything. It had been at least two weeks since we'd had sex, neither of us feeling particularly in the mood. Amulii wasn't lying about the cost of keeping the human form. Sometimes the hunger would get so intense we'd eat the butcher's scraps I kept stocked in the mini-fridge, just in case. As I watched Amulii drift off again before snapping alert, his face emotionless, I couldn't help but feel guilty.

We couldn't stay here much longer, or we'd probably wither away. Now that we had laid low for a while, I was confident we'd be able to leave and head further southwest. Perhaps we could find another forest cave to live in undisturbed until December.

I glanced at my cell phone on the table. It had been charging all day but remained off. Despite knowing the risks, I contemplated getting my fix of social media for a few minutes. Any connection outside of this room was welcome. It didn't matter if we were in a cave or a seedy motel, this was the human world, and we had no business being in it.

I grabbed the phone and held it to my face. It would just be a few minutes, what could it hurt? After a few more minutes of contemplation, I pressed the side button until the screen lit up. It was the first time I'd used it since moving, and as the cell phone cycled on, fifty messages and a voicemail notification popped up.

Skimming through all the texts would take too much time, but the voicemail may have been important since I rarely got them. The phone clicked, and the menu blasted through the speaker. Despite being AWOL for two months, there was only one message. It was from back in early November when shit hit the fan.

Mike's voice came through the speaker, and it got hard to breathe.

"Hey man. I know you're probably still pissed, but you haven't replied to my texts. So, I'll just tell you, and hopefully you hear it.

I miss you. It's so boring without you here, and I'd give anything to have another movie night. I know I was an ass, but please don't be mad at me anymore. Come visit sometime, or maybe I can drive up there if you want. Alright, I won't make this too long, so have a good one. I hope you're doing okay."

The message ended, and I turned off the phone, setting it back on the table. Tears soaked my face as I wondered what he thought of me now that I hadn't spoken to him in months. It was too dangerous to visit, but I wanted to see him again. Hearing his voice for the first time in a while made this forced isolation even worse.

I stood and wiped my face before crossing the thick carpet toward the bed. Amulii gave me a sad smile and held out his arms, which I gladly fell into.

///

"I'll be back in a couple hours. Are you sure you don't want to come with me?" I wrapped my arms around Amulii's neck as he sat on the bed, his eyes once again glued to the television set. I planted a kiss on his scruffy cheek, trying to grab his attention.

He shook his head. "You go. I am tired."

"Okay," I said, walking toward the door. As I stepped outside, I took another look at the melancholy distance in Amulii's expression. Today, I was going to brave the inner city to get him something special.

Amulii always stayed in the room these days while I went shopping. He couldn't handle the chaos that I grew up with, and while I wanted to get him out of that room, I was glad he didn't take me up on my offer today. Tomorrow was the twenty-sixth of January, his birthday. He probably thought I'd forgotten, considering he only mentioned it once back at the cave.

I wanted to get him a cake, but it couldn't be the usual because I discovered what too much refined sugar does to us.

Two Maw'cha, One Toilet could have been the title of the horror show that played out our first night in the motel. I had picked up milkshakes and some fast food to celebrate being human again. What happened later would affirm that I was merely wearing human skin, nothing more. It was terrible, and at one point, we both needed to use the bathroom at the same time. I had to go in the tub.

Never again.

Amulii said it was the first time he'd ever been sick like that in almost eighty years of being alive. It made me wonder what the hell was in human food to make two nearly immortal werewolves almost shit themselves to death. After some unfortunate experiments, I found out it was the sugar. It was in everything, apparently, and the best course of action was to avoid any food other than meat.

The birthday cake I had in mind was custom ordered from the deli, and I was on my way to pick it up. It was four smoked briskets that I'd stack on top of one another and put some candles in. It was Amulii's favorite human food, but nothing came close to Dad's.

I held my stomach as it growled. The thought of a nice brisket made me hungry, but I knew it wouldn't satisfy. It had been a week since I last shifted and ate raw meat. When I got back to the motel, I'd need to grab some entrails and organs from the fridge in order to stop me from losing my mind again.

Keeping to the back alleys and away from the busier streets made traversing this part of Calgary easier. I was close to my old house, and part of me wanted to see it again. But I knew it wasn't a good idea for my mental health to see new people living in the place I'd called home since middle school.

After an hour of walking the long way, I rounded the street corner to see a familiar red-brick building. A giant sandwich and an olive were printed on the blue vinyl awning that shaded the entrance.

Nostalgia hit me as I strolled up to the automatic doors. They slid open, and the fragrance of my early adolescence wafted into my nose.

My friends and I frequented this place on the weekends before hanging out at the skatepark. They had the best Reubens in the province.

Orange booths lined the outer walls, familiar high schoolers packed into them. Some of the varsity football team was there, and I wondered if Mike was among them. I wouldn't risk it, but it would have been nice to at least catch a glimpse of him. It's not like he'd recognize me anymore.

It was disconcerting to walk through this place feeling like a complete stranger—an outcast everyone would fear if they knew what I was. Barely being able to hang onto my human form every day made these trips more harrowing than routine. I longed to go back to the wild and feel the power of my paws against the snow as I hunted.

God. When did I completely slip away from humanity?

After tearing a number from the ticket dispenser, I waited away from the crowd that gathered around the display case. This place was always busy, and the meaty scents tantalized my nose, making me hungrier than I already was. Though I had only planned on picking up and leaving, I had to order a sandwich for old time's sake.

"Seventy-three," an older woman I didn't recognize in a black hairnet called out, and I stepped to the counter.

"I called in an order," I said. I'd already paid over the phone, giving them my real name by mistake instead of the fake one I'd often use. After glancing at the rowdy teenagers in line, I lowered my voice. "For Alex Hunt."

"What was your name again, hon?" the lady shouted, cupping her hand behind her right ear to hear me better.

"Alex," I said, looking both ways before lowering my voice again, "Hunt. Also, could I get a classic Reuben to go?"

"You got it, sweetie."

"Alex?"

Mike's voice. I swallowed hard and turned toward my estranged best friend, whose gorgeous brown eyes narrowed to confusion.

"Mike," I responded, trying to catch my breath. "What's up?"

"What's up?" he asked, shaking his head. "I—I kept staring, wanting to say something, but you look so different. Dude—"

"Uh, yeah. I guess I'm a bit of a late bloomer." I flashed back to all of those awkward conversations I had with Mom.

"You're taller than me now, and how'd you get so ripped? It's only been three months. You're not taking gear, are you?" My anxiety returned with every one of his questions. I didn't know how to answer any of them, and I was terrible at making up stories on the fly. His cheerfulness faded as he studied me. "You don't look too happy to see me. Are you still mad?"

"Of course not," I said, trying to keep my voice low.

"Then why didn't you return any of my messages?"

"A lot of things have been happening in my life. I've been spending most of my time out in the woods camping and stuff. I don't get a cell signal out there, and the internet is slow at the house. I guess I kind of fell away from everything, especially after our fight." I lightly punched his shoulder. "You're the one that didn't respond to me first."

"I was upset for like two weeks, but I missed you. Everyone misses you." His face brightened again as he turned to the crowd. "They're gonna freak when they see you now."

I grabbed his arm. "Don't tell anyone I'm here."

"Did you move back? Are you coming back to school?"

"No, just visiting. We're gonna be leaving soon." Talking to him again made me smile. I forgot what it was like to have conversations with other people my age. Amulii and I were close, but he was still an alien from another world.

"So, you're here, your family's here, and no one came by to visit?"

"My parents are still in Jasper; I'm just passing through."

His unusual, sly reaction meant I'd need to make up more stories.

"Alex," the woman from the counter called out while holding up two large bags. It was perfect timing, allowing me a few minutes of reprieve from Mike's grilling. As nice as this was, I still had to be careful with what I said. Mike could always tell when I was lying. He followed close as I paid the cashier for the Reuben.

"Let's go somewhere." His firm hand fell on my shoulder. "You owe me after ditching our plans that day."

I wanted so badly to say yes, but I knew how this would end. With my sensitive hearing, it was hard to hang out at all the loud places we used to frequent. Plus, there was always the chance I'd accidentally shift. I wouldn't make that mistake again. Amulii wouldn't be there to stop me, and if I did something terrible to Mike, I'd never be able to live with myself. "I can't. I wish I could, but someone's waiting for me."

"No." He grabbed me by the arm and pulled. "Don't blow me off anymore. We've been close too long for this shit." Typical Mike. My refusal only bolstered his insistence. "If you don't wanna go anywhere, then let me drive you. Still don't have your license?"

Did I want to go back to that motel room alone with Amulii as we sat and watched TV like a pair of lifeless husks, or could I spare fifteen minutes to spend time with the person I had been aching to see for months?

"No, I don't. Never had time to get one." As we walked outside, I couldn't stick to the alleyways and backstreets; instead, we strolled right into the busiest area. I coughed as fumes wafting from exhaust pipes suffocated me, and the sounds of tires, horns, and people shouting made me want to cover my ears and run. I tried to pretend everything was fine while we strolled along the frozen walkway, but Mike caught on quickly.

"Are you okay?"

"Yeah," I grunted, squinting my eyes as an ambulance rolled by, its sirens blaring. It was like hearing shockwaves from an explosion over and over again. Nothing about civilization suited what I had become.

The area I used to rollerblade in as a younger teen was now an alien hellscape.

"Alex? Hello? Where are we going?" Mike's question startled me. Was he talking the whole time and I couldn't hear him?

"Uh, Lodgepole Heights Motel," I said, coughing again as a diesel truck rolled by. "That's where we're staying."

Mike grinned. "That's the second time you've said 'we're.' A cheap motel and no parents." I knew where he was going with this. "You're gettin' laid, aren't you? Is she someone you met in Jasper?"

"Oh boy," I muttered, opening the door of his car before sliding onto the ripped leather seat. I placed the bags of food on the floor and pulled the seatbelt over my chest, buckling it in place. The vehicle was a clunky old mustang with faded silver paint peeling from the hood to the roof. I'd never felt safe in that thing, and I was surprised it still ran at all. When Mike jumped in and started it up, I remembered why I hated riding with him. The obnoxiously loud muffler drowned out any conversations we'd have. It was a hundred times worse now as my head pounded with each rumble and pop.

"Well?" Mike shouted, putting the gear in first before peeling out onto the road. "Who is she?"

I blushed as I tried to come up with a way to ease him into the secret I'd been holding onto for years. I didn't want to keep screaming *I'm gay* when we could barely hear each other, turning what might be a serious moment into some kind of cheesy comedy sketch.

"I'll explain when we get there."

After several minutes of feeling like my head was being repeatedly struck by mallets, we pulled into the parking lot. When he cut the engine, all sound faded save for a persistent ring that lingered for a minute. He opened the door, but I grabbed his arm, pulling him back inside.

"Wait." I couldn't let him go in that room. "We need to talk."

"What's going on with you? You've had this look on your face like I'm taking you to a firing squad or something."

"I'm not with a girl," I blurted out, looking down at the deli bags. It was better to rip this bandage off rather than draw it out. "I'm not into girls. I never was."

A wave of heat traveled down my face to my body, followed by a chill. I could almost feel his stare, but I didn't want to look at him. Was he judging me? Did he feel betrayed? Maybe he was disgusted since I'd slept over at his house so often, sometimes in bed with him.

"Alex—"

"I'm with a guy. Sorry for the bombshell," I muttered, opening the door before grabbing my bags.

"Hold on," Mike said, grabbing my hand, pulling me back down into the seat. For whatever reason, he seemed more devastated than shocked. "Why? Why didn't you tell me all these years?"

This wasn't what I expected. For once, the worst hadn't happened.

"Well, I mean, it was hard for me. I didn't want to believe it for a long time, and my dad had a hand in that too. Plus it would just be weird for us."

"No it wouldn't," he shouted, surprising me. He caught himself, lowering his voice. "I mean . . . I would have understood. God, you don't act gay. I didn't know."

I looked at him and laughed. "Seriously?"

"You know what I mean. I guess it would have been nice to know," he said, looking at his lap.

"Being gay just means I like guys—it doesn't mean I turn into a stereotype."

"I know, man." He looked back up and seemed to force a smile. "I wanna meet him," Mike said, opening his door again.

"That's probably not—"

He slammed the door shut, cutting me off mid-sentence and stood outside, staring at me through the dirty windshield while crossing his arms. I grabbed the bags and opened the door.

"I'm not going away. I haven't seen you in like four months, and I wanna meet this guy. Size him up and all."

This was going terribly wrong, and part of me wanted to piss him off so that he'd leave. The other part of me craved his company. As long as we remained human, this probably wouldn't be so bad.

"Interesting choice of words," I said, a grin returning to my face. He blushed as he realized what I meant. "Alright, but you should probably know something before you meet him."

"Is he in a dress or somethin'?"

A snort left my nose as I tried to picture that, but my brain wouldn't cooperate. Had Mike always been this ignorant?

"No. This guy is . . . obviously not what *you're* expecting. He gets nervous around other people, so just be patient with him." I noticed him hesitate for a moment. "You know you don't have to do this."

"I'm not nervous or anything. This is just a bad part of town. I'm afraid to leave my car out here."

"I promise, no one's going to look twice at this piece of shit," I said, patting him on the back as we walked along the salt-covered cement path to the door of the motel.

"Not everyone's got doctor money."

I reached for the knob and took a deep breath, hoping this would work out, but I also knew Amulii's temperament. The door slid open, and I noticed he hadn't moved from the bed since I left. Another pang of guilt hit me as I watched his gloomy focus slowly shift from the cartoon he was watching. Amulii's eyes went wide as I walked into the room with Mike trailing so close, he was almost touching me. I could sense the nervousness from both of them.

"Hey Amulii, this is Mike, my best friend. I ran into him while picking up a surprise."

"Amulii," Mike said as he jogged over, extending a hand. "That's a cool name." He looked back at me and mouthed the words "He's fucking huge."

"Greetings," Amulii said, grabbing Mike's hand. "It is nice to meet the best friend of Alex." He flashed a genuine smile, and I breathed a sigh of relief.

Mike turned away from Amulii and wandered to the table before plopping down on one of the chairs. Though he grinned, I couldn't help but notice he was holding back tears. Perhaps it was his allergies. I hadn't yet vacuumed all of our shed fur from the carpet.

"I wanted to surprise you with this tomorrow, but I couldn't wait," I said, placing the bags on the bed in front of him. In all the excitement of seeing Mike again, I'd forgotten candles. I leaned in and planted a kiss on his lips. "Happy birthday, on'she."

His face suddenly regained a bit of color, and it had been a while since I'd seen him smile like that. Perhaps this wasn't the worst idea.

"You remembered. This means so much." His breathy voice quieted as he leaned in. "Later, I will return this gesture, if you are willing." He returned a much more passionate kiss, but my eyes kept wandering to Mike, who awkwardly glanced down at his fidgety hands resting on the table. I broke away and walked across the room, able to stand a little more confident now. I realized at that moment that I was finally happy being who I was. Mike's acceptance only bolstered that. "Both of us have been kind of down lately, and I had planned on trying to make the evening special."

"Oh," Mike said, shooting up out of the chair, fumbling with his keys which fell on the floor. "That's why you didn't want me to come in. Dude, I'm sorry. I, uh, didn't mean to stop you guys from, you know—" He smirked, flashing his brows. "Doin' it."

"Shut up and sit down." I laughed, pushing his chair toward him with my foot before picking up his keys and tossing them across the room. They landed with a jingle on the king-sized bed.

"Finally, the Alex I know," Mike said, taking a seat.

Amulii jumped out of bed and walked over, setting the bags of meat on the table before plopping down on another empty chair. I didn't expect him to be so ecstatic about this, but the way he looked at Mike was promising.

"So, let me guess," Mike said, meeting Amulii's eyes. "You're his personal trainer, and one day you were spotting him when you noticed a slight bulge in his pants."

Amulii looked over at me and shrugged. "I . . . do not understand those words in such a context."

"Goddammit, Mike." I let out a laugh while opening the bag on the table. "No, we didn't meet like that, but your description makes me really curious. I want to look at your browser history."

Mike actually started to blush. "Don't read too much into that."

"Do you want some brisket?" I asked, though I didn't know what I'd serve it to him on. Amulii and I usually ate with our hands.

"Nah, I ate before running into you." He gritted his teeth. "Oh shoot. I kinda left the guys back at the deli without saying anything."

Amulii picked up an entire slab of meat and began gnawing at it. Mike watched, mouth wide, as Amulii made a seven-pound brisket disappear in moments. My stomach growled, and I contemplated eating the sandwich. However, after another few seconds I recognized the signs of real hunger. I froze as the room dimmed a reddish color.

"You okay?" Mike asked, rubbing the back of my neck. His voice sounded far away.

I tried to hold it down. If I could just get through this . . .

"Yeah, I'm fine." My tone shifted to a growl, and Amulii snapped toward me.

"Mike." Amulii stood, dropping his meal. "You must go."

"I can handle it," I said. A prickling sensation nipped at my skin, and I jumped up before running toward the bathroom.

"What's going on?" Mike's voice called out from behind.

Of all the times for this to happen. I'd been under so much stress lately that this came on sooner than I thought it would. Mike must have been the breaking point for me. I had to eat, but I couldn't eat bloody entrails and organs in front of him. After sprinting into the bathroom, I slammed the door shut behind me, locking it.

"What's wrong with you?" Mike asked, his footsteps approaching.

"I am sorry." Amulii's whispered voice was muffled as he kept it low. "You cannot stay."

"Why? What's wrong with him?"

Amulii said nothing for a few seconds before tapping on the bathroom door.

"It is up to you. Do you wish to tell him?"

"No," I shouted, my tone growling as I fought to hold down the bloodlust.

I heard Mike's tongue click from the other side. "Fine. Keep it all to yourself like you have for years. What the fuck do I matter anymore?" His footsteps faded toward the entrance of the motel room. "All I've thought about is you for months, but I guess since you got a boyfriend now, you can throw me to the wolves." The door squealed open before slamming shut.

"Fuck," I cried out, removing my pants and shirt before opening the door and running for the fridge. I reached into the bags of dark blood, pulling out organs. On cue, the shift happened, and Amulii put his arm around me. "Of course." Human whispers became bestial grunts as my body grew and changed. I bit into a floppy red liver, blood pouring from the sides of my lower jaw.

"I should join you. I do not want to wait for the hunger." Bones snapped and popped beside me, as Amulii shifted.

"I guess that's it," I whined out, finishing what I was eating. "That was the last good thing from my human life the maw'cha destroyed. I guess nothing's really tying me to this world anymore."

"Alex," Amulii said, nuzzling my neck.

The door slammed open and both of us jerked our heads toward the entrance.

"Forgot my ke—" Mike froze in the doorway, his eyes and mouth wide. He took a shaky step back, but not before Amulii lunged at him, pulling him back inside before closing the door as someone walked by outside.

"Oh fuck, please," he cried out, trying to pull away from Amulii's grip. When he wouldn't stop screaming, Amulii placed one of his massive hands over Mike's mouth.

"Calm yourself," Amulii grunted, shaking the poor guy until he went limp.

I dropped the bag of entrails onto the floor and pressed a hand to my forehead. "Be careful with him, please."

"Will you stop screaming?" Amulii asked, his hand still tight across Mike's mouth. His bulging eyes shot sideways toward me before he gave a silent nod. "I will let you go, but you cannot scream."

He let his hand slip from Mike's mouth before releasing him completely.

"A—Alex?" he choked out.

"I guess I've got more shit to tell you." I trudged across the room and placed a hand on his shoulder, causing him to flinch. "I didn't want you to see this."

"How? Did—did he bite you or something?" His voice squeaked as he watched Amulii sit back down at the table.

"What is with humans and your fascination with being bitten?" Amulii asked, his brow furrowing as his gaze met mine. "Is this more we should explore in bed?"

"Amulii, Jesus Christ," I muttered, before turning my attention toward Mike. "No, it wasn't a bite, but he did do this to me. I don't wanna get into it right now." I patted him on the back with my rough, padded hand. He tensed, looking at the door as if he were ready to make a mad dash for it. I knew I had to do something to calm him down. "Look at me," I said jokingly. "Watch this." My best friend studied my movements with terrified suspicion. "I'm a gay werewolf," I said in a bright, growled lisp, shaking jazz hands in front of me while opening my mouth wide, letting my long tongue flop out and off to the side. "Surpriiiiise."

Mike looked away and snorted as a smile spread across his face. "Dude," he whispered before breaking all the way into loud laughter.

"That went better than I expected," Amulii said as I lay in his arms. I shifted back to human so I could walk Mike out to his car and say goodbye. The transformation was much easier now since I'd gotten the hang of it. Less painful too.

Amulii spent the night in maw'cha form, which made him happier. Tomorrow was his birthday, and I didn't care if he wanted to stay like that. We were inside all the time, anyway.

"I don't know," I said, fixating on the TV. I'd been watching for a while, but I wasn't paying attention. My mind had been elsewhere for the last hour and a half after Mike left.

"He seemed to be okay." Amulii gave me a nudge. "Come on, smile. It was a good day."

"Yeah," I whispered, the intense conversation we had in the parking lot before he left repeating in my head. I didn't want to trouble Amulii about that tonight, especially before his birthday.

The moments passed and he nodded off next to me. I flipped through the channels but stopped when I saw a mugshot of Dad on the news with *Trouble in Jasper* as a headline caption. The heaviness in my chest got worse as I turned up the volume.

". . . this afternoon. Forty-five-year-old Robert Hunt was detained for aiding the escape of a person of interest in the two thousand and nine slaying of Joseph Davis. Hunt, a former sheriff's branch officer, was peacefully removed from his home after a warrant was issued for his arrest."

"Amulii," I yelled, shaking him awake in time to see a video of my father being escorted to a police car in handcuffs. He sat up and stared at the television, rubbing his eyes.

"His son, Alexander Hunt, is wanted for aggravated assault and two attempted murders. He and the other suspect are traveling together and are still at large. If you see them or have any information on their whereabouts, do not approach. Contact the police immediately. They are considered extremely dangerous."

An image of Amulii and me near the lake appeared on the screen, and I knew the plans I had patiently made over the weeks to get us out of the city were no longer feasible. They knew we were here, and though I had changed since that picture was taken, they had Amulii's face. The city was now a trap.

The news feed changed to pre-recorded video of Jasper's mayor standing next to a rotund older man with a gray beard and cowboy hat.

"I recognize that man," Amulii said, leaning in to get a better view. "The one in the silly hat."

I turned the volume up as the old man spoke, glowering into the camera.

"I'm offering a large sum of money to whoever turns these *people* in. One hundred thousand dollars goes to the first person who calls us with leads that result in their capture." His southern drawl made the ire in his tone less impactful, but it was intimidating enough. "We know they're in Calgary somewhere, but—"

Amulii turned the television off, his wild eyes locking with mine. "Now what?"

CHAPTER TWENTY-THREE

Nowhere Warm

I paced the room, holding my bag while frantically shoving our belongings inside. The level-headed leader I tried to portray whimpered like an injured dog the moment they threatened my family.

"Who was that guy?" I asked, stopping to peek out the window before dashing to the other end of the room to grab more of our things.

"I do not know. I have seen him sometimes with the other hunters."

Paranoia scattered my thoughts as I cut the lights and cracked the curtains open again. It was black outside, save for a few streetlamps dotting the road.

"Shit," I whispered, wiping my eyes. "Now they're going after my parents to smoke us out."

"Alex, I—"

"Just stop," I interrupted, holding a hand to my forehead. "Whoever these people are, they have the police, the mayor, and news stations in their pockets. They might even have the whole fucking province.

They've got Dad, and they know we're here." That news broadcast—it was a re-air from six o'clock earlier that evening. "They might even know exactly where we are by now."

"Calm yourself," Amulii said, pointing to my arms, now covered in fur.

"Who cares? We have to get out of here. We may as well shift back, so we don't freeze to death out there." My voice went from human anger to booming as I finished my transformation. "Grab what we need. I may as well take this," I continued, snatching the blanket from the bed so we'd have more to keep us warm.

Amulii remained quiet as he gathered our clothes. I tried to clip the pack harness around me, but it didn't fit in this form. I let the straps hang loose before draping the blanket around my neck.

We were becoming experts at packing and running away. I'd have given anything for a few months of settling in one place without worrying all the time.

"Let's go," I muttered, stepping outside.

The night was calm, which both helped and hindered us. It would have been harder to track us in a snowstorm, but it was easier to travel quickly when the weather was mild. I chose this motel because it was on the south side, near the river. There were trees everywhere and no buildings beyond them, so if we had to make a maw'cha escape, there was less chance of being seen. However, beyond the trees was open plain making it harder for us to stay hidden.

Amulii and I slid across the shallow, half-frozen river, heading for the woods. We were out in the open here, exposed, but at least it was dark enough that we had a chance.

As my paws left the ice, I stopped and looked back at the bright skyline in the distance.

"We cannot stop," Amulii said, turning back toward me. "We must keep going."

"What are we doing?" There were no tears in my eyes, but despair chipped away at me by the second. "If that guy has the police under his control, I can't leave my dad. If I turn myself in, I don't know what they're gonna do to me, but if I don't, what's gonna happen to him?"

"You are not considering that, are you?" Amulii said, rushing to get in front of me. "No, you will not do this. They will kill you."

"If you had a chance to save your dad, what would you do?"

"I would not sacrifice myself. That would make everything pointless. Parents give their lives so their children can live. My father gave up his life so I could live, and I will not throw that gift away. Robert knew the risks, and he did this for you."

"Did he really? He didn't know that you killed someone, or that I tore a guy's arm off."

"We have to keep going. We can discuss this later." The moment he turned around, I heard a whistle before something jabbed me in the calf. A second later, my entire leg went numb as I reached behind and pulled out a pink-feathered dart.

"Amulii," I cried out, limping ahead of him away from the woods. "They're here, run."

Invisible sedatives zipped at us from every direction. Another dart hit my shoulder, and I was already too sluggish to dodge anything more. I turned to the right, and men in uniform ran in a line as they emerged from the trees. Crunching snow from the left caught my ears as more approached. When a third dart hit my lower back through the blanket, I lost my balance and fell to the ground. Amulii tried to lift me from behind.

"Alex," he shouted, his speech slurred. I glanced up to see two pink darts jutting from the side of his neck. "I . . ." His eyes rolled back and he fell on top of me.

///

It was a strange feeling going in and out of consciousness, like I was both floating through the air and sinking into the ground. When I opened my eyes, the men and women who were once standing at a distance were on top of us, observing with their guns still drawn.

"The lead we got was right," one of the men said, kneeling to look at my face. The vision of him blurred, and I couldn't make out any features. "Alert the other squads; they were on the east side."

Something clamped hard around my neck, and I felt Amulii's hefty body being dragged off of me.

My nose went numb after being sprayed in the face with a strong-scented chemical. After that, every scent vanished, and I was still awake enough to feel what was happening to me.

Though hazy, I could make out the twin red halos of taillights as several men lifted and slid me across the textured lining of a van floor. Amulii wasn't around. Had they put him in a separate vehicle? They were so efficient that my mind had no time to catch up to our predicament. I still didn't understand what happened.

People talked amongst themselves before shutting the rear doors, but I couldn't understand a word. The thing on my neck emitted a low-frequency noise that canceled out all other sounds. My ears were stuffy, like they were filled with water.

As a maw'cha, I may as well have been blind without the ability to hear or smell. Not only did these people know our exact location, but they knew how to completely shut us down.

The world faded to black again as the vehicle I was in rocked into gear. I thought I'd only closed my eyes for a second, but somehow, the van turned into a gurney being wheeled into someplace cold. I squinted as white lines of fluorescent lighting passed over my head, one after the other.

There was a pulsing ache all over my body as I regained more of my consciousness and muscle movement. A blonde woman wearing a surgical mask and a white coat glanced at me for a moment before her eyes darted to the side. She spoke frantically, but her voice was a garbled mess. A male voice responded to my left, but I couldn't turn my head enough to see him. Armed guards surrounded me as they continued wheeling the bed deeper into whatever this place was.

There was a heaviness on my arms, and I jerked one of them upward, breaking thick leather straps that held it in place. The bed stopped and everyone scattered. Before I could blink, there were five unsteady rifles pointed at my head. I froze and swallowed hard, letting my arm fall back to my side.

The bed moved at a slower pace this time as every eye in the hall watched me, barely blinking. Every instinct urged me to break free, but I had to control it. All it took was one anxious trigger finger to end me, and these guys were all on edge. I couldn't smell the fear from them, but the wary-eyed expressions and shaky sideways glances they'd give one another were enough of an indicator.

The doctors wheeled me into a room surrounded by thick glass. It looked like a cross between a medical examination room and a chemistry lab. A smooth black countertop took up the wall space that wasn't glass, and brown cabinets lined the area above it.

The device around my neck snapped loose, and two men in uniform kept the barrels of their guns pointed at my face. A rush of sound filled my ears.

"Alex? Are you . . . in there?" a man asked, his voice sounding familiar. I couldn't quite pick up on the tone as everything was still ringing.

"Where am I?" I was hoarse from whatever sedatives they'd used on me.

"You're safe now," he said, laying his hand on mine.

"Who are you?" He removed the mask, and I exhaled in relief. The last time I saw him, he wore pale make-up with fake blood dripping from his mouth. This time, he was dressed in green scrubs with a white lab coat. He was well into middle age but still rather good-looking, the salt and pepper graying of his hair making him look more distinguished than old. He'd always taken good care of himself. "Dr. Mitchel. Thank God."

He reached for an otoscope hanging on the wall before inserting it into each ear. "This is incredible. I can't believe what I'm seeing."

The gunmen in blue uniforms at either side of me were even more alert than before. If I so much as breathed heavier, their eyes and hands twitched. When the barrel of one weapon grazed my forehead, I knew I needed to say something before someone killed me.

"Can you guys . . . not point those at me anymore?"

"He's fine," the doctor said, pointing to the door. "Wait outside until the examination is over."

The men said nothing as they lifted their weapons and walked out of the room.

"They'll shoot you if you try anything. I know you won't, but I need to warn you."

"What's going on? What is all this?"

"Your mother contacted me a couple of months ago, and what she told me about you—" He paused before shining the light of the scope in each eye. "I thought it was impossible. I'd always suspected the beast could spread this, but how?"

"Why the hell is Mom calling you?" I asked as he took my heavy arm in his hands, binding the upper half in a latex tourniquet.

"We've always been close colleagues, and after what happened at the party, I knew she could be my eyes and ears, letting me know what was happening between you and that creature." He grabbed electric clippers and shaved the fur from the inside of my elbow. "We had hunters out there for years, waiting for him to make another move. But we had no idea he could take human form. No wonder we weren't getting anywhere."

He sat the clippers down. "It looks like you're another one of his victims too, but he did something way more incredible than kill you. I promised your mom I'd do what I could to help."

From the small table next to him, he grabbed a syringe that lay beside a stand with eight vials. He ran his fingers across my shaved skin, finding a vein before swabbing the area. I cringed as he inserted the huge needle.

"I'm going to keep that promise, but if I'm going to fix you, I need to figure out how all of this works. Biologically, none of this should be possible. How does one rapidly transform, doubling or tripling in weight? Where does all that mass come from?"

"You're wasting your time." I shook my head. "Science can't explain this. I don't think anything in his world makes sense to us."

"His world?" He narrowed his eyes and grabbed another vial, collecting more of my valuable blood. I didn't want to elaborate on something I didn't know much about.

"Nothing," I muttered. He placed the last full tube on the rack and slid the needle out. He was going to put a bandage on it, but the bleeding stopped, and my fur began to grow back.

He raised his eyebrows in amazement.

"I knew about the rapid regeneration, but to see it in action—" he said as the fur finished growing. "I didn't know it was this fast. You have super strength, incredible senses, speed, and agility that rivals any living being on Earth, and you're able to heal in seconds. You're an unstoppable apex predator, and if there is a world full of beasts like you and that other one, we'll be in trouble if more pay us a visit."

Dr. Mitchel freed my other limbs from the straps I hadn't broken and grabbed a brown bottle sitting next to some paperwork on the table.

"But they have one major weakness. Hold out your hand, please," he said, unscrewing the lid while sucking a clear liquid up into an eyedropper. I did as he asked, and he released a tiny drop onto my padded skin. It began foam and sizzle as foul-smelling steam wisped from my hand. That was when my flesh blistered and fire shot up my arm.

I roared in pain, and the doctor rushed me to the sink.

"Wash it off," he said, turning the water on. "I didn't expect that violent of a reaction."

"What the fuck was that?" I growled, rinsing my hand. When I examined it, the small blister in the center where the liquid had touched me began to disappear.

"Silver nitrate," he said, wiping his hands with a paper towel. I'd gotten silver nitrate on me before in chemistry class, and all that resulted was a brown stain on my skin that lasted a few weeks. That tiny drop alone felt like I had shaken hands with Satan. "Your bodies have an awful reaction to silver, and no, not just silver bullets. Even when the metal contacts your skin, it can cause third-degree burns and worse."

"Let us go," I whined out, massaging the skin on my palm. "We just want to be left alone."

He leaned back and shook his head.

"You guys are in some big trouble right now. You're too dangerous to be free out there where you might kill someone."

"I've got it under control now, I swear. Amulii helped me learn to control it."

"Oh yeah. I'd almost forgotten the beast had a name."

"That beast is a person too."

"None of this is up to me," Dr. Mitchel said, placing a sympathetic hand on my arm. "Stand up and take off your clothes."

I'd been reduced to a lab animal they would examine and experiment on. Frightened and defeated, I removed my tattered shirt and pants, letting them fall to the floor.

"Christ almighty," he remarked as he examined me. It was humiliating, but far from the most embarrassed I'd ever been since meeting Amulii. He put on a fresh pair of rubber gloves and lifted my tail before sticking a Vaseline-coated plastic stick into my rectum.

"The fuck are you doing?" I asked, wanting to push him away, but my focus shifted to the men outside watching this happen through the glass.

"Relax, I'm just getting a sample," he said, removing the strange tool. "See? Quick and simple. So, how did this happen?"

I yanked my tail out of the doctor's hands and faced my rear to the wall so there wouldn't be any more surprises like that. He carefully placed the sample in a bag and sealed it before removing his gloves.

"I don't want to talk about it. I want to know if my dad and Amulii are okay. I want to know who you people are."

Our attention shifted through the glass when a few armed guards ran by before vanishing around the corner.

"Your friend made an enemy he shouldn't have. Did he ever tell you that he killed someone?"

I nodded, looking at my feet as I fidgeted.

"Well, the person he killed was the son of Daniel Davis. He's got bottomless pockets, and he's been funding this for the better part of a decade. He preferred the monster found and captured alive, and it's been my job to examine the samples left by your friend so I could get a better genetic understanding of the species. But he'd practically vanished for years until recently."

"Oh no," I whispered, feeling like I'd throw up any minute.

"So, you understand now," Dr. Mitchel said with a heavy sigh. "I don't know how much I can protect you after what you did, but I'm going to try. Mr. Davis is usually a reasonable man."

I turned away, holding my stomach.

"Liam's still alive?"

"Yes, though one arm short." For the moment, I was relieved. "He's been in rehabilitation and getting therapy after what happened. You're lucky you didn't kill him, because I wouldn't be able to save you."

"I have Amulii to thank for that. He's the one that stopped me. None of this sounds like him at all. He wouldn't kill someone without a good reason."

"I've seen pictures of the corpse, and it was pretty damning. Have you ever seen what a human looks like with an enormous chunk of their neck missing? That's what your friend did." He pulled his phone out to stop it from vibrating, glanced at it, then focused on me again. "None of this is up to me, anyway. He didn't kill one of *my* kids." The doctor ambled toward the door. "You should probably say goodbye to him because I don't think they're going to let him live."

"I don't want him to die," I said as tears swelled in my eyes. "Can't you do anything?"

"I'll try to get *you* out. That family has been waiting ten years to see justice done, and these people are from Texas."

I followed him into the hall, and the guards trailed close behind. We made a sharp turn left, and I saw a large, black lump of fur in an empty room through thick panes of glass. Amulii lay on the floor, tied to a hook by what appeared to be a wire.

The doctor swiped his clearance card, and the doors whirred and clanked. The sound of metal against metal reverberated throughout the mostly empty chamber.

"You have a couple of hours before Mr. Davis arrives. I don't know what's going to happen after that. I wish it didn't have to come to this."

I nodded and sauntered into the room before the doors clanked shut behind me. The patter of my claws against the frigid, metal floors echoed from the white concrete walls. Amulii didn't respond to my footsteps. My sense of smell hadn't returned, so I couldn't determine much about his emotional state beyond what I could see in front of me. What I'd thought was wire around his neck was something else entirely. The material was unfamiliar and transparent, like a bunch of fiber optic cables braided together. I tried to pull it apart until it broke, but it was too strong.

Amulii stirred awake, and I sat beside him.

"Alex," he whispered. They must have shot him up with more drugs to keep him sluggish and subdued. He sat up briefly before his head hit my shoulder. I moved him into my lap and stroked his head.

"It's okay," I choked out. "I should have listened to you and run for the portal. I thought I could save us."

Amulii turned so he could see my face. He struggled to lift his arms before letting them fall to his sides again.

"No." He shook his head. "Nothing was your fault. Nothing. All of my mistakes are catching up with me, and I got you tangled in all of this."

"Why did you really do it?" I asked, wiping my eyes. "I don't understand. None of what you told me sounds like you at all. Tell me the truth. Don't lie anymore."

A slight high-pitched whimper left his lips as his eyes watered.

"I am good at lying, it seems, and I did not care about the theft. Such a petty thing is not worth a life. It was what he took, and the little time I had to act that determined the outcome. The moment those crystals touched his skin, it was over for him."

"Crystals? Like the chélanc?"

"This was before the chélanc, but the concept was the same. Those were not for human contact. They were so I could experiment in this world using the potent magic stored in them while I wasn't studying humans. I was to report my findings to the shamans.

"There were many around the area that summer. If I had let that human go, he would have turned into a real monster. He was already showing signs as I held him, writhing in pain from what was happening to his body."

I lifted my hand to stop him. "If you knew what the crystal did to people, why did you break mine? If it was too late for me, why would you put on the act?"

"That was no act. The chélanc works gradually, not giving everything at once. It keeps the spirit intact, but too much can destroy a human. The night you changed, when I heard your howl, I knew time would be running out. In fact, when I saw how much of yourself you'd lost, I thought I was too late."

He grimaced and squeezed his eyes shut, his fur soaking up his tears.

"I should have never given you that cursed thing. The bond is a natural way for a maw'cha to change a human because both accept each other," he continued. "Therefore, there is no resentment or bloodlust. That is different for those turned by blood, as was the man's case—and yours. I lied when I said you were the first changed this way. It had been done a few times before, and I knew very well what would happen to that man."

He shook his head as if wanting to fling the thoughts from his mind. "I do not want to die knowing you will hate me again. Please, do not burden your mind with any more of this." He sniffed as I rubbed the side of his face.

"I want the whole story," I said, giving him a reassuring smile. "I don't care how bad it is, but I have to know."

After another tense moment of hesitation passed, he relented.

"Please remember that I struggled with this decision after it was done, if that means anything," he whispered as his ears clung tight to his head. "The blood ritual would have changed you temporarily without the bond, but eventually, it would have to take place. Being enchanted by the chélanc would have made you . . ." he nervously cleared his throat, "willing."

"Willing?" What he said sent a shudder through me. "Would— would make me willing? You wanted to brainwash me?"

"I cannot deny that was my original intent."

"Okay," I said, turning away from him.

"I have broken you," he said, reaching up to turn my chin. "It was the worst decision I ever made. I regretted it soon after slipping it around your neck for the first time, and as I grew to love you more, my decision haunted me."

The world crumbled, but I chose to know this truth. It would be my last memory of him, and that tore me apart.

"Now you understand. There was no time to make the bond with that man, and even if there was, his mind was ruined and could not be willing. Many lives would have been lost if I had let him go. I also knew what blood magic would do to you in time, but I thought I could control everything. I thought I understood more than I did. That ignorance cost you dearly." Amulii wailed, drenching my lap in his confession. "Your mother was right about me. I am a terrible creature, beyond redemption. I stole your life, and I ended an innocent man's. I deserve to spend eternity paying for what I have done."

Now that the truth lay bare, what could I do with it? Did I try and hate the person I loved more than anything, now weak in my lap, hours from death, or did I forgive him?

Amulii had the luxury of dying, whereas I would languish in a world I no longer belonged, imprisoned for life through no fault of my own. I could hate Amulii, even after he died, but what good would it do? It would only hurt me more.

The past was gone. I loved him, regardless of what he wanted to do to me back then. That wasn't him now.

"You know, it doesn't work like that," I said, pulling the heavy werewolf up against my chest as I rocked him side-to-side. "Everyone hopes there's eternal punishment for people who've done them wrong, but no one's punished forever for mistakes made in one stupid life. I don't know what the point of anything is, but I know I don't wanna live without you.

"Chélanc or not, I believe we were meant to be together, but I don't think this was the way it should have gone." A memory of Amulii's father returned for a moment. I could almost hear his voice in my head.

"You make mistakes. You're complicated, selfish, and manipulative, and you don't think anything through." I let out a painful laugh. "But that doesn't cancel out everything else I fell in love with."

His smile was just as warm as the day he looked at me from that boulder on Spirit Island. I wished I could go back to being ignorant. I wanted to return to a time when I thought Amulii was innocent, when none of this had happened.

I barely blinked, wanting to take in as much of his eyes as I could.

"I love you, on'she," Amulii choked out, shuddering as he reached for my face, his palm caressing my cheek. "I love you, and I am so sorry."

"I forgave you a while ago." I squeezed him tight against me. I hoped he could find the redemption he sought in my arms. It was all I could do for him. It was all I could do for both of us. "I love you too, so wait for me, okay? We found each other in this life. Maybe we can do this right in the next one." I knew it didn't work like that either, but I had to give him some comfort.

Amulii nodded as I combed my fingers through the mane on his head. Our steady breaths were all I could hear as exhaustion caught up to me. Leaning back, I closed my eyes, drifting into a storm of nightmares.

CHAPTER TWENTY-FOUR

A Father's Vengeance

Boiling metal clung to my neck, torturing me awake. A choke tore from my parched throat as I was dragged across the smooth metal floor with a heavy chain. Amulii roared, nearly ripping the hook out of the ground as he tried to reach me. Everything happened so fast, and though I was wide awake, I couldn't place where I had felt this kind of molten pain before.

"Sit down, beast," an older, stocky man shouted, firing a bullet into Amulii's stomach. It barely fazed him as he tried to lunge at the shooter, who unloaded another round into his leg. Amulii fell to the floor.

This was the man we most feared, the man leading the hunters who hounded us these last three months. He stood tall and heavy in the middle of the room like a long-awaited punishment. This time, he wore no hat, instead revealing his short white hair. He was clean-shaven, and there were deep rings around his eyes, as though he hadn't slept in months.

The shrapnel from the ammunition hit the floor with a jingle as Amulii's body expelled it, the wounds swiftly healing. Those bullets obviously weren't silver, but the chain around my neck was. I remembered the agonizing sensation from my experience with the silver nitrate earlier. My hands sizzled as I grasped it, trying to pull it away from my body so I could get some relief.

The men behind me secured my legs and arms to the floor hooks, using the same transparent leash that held Amulii in place. The chain loosened enough for me to pull it over my head and throw it at the men holding the other end. I gasped and fell to my stomach, sobbing.

Dr. Mitchel dashed into the room and hurried to my side, wearing the same clothes he had on earlier.

"I'll take him back for study," he said, reaching down to undo my bindings.

"You leave that animal right there, Paul," Mr. Davis said. He walked five paces across the room, tucking his revolver into a well-fitted tan blazer.

"That one over there killed your son. Alex is just a kid—a victim himself."

I had expected pity from him, but instead, he regarded me with the same disgust.

"I don't give a damn who he *was*. That thing is not a person right now, is he?" He sniffed, holding a red paisley handkerchief over his nose. "They smell god-awful."

"You can't kill him," Dr. Mitchel shouted, stepping in front of Davis. "He's only seventeen. I've known him since he was a baby."

I wanted to shift and maybe garner some sympathy, but to do that required concentration under stress. That was impossible at the moment.

"Get him out of here," the old man shouted to the guards near the door.

"Don't do this." The doctor struggled to shake free from the arms that held him. "You'll go to prison for this, I'll see to that." His screams reverberated through the building as they dragged him into the hall.

As the commotion died down, the man I'd been dreading to see again walked in.

"Liam . . ." His eyes burned hotter than silver as he stepped into the room, and his missing right arm was now only a scarred nub peeking out from under his blue polo shirt.

He stared me down, a revolted sneer twisting his face. I refused to look at him, instead, keeping my gaze fixated on the floor.

"What's the matter, Alex? Don't wanna look at it?" A steel-toed boot struck me below the jaw, knocking my head up before I fell back to the floor again. "Look at it," he shouted.

Two men grabbed handfuls of fur around my upper back, pulling me into an upright position. A thick rope slid around my neck, holding me in place so I couldn't look away.

"Look what you did," he said in a calmer voice as he knelt next to me, pointing to the bruised stump. I squeezed away tears while staring at the aftermath of that night. In my memories, there was always a distance between me and the attack; I saw nothing more than a disembodied arm afterward. Yet, I'd changed this man's life in such an awful way that no amount of explaining would soothe his hatred. "The playin' field's even now, and yer cryin' like a little kid. But you're not a little kid. You're a fuckin' demon." He choked on his words. "That evil look on yer face—I can't close my eyes anymore without seein' it. I'll never forget it." He calmed his voice. "I thought I could help you, but you're beyond help."

Liam grabbed the chélanc and tore it away from me, kicking me in the face again. The pain only lasted a moment before I healed. I was fine taking that over the chain.

"No," Amulii shouted. "Kill me. Torture me. Please—he had no control over what he did. That was me. All of it." His gruff voice shook with resolve as he tried to convince them. "I turned him into this. Spare him, please."

Liam's scowl deepened as he glared at Amulii. "You." His voice cracked as raw abhorrence dripped from his face. "He was screamin' and beggin' for his life . . . remember? You remember what you did to my brother? You didn't give a shit, why should I?"

"I will not beg for my life. I will accept any punishment you wish to give me. What I did I still live with to this day, and it is useless to explain why I did it. You crave vengeance, so have it. Do with me what you will. But he is a victim of my stupidity. He has killed no one."

"Yet," Davis said. "He hasn't killed anyone yet. It's a mercy to put down suffering animals." He faced me again. "You don't wanna live like this, do you, son? Half man, half dog, can't control himself. These scientists will poke and cut and probe every inch of your body for the rest of your miserable life."

I let what he said sink in for a moment. Earlier I thought Amulii would be the one getting off easy because he'd be dead, and I didn't want to live like that. My body gave in to what he was suggesting, and I hunched over, ears drooped while shaking my head. "No," I whispered, keeping my focus on the floor. What was the point in all of this? Had everything I'd learned, everything I'd gone through, been for nothing? Vol'drik gave me a second chance at life, and I learned to love and live as something more than human. Was this really how it was supposed to end?

Davis knelt next to me.

"You know, maybe Jesus might take you in after all, if you ask his forgiveness." I couldn't believe the hypocrisy. He was proselytizing while in the same breath threatening to kill me.

"Thanks for your concern about my soul, but shouldn't you be worried about your own? You're breaking the sixth commandment after all."

He shook his head.

"I think that just applies to people, not whatever the hell you are."

"Didn't you just say all I had to do was ask for forgiveness? Which is it, sir? Am I a person that gets to be saved, or am I a beast that deserves to be killed by a *good* Christian?"

Davis pulled away from me, folding the handkerchief he held in his right hand before stuffing it back in his pocket. "I'll think it over." He nodded to his son, who now held a polished machete in his one hand. I saw my own horror in its reflection. "Now, I do believe the Bible mentions a little something about an eye for an eye—or in this case, an arm for an arm."

"I didn't mean to," I screamed out in tears as Liam dropped to a knee next to me again, balancing himself as he held the weapon like a cane in his left hand. "I wasn't me."

"Hunter," Amulii yelled. "Take my arm instead."

"Nah," he said, smiling. "I want you to watch this like I had to watch you rip my brother's throat out." He turned his head toward me and smiled. "I ain't a leftie, so you better hope I don't slip and get more of ya."

Liam nodded to the guards behind me as they grabbed my arm. Three men were not enough to hold me in place as I thrashed about, desperate to move away from the sharp blade in Liam's hand. They placed the discarded silver chain back around my neck, each pulling it tighter toward the ground as I squirmed beneath them. They kept my right arm in place as I let out quavering howls.

There was no scent of burning flesh, but the poisonous metal chain cut through my fur like a high-powered laser, branding the skin around my neck in heat blisters.

"Hold him still, boys," Liam said, raising the blade high, his eyes wild and stained red. Amulii thrashed, snarled, and shouted, but his voice, along with every sound in the room, faded. The blade swung downward, and I squeezed my eyes shut. A whipping noise whooshed by my face, and a slight breeze from the movement tickled my nose. In a split second a metal clank reverberated from the floor as the machete slammed into it, and a muffled thud soon followed. I expected to feel a different kind of pain, but there was nothing at first. It was as though he'd missed the mark, but after another second ticked by, the molten, blistering heat shot from my right elbow. I snapped my eyes open and saw a lifeless, furry forearm on the floor next to me in a pool of my blood.

The pain caused me to lose consciousness for a moment as they removed my restraints. Blood soaked into my fur as more gushed from the wound, and I let out a choked howl that sounded more human than beast.

The wound soon healed, the blood a mere trickle, but an arm couldn't grow back as far as I knew.

"Look at the time," Davis said. Though he feigned indifference, he seemed shaken as he glanced at his gold Rolex. "It's almost four in the morning, and we all need our rest, including you beasts."

Liam stood, hocking spit at my face before stumbling toward the door, tears staining his eyes. "Welcome to the no-arm club, motherfucker," he cried out before disappearing into the hall.

"What we talked about earlier," Davis said, making his way toward the exit. "I'll pray on it."

When the doors slammed shut, I turned my head and retched. Those humans were just as callous as the monster inside of me that lay dormant.

"Alex," Amulii cried out. It was impossible to answer him, and I was too weak to sit up. All I could do was curl into a ball on my side and sob as the white-hot pain from my arm and neck continued to rip through me.

The doors opened, and hurried footsteps neared, but I no longer cared to look. I just wanted to stay there in my tight, furry ball until I could finally die.

"Oh God," Dr. Mitchel said, laying his hand on my head. "You guys heal fast, so I'll try reattaching it."

I didn't look at him. I was lost in a mire of hopelessness, and I wasn't sure I'd be able to get out again. What was this feeling?

"I didn't know they'd do this," the doctor said. With one eye open, I peeked at him as he scooped up the disembodied limb, cradling it before dashing out of the room.

I turned my head to the floor, and Amulii rustled about as he tried to move as close as he could to me.

"There is nothing I can do. I am useless to you," he cried out. "You have suffered too much." As the pain went from searing to a dull ache, I tried to relax. Rolling over, I gazed into the shimmering eyes of my mate.

It wasn't fair.

If my parents had gotten along, and my dad wasn't fucked up, we would have never moved. I would have been in a warm bed tonight, resting for school in a few hours. If only I had listened to my gut and avoided Amulii, I'd still have my arm and my humanity—and my life. What was the lesson I was supposed to learn from this? Don't fall in love? Don't trust anyone? When I jumped to my death, the ghost of Amulii's father made me believe this life was worth going back to.

Did he enjoy watching this? I wondered if my life was a cosmic soap opera, entertaining celestial beings as they observed every part of me unravel.

"You asked me if I cried the night we bonded," Amulii said, his voice hoarse. "And I did. I felt your memories. Everything from your past and that night of your first transformation. I had never felt anything like that. No living creature should ever feel the kind of pain I put you through." He dropped to his hands and his head hit the floor as he bowed. "And now this. More pain. More suffering. I wish I could take it all away."

The door opened again, and my eyes narrowed on Dr. Mitchel as he wheeled in an operating room's worth of surgical equipment on a gurney.

"Don't worry, this won't hurt," he said, kneeling next to me with a handful of syringes filled with clear liquid. The needles went in one after the other, and the burning I experienced was laughably tame compared to the amputation. The skin and fur had already grown back, and my wound was covered.

The doctor pulled out a scalpel and began cutting into the stump. "You might want to look away." I did as he said, turning my head toward the wall. All I could feel was light pressure as he worked. "Incredible," he said in an almost breathless tone.

Barely able to move anymore, I shifted my eyes back to the reattachment, curious to see what was happening. He held my severed arm close to the wound like one would a cleanly broken handle to a ceramic coffee mug. Blood spurted from the area where the doctor removed the skin; muscles, arteries, veins, and ligaments stretched outward toward the arm like a symbiote alien in a horror movie, pulling it into place. If I weren't so foggy, I would have shown a bit more intrigue. There was so much more to this body I should have learned about.

More of my blood squirted from the circumference of the gash as new skin sealed around it. I lay my head back down as the arm continued to reattach itself with no further aid. I was glad to have my arm back, but I still couldn't bend my elbow or move my hand.

"Poor kid," Dr. Mitchel said as he stroked my head. "I'm going to get you out of here." He paused for a moment. "I'll get you both out."

I nodded, but didn't reply.

"I'm sorry Alex," he whispered, undoing my bindings.

After a few moments of silence, I cleared my throat and spoke up, annoyed by the apologies everyone seemed to give me lately, all while making decisions that put me in harm's way. "If someone makes a movie about my life," I mumbled, my words slurring, "they should call it *Sorry Alex*." I glared at Amulii. "Everyone keeps hurting me."

The doctor rested his hand on my back as I curled up again. My right arm was still unusable, so I used my other one to pull it in place. Even at my worst, I'd never felt so hollow inside.

"Amulii, I need you to turn human when I get back. I'm going to disable the cameras in the room and get you a security uniform. We won't have much time after that." He pulled out another syringe.

"What about Alex?"

"He's going to be 'dead,' and you're going to help me dispose of his body." The doctor used air quotes while speaking, but I could hear Amulii's desperate movement.

"After all of this, you are going to kill him now?"

"He doesn't understand," I whispered.

"He's not going to die. I'm going to grab another gurney and some more supplies. This will help him sleep." He put his hand on my arm and leaned close. "Is that okay? I know you've been through a lot already, but you need to be convincing as a corpse now."

"I guess the only thing worse is being an actual corpse," I muttered, closing my eyes as he lifted my disabled limb, shaving it with clippers like he did earlier. There was still no feeling in my arm; it seemed every nerve had been severed with no way to heal. I couldn't tell he'd slipped the needle into my vein until the room darkened.

I was warm, and sunlight poured through my slitted eyelids. Unable to move, I gazed up and out the window to see a clear azure sky and an icy evergreen canopy whipping by. It had been a while since I'd seen such a beautiful day. We were out of the city and hopefully far away from whatever that place was.

Everything had a fuzzy halo around it, and I must have been unconscious for hours. The plan had obviously worked because I was in a van and not chained to a floor, waiting to die. My sense of smell returned as I caught the scent of Amulii and another human close by.

"I still don't understand this 'Segolia.' What is it, how does it work?" Dr. Mitchel and Amulii must have been talking the entire trip. I couldn't imagine the doctor sitting in silence as the two sat up front together. He was always the talkative type, even when I was a kid.

"I do not know. Why do you keep pestering me for answers to the same questions?" Amulii's human voice dripped with exasperation. "Your world and ours travel the same path and meet once a year. That is all I know."

"It just seems far-fetched. I've been to that lake many times and never saw anything like you describe."

"Very few can see it, even my own kind. I do not understand why some can see it while most cannot. My people have always suspected it had to do with being connected to two different worlds, but that is not something we can prove."

There was quiet once again from the cabin, and I could finally turn to my side, not wanting to take part in their banter. I didn't want to hear Amulii's many apologies or answer a barrage of questions from a guy I hadn't spoken to since childhood. It didn't matter where we were going; we'd probably end up dead in another month or so.

Every feeling was a dark, hopeless cloud. I hated it, but I also didn't care to resist it. If we somehow evaded capture and survived long enough to pass through Segolia, what then? I had forgiven Amulii, but I couldn't let go of what he told me.

"How long is he supposed to sleep?" Amulii asked. I heard him shuffle in the front seat of the van, but I kept my eyes closed.

"I don't know," the doctor replied. "He's not well, and I don't just mean physically. I don't know how I'm going to explain this to his mother."

"That was my doing," Amulii said, his voice quieter as his mood shifted. "I may have broken his mind and spirit."

"That was that crystal you talked about, right? The one you gave him?"

"Yes." The two stopped conversing. I knew Amulii would have done anything to help me now, but time was the only doctor in that van who could heal. Time was also the killer, chasing me with a silver machete.

The despair I felt wasn't ordinary depression. My hope for sanity lay in that crystal, and Liam had ripped it away. Now that it was gone, I knew what was going to happen. The horrible twist to our rescue was that instead of Liam or his dad killing me, Amulii would have to, once I lost my mind.

"How long will we be traveling?" Amulii asked.

"Not much longer. Another thirty minutes and we'll be at my cabin in Taft."

So that's where we were headed. I'd have more peace of mind if we were going to the Yukon instead of British Columbia, but at least it was a place we hadn't been yet. Taft was barely a town, so we'd be away from most people.

Sitting up, I glanced out the window to get my bearings. Winter covered the mountains and trees in thick blankets of white powder. The traffic was light on the highway, despite the clear weather. There weren't any buildings around, just a black road winding through endless peaks and trees.

"Alex," Amulii said, seeing me upright. "How are you feeling?"

I turned away, looking back out the window, my throat still sore from all the screaming and that silver noose.

"Okay, I will not bother you now," he whispered before turning back to the front. Amulii wasn't stupid. He knew I was going to need time. Right now, I wasn't sure if I was strong enough, and not having the necklace anymore added to the stress.

The chase was on, and I wondered who would get me first—the hunters, or the creature dwelling in the darkness of my thoughts.

We had ten long months to wait and see.

CHAPTER TWENTY-FIVE

BIRTHDAY BLUES

It was a grueling thirty-something days, and the monotony made it all blend together. I'd done little over the past month, only lying on the couch watching whatever was on television. It was much better than a cave, and at least I was warm.

I soon realized that without the chélanc, it was impossible for me to shift back to human form. Amulii tried to talk to me but couldn't hold my attention for very long. At one point, he attempted to get me in the mood for sex, but as expected, nothing happened.

My right arm still didn't work, and it was likely permanent nerve damage according to Dr. Mitchel. Amulii assured me that when I got back to his world, they could fix it, but he often promised the moon to make me feel better. A silver blade severed me. I was lucky the arm healed as much as it did.

Amulii hunted for our meals, trying everything he could to get me to join. Despite feeling hungry, when I'd try to keep anything down,

I'd get sick and throw it back up. The other day, I lay on the roof when the weather cleared to soak in the sun, hoping it would help. I ended up falling asleep, waking up hours later in a snowstorm with Amulii scooping me in his arms, carrying me back inside.

The past week, I preferred to stay inside with the curtains drawn. The light hurt my eyes now, and I'd become increasingly paranoid, occasionally seeing Liam's face through the windows. Not knowing their next move drove me crazy. I didn't live anymore; I existed.

Amulii had been working on something for two weeks, and he was patient enough to give me space. He didn't pressure me into doing anything, and when the anxiety was too much, he'd let me lay against him. We'd stay like that for a little while as he stroked my head and attempted to sing songs to me in his native language. I say attempted because he couldn't carry a tune if it came with handles, but it took my mind off of being slowly tortured to death by hunters. He was all I had, and he was trying to help me. Despite my emotional distance, I needed him close.

The drivel that aired on TV also helped take my mind off of the bad. Growing up, my parents restricted the amount I could watch, and it stuck with me through the years. I never developed the habit, opting to read most of the time instead. There were no books in the cabin, and with my fuzzy vision, I wouldn't have been able to focus on text, anyway.

"On'she," Amulii whispered, startling me as I dozed off. I fell into an unpredictable cycle of unconsciousness and alertness. One moment I'd be watching Laura Ingalls running through a field, and the next, I was waking up to Judge Judy screeching a verdict in a thick Brooklyn accent.

The blurry black image sharpened to Amulii's face, and I noted his unusual smile. It was a rare thing for either of us to do that lately but seeing him so cheerful was just the right amount of contagious. He knelt next to the couch and licked my forehead.

"Today is your birthday. I know you probably have not kept track," he whispered. The day had slipped my mind. It was already the end of February and I had no idea. "I did not forget."

After struggling to sit up on the plush, leather sofa, I patted the area next to me with my left hand, beckoning my neglected mate to sit. His ears stood erect as he got up off the floor.

I started to speak but had to clear my throat, having not said anything in days.

"Yeah, I forgot."

"The last time Dr. Mitchel was here, he brought what I requested, and I think you might enjoy what I have done," he said, sliding his fingers between mine. "Are you feeling well enough to take a walk with me? I will understand if you do not."

As much as it hurt to drag myself out of that cabin, he had been working hard on something. I nodded and struggled to stand, feeling weak from hunger. Amulii wrapped his arm around my waist, supporting me as I walked through the scarcely furnished living room toward the door and out into the blinding daylight.

"I am hoping this will enhance your appetite so you can eat something more nourishing. I have worried about you over the weeks, and I want to give you something to make you smile."

The wind changed and a familiar scent wafted into my snout as we got closer to our destination. Drool seeped from my lips as a bit of joy pulled my mood from the shadows. There was smoke billowing from what looked like a shoddily built outhouse in the middle of the woods. It was made of treated planks of wood, but everything leaned awkwardly to the left.

"Dad's brisket," I said, Amulii's starry-eyed expression reminding me of happier times. "You did this by yourself?"

"Yes," he said. "I never got to finish the one at our old cave, but I remembered everything your father taught me." We turned toward the smoker as a loose plank of wood fell from it. "Kind of."

"This is really sweet," I said, reaching for his hand as we walked closer. "It makes me feel kind of bad for getting you second-rate brisket for your birthday."

He stopped and pulled me toward him. A brief jolt of energy caused a domino-effect throughout my body. It had been a while since he'd embraced me while giving off *that* scent.

"It was a wonderful gift. Not only did you bring brisket, you brought good company. I wish I could have gotten people you love to visit, but it is too risky right now. The doctor Mitchel told me when he was last here that he would not be back for a while. They were after him."

I didn't want to focus on the worry. Electricity coursed through me, and I leaned in, surprising him with a forceful kiss. He caressed the base of my head as we stood there among the trees, sharing our first intimate moment in over a month. I needed to feel something good. Anything good.

We stood pressed against one another for several minutes before breaking away, all the emotions we'd bottled up surfacing at once. A surge of vigor rolled through every muscle, and before I knew it, I'd knocked Amulii to the snow under me. I straddled his hips, the claws of my left hand raking through the thick, black mane on his chest.

With no preparation, I positioned myself over what was growing hard beneath me. I had never been so eager, and I ignored the pain as he went deeper, using the natural lubrication of his body. We would do this right there in the snow with no hesitation or inhibitions. I didn't care if anyone saw. Animal desire wouldn't wait for us to make it back to the cabin.

Amulii's arms wrapped me tight as he turned, pushing me under him before grinding his hips. I moaned as each thrust went from gentle to rough in moments.

I needed this. Stress and crippling dread turned to ash and blew away as lust consumed them.

Amulii and I hated being called animals, but there on the forest floor, that's all I wanted to be. I didn't want to feel the emotional pain anymore. Every square inch of my being cried out for relief, and Amulii was more than eager to give me that.

We both finished faster than usual as I howled and he collapsed exhausted on top of me. Our mouths connected again as we released weeks of pain, stress, and frustration in violent pulses. One of the best things about being a maw'cha was how long this could go on, especially since we hadn't done it in a while.

We were locked together, and Amulii lifted me in his arms, turning us so that I lay on top of him. I rested my head against his chest, listening to the relaxing rhythm of his steady pulse.

"You are full of surprises," Amulii said, his hand resting on top of my head as claws scratched the backs of my ears. "If I had known you wanted to mate, I would have offered myself again like last time."

"No." I panted while gradually coming down from the high I was on moments ago. "I needed this."

He let out a contented laugh, letting his head fall back against the snow. "Then I am glad I could give you something you needed." He tried to pull himself out of me, but whined when he was unsuccessful. "Now if only I could calm down enough so we could eat."

///

We lay together on the bed, full of brisket and the deer Amulii had hunted after. He'd perfectly mimicked my father's recipe, which was a wonderful surprise. I knew we wouldn't be able to eat smoked meat all the time, but it was nice having a taste of home and someone who could cook.

"Thank you," I whispered, clasping my hand around his, "for giving me a great birthday."

He smiled. "We share everything now. I celebrate the day of your birth because I am thankful you are in this world and by my side. I only wish I had not also shared pain with you."

"Amulii, I already forgave you."

"No." He looked up at the ceiling as he spoke. "I know that is not wholly true because no one is that strong. When I say I struggled every day after giving you the chélanc, I mean it. It was hard to sleep knowing I thought so little of you that I wanted to mold you into what I desired by force. I justified it as me liberating you from humanity, but I would have taken away much more had I let the ritual finish. I still do not know why I let the others in the sect convince me. My parents would have never approved of my choice."

"You realize it now," I said, trying to think of a way to put what I felt into words that wouldn't hurt him more. "Yeah, there will always be a part of me that's angry, but it'll get better. You know it was wrong, and you're trying to make it right. That's all any of us can do when we make a mistake."

His ears drooped as he looked into my eyes.

"I was prepared to die for you, and that would not have been enough. I kept the truth hidden because I was a coward and could not bear to face you. You have a strength that I wish I had." His other hand caressed my cheek, his thumb rubbing against my muzzle. "You are the one that makes me better, not the other way around. I do not know the future, but I want to keep growing with you. Sometimes I forget you are much younger than me, today marking only eighteen years of life. But humans are smarter, learning faster than us."

I couldn't tear away from him. The timing was never right for this conversation until now, and I wouldn't have been as receptive from the dark places I'd dwelled over the weeks.

"What kind of ceremony are we gonna have?" I asked, changing the subject. "When we get to your world, I'll take your name."

He beamed, the fur around his eyes soaked. I loved that about him. I wondered if all male maw'cha were as emotional as Amulii, or if he was unique. I wanted him to be my rock again, and I wanted to be his.

"Bonding ceremonies take place over three days. On the first day, we will dress in traditional clothing, and you will stand before the elders as they determine your affiliation. The next day, we will become one at the place of your element. And finally, on the third day, there will be a feast with dancing and music with many in attendance, including my mother who will be eager to meet you."

That seemed elaborate for a simple wedding, and I'd never enjoyed going to them. I couldn't picture myself having one either, but if that was what Amulii wanted, I'd try to enjoy it. Hopefully, it wouldn't be stuffy and boring like traditional human weddings were.

"What kind of person is your mom?"

"She is one who listens and is wise. Any time I have doubts, she helps me make the right choices."

A sudden knock on the front door startled us, and I scrambled out of bed before Amulii pulled me by the tail. Exerting minimal effort, he shifted to human form before his feet touched the floor. His body did that so effortlessly now since the first day he transformed in front of me.

"Stay. Calm down," he whispered, grabbing a pair of pants that lay crumpled in the corner. "I will see who it is."

I held my breath, swallowing hard as I lay back in the bed. In my irrational mind, the hunters had already found us. But why would they knock? What I experienced lately wasn't merely episodes of panic.

Amulii tiptoed through the house, the loose wooden panels on the floor creaking with every step. The noises and anticipation only added to my crushing sense of dread.

"Open up, it's me," Dr. Mitchel shouted from outside. When I heard his voice, I collapsed back into the pillows. Amulii's pace quickened as he opened the door and let the doctor inside. "It's so dark in here."

"We can see in dark places. I will turn on the light," Amulii said. The living area of the small cabin went from drab to cheerful when I heard the click of the lamp switch. "It is rather late. If you had come earlier, we would have had brisket for you."

"That's okay. I need to talk to Alex," he said. There was an air of seriousness, and his state of mind wafted through the air as a very distinct scent. He walked through the bedroom doorway and flipped the light switch. I squinted, allowing my vision time to adjust. "How are you feeling?"

"Much better today," I responded, giving Amulii a smile. "What's going on? Are they still following you?"

Dr. Mitchel sat on the edge of the bed and rested his hand on mine.

"No, but I needed to stay away until I knew for sure." His demeanor darkened. "I would have called earlier instead of driving out here, but this isn't something you should hear over the phone."

More of this. More bad news. I now understood his scent, and it got stronger as seconds passed.

"It's about your dad," he said, carefully considering what he would tell me next. "He died a few days ago at the hospital after having a heart attack."

Every racing thought in my head stopped in an instant and faded as I processed what he told me. My eyes shifted toward his as I shook my head in disbelief.

When I glanced at Amulii, the shocked look on his face made it my stark reality. It got hard to breathe. My vision dimmed, and I could only see a point of light. The bed dipped as Amulii sat next to me.

"This wasn't a good day to tell you this, I know."

There were no tears, which surprised me. I should have been crying, but I wasn't.

"We just . . . we just started getting along," I whispered. "And now he's gone."

He was in his mid-forties and in good shape. How did he die of a heart attack? We may have had some barbecues now and then, but most of what we ate was healthy. Could the stress of everything have pushed his body to the limit? I considered a more sinister reason. Was this my fault again? He'd put himself at risk to save us, and he may have paid the ultimate price for that.

I left the bed and stumbled toward the living room, Amulii and Dr. Mitchel following close behind.

"Can I be alone for a while?" I asked, not looking back. "I'll be fine."

"Okay," Amulii whispered.

The doctor reached over and placed his hand on my shoulder. "Take all the time you need. We'll be right here."

"Why?" I asked, looking up at the night sky. "Why do you keep taking more from me?" It was meaningless to talk to no one in particular, but I had to say it. Someone on the other side, my father or Amulli's father, might have been listening. They couldn't answer back, but I felt better assuming they were listening.

The cabin was several kilometers away from the broad mountainside where I sat and looked out across the dark valley as the almost full moon peeked above the eastern range. Countless stars of the Milky Way blanketed the void like a line of shimmering sea foam coating a celestial shoreline. A relentless icy wind lapped at me, freezing the tears in my eyes and the condensation around my snout.

"When does it all get better?" I asked, chucking a stone into the black vale below. I froze as I felt a familiar and unwanted presence stir within me.

They killed him you know. The humans who hunted us killed dear old Dad.

I gripped my chest and jumped to my feet when I heard the monster's voice. This time it sounded different—intelligent. It sounded like my human voice.

"Get the fuck out of my head." When I shouted, my deep roar echoed in the blackness like a thunderclap. I tried to howl for Amulii, but nothing would come out.

What do you mean? I am you.

With my one functioning hand, I pulled at the fur on my head, trying to cause enough pain to make the voice leave.

I've gotten stronger. I can help us. Together, we can put an end to all of this. You want revenge, don't you?

"I want you to leave," I shrieked as I fell to my knees, pushing my forehead into the snow. "Leave." This wasn't the monster I knew. It was a lot more deadly.

This is what you want. They took Dad. They took our arm. They took your peace of mind. How long will it be before they take our life?

"This isn't—" It was harder to speak as I lost control of my tongue. "I don't feerr rright."

Free yourself. I can fix everything. They have the numbers, but I'm an army. I can silence them.

"Ssssstop." With every second the monster's deceptively gentle voice echoed within me, I had a harder time staying on the surface. It was as though I were being dragged into an undertow of tar.

Let me handle it all.

A blue light emanated from my eyes as it reflected off of the snow. Invigorated, I reared up like a bear, everything sounding and even smelling different. There was only one thing on my mind, and that was finishing what I'd started.

There was a smorgasbord of human flesh back in Jasper. Every person who wore a uniform would sate my hunger, but my main course would be Liam and his fat, juicy fuck of a father.

"Ah, this is better."

I don't want to do this.

"Stop worrying. We'll love it when the deed is done. Second thoughts might kill us though, so be careful."

I don't want to go back.

"You never deserved someone as strong as Amulii. I saw his power, what he's capable of. When he brought down that helicopter, he could have done a lot more, but . . ."

A grin slipped across my maw as I leaped from rock to rock, down the mountain toward the east.

"He had to worry about you, because even after having this amazing body for months, you still haven't learned how to use it. I'll show you, though. I don't even need two arms."

I am not a murderer. Give me back control.

Insane, howling laughter erupted from my gut as I landed on flatter ground. I gave the air one more sniff before sprinting toward the place of delicious pain. I'd never felt such heat, such power, and I knew I couldn't maintain such high speeds indefinitely. I'd eat anything I saw between here and Jasper, and there would be no time for rest.

"When have *you* ever had control?"

CHAPTER TWENTY-SIX

FULL MOON MASSACRE

arm, wet, delicious. I savored the kill. They feared a demon, but I would show them something much worse. I spent a day pushing through blizzards and impossible terrain, my sole motivation being the many human corpses that would lie beneath me like the bloody one under me now.

When my sense of smell vanished, I knew I was close to the rest of the militia that had hunted us ruthlessly for months.

My maw'cha body was remarkably adept and could heighten my other senses whenever I lost one. Though I couldn't follow trails of scent, I could feel living creatures as vibrations that traveled through the ground and the air. Their heartbeats were like bass drum cadences, and the faint sloshing of their circulatory systems pleased my ears, bringing out more of the hunger I once tried to control.

The human under me was unfortunate, but easy to take down. His lifeless eyes would remain frozen in the horror I'd inflicted in his last moments until buzzards ate them. I made sure his death was quick, clamping my jaws around his neck before severing his spine. I was hungry but had precious little time to spare eating nobodies, so I dug a shallow hole in the snow before dragging the body into it, leaving a trail of blood behind.

Liam was the only hunter I was interested in eating, and I wasn't completely out of my mind with revenge. I resigned myself to being a monster, but there was a limit to what the human inside of me would allow. Alex—my true self—had just enough control to put a damper on my fun.

There were two humans walking along the icy shore of Maligne Lake, and I shadowed them through the trees. Spirit Island was further to the north, and most of the park was dotted with temporary stations and blinding crane floodlights which put me at another disadvantage. I had to wait for my chance to attack, or I'd alert the other hunters to my presence. Having one arm hampered me, and there were only so many humans I could take down at once. All it would take was one silver bullet to put an end to my pleasant evening.

When does murder feel good? All I feel is sick.

Alex felt sick, but I was hungry for more carnage. When the men had put enough distance between themselves and the tents of other hunters, I leaped from the brush, my powerful jaws snapping one's neck before he could react. In a split second, my sharp teeth were already ripping through the other's arteries, clamping down on his windpipe so he couldn't scream. His body convulsed as my jaws locked. My tongue lapped at the thick, iron-rich liquid that gushed from the fatal wound. It wasn't meat, but the nutrients in the fresh blood kept me going for now. As my deranged hunt continued, I'd need to consume a body, eventually.

After twenty minutes of stalking, there was a familiar voice in the distance, and I let another limp corpse drop from my saliva and blood-soaked maw. Though the sound was a mere whisper among booming voices, I knew it was him on the other side of the lake.

A burst of energy propelled me into a mad dash on my hands and feet. The surface of the lake had frozen over, giving me easy access to the other side. If it weren't, I'd have swum the icy waters to get to that man. My heart thumped as I dashed toward the sounds of talking and metal scraping metal.

A vehicle door slammed and a cold engine sputtered to life. I was almost there. The soft crimson halo of taillights illuminated the snow around a jeep that had a tall white trailer hitched to the back. It wasn't able to move more than fifteen or twenty kilometers per hour over the cleared snow path because of the rough topography. The vehicle was no match for my speed out here.

I would have torn open the door to drag him out, but the trailer gave me an idea. Would he lead me to his father? Maybe he'd lead me to a compound where the militia slept. Saliva roped from my mouth as I thought about the gore I'd leave behind.

I ran ahead of the jeep while staying in the shadows. Using my powerful legs, I jumped up a bare aspen, climbing across the branches that draped over the path while gripping tight since I was one arm short. The thin tree creaked and snapped under my weight. It held long enough for the jeep to pass under, and I dangled from the branch for a second before dropping onto the flimsy aluminum trailer with a loud thud, making a maw'cha-sized dent in the top. After thirty minutes or more of bumpy terrain, the ride finally smoothed as tires turned onto asphalt.

We were headed for Jasper, and I lay flat against the top, punching a hole in the trailer top to keep my grip. This time when I went into town, I would have the night and my acute senses to keep me hidden.

About ten minutes later, the jeep parked in front of a wooden lodge. Anticipation for the kill was building inside of me, but I'd been patient so far. Amulii's hunting lessons worked just as well for revenge.

Liam climbed out of the driver's seat, and with an infuriatingly confident gait he made his way to the front of the tall log building. The roof was steeply angled, and enormous windows above the entrance revealed a giant chandelier lighting the lobby inside. I recognized the place. It was where all the mega-rich fucks would congregate on their brief day trips to the mountains. Pushing myself up with my one good arm, I jumped down and circled the perimeter.

There were too many lights on, and I needed to find his room and wait for him without being seen. I peered through windows to keep track of Liam, searching for signs of his father. So far, my hunt yielded no results. The feeling of disappointment was brief, though, because I knew at least one of my enemies who tortured me would die tonight.

Many of the windows wouldn't budge and curtains blocked my view, so I couldn't see what room my meal would end up in. I could still hear his heartbeat and footsteps through the walls as I followed his sounds.

It wasn't too difficult to find an open window, and I jostled one loose, carefully pushing it upward. The room was dark, and I could sense a sleeping child in the bed in front of me. My stomach growled as I approached, but I turned away from the easy meal as the voice inside of me screamed. I obeyed it, for now. How long could my human side keep this up?

A child? You'd eat a little kid? Sick son of a bitch.

My sense of smell had returned, but I'd never lost Liam's signature heartbeat. I followed the sound, keeping out of sight as I crept along the narrow halls and ducking into closets when I heard or smelled another human close by. The challenge now was getting to him without alerting another to my presence, but that was also part of the fun.

I was the monster in the scary movies, skulking unnoticed amongst my unsuspecting victims. It was exhilarating. There wasn't a person here I couldn't kill with ease. As I homed in on his location, I sensed another presence in the suite. Could it be?

The voice was unmistakable. Southern, pompous—infuriating. The man could have been a politician considering his wealth and charisma. The thought of his preaching in the lab, and the way he flaunted his hypocritical religious views only added to my ire.

He wanted to go to heaven, but I was more than eager to make him experience every glorious moment of hell. The humane and empathetic part of me knew all of it was wrong, but that part no longer mattered and would disappear given enough time without that crystal.

I tested to see if the door was unlocked, and to my joy, it was. Liam finished speaking and his feet scuffed along the wooden floor toward the bathroom. As water hissed through the pipes, I knew it was time to make my move.

I opened the door and slipped inside, sniffing the air. The room was a master suite with cathedral ceilings and so spacious that the entire first floor of my parents' cabin could fit inside. The entryway was narrow, concealing my presence, but I could see Davis sitting on a white sofa in the living area. The entire side of the suite facing the mountains was one giant wall of glass with a sliding door leading outside to a deck.

I grinned and let the door click shut. Startled, he jerked his head toward me before jumping from the couch. I darted from the entrance and snatched his throat with my left hand. When I saw the shock in his eyes, I pictured the ways I'd tear him apart while keeping him just barely alive. His terrified expression was a far cry from his smug look the day his men chained me to the ground. He had no one now.

"Alex." His voice was high and throaty as I tightened my grip on his soft, flabby neck.

My smile stretched further across my blood-caked maw as I forced him to sit in a white recliner close by. "If you scream, I'll make this much worse for you." I struggled, not wanting to give in to the need to gut him like the pig he was. Pacing the floor, I thought about what

I wanted to say before ending his life. How he reacted to my bluff would determine how he would die.

"I was told something about your involvement with my father's death. Maybe if you can prove your innocence, I'll let you go." I looked at the bathroom door. "You have until he gets out of the shower to make it convincing."

"Don't believe what Dr. Mitchel told you, I—"

"Dr. Mitchel didn't tell me shit. I heard this from your own people—before ripping their throats out," I said, pointing to the dried blood coating the fur around my mouth. I was a living lie detector, and if I got a whiff of dishonesty, he would suffer longer.

His racing heart and shaky breath confirmed my suspicions. I cared little about how he did it, all I knew was he was somehow responsible.

"I didn't kill him," he pleaded. I didn't want to believe it, but as his pulse slowed, I knew he was telling the truth.

"Did you order someone else to do it?" I asked, kneeling next to his face, sniffing him as he spoke. He turned away from me in disgust as a familiar scent wafted from the folds of his flesh.

"No. I had nothing to do with it." The stench and deafening heartbeats coming from him made the lie more apparent. "And I'm sorry for your loss." Another apology. Another useless apology.

"That was all I needed to know," I whispered as I reached into his jacket for the revolver he carried. I nearly forgot about it, but the stink of gunpowder gave it away. "Sit quietly now. I have some business with your son."

"Don't kill him, please." Davis went to sit up, but I shoved him back into his seat with my knuckles while I clutched the gun in the same hand.

"Shh." I grinned, thinking of the perfect thing to say. "Maybe I'll give him a few moments to talk it over with Jesus."

I padded toward the sliding door and held the gun between my teeth as I unlatched it and stepped outside. After tossing the revolver off the deck, I lumbered back over to the chair Davis was sitting on and waited next to him for Liam to emerge.

We exchanged no more words, and I didn't make eye contact, despite him glancing in my direction. There was a presence in the room that disturbed me, pushing down some of my rage. I shrugged it off as much as I could, but it was getting harder to ignore.

The bathroom door opened, and Liam emerged in a pair of shorts and a white T-shirt, holding crumpled dirty clothes in his left arm. He froze, dropping everything as he came face-to-face with the monster he feared more than Amulii.

"Oh shit."

"Did ya miss me, sweetheart?" I howled with manic laughter.

"You . . ." I could tell he was trying to assess the situation, but the hopelessness in his eyes brought me more enjoyment than his father's reaction did. "No big bad boyfriend this time?" He looked at my right arm and sighed. "I guess you can grow things back too, huh?"

"Nope, just little ol' me. And also, no, it was reattached. It doesn't work anymore." My nose wrinkled into a snarl as I bared my teeth, lifting my dead arm with my other one before letting it fall limp to my side.

"I guess you won the hunt. You can live like a monster now after you finish what the other one started," he muttered. "Did you come to get your little crystal back?"

That was the presence I'd been feeling, and the damn thing was pulling Alex closer to the surface. Until Liam mentioned it, I'd forgotten it was in his possession. It was nearby, and I needed to kill them quickly before—

"I don't want it," I said, my attention shifting to the other side of the room. I was losing strength, and I'd need a little more time. Every moment I was in that room, my ferocity diminished.

The front door swung open, and I expected police or militia to run through. Instead, it was Amulii in human form with Dr. Mitchel.

They were dressed in the same clothes from last night, though Amulii didn't have a shirt on. I knew it was only a matter of time before they found me.

With a swift, desperate motion, I grabbed Liam's throat, my teeth now inches away from his face.

"Alex," Amulii shouted, walking closer but stopping as I opened my jaws.

No. No more.

I pulled back and closed my mouth, then opened wide again. No matter how hard I struggled, I couldn't get near his neck. Dropping my head, I concentrated as I tried to retake control from Alex inside.

"How did you find me?" I asked, my eyes never leaving the trembling man I held by the neck against the wall. "I didn't exactly leave a scent trail for you to follow."

"Amulii was looking everywhere, and he finally caught your scent and paw prints . . . with the bodies." Dr. Mitchel swallowed hard. "When they disappeared and he saw tire tracks, he ran back to me. I knew you'd be here." He nodded to Amulii. "I see we're not too late."

"The chélanc," Amulii said, dashing toward a wooden hutch in the corner; he must have been able to feel its presence too.

"If you come near me with that thing, everyone dies," I said, stopping Amulii in his tracks. I glanced at the doctor. "Everyone, including you. I'm not going back to being weak. I won't be captured and tortured. I control my future now. ME." I pulled Liam close before slamming him back against the wall.

"I do not know what entity has taken you, but it is a coward. You are much stronger than this. The longer it has you under its control, the more you lose," he said, reaching into a drawer to grab the necklace. "I have always been drawn to your kind and beautiful spirit. That is who you are, not this."

Let me go.

I grunted, squeezing Liam's neck before lifting him from the ground. "A coward? You could have ended it all years ago, but you didn't have it in you, and I suffered for it." I paused, gritting my teeth. "My dad died because of you. This is all your fault."

Liam thrashed around, hitting me in the face with his fists, but his struggles slowed as he lost consciousness. Alex resisted, holding me back again.

"Please don't kill him," Liam's father shouted, but I ignored him.

"You interrupted my meal, Amulii. Do you want me to starve?"

He appeared behind me, grabbing the nape of my neck, bones cracking as he transformed in mere seconds. Liam fell to the floor and began gasping for air as my body locked up. How the hell did he move that fast?

"Doctor, I need your help. I cannot let him go or he will frenzy. I need you to tie this around his neck," Amulii said, dropping the crystal to the floor before pulling me away from Liam.

"Don't you fucking do it. I will tear you to pieces. All it'll take is a second if Amulii loses his grip. Do you want to risk your life for theirs? After all, haven't they been hounding you too?"

As the doctor knelt to pick the crystal up off of the ground, I bucked, startling them both. Amulii gripped the loose skin on my neck with both hands and shoved me to the wall.

"He is . . . much stronger than before," Amulii said, out of breath as he struggled to keep me still. "You need to hurry; he is hard to hold."

The doctor shuffled behind me and tried to fasten the necklace, but he got too close. I snapped at his hand, grabbing it in my jaws. He shrieked in pain and dropped the necklace as I clamped down harder. The sound of cracking bones and screaming made me forget about Davis standing behind me. Leather straps tightened around my neck as the crystal fell against my chest. I let go of the doctor and looked over to see that man securing the necklace with a knot before putting his hands up and backing away.

Amulii dared not let go of me until he was certain I was back. It took several minutes for me to feel the soothing effect of the crystal this time. It was worrying, but worry was the first sign of normalcy. My mind cleared, and I surfaced, shaking away the nightmare of being controlled by whatever that was.

"Amulii," I whispered as tears fell from my face. When he saw my emotions return, he let go before pulling me against him.

"It is okay. You are okay," he said, squeezing me tighter. "This has all gone so far. I must try to put it right, if I can."

As he helped me to the couch, he looked back at Dr. Mitchel, who clasped his bloody hand against his chest.

"How bad is it?" Amulii asked, running over to inspect the mangled mess I'd made of it. I felt a wave of guilt knowing I had done that, and I wished I could take it back. I wished I could take back everything I'd done tonight. How was I going to live with myself now?

"It's nasty, but . . ." he stammered as he tried to catch his breath. "I'll live. I need to get to the hospital, though." His eyes met mine when I started to cry. "It's not your fault, Alex. None of this is your fault."

"I'm so sorry," I whispered.

I couldn't say anything more to him. How could I truly apologize? That cunning, well-spoken monster was a part of who I was now. Deep down, I had wanted to give into it on that mountain. That second of weakness was all it needed. How much more powerful would it get the longer it remained?

Amulii watched as Liam scrambled to his feet. "Can you help him?"

"Suddenly the good guy, huh? The kid might not have been in control of himself, but you were. Why do you care if he gets help?"

"I cannot change a decade of your perception of me. My reasons for what I did that day will probably not assuage your hatred, but I owe you both an explanation." Amulii paused as the sounds of Dr.

Mitchel's dripping blood pulled him back to the present. "However, he needs help now. Your father and I must have words."

"I'll get him to the entrance and call an ambulance, but I'm comin' back. You kill my dad and I'll—"

"No one else will die," Amulii interrupted. "Now leave."

Liam reached into a suitcase and pulled out a white T-shirt to wrap the doctor's hand in to stop the bleeding.

"Someone that has two working hands fucking help me."

Amulii ripped the shirt and tied the fabric with enough care not to hurt Dr. Mitchel further. When he was done, the two men left. Three of us remained: me, Amulii, and the man who murdered my dad.

"You just experienced a fraction of what an out-of-control maw'cha can do." Amulii glanced at me before placing his hand on Davis's shoulder, pointing to the chair. "Sit, please."

Davis glared and nodded before plopping onto the recliner, sinking into the cushions.

"When I killed your son, it was not out of spite or hunger, it was because I felt it was the only way. He had taken something dangerous that was not given to him. He would have changed into what Alex is, only he would have lost all of who he was. Nothing would have remained of his humanity or his mind. He would have killed many people had I let him go. You and your other son would be dead, or you would have to deal with the pain of killing him yourself."

Amulii bowed his head.

"I did not know what else to do. Should I have let your son live, and sentence many humans to die? That has been something I have struggled with since that day. I have never forgotten his face, and the guilt of my decision still haunts me, eats at me. I do not expect your forgiveness, nor do I want it, but I hope to have your understanding. It was a terrible choice that maybe I had no right to make. Perhaps I should have let him go and left you to deal with the consequences of his mistake. After all, he was the one that took what he should not have. It would have been easier for me to let him go, but would I have been able to live easier with that choice?"

We sat in silence as Davis broke down, tears filling his once cold, vengeful eyes.

"His name was Joseph, and he was my oldest," he said, pulling out a cloth handkerchief, wiping his eyes and nose. "He was smart as a whip, and I was so proud of him. He had a bright future, but you took that in the most awful way. If you didn't exist, he'd still be here. I'll never forget when I had to identify his body—"

"Amulii killed your son because he had to. You killed my dad because you're a fucking murderer," I said, my voice unapologetically harsh. "I know you did; I could smell you lying to me. What's your excuse?"

"I don't have one. I would have done anything to see the beast that killed my boy punished, and I thought it would lure both of you back," he said, now making eye contact with me. "I made peace with myself when I gave the order."

The beast inside clawed at my mind, and I wanted nothing more than to kill him now that he'd confessed. Sensing danger, Amulii gripped my shoulders from behind.

"I had no control over anything I did, but *you* made a decision to kill an innocent man." I stood and walked a few paces across the living room so I could get a better look at his face as I spoke. Amulii followed close, his hand slipping to the back of my neck. "I hate you and I still wish I could kill you, but—" It was hard to let the pain roll off of me as I watched my father's murderer sit there, healthy and intact. "I did enough of that sick shit tonight. I just want this to end. We're leaving soon, and I'm tired. I didn't choose to be what I am, and I didn't kill your son. I'm just the one that paid for it, though. Like you give a shit."

My legs shook as exhaustion and hunger finally took hold. I had to kneel next to him, letting the arm of the recliner support my weight.

He looked at me with sympathy instead of disgust this time, but I still couldn't shake my desire to rip him apart.

"I . . ." Davis choked on his words. "Maybe I'm worse than you," he said, glaring at Amulii. "Since you're leaving, I'll call it all off. This cost me a fortune, and it nearly cost me my other son. Alex doesn't have to forgive me, but I'll never accept your story. I don't care what your reasons were."

Amulii wrapped his arms around my chest and pulled me off the ground.

"I will take Alex and leave this place. I will hold you to your word that you will call back the hunters and no longer pursue us. We need not see or even think about each other again. We must move on. Robert was my friend, and I share in Alex's pain. I will mourn him, and I will continue to mourn your son."

My legs buckled again, and Amulii lifted me into his arms. I'd run at top speed for hundreds of kilometers without stopping and used up the last of my energy struggling with Amulii as he kept me from making another tragic mistake.

"You have my word, beast," Davis muttered. His expression shifted when he looked at me. "And I am sorry, Alex."

As my mate carried me toward the sliding door, I stopped him, thinking on the man's apology.

"I died once already, and I've seen what's waiting for us. It's not what you think it is. There's no God to punish you. That's not what happens. Your soul will be fine. It doesn't care what you did because this life only matters now, not for eternity. I don't expect you to believe me, but maybe instead of apologizing you can do something that's actually useful. You're lucky enough to have the power and money to do some real good in this world while you're alive. Obviously, God wasn't enough of an influence to make you do the right thing so far in life, so try digging deeper into yourself for the answers. If you still can't figure it out, then maybe you just fail at being a decent human being, God or no. Take that however you want."

I tapped Amulii on the shoulder and he carried me outside before jumping from the deck.

///

"I never thought I'd be so happy to see this place again," I said as Amulii lowered me onto the fur bedding in the middle of our old cave. Everything was still here, left untouched since the day we had to run from my parents' house. "I think this is the second time I've thought that."

"I will be back; I need to hunt." He rushed toward the cave entrance.

"Don't leave me, please." I remembered what was out there, bloody and buried in the snow.

He stopped, eyes wide as he approached the bed. "You need food," he whispered, kneeling down to stroke my head. "I will not be gone long."

I pointed to a bag I brought to the cave over a month ago. "We have a lot of jerky in there. Let's eat that, and we'll hunt tomorrow," I said nervously as I rested my head. "I did awful things tonight." Images of blood-soaked human bodies made me wince, a parting gift from the monster that had me in its clutches earlier. "I need you right now, okay? I can't be alone with myself."

"Of course," he whispered, grabbing the bag, an orange crystal for light, and our tattered old blanket before climbing into bed. He pulled me into his warm body and nuzzled my neck. "I will not leave you."

CHAPTER TWENTY-SEVEN

PRECIOUS MEMORIES

My feet scraped along gravel as I climbed out of the back of a black Lincoln Continental. Despite the early snows last month, I was glad the weather had warmed enough lately to melt it all. It was mid-October, exactly one year since the morning that changed my life.

I inhaled the familiar scents of pine and chimney smoke as the chilly breeze nipped at my face. A pang of grief hit me as I scanned the overgrown yard. There were no signs of human life here anymore—no smoker or grill out front, Dad's truck and Mom's car missing from the driveway, and the rickety old shed that once housed my four-wheeler stood empty. It was tough to come back here again, but I had to.

Amulii shut the door on his side and stretched, having been in the car for several hours. We were both human, and we'd been planning a trip back for a while to not only celebrate our anniversary but to help heal the unresolved trauma of the past.

Thick black coats and jeans kept us warm, and I was able to get Amulii to wear shoes, though he still hated the feeling. It was hilarious when he'd tried walking in them for the first time in almost a year, and I took video of him goose-stepping over carpet.

Mom rolled down her window, flipping the fuzzy hood of her blue parka up over her head as a frigid blast of wind hit us. It had taken months and many human visits for her to finally warm up to Amulii, but the scornful look on her face as he wrapped his arm around my waist meant she still had a long way to go.

"What time do you guys want me to pick you up?" Dr. Mitchel asked from the driver's seat, preparing to set an alarm on his phone.

"How 'bout five? We wanna walk around for a while."

"I'd tell you to be careful, but that would be kind of stupid," Mom said, stepping out of the car. She hugged me, shoving Amulii away. It was sad watching his shoulders slump, especially after he'd tried so hard to win her over. "We're not going far. We'll be at the lodge downtown."

"That sounds boring. What's at the lodge?"

"Bedrooms."

"Gross," I muttered under my breath.

She rolled her eyes and laughed.

"Imagine, if you will, your son having gay werewolf sex, and having that described in detail." She cocked an eyebrow, glaring at the slouching man behind me. "If I can deal with that, you can sure as hell deal with this."

She had a point. Amulii was seldom coy when he discussed our relationship with my mother, never leaving out the dirtiest details sometimes. I learned it was a cultural thing for his people, and oversharing a bond with family brought about a sense of pride rather than shame. It did little to score points with Mom though, and there were moments I wanted to put his head through a wall.

"When are you guys supposed to go on your honeymoon, anyway? You've been married what, three months already?"

"We've been saving that for after you leave. I'll need a trip around Europe to take my mind off of everything," she said, her mood darkening.

"Mom, I'll be back in a year. It's not like I'm leaving forever. Think of it as me studying abroad." I looked back at Amulii, who pinched my jacket and tugged. "I guess, have fun at the lodge 'playing video games', or whatever," I muttered.

"And you guys have fun 'hiking,'" she retorted in kind, giving me one last hug before getting back into the car.

As the sedan disappeared down what used to be our driveway, I turned back to the place I'd called home for barely a couple months. The cabin hadn't been occupied, and Mom had a hard time selling it. It wasn't because there weren't any buyers. Dad was gone, and I'd be off in another world. This was the last place we all lived together as a family, even if we were broken.

We slowly approached the two-story cabin, and I noticed the cracking paint of the front door, still dented from where Amulii pounded it.

"It feels like we haven't been here in a lifetime," I said as we ascended the bowing steps. "This is where I first saw you. You were such a beautiful wolf."

Amulii smiled proudly. "I still need to teach you that form, though I don't use it that often. It can come in handy."

"Remember when you brought me that hare?"

"Ah yes, I was so nervous to see you that day, especially after you got mad at me the evening before. You were the first human I ever followed."

"Yeah." I clicked my tongue and glared at him for a moment. "I fell in love with my stalker. How cliché."

"Knowing what I know now, I can see why you were upset with me."

Amulii opened the door, which was still off center after he broke it the day we met. I couldn't believe Dad had never fixed it. Normally, something like that would have driven him nuts, but I suppose there were more serious things occupying his thoughts.

"I wonder if Mom will ever be able to sell this place," I said. Floorboards groaned under our weight as we entered the empty living room. The place seemed smaller without furniture in it. Dust had gathered on the wood floors and molding, and there were a few cobwebs in the ceiling corners near the dining room. The hastily patched holes I punched in the wall the day Mom rejected me had claw marks next to them. "There aren't a lot of memories of this place, and most are pretty bad."

"We can leave," Amulii said, grabbing my hand again. "If this becomes too painful, let us leave, okay?"

"I'm fine. They aren't all terrible; in fact, some of them were the best ones I've ever had." I walked over to the front door. "Dad stood here and told me he loved me for the first time. And in my bedroom, I saved your life, and I ended up falling asleep in your arms. Over there, where the table was, you burned your mouth eating lasagna."

"Hey. That was not a pleasant memory," Amulii said. "That was the most painful meal I have ever eaten." He paused for a moment as his thoughts likely wandered back to the motel in Calgary. "Well, it was the second most painful meal."

"You were creepy, but adorable, not really knowing what the hell anything was. You ate with your hands and stuck your head under the faucet to drink." I opened the front door again, and Amulii cocked his head.

"Are we not going to your old room? I have good memories of you there."

Shaking my head, I stepped back outside.

"There are things I don't want to be reminded of. The night I transformed was worse than getting my arm chopped off. I get sick to my stomach just thinking about it."

"I wish we would have bonded naturally. My mother never mentioned her first transformation being so awful. I do not understand why it was painful for you, but I have a lot of questions that I will demand answers to when we go back to my world." He followed me out and forced the door shut. "I know I have said this a lot, but had I known how awful everything would be for you, I would have never done this."

"I know, but it's not awful now," I said, giving him a soft pat on the shoulder. "So much fucked up shit happened to both of us, but it's over. It's been a lot of fun these last few months, and I love being a maw'cha now. We have a nice cabin, a comfortable bed." I smiled when I thought about that crooked thing Amulii built on my birthday. "And we have a smoker."

"*Had* a smoker, remember? I am not very good at building things. It caught on fire the second time I used it."

"Oh yeah, I forgot about that. I thought you rebuilt it."

"I will build one in my world. I will bring bags of the seasonings your father used to smoke his brisket," he said as we walked off toward a familiar route.

"Do you even have brisket in your world?"

He scratched his head. "I have never tasted meat like that, and I have never had it raw. I will need to experiment with different game to see what parts taste the closest. Prey is similar but different in my world."

We walked for twenty minutes before ascending the mountain path we used as a shortcut on our first hike together. I wasn't out of breath this time as we trekked along the steep, craggy slope.

"This was where you almost fell," he said, pointing to the broken rocks. I couldn't believe after all the snow, the scree remained mostly undisturbed. Turning back and glancing down the slope, I saw exactly what I saw the moment I thought I was going to die.

"How do you remember this stuff? Like, how do you know the exact spot I fell and what day it is without looking at a calendar?"

"I do not know. I have always had an excellent memory. It is odd that so many people cannot remember the details I can. When I was younger and became aware, I thought everyone remembered as I did, but that was something unique."

It was good to know that his vivid memory wasn't a common trait among maw'cha. That would not only be frustrating, but it would make me feel really stupid.

"If you do not mind, on'she, I would like to play out the memory I have here. It was one of the best back then, outside of our bond, that is."

"That's what we're here for."

He reached down, placing one of his arms behind my legs while another supported my back. With a swift motion, he lifted me and began running up the mountain.

"Oh, this was what you meant." With my left arm, I reached around his neck and held on, this time not in pain or fearing for my life.

"You have gotten a lot heavier since then," he said, as he leaped from rock to rock. "Ah, the memories. I loved the moment I carried you. It was my first time being so close."

"Yeah, I remember this being the weirdest moment of my life," I said, leaning into his chest with a content smile. Since I was taller, it didn't feel the same as it did then, but I still loved it.

"We are almost to the place." He jumped up a few more outcrops before we reached the summit. "Here it is," he said, setting me against the trunk of a familiar lodgepole.

"It's our tree," I said as he sat down next to me, our shoulders touching. Everything he acted out stoked another memory.

"I liked your scent," he said. The phrase that creeped me out a year ago had a different meaning now. I couldn't understand it when I was human, but as Amulii sat next to me, his unique, musky scent sending jolts of joy to my brain, I grew to love that smell.

"I like your scent," I responded, leaning in to kiss him. "You turned out to be a wonderful guy, despite everything."

"And you too." He reached down and rubbed my ankle. "I will forget none of this for as long as I am alive. You taught me many harsh lessons, whether you meant to or not. As long as we have one another, we need nothing more."

"Well, baths are nice," I said, half-jokingly.

I was trying to hold back a lot of sentiment as he spoke, in case the tears started again. There wasn't a person on the planet I loved more than the maw'cha next to me. Even if I believed that we were fated to be together, it wouldn't have happened without a lot of pain and compromise.

"I'm scared about leaving."

He covered my hand with his and our fingers locked together.

"I will be honest; I am nervous about going back with you. We have not been very fortunate in recent endeavors, and I worry your mouth will get the better of you."

"It's not the first time I've ever heard *that*," I said, laying my head on his shoulder. "I'm not so much scared of living in your world as I am about missing out on mine. Also, this may sound weird, but I'm scared of living so long. I know I'll wake up one day and realize everyone I've ever known in this world is gone."

"Oh," Amulii said, as he took in a sharp breath through his nose. "That is something I had not considered. My world does not change much because the same beings who helped shape it did not die that long ago. Humans have short lives, and time still flows similarly to you though you are no longer human. Maybe this will be something you can discuss with my mother. She is more familiar than I."

"I hope she likes me," I said.

"She will love you as if you were her own pup. She has been looking forward to the day I bring home a mate."

/ / /

"There's no sugar in this glaze, right?" I asked, about to take a bite of ham, but parked the fork in front of my lips. "If we eat too much sugar, all of us will regret it."

I glanced at Mike, who sat at the other end of the long dining room table. It was strange being in Doctor Mitchel's house as his stepson. The five of us sat around the table; it was covered with a burgundy tablecloth, barely visible through the mountains of food. Mom didn't cook that often, but she always went overboard during the holidays.

"Relax. Amulii and I smoked those hams. They don't have glaze," Mike said, mid-chew with a mouth full of mashed potatoes. "Man, everything tastes awesome, and I get to do this again in five days."

"You're such a pig," I mumbled, as I shoved the fork into my mouth. "What's college like?"

"Believe it or not, the same as it was in high school, only now there really is a permanent record."

It was hard to admit that I was jealous of him, especially since I never got to graduate. To think the student with the highest GPA would end up being a high school dropout. Knowing I was just months from earning my high school diploma drove me crazy. It was like knitting an entire sweater, but never having time to finish that last sleeve.

"It's weird how much more freedom you have in college, but it's kind of a trap. You're free to do whatever you want, but if you fail, it's your money."

"Well, don't fail," I muttered, before gnawing on a gravy-soaked piece of turkey breast.

"Not everyone can ace every test without studying like you can."

He'd often had that misconception because I'd never studied in front of him, but none of my grades came easily to me, especially in college prep and advanced placement courses.

"What are you doing for Christmas, Mike?" Mom asked, setting a platter of croissants in the middle of the table.

"Not much, just visiting my grandmother and all of our annoying extended family, but my grandma's cooking will make the pain worth it."

We all went quiet again, and I looked at Amulii, whose cheeks puffed out from the massive amount of food he was scarfing down. The way he ate always made me laugh, and he had finally learned to use a fork.

"Are you ready for tomorrow?" Paul had been rather quiet at the table, so it was startling hearing him speak out of nowhere. Everyone stopped eating and stared at me.

Tomorrow was the big day, and it always seemed so distant until it wasn't anymore. We had Christmas early because it would probably be the last human holiday I celebrated for a while. Both of us received a lot of practical gifts that would come in handy in a strange world.

As anxious as I was feeling, Mom was probably worse. She said that she had come to terms with it, but I could tell with every passing day, it got harder on her. At least she and Amulii were getting along better, but she still had a lot of unresolved anger.

"No, but I've gotta go anyway." I smiled at Amulii. "I know *you're* excited."

"It will be good to see my friends and family again, and I get to boast about you."

After dusting the snow from the marble and setting the now frozen poppies on the ground, I kneeled next to the grave. It was a beautiful headstone, with a picture of an American bald eagle carrying a

Canadian maple leaf in its talons and a lyric from one of Dad's favorite songs. Since he was a dual citizen and served in the US Marines, it was a fitting grave.

Robert Andrew Hunt
Risked his life for his country, gave his life for his family.
June 22, 1974 – February 25, 2020
And when the fight was over,
And Old Glory raised,
Among the men who held it high,
Was the Indian, Ira Hayes.

It was a quick run here from the house, and I needed to clear my head and visit Dad for a little while. I stared at the lonely plot, remembering his truck driving away after he left us in Canmore. I never thought those would be the last words he ever said to me.

"I love you," his voice whispered in my mind.

"Hey Dad."

The biting December air burned my nose as I took it in, and I smiled while looking up at the sky. It was clear, and the stars were bright, even with all the city lights drowning most of them out.

"Tomorrow's the day—we're finally leaving," I said, choking up as the words trickled out. "I'm scared. I don't know what's over there, and even though Amulii says I'll be back, part of me knows someday there won't be anything to come back to." I forced a smile and wiped my eyes with the back of my gloved hand. "But I guess it's good to know that even when everyone I know in this life is gone, I'll still have Amulii.

"A part of me still wants to blame him for everything, even what happened to you. He blew in like a tornado and tore our lives apart, but I know he never meant for any of this to happen. He really liked you. He still brings you up all the time, and—" I crawled a closer to the headstone before lying next to it. "He's sorry. He tells me that almost every day it seems."

I lay quiet for several minutes as I stared at the shimmering stars, thinking about what I really wanted to say. "You were an awful father. You knew it, Mom knew it, but you were there when everything fell down. If you hadn't been, I wouldn't be alive." A meteor streaked across the sky before disappearing behind the high-rises. "All's forgiven, Dad, and I've let go of the anger. I love you."

///

"We will come back," Amulii said, leaning his furry forehead against my own. "Soon you will meet more family and friends. Eventually, it will not be so hard to leave when there are those who love you on both sides."

"I know."

I reached down to grab my hiking pack loaded with clothes and things I had gotten for Christmas. There were also some family photos, favorite books, and a bunch of leftovers in plastic bags. Amulii helped me thread my right arm through a strap, and the large, heavy satchel fell comfortably onto my back.

We were in maw'cha form but kept our pants on while we were here. I wasn't about to hug Mike with my junk hanging out. Everyone but us had already gathered at Spirit Island, but we had to stop at the cave to make sure we got everything. Amulii packed his crystals and books, and I made sure to grab our blanket. The thing still smelled terrible, and I had to put it in its own bag inside of a bag until I could get it washed. That tattered blanket got us through a lot of terrible times and freezing nights outside. We made our first bond on it too, and while that was romantic and all, it only bolstered my desire to wash it well before using it again.

"It is time to truly begin our lives together," Amulii said, leading me out of the cave. Snow had built up along the outside, and we kicked some of it out of the way as we descended into the clearing, the icy, shimmering lake coming into view. "I will finally be able to go home a bonded male, my on'she next to me. I have been dreaming of this moment for most of my life."

"You sure are laying this on thick," I jabbed, laughing as I hooked my arm through his.

"As usual, you know how to ruin a moment." He smiled, leaning over as he pressed his thin, black lips into mine.

"Yeah, I'll probably keep doing that a lot from now on."

The lake was half-frozen, and the waters glimmered in the sunlight, the strong winds from the north disturbing the surface. It was a gorgeous day for a send-off, though clouds were gathering in the distance. I worried there'd be more blizzards in the forecast, but it cleared up in time for me to say a proper goodbye to everyone.

Mom, Mike, and Paul stood near the land bridge, waiting for us to leave. As we got closer, I saw Mom crying. I hated leaving her, but at least she wouldn't be alone. I was glad that she and Paul had married, though I often wondered about how close they were before Dad died, considering how fast all this happened. It wasn't something I wanted to give much thought. Dad was gone, and Mom remarried. Life went on, and past mistakes were in the past where they belonged.

"Well, this is it," I said, looking toward the island. "Isn't there supposed to be some kind of portal?"

"You will see it when we get closer," Amulii responded, looking at Mom. "I know you dislike me, and you think I am stealing your child from you, but I will make him happy. I will love and protect him, and he will never want for anything. I swear this."

Mom wiped her eyes with a tissue.

"I know you will." She sobbed harder, struggling to catch her breath. "But you better bring him back next year."

"I will," he said. She grabbed him and wrapped her arms around his waist, unable to reach all the way around. He returned her affection, kissing her on the head. "After all, you are my family now as well."

That was surprising, but it was a pleasant way to leave things in this world. She walked over to me and gave me a hug. I should have turned human for that, but it was too late. The last she'd see of me for a while would be a brown maned maw'cha that looked nothing like her son. Perhaps it was better that way.

"I love you, sweetheart," she said, her voice cracking as more tears fell from her eyes. "Be careful over there."

"I love you too, Mom, and I'll be fine." I wrapped my left arm around her and squeezed before letting go.

"You're a good kid," Paul said, extending his left hand to shake mine.

"What's this? We're family now." I smiled, pulling him into a one-armed hug. "Take care of my mom, or you'll have two angry werewolves after you."

He held up his left hand, which still had scars and puncture holes in it from when I attacked him.

"I definitely do not want to piss you off." He let out a nervous chuckle.

"Well," Mike said, tapping me on the shoulder. "I'm gonna miss our late-night conversations, and all the times I kicked your ass at every video game we've ever played."

He tried to put up a front, but I could tell he was about to break. There was something else that had been eating at him for months when he'd visit, but whenever I'd try to talk to him about it, he'd change the subject.

"Have fun in college, and don't drink too much," I said, my eyes watering again. "I'm gonna miss you a lot."

He grimaced and threw his arms around me, holding me tight. "You're my brother," he whispered, barely able to speak. "I don't want you to go, but I know you have to. I wish I could go with you."

Our hug lasted much longer, and I felt like I'd crumble if we stayed like that a moment more. He was closer than a brother, and I was leaving him all over again. He let me go, and the tears I'd been holding back blurred my vision as I turned away from him toward the island.

Amulii held my trembling hand as we made our way across. I couldn't see anything resembling a portal at first, only a tiny pinprick of light. The light intensified as we approached, the daylight around us turning a fiery orange. A warm breeze flowed from the ethereal, swirling gateway, which roared with the sound of a gale. We stopped just shy of the maelstrom that revealed a strange navy-blue sky with three moons. We faced one another.

"I love you, on'she," he whispered, his amber eyes reflecting glimmers of starlight from an endless universe beyond reality. A warmth and completeness washed away any doubt, freeing me from the tumultuous seas that tossed me to the depths at our journey's beginning. He used to be a black hole I couldn't escape from, but now he was my sun I couldn't live without.

"I love you too."

We took our final steps toward the next chapter of our lives, unwritten by fate, unknown by our fathers watching over us. A year of trials led us to this moment, and I was more prepared than I'd ever been. The one I was destined to walk with did so proudly, squeezing my hand as echoed chants of an old shaman prayer whispered to us from the world beyond.

The tempest enveloped us in a blinding light as we took our long-awaited steps through Segolia.

GUILT

Mike's Perspective

A flash of orange light hurt my eyes as both of them disappeared. He was gone so fast. I wanted to comfort Mrs. Hunt somehow, but what could I say that would make any damn difference?

This sucked. All of this sucked, and now I was without him—again. It was impossible to like anything about their relationship, even though I pretended it didn't bother me these last few months.

That night outside the motel, when Alex told me everything, I lost it. He was the smartest guy I knew, but this was just plain dumb.

"Come on, man, don't be upset. I didn't tell you this to get you riled up, but I had to tell someone. I've forgiven him now, and we love each other."

"This is nuts. He forced you to do this. Don't you see what this shit is? This is the same fucking plot as Beauty and the Beast."

"You've got the wrong idea, he—"

"No. I don't care how you try to spin this; he's a piece of shit who got into your head. After what you just told me . . . how?"

"Let's not end tonight like this. I've missed you, and with everything going on, I don't want us to leave on bad terms again. Okay?"

"Fine. If you're happy, I'll drop it. But I need to know that you're really cool with this."

"I am. I swear."

We were supposed to be adults together. We were gonna apply for the same colleges. Alex promised me he'd go to whatever school accepted my awful grades and low test scores. There was nothing I wouldn't do for the guy—that's how close we were, closer than brothers. Maybe closer than I could ever admit before he came out.

It still stung that he never told me until it was too late. I let him suffer with that alone, never once thinking he was different. He was the same Alex I was assigned seats with on the bus in middle school the day we met.

There were some hints that something wasn't right when I was around him during school, but I ignored them. The coldness between us got worse when I joined varsity football, and I always wondered why our friendship seemed to change overnight. Sometimes he'd walk out of the boy's bathroom, his eyes swollen and red, and I knew he'd been crying.

He would look up and smile, then walk away. I didn't think to ask him what was wrong; I just assumed that since he hid it, he didn't want to talk about it. Looking back now, I think he was protecting my reputation.

None of that petty shit mattered to me, but it bothered him enough to push me away. I wish he would have known what I felt. If only I could go back in time and tell him. I loved him; there was nothing that could change that. I loved him.

He called me his rock when his parents fought, and it was always fun when he came over to spend a night or two. I'd never laughed as hard as I did around him. I'd give anything to have those days back. I really wanted him to live with me instead of move away.

Damn. I was going to start crying.

"He's going to be back, okay?" Dr. Mitchel put a steady arm around Alex's mom before his eyes shot to me. "The year will fly by, and we'll see him again."

"I can't believe my baby's gone." She pressed her head into her husband's chest. "This wasn't supposed to happen. I wanted to see him graduate and become a man. We shouldn't have moved out here. Why did I move us here?"

Bitter winter air hit us as the sun disappeared behind thick clouds rolling in over the peaks.

"Shh, he's safe and happy. That's all that matters." He looked out across the lake. "It's supposed to snow again. We should get home," Dr. Mitchel said, shivering as another burst of wind dropped over the lake through groaning branches of pines and firs.

"I'm gonna stay a little longer. I'll put the snowmobile back in the shed when I get to the cabin." I tried to sound more together than I was. Painful emotions blurred my sight, threatening to come out. Mrs. Mitchel shook her head and began to speak, but I cut her off. "I'll be fine. Only gonna be another ten minutes or so."

She dabbed her eyes with the sleeve of her jacket and had a sad smile on her tear-stained face. "Are you sure? He was closer to you than anyone else."

"I'll live." A single warm stream crept down my cheek. I wished they would hurry and leave so I could let out a damn good cry. "I just need some alone time."

She walked over and wrapped her arms around me.

"Remember, you can come visit anytime. That's not a shallow invitation either." She paused and took a step back. "So please visit, okay?"

"You got it Dr. Hunt, er, Mitchel. Sorry."

"Alright. Don't stay out here too long."

I nodded.

They returned to their snowmobile and as they rode into the woods, everything I held onto ripped from my body. I ran toward Spirit Island, crossing the narrow strip of land.

"You piece of shit," I shouted, kicking clean the larger set of paw prints where they'd disappeared.

Alex had to leave everything behind, and though he said he was happy, I wondered if those were his words or Amulii's. What he told me—the terrible things that creature did to him—it wouldn't be possible to forgive someone like that, let alone love him.

But I was a hypocrite.

"I hate you." I whispered through clenched teeth, stumbling toward the lake. "I fucking hate you."

When I caught my reflection in the thin ice, it reminded me of someone worse. The person I hated the most.

"I'm sorry, Alex. I fucked everything up for you so bad." I dropped to my hands and knees as freezing tears fell onto the snow.

When they first contacted me, I hadn't spoken to Alex since he left Calgary. They were vague but said if I saw Alex to call them, that they would help him. They never gave me the details; they just told me he was with someone dangerous. All of it was sketchy, and I wasn't about to call them back. I forgot about it until the day I saw Alex again.

After learning what Amulii did it to him, I knew Alex needed help getting away from that monster. I didn't know what would happen, but I had to do something to get my best friend back.

Nothing felt right after I made that call. I never was smart.

The guilt ate me alive for months, and I wanted to come clean. If I did that, I'd lose him, and that would hurt more than anything. Mirrors were my enemy because I'd see a traitor and a coward staring back. Every night since I left home, I drank alone in my dorm, trying to numb my loneliness with the cheap vodka I'd get my older friends to buy me. Nothing was ever enough. It got harder to make eye contact with Alex as he held onto that dead arm. I may as well have chopped it off myself after hearing what those people did to him.

I wasn't okay, and after this, I wasn't sure where I was gonna end up. Amulii may have taken my best friend, but I nearly killed him. Now that Alex was gone, I had nothing left.

"You trusted me. I'm so sorry."

Something grabbed the back of my neck and kept me from turning. A shriek escaped my throat, followed by a scream as whatever had me gripped tighter. My call for help was cut short when a huge, rough hand covered my mouth, pulling me from the ground. A furry arm wrapped tight around me, pulling my back against a mass of muscle. The creature's hot breath tickled the skin of my ear as he growled out a strange language.

Claws raked through the jacket and shirt I wore, exposing bare skin. A monstrous palm slammed into my chest pressing a solid, hot object into me. My thoughts burned away one-by-one as numbing warmth spread to every limb. When he let go, no matter how much I wanted to run, my legs wouldn't budge.

The hulking figure finally revealed his appearance. He was a were-wolf, covered in silver fur and nearly as tall as Amulii, a dark gray mane coating his chest and groin.

I had no idea where he came from and hadn't heard a thing before he attacked.

He dangled a deep red crystal in front of me from thin leather straps. With a crooked grin, the monster stepped forward and wrapped the straps around my neck before tying them tight. The jewel fell in place, but he lifted it once more in his palm before looking into my eyes. It was kind of sick the way he did it.

"We . . . leave . . . now," he grunted, releasing the necklace.

My eyes burned as the landscape glowed. When my vision adjusted, I glimpsed a fiery hole in the world as it swirled and twisted in a torrent of light, revealing a navy-blue sky of stars and moons. The beast grabbed my hand and pulled me along. No matter how much I struggled and wanted to scream, I couldn't.

Someone . . . help me . . .

ABOUT THE AUTHOR

Aeron Dusk is a native of Florida who has spent most of his life loving nature, wolves, fantasy, sci-fi, and the paranormal. When he was young, he collected photos of beautiful landscapes from all over. Every picture told a tale of magic, mystery, and romance. The only things missing were the words.

To learn more about Aeron, visit: www.howlingdusk.com

www.ingramcontent.com/pod-product-compliance
Lightning Source LLC
Chambersburg PA
CBHW021242200726

48288CB00014B/201